A VAMPIRE WALKS

I love pizza. If I smell pizza, I have to stop and take a good whiff; I have to look at it, see what kind it is, and watch a lucky bastard take a few bites. Chicago pizza, Italian pizza, brick-oven pizza, anchovies, pepperoni, olives, mushrooms, peppers, kiwi, it doesn't matter to me, so long as it's pizza. I think I miss pizza more than I miss the sun.

I smelled pizza the instant Lillian smuggled my lightly toasted, stinking, quilt-covered ass in through the back entrance of the Demon Heart. The tangy Sicilian aroma made my mouth water, by which I mean blood filled my mouth, a poor imitation of saliva. It's Mother Nature's way of reminding me that I'm a walking corpse that hasn't fallen down yet. Thanks, Mom. Shower forgotten, I followed the smell of the pizza down the hall to the girls' dressing room behind the stage.

I opened the door and found Candice eating a slice of pepperoni. She was mostly naked, and when she saw me, she began ostentatiously licking the side of the pizza to remove the excess cheese. My fangs came out and a certain lower portion of my anatomy paid attention, too. If she had been wearing her glasses or her contacts I think she would've had a harder time keeping up the act. Even so, when the smell hit her, the revulsion was hard for her to mask.

"Good Lord, Eric. What have you been doing?"

Staked

J. F. LEWIS

Pocket Books
New York London Toronto Sydney

Pocket Books
A Division of Simon & Schuster, Inc.
1230 Avenue of the Americas
New York, NY 10020

Copyright © 2008 by Jeremy F. Lewis

First Pocket Books trade paperback edition March 2008

POCKET and colophon are registered trademarks of Simon & Schuster, Inc.

For information about special discounts for bulk purchases, please contact Simon & Schuster Special Sales at 1-800-456-6798 or business@simonandschuster.com

Designed by Mary Austin Speaker

Manufactured in the United States of America

10 9 8 7 6 5 4 3 2 1

Library of Congress Cataloging-in-Publication Data

Lewis, J. F.
    Staked / J. F. Lewis.—1st Pocket Books trade pbk. ed.
        p. cm.
    1. Vampires—Fiction. I. Title.
    PS3612.E9648S73 2008
    813'.6—dc22   2007032930

ISBN-13: 978-1-4165-4780-8
ISBN-10:   1-4165-4780-0

The book is dedicated to four very special women:

My mom, Martha

My wife, Janet

My mother-in-law, Virginia

and

My good friend, Mary Ann

ACKNOWLEDGMENTS

The author would like to acknowledge every single person who made this book possible, but he's quite certain he left someone out. If it was you . . . oops.

With that said, I'd like to thank my writing group, WTF (Write the Fantastic): Janet, Rob, Mary Ann, Dan, Karen, and Virginia. Thank you for the many Tuesdays you've sacrificed on my behalf and for letting me go out of order every single time I was up against a deadline. Mom and Dad, thanks for the child care that made those editing sessions possible. Sandra and Rachel, I know you aren't technically in the group, but for your feedback and general ability to put up with me, I thank you. Rich and Shea, I know editing's not your thing, but thanks for your support during the whole process. Having friends helps.

Thank you to my agent, Shawna McCarthy, for rescuing me from the slush pile and letting me know what genre I was actually writing. Your advice was invaluable.

Thanks to my editor, Jennifer Heddle, not just for buying *Staked* but for going above and beyond the call, sanding the rough edges, and making the novel shine.

Thanks also to my copyeditor, Chris Fuller, for his detailed character sketches, time line, and especially fine attention to detail.

And thanks to you, the reader, for picking up this book. I hope you enjoy it. (Buy two!)

Staked

1

ERIC:

THE ALLEY

Somewhere in the middle of my rant it occurred to me that I'd killed whoever it was I'd been yelling at, so arguing was no longer important. I looked down at my victim's broken headless body and winced at the unnatural odor of rapidly rotting flesh. It never smells right to me when a vampire dies. I've always chalked it up to bowels. If you don't eat, you don't shit, and death just doesn't smell right without it.

Whoever this guy was, he'd obviously been a Master vampire, because Drones and Soldiers don't get the quick rot treatment. They turn to dust and blow away . . . which smells even less natural. And if he'd been a Vlad like me, he'd still be kicking.

I glanced around the dingy back alley where we'd been arguing and couldn't remember exactly where I was, what we'd been fighting about, or what I'd done with the guy's head. From the way the neck muscles had been ripped, I was guessing I'd torn it off. If he'd been human, I would have been soaked in blood, but vampires don't bleed easily; my fingers were barely damp.

Out of curiosity, I went looking for What's His Name's head and found it lying next to the Dumpster at the back of the alley. I figured I ought to see if I recognized him. In spite of the unnaturally rapid decay, he looked vaguely familiar, like I might have seen him around town. Other than that his face didn't ring any bells.

A homeless man was curled up against the wall of the alley, shaking like a leaf and staring at me. I tucked Dead Guy's head under my arm and slipped the bum a twenty, mostly to screw with his mind, but also because I was sorry he'd seen whatever it was he'd seen. Besides, the homeless guy kind of looked like Alex Trebek and *Jeopardy!* is a damned good show.

"Do you want me to tell the police somethin' in particular?" asked the bum.

"Don't talk to me, you dirty little fucker," I snarled. I flashed my fangs at him and let my eyes do the whole glowing red bit. "I'm not paying you to do anything. The body will burn up when the sun hits it. Tell the cops whatever you want. If they believe you at all, they're well paid to do the right thing. This is Void City, sweetheart."

Norms don't notice the supernatural here unless they

aren't really normal. The spell that hangs over this city doesn't work on crazies, though. In this case I suspected the bum might remember what actually happened rather than thinking he'd seen a mugging or a gang fight or something.

I can't see magic, but I know that's how the spell is supposed to work. Your average Joe or Jane will forget the undead, the werewolves, even the demons that roam Void City and call it home . . . or sometimes they remember it wrong, their memories haphazardly replaced or jumbled by the spell. To see vampires and remember it later, you have to be crazy, be supernatural yourself, or be part of the scene, focused on being "in" with the undead crowd.

The cops all work for some high society fang I've never met and have no interest in meeting. I forget his name. If the police in his pocket have to cover up your crimes, you get a bill in the mail or a demand via phone from Captain Stacey with the VCPD. Everybody calls it the fang fee, because vampires get hit with the most of them. It's just one of the extra headaches of being a vampire, right alongside having to drink blood, staying away from holy objects, avoiding sunlight. . . .

Sunlight. I looked at my watch and cursed angrily. You'd think a vampire could remember to be in by sunrise, but my time sense has always sucked. Dropping the vamp's head and ignoring the bum, I dashed for my car only to see the driver's side door already glowing cheerily with the first lovely rays of dawn. I stopped for a moment in the shade of the alley to watch the sun's reflection in my Hummer's windshield. I used to love the sun. I still do, but now she doesn't like me so much. Which makes her not that much different from any number of women I dated back during my living years.

I strolled back down the alley and glared disapprovingly at the bum. In the increasing illumination I could see him much better, and he didn't look a damn thing like Alex Trebek. "You could have told me how close to sunrise it was," I complained.

The bum smiled, and began to grow fur.

It rippled across his body, fingertips first, in a wave so fast the brown hair breaking the skin made little musical tinkling sounds like a giant rainstick. In the movies, the transformation always looks painful, but the bum's eyes rolled back in his head, eyelids fluttering in what looked more like pleasure than pain.

"If I'd have done that, it would've been a fair fight, dead boy." He growled, his skeleton distending with a sound like a hundred knuckles popping all in order, smallest to largest. The human teeth fell out of his muzzle as it lengthened, replaced by a mouthful of sharp pointy teeth. The better to blah blah blah me with.

"If you put those under your pillow, does the tooth fairy still pony up?" I asked.

"She pays more for vampire fangs," he retorted.

What a pistol, that guy! I was laughing even as I picked up the Dumpster and emptied its contents over his head. Two more dead vamps rolled out to join No-Name. Their bodies weren't like Headless Guy's. They were little more than skeletons, the quick rotting flesh having bubbled away, leaving only a thin layer of gray scum. The bones had been gnawed on; the rib cages were splintered, gaping open where their hearts had been ripped out. They stunk even worse than Headless Guy did.

Normal animals won't touch vampire remains, which left Werewolf Bum the obvious culprit. I'd have guessed even a low-level Master to be equal to one werewolf, so either this guy'd had help or he was really something special.

The werewolf launched himself from beneath the garbage, sending gouts of filth into the air and scattering refuse everywhere. The dead vamps' peculiar odor problem ceased to be an issue. Now the whole alley smelled like human waste of all types, foreign and domestic. I smiled, though. After all, Wolfy had to have a much more acute sense of smell than me. Heh.

"Damn it!" he roared, then sneezed pathetically and swatted at his nose.

I've always had trouble taking werewolves seriously. They all look like one of Ray Harryhausen's stop-motion creature effects to me; you know, fake looking. I keep expecting Sinbad to show up and pretend to duel with them, like he did with the skeletons in *Sinbad and the Eye of the Tiger*. Normally I could probably take on four or five of them. This guy had no chance. I was still thinking that when Wolfy sank his fangs into my shoulder. The Dumpster fell backward out of my hands. He should have bitten my head or my neck; he wouldn't get another shot.

Time seemed to slow as I reached up and grabbed the werewolf's jaws, forcing them apart until I felt the joint give. Then I let go and rolled backward, coming up beneath the falling Dumpster, and catching it before it landed. It always makes me feel like a superhero when my vampire speed kicks in. Some vamps are able to use that speed all the time, but mine has always been sporadic for some reason.

I knew that I should kill Wolfy, but I really wasn't interested. Werewolves tend to stick together. Kill one and you might wind up fighting the whole pack, or worse. Besides, I didn't care about the other two vamps he'd killed. Wolf Bum was just doing what came naturally to him, so if I could, I'd let him go with a warning. I swung the Dumpster in an arc and knocked him into the air with it.

Time sped up again. I watched the blood spurt from his jaws, splattering when he hit the wall of the alley with a wet cracking noise. Bones had broken when he landed. Some of them sounded important. My twenty-dollar bill hit the ground and I dropped the Dumpster to pick it up, the crash of metal on concrete reverberating in my ears.

Wolfy was still breathing, but he was down for the count. With a grimace, I walked over and tucked the cash into his hand, then added another twenty to it. His jaw was really going to hurt if it healed that way and had to be re-broken. Adding a third twenty, I shook my head.

"Walk away," I told him. "You gave it a good try."

At least the buildings on either side of me were tall enough to keep most of the alley safe from the sun, but not for long. I had to get out of here somehow. I ripped off the lid of the Dumpster and dropped the bin down over myself. "God, this stinks," I complained.

The front page of the *Void City Echo* was stuck to one

wall of the Dumpster. I could make out a headline about the decrease in crime, the record drop in the murder rate on East Side. It was bullshit, of course. There's a reason the paper is called the *Echo*. It's a fang rag, heavily influenced by vampires who want to keep Void City's human populace fat and happy. On the plus side, the captions jogged my Swiss cheese memory and I suddenly remembered where I was, and for that matter, which alley I was in. My club wasn't far from here.

I put my hands on the brownish sludge caking the walls of the Dumpster and felt it squish between my fingers as I began to push my makeshift sunblock toward the end of the alley.

Tabitha was going to find me so appealing when I got back to the club. The thought of her pretty little nose turned up in disgust brought a smile to my lips. A wet clump of refuse fell from the Dumpster's upturned bottom, slapping me messily across my hairline. "Shit!" If it wasn't, it certainly smelled like it. I wiped whatever it was from my face, leaving a trail of brown sludge in its place.

I put my hands back on the Dumpster wall and began to push, leaving long scratches in the road as I went. The sound of metal on asphalt was earsplitting, but I picked up speed anyway. The strip club was only three blocks away and all I could think about was washing this shit off and making Tabitha help. Tabitha was one of a long line of human girlfriends I'd had. There were always girls willing to do anything a vampire might want as long as they thought there was a chance they might get immortality out of it.

My Dumpster-pushing progress came to a sudden halt as I slammed into my Hummer. It was new, only a couple of weeks old. My car alarm started going off. It was the last straw. The next thing I knew, I was punching holes through the Dumpster with my bare hands. It came apart like tissue paper. It was all very satisfying until I caught fire. Note to self: The big burning ball of gas in the sky is the sun.

I walked back into the alley, rolled on the ground, and beat my head against the wall to put out the remaining flames. Then I checked on Wolfy. He was still unconscious, so I pulled out my cell phone and called my club.

Roger answered the phone. "How refreshing! Did you actually remember the phone number or did you have to look it up?" He sounded tired and angry, as if he'd answered the phone only because he'd recognized the name on the caller ID. I decided to let it slide. After all, Roger needed more sleep than I do and he was my best friend. I also needed a ride.

"Remembered," I said.

"Thank heavens!" Roger's voice dripped with sarcasm. "It's Eric," he called to someone else on the other end. "Safe and sound, our lost little lamb. We were all so worried about you." In the background I heard a woman let out one scornful "Ha!" I ignored it.

"I'm three blocks away, in the alley at Thirteenth Street and Fifth Avenue. Bring the party van around to pick me up."

"Sun's up, pal. I can't come get you," he said more seriously. "I'll send Candice over."

Candice is the kind of golden-hearted stripper other strippers pretend to be. She's working on her nursing degree, and if I were still human I'd be all over her. As it is, I just pay for her college and watch her dance naked in the club. And, okay, sometimes I pretend I'm with her when I'm with Tabitha. It's just better for all involved.

"I smell pretty bad. Is Lillian still around?" I asked. Lillian had come in late three days in a row, just in time for the evening rush. If she thought early afternoons were shit duty, I'd show her shit duty.

"Yes," Roger answered, laughing. "Don't want to smell bad in front of your little groupie?"

"Lillian's more deserving," I said. "Send her over, then tell Talbot he's going to need to get the van cleaned up after we're done with it."

Roger hung up and I waited for the van, admiring my handiwork on the Hummer. From the damage, I must have really picked up some speed before impact. I took a perverse joy in having demolished the shiny new SUV. Roger had talked me into buying it, but to be honest, I hated the thing. I'm only comfortable in my Mustang. It's old, but so am I, and we both have plenty of miles left in us.

A few minutes later, the party van rounded the corner, screeching to a halt just inches into the shade. Lillian glared at me through the windshield, bleary-eyed through her half-removed makeup. She looked really pissed. As I walked toward the van, I found out the hard way that the werewolf had been playing possum for the last few minutes. I'd never known what it was like to be picked up by the ankles and slammed face-first into a brick wall. The experience isn't much to write home about.

He swung me back around to repeat the process and I felt time begin to slow down once more. I was giving Wolfy too many chances to kill me. I'm pretty damn hard to wipe out, but I supposed he could get lucky. After all, he'd killed those other two vamps somehow.

I bent backward at an angle usually reserved for circus acrobats and grabbed his jaw. He would have whimpered if he'd had the time. The jaw had healed broken; each portion pointed in opposite directions at odd angles. I re-broke it for him and slammed it shut on his lolling tongue.

As time shifted back to normal, he screamed. It was part pain, part fear; a real little-girl scream. He dropped me, and I rolled to the ground and came up facing him. Wolfy smelled scared. I guess he finally realized the first round hadn't been a fluke and the little five-foot-ten bastard he was up against actually could kick his ass up and down the alley. He held up both paws and backed away from me. My twenties had scattered across the alley, mixing like dried leaves with the trash. For some reason, it pissed me off.

The edges of my vision began to blur. It happens sometimes when I get really angry. The werewolf tried to say something despite his mangled tongue, but I couldn't quite make it out. It was too late for talk; I was too far gone to rein the anger in.

The next thing I knew, I was knee-deep in werewolf, shoving bloody twenty-dollar bills into my jeans. His chest had been cracked open like an oyster and gutted. I was standing where his organs ought to have been, but they were scattered about the alley like mismatched socks. I never remember what happens when I'm really mad. I black out.

I couldn't decide whether the scene would be more or less disturbing when the sun rose high enough to fill that portion of the alley and his corpse turned human. A dead werewolf reverts to human form in the light of day. Too bad it doesn't do the same to live lycanthropes. Part of his stomach was under my left shoe, the bile already staining it beyond recognition. At least the blood had washed some of the garbage off. Lillian, her face contorted in disgust, climbed out of the van, opened the back, and threw me a towel.

Sometimes being a vampire is truly fucked up. If you don't believe me, ask the poor vamp I'd killed in the alley earlier. I couldn't remember why the hell I'd killed him, much less why we'd been arguing. For all I knew, it was about football. Definitely fucked up.

2

ERIC:

DEMON HEART

My strip club, the Demon Heart, is in downtown Void City in a district lovingly referred to as East Side. I couldn't tell you why, because it's actually on the south side of town. The club sits on the corner of Thirteenth Street and Eighth Avenue, across from the old Pollux Theater. The Pollux is a beautiful art nouveau popcorn palace that dates back to the days when there was a cartoon and a sing-along before the movie and a nosebleed section for the folks white people didn't want to see.

I bought both buildings cheap since hardly anybody gives a damn about East Side anymore. Roger says Sable Oaks is where all the high society vamps want to build. If you ask me, it's too far from Void City. I'm not commuting an hour into town to hunt.

The Demon Heart kept me close to people nobody would miss and the Pollux gave me a place to be by myself. Besides, I hate society vamps. We have a nonaggression pact. If I don't see them and they don't see me, then there's no need for aggression.

I considered buying a pizza parlor once, but I decided I would go crazy from the smell. I love pizza. If I smell pizza, I have to stop and take a good whiff; I have to look at it, see what kind it is, and watch a lucky bastard take a few bites. Chicago pizza, Italian pizza, brick-oven pizza, anchovies, pepperoni, olives, mushrooms, peppers, kiwi, it doesn't matter to me, so long as it's pizza. I think I miss pizza more than I miss the sun.

I smelled pizza the instant Lillian smuggled my lightly toasted, stinking, quilt-covered ass in through the back entrance of the Demon Heart. The tangy Sicilian aroma made my mouth water, by which I mean blood filled my mouth, a poor imitation of saliva. It's Mother Nature's way of reminding me that I'm a walking corpse that hasn't fallen down yet. Thanks, Mom. Shower forgotten, I followed the smell of the pizza down the hall to the girls' dressing room behind the stage.

I opened the door and found Candice eating a slice of pepperoni. She was mostly naked, and when she saw me, she began ostentatiously licking the side of the pizza to remove the excess cheese. My fangs came out and a certain lower portion of my anatomy paid attention, too. If she had been wearing her glasses or her contacts I think she would've had a harder time keeping up the act. Even so, when the smell hit her, the revulsion was hard for her to mask. "Good Lord, Eric. What have you been doing?"

"Eat your pizza," I snapped. It was all I could do not to jump on her, so I left the room and headed for my shower. Maybe I'd been rude to Candice, but it was better that way. If she was smart, she'd quit in a huff and go start a normal life somewhere the hell away from me. In the end, a friendship between a vampire and a human is like a friendship between a dog and a chicken nugget. Sooner or later, the nugget is going to get eaten; the only real question is how many bites it will take.

On my way down the hallway, I caught Tabitha's scent. Fresh out of the shower, she smelled like fizzy citrus-scented soap. She opened the door of our bedroom wearing nothing but a bathrobe. I don't know if she was on her way across the hall to borrow some lotion or to see if she could score a slice of pizza, but it didn't matter since she wasn't going to do either.

I kissed her, filled with the need for sex and blood. She didn't even mention the smell, answering the urgency of my kisses with her own, pushing me out into the hall, pressing my back against the wall. When we kissed, her heat washed over me all at once. Her robe came open, revealing the smooth surface of her sex. She'd just waxed.

"Are you okay, baby?" She asked the question between kisses, but I didn't answer. She didn't ask again, didn't complain or wrinkle her nose as I left trails of blood and grime along her breasts. I would have had sex with her right there, but I was afraid the gunk from the Dumpster might make her sick. I carried her into the bathroom, the tile still slick with moisture, mirror still cloudy, and got into the shower.

Tabitha was the only kind of girlfriend I let myself have anymore. She had a great body, a bad attitude, and extremely low self-esteem. She wasn't dumb, but she wasn't smart, and she thought that she wanted to be a vampire when she grew up. I knew she had a sister named Rachel whose photo she carried in her billfold, and I guessed she had parents, but they never seemed to be around. In short, if I broke her by accident I wouldn't feel too bad about it and no one would really miss her. It's cruel, I know, but I am a vampire, remember?

I meant to have sex, but that's not what happened. We made love instead. It was passionate, tender. It was a mistake. When we got out of the shower, Tabitha wore that stupid look she gets when she thinks she's being sly. I turned away and rolled my eyes; my memory, for once, clear as crystal.

It was like a formula with her. Before she even opened her mouth I knew the basic ploy. She would compliment me on the act, even though I'd know she was faking it for my benefit. Even when she wasn't, she always put on a big show. I guess the whole preternatural senses thing hadn't clued her in to the fact that I could tell. I didn't blame her for faking it a little; unless blood turns you on, having it stand in for all the normal bodily fluids can get a little nasty, especially during sex.

After the compliments, I predicted she'd snuggle for a minute and then ask me how old I am. I'd answer and she'd pretend like she'd forgotten. She'd tell me how cool it is to be immortal, how wonderful it must be to know that no matter what happens to the rest of the world, you will go on, forever. I'd attempt to disabuse her of the notion. She would tell me that she heard one of any number of a recycled little list of activities is much better when it's between two vampires. She'd insist it would make us feel so much closer, claim we'd be able to read each other's minds. I'd disagree.

She'd say it would be different with us because we're in love. I'd point out that I don't love her and then I'd wait to see if she cried or started yelling. If she cried, I'd leave. If she yelled, I'd leave. So predictable.

"You are so good at that, you know," she started up. I sighed. She walked across the room still damp from the shower and I thought about taking her again to see if she would take another shower and leave me alone when we were done. I let her rub up against me.

Tabitha was an extremely attractive woman; she was big where she was supposed to be big and narrow where narrow is good. Her long and luxurious hair was the same dark black I dyed mine, only hers wasn't a dye job. Cutting it would have been a crime. She had the sexiest green eyes I'd ever seen, though she claimed she wished they were blue like mine. Tabitha's smiles took complete advantage of her full red lips. Other girls had to use makeup to achieve the qualities she already possessed.

Tabitha would go to great lengths to vary her soaps and

perfumes, to wear just enough that I would notice, but little enough that it rarely annoyed me. She even got a tattoo at the base of her spine where I once mentioned one might look sexy. I designed it for her: a multicolored butterfly. She'd be a great woman if she didn't act so dumb.

"... and I mean my legs were so totally shaking." Oops, I missed part of it. It sounded like we were still in the "what a sex god" section, though. She hugged me from behind and I felt her breasts against my back. Her warmth overwhelmed me again. Vampires don't generate any body heat so we're always cold unless we've just fed. Even then, humans feel warm by comparison.

Despite her flaws, she was so *alive*. Maybe it was that I could still smell pizza in the distance, or maybe it was her perfume, but I began to feel a knot of panic in my chest.

"How old are you?" she asked.

"I'm not even a hundred, Tabitha," I told her halfheartedly. "You know that."

She kissed my neck tenderly. It wasn't a sexual kiss, more a touch of possessiveness. Oh, shit.

"I always forget. You seem so much older. God, it must be so cool to be immortal. Time wears down mountains and changes the flow of mighty rivers, but not you. To be changeless, forever ..."

I felt caught, trapped. It was like a snare closing in around me. What the fuck was wrong with me? This crap didn't work on me. I'd heard it a thousand times. It was all bullshit. I didn't believe a damn word of it. I knew she didn't believe it either. Then I realized that this morning had been different.

I could hear her breath, her heartbeat. She'd meant it all, and it was too late to do a damn thing about it.

"Maybe," I said finally. There is nothing more terrifying than the heartbeat of a woman in love. It complicates everything.

I could hear the muscles in her face draw her lips into a smile. Her heartbeat sped up and I felt it as if it were pounding in my own chest. Her breath was a little faster, too. She knew something was different. Was it the way she helped clean me up after the fight?

She hadn't looked disgusted once. Not when I'd walked in covered with blood and filth, not when I'd pulled her close before we'd even made it to the shower and not when the act was complete and my blood swirled down the drain. She was into it. It hadn't been fake this time. If it wasn't love, it was a close cousin. I was so fucked.

"I want us to be together, Eric. I've heard that—"

She was so alive, so warm, and I was so dead, so cold.

"Shut up," I said softly.

"What?" I felt her heart skip a beat.

It won't be what you're expecting, I wanted to say. If I make you a vampire, you won't be warm anymore; you won't smell like you anymore. Before long, you won't even act like you. Just looking at you will be a painful reminder of what I am and what you used to be. And then you'll have to leave.

Instead, even more softly, I said, "I'll do it."

When women truly fall in love with me, I can't say no. It's like a sickness.

She hugged me so tightly her entire body seemed pressed

against mine, squealing as she did so. I smelled her excitement for almost the last time. I was so stupid. I was dumber than she was. I knew better. I'd seen what happens. The transformation changes people. Even when they turn out just the way you want, there are problems. Like with Greta . . .

"Can we do it right here, in the bed?" she asked.

"Hell, no." I scowled. "I don't want your crap all over everything." I shook free of her and picked her up in my arms like a damned newlywed, as though the act could make murdering someone romantic rather than monstrous. "We do it in the bathroom, on the pot, so there's less to clean up."

My inner voice told me exactly what I needed to hear. I didn't love this woman. I only cared about her because she was a moist warm tightness with the appropriate attachments. She wouldn't be the same. She'd be a dead thing like me, a walking would-be body bag occupant.

I wouldn't be able to live vicariously through her. I wouldn't be able to feel and smell the sun's heat on her skin when she came in from outdoors. No more making her eat the food I craved just so I could watch her eat it. I wouldn't even be able to listen to her breathe while she slept because she wouldn't breathe autonomously anymore. I tried to think of everything she'd be giving up, all the things I'd miss, and none of it mattered because she loved me. How twisted is that?

I should have just broken her neck and found a new girlfriend, but I didn't have the balls to do it. Somebody should have put a stake in me, or better yet, gotten a good strong muzzle . . . one of those masks like Hannibal Lecter wore in the movies. It was all wrong, but that morning I no longer cared enough not to do it, or perhaps I cared too much, wanted both of us to live her crazy fantasy, though I knew damn well giving her undeath wouldn't just shatter those illusions, it would grind them into the dirt.

3

ERIC:
EVENING AFTER

I usually wake early. In fact, as far as I can tell, I barely sleep more than an hour or two each day. Even then it's easy to wake me. I rolled over and was momentarily surprised to find Tabitha beside me. I was even more surprised to see the time display on my alarm clock—18:43 . . . after six o'clock. I never sleep until six. I knew why I'd overslept today, though. The reason was still lying next to me.

She was pale, a little thinner than she'd been, but not unattractively so. The sudden additional slenderness made her breasts look bigger than they actually were and the skin and muscle all over her body had tightened a bit as the transformation took hold. She looked better than she ever had in life. I could picture how pleased she would be when she woke up. I smelled a strong odor from the bathroom and rolled out of bed. There was blood caked to my lips, trailing down my face, across my neck, and down my chest. It had dried there during the day.

I opened the bathroom and retched at the stink. The transformation flushes the body clean. That's twenty-five feet of intestines with five to ten pounds of solid waste. The process isn't pleasant or comfortable, either; I had a vague memory of Tabitha screaming. The toilet clogged when I flushed. Hastily grabbing the plunger, I took care of it before the putrid brown water poured out onto the floor.

A narrow trail of fluids led from the toilet to the sink, but I left it alone for the moment and opened the shower door. My clothes from earlier were already piled in there. I must have rinsed them out before I went to bed. I didn't remember doing it, but I was glad that I had. Most of them looked recoverable.

When I'm in top form, I can usually shapeshift into an animal, and then use a little of the residual transformation mojo to fix my clothes when I change back, but it can be very draining. The worse the damage is to the clothes, the greater the drain. This morning it had been worth the possible loss of the clothes to save that energy, to make sure I only woke up hungry, not starving. I had no desire to go on a feeding frenzy after the blood-and-energy-intensive cost of turning Tabitha.

I turned the shower on hot and washed myself, scratching at the dried blood with my fingernails to get it all off, and as the water turned scalding, I started to feel better.

I got out of the shower and squared away the rest of the room using the cleaning supplies Marilyn kept under the sink. Marilyn and I had been lovers before . . . when I'd been alive. We'd come within three weeks of getting married.

My wallet sat on the edge of the sink; I checked it quickly to make sure it hadn't gotten wet. When I opened it, Marilyn's picture smiled up at me. She wore a leather biker's jacket and sat with casual disdain on Roger's motorcycle, a 1964 Harley-Davidson Duo-Glide. In shades of sepia, the photo didn't show her red hair, but it captured her look, smoldering like Cyd Charisse, a Marlboro at the corner of her lips.

Forty-three years doesn't seem like a long time for a vampire, until you look at one of your living contemporaries. My Marilyn was more like my nanny now.

I laughed, imagining Marilyn's reaction to the whole Tabitha thing. At least it would get a rise out of her, and that was always fun.

I wasn't looking forward to telling the others, though. Candice's feelings would probably be hurt and Talbot wouldn't say a word; he'd just glare at me. Roger, on the other hand . . . Roger would probably never let me hear the end of it. He still gave me shit about turning Irene some twenty years ago.

Greta would probably take it all in stride, if she ever found out about it. Greta's my daughter. There was a picture of her in my wallet, too, but I kept it behind Marilyn's. Once I'd decided to make my own little vampire children: a girl and a boy. Greta and Kyle. It hadn't worked out. Greta took to vampirism just fine, I guess because I'd raised her, more or less, from the time she was nine, but I'd only known Kyle for a year or two when I'd turned them both. After the change Kyle wasn't the same anymore: the jaunty step he'd had in life disappeared, leaving him a shadow of his former self, a Drone, so hard to look at that I eventually sent them both away. Thinking of Greta and wondering how she was doing, I looked at the bathroom mirror and wiped off the condensation with a towel.

Nope, still no reflection.

A longing in the back of my throat told me I was hungry. It was followed quickly by a fiery pain in my gut. Turning someone takes a lot out of you even if they don't drink very much. The wound you feed them with can grow dark and inflamed; sometimes they even scar.

It takes a lot out of me to make a vampire. In the movies, it's simple: you just drain a human and then have her drink your blood. If it really worked that way, I had no doubt that Tabitha would have saved up some of my blood, slit her wrists, and turned herself a long time ago. For starters, draining the human is just common sense, not a requirement. Drinking their blood first gives you more blood to spare, but the change, making the human become a vampire, requires an act of will. It doesn't happen by accident.

I left Sleeping Beauty on the bed and walked out into the hallway before I realized I was naked. Back in my room I pulled on jeans and one of my favorite T-shirts. A few years back the Void City Music Festival swapped suppliers; instead of *Welcome to the Void City Music Festival* all ten thousand T-shirts said *Welcome to the Void* in white letters on black material. The misprint was so popular they claimed it was intentional and kept right on printing them that way every year. I have dozens of them.

Sitting on the edge of the bed, I tugged on a pair of dark socks and my work boots. My favorite belt was still lying in the shower so I went without one even though it irks me. It's a hang-up I have. Maybe I got pantsed once too often as a child. I don't know. After a little searching, I found my watch under my nightstand and slipped it on my wrist.

I checked the backstage dressing room on my way down the hall. Sheena and Desiree both gave me polite smiles. Sheena was dressed for work, ready to go onstage in a perky cheerleader uniform complete with pom-poms. Desiree, having finished her set, was slipping into a slinky French maid's outfit to wear while selling drinks and lap dances. I gave them a half smile in return and walked back out into the hall, then out into the club itself. Often the sounds and lights make me feel better. Even though the music usually hurts my ears, it excites everyone else and the more alive they feel the more I can leech off of their excitement.

I didn't see Marilyn, which only vaguely concerned me. Maybe she was at another doctor's visit. Old people get sick a lot, and Marilyn had grown old. We'd known each other since we were kids. We'd been friends, lovers, fiancées. I've been told that when I rose as a vampire, she was there, standing over my grave crying. I don't remember any of it, but it must be true, 'cause she's been with me ever since.

She's the one woman I've ever really wanted to turn, but she's always said no. Something about her immortal soul, which is odd, since she claims to be an atheist. The real reason is probably a secret. All Marilyn's secrets are safe from me. I can't even make her tell me what she's getting me for Christmas. When she dies, I'm pretty sure I'll go crazy, but only time will tell.

I looked around the room, soaking up the atmosphere. Sarah was doing an uninspired bit of stripping while Kelly and Lillian worked the tables. Talbot stood off to the right of the stage. There were a lot of people in the club for a Wednesday. I glanced at my watch and realized it was Saturday. Damn. My sense of time was getting worse. I think that's why Marilyn bought me a watch that displayed the time, date, and day of the week. Talbot headed my way and I headed back the way I'd come, straight toward the nearest exit. Talbot was big, black, bald, and too well dressed to be a bouncer in a place like mine.

The Demon Heart was no dump, but it didn't pretend to be anything it wasn't. Clean but faded, it was the kind of club that looks better in dim light. The outside still looked like a department store, which is what it had been, I guess, back when the Pollux was open across the street. I'd had the interior redone in red, black, and chrome. It reminded me of a 1950s burger joint gone wrong.

Talbot sped up to catch me and I let him. It would look a little silly to run away from my own employee, wouldn't it? Even if that was exactly what I wanted to do? I was ashamed of what I'd let happen and I didn't want to face it yet, not until I'd eaten, maybe not even then.

He reached me just as I started down the hall toward the back door. "Tabitha didn't come up to help open the club," he said abruptly.

I turned to look at him and couldn't say it. "Hire someone else," I snapped, instead. "Get one of the other girls to fill in for now."

He waited for an explanation and I just stared at him. Figure it out, damn it! Talbot has been with me for close to twenty years. By now, I expected him to know when the boss has fucked up. Then I saw it in his eyes. The bastard knew exactly what had happened. He just wanted to make me say it, to watch me be uncomfortable, the bastard.

"I fucking turned her last night, okay? And I'm too hungry to snack on anyone here. I'd drain them down too far and I don't want to have to deal with a dead body in the club tonight, so get back there and keep an eye on her for me. If she wakes up before I get back, you can damn well feed her yourself!"

His brown eyes turned green for a moment and his pupils narrowed into slits. Cats' eyes. He took a couple of breaths and his eyes turned back to normal. I usually knew not to goad him like that, but I was fucking up so consistently that I didn't want to interrupt my streak.

"I can do that, sir," he rumbled. Then he smiled, regaining his composure. "I was just talking to Roger about a rumor he heard . . . supposedly a vampire killed a werewolf three blocks from here . . . around dawn . . . down at Thirteenth and Eleventh Avenue."

"Good for him," I growled.

"He said that was where Lillian picked you up last night. Is that so?" Talbot asked.

I didn't remember. It sounded right. "Maybe." I sighed.

"Rumor also has it that the dead wolf was important to his pack," Talbot added.

I looked away for a moment and rubbed my eyes. I could feel the beginnings of a nice happy migraine coming on. "How important?"

He pursed his lips and made a whistling noise. "Pretty darn."

"Yeah, well, that's just wonderful! With my luck, it was the fucking Alpha."

He laughed. "Actually, it was William's eldest son."

"William's the Alpha?"

He nodded.

"Shit."

Enjoying my dismay, Talbot continued, "The van cleaned up well, but the Hummer will be in the shop for a while."

"Sell it for scrap," I said harshly. "I don't even know why I let Roger talk me into buying it."

Talbot has one of those infectious laughs that can make anyone laugh in return. It didn't work this time, maybe because I felt he was laughing at me, at the mess I'd made. When I didn't share in his amusement, Talbot grimaced. "What else are you not telling me, Eric?"

I waved him off and walked out the door. My Mustang was waiting for me. Even though Ford didn't make a distinction between the 1965 and the 1964½, I could tell. I'd bought it new in late April 1964, and had it loaded with options. I don't know if it was the first vehicle with a power convertible top, but for fifty-four dollars and ten cents, I'd said hell, yes. That Mustang was the first car I ever owned that had an air conditioner.

I ran my hand along the long blunt hood and grinned from ear to ear, picturing the 271 horsepower V-8 engine underneath. I understood why Roger wanted me to get used to a new car. The Mustang couldn't last forever, but I wouldn't let it go yet. Marilyn's first time was in that car. They don't make cars like that anymore.

"Hey, asshole," Roger shouted from the club's rear door. That I hadn't sensed him only slightly surprised me. The first and second tier of vampires can sense each other when they come into range. Roger's second tier, a Master. I'm a Vlad and a Vlad trumps a Master. My not sensing him meant that he'd been within my range before I woke up. Technically, I must have sensed him in my sleep, but since it was Roger, it hadn't woken me.

He was dressed better than me, as usual, but he looked harried, every hair out of place. "I just heard that guy who owns the Demon Heart turned another one of his girlfriends last night. . . ."

"What a prick," I said dryly. If Roger was trying to cheer me up, he was going about it the wrong way.

"Tell me about it." He walked over to the car, thoroughly enjoying pissing in my Cheerios. "I hear he crashed his new Humvee, too."

"Sounds like a real fuckup. What do you want, Roger? I'm hungry."

"I hear he's eating out tonight."

"I figure I'm on a roll . . ."

". . . so why not let it ride?" he said, finishing my sentence. The last time I could remember Roger being all buddy-buddy like this was in Vegas. We'd hit it big, or I had, and I'd taken care of his losses, paid for the whole damn trip, actually. Roger's always happier when he's spending someone else's money.

"You want to come with?" I asked.

He shook his head no, the prospect unthinkable. "Look, buddy, I know it's not my place to say—"

"But you're going to anyway." That drew a smile, but not the friendly one for which I'd hoped.

"Why don't you go ahead and end Tabitha? Spare yourself a little heartache and get it over with, huh? She's not worth it." It was Roger's same old song and dance. He was right, of course, but that didn't mean I wanted to hear it.

"Speaking of girlfriends," I said, "are you still fucking Froggy?" It was nasty and I shouldn't have said it, but I wanted him to go away. If he didn't want to be teased about having a girlfriend vamp who could only turn into a frog, he should know better than to start poking at me and mine.

Besides, I needed to eat. No vampire is hungry and nice. Nice and hungry, sure, but . . .

"Look, just hunt away from the club tonight, okay?" he said.

"I was planning to."

"Oh, you were planning?" Roger smirked. "Where were you planning on going then, if I might ask?" He emphasized *planning* like it had air quotes around it. Still, I'd asked for it, by mentioning Froggy.

"North Side," I blurted.

"Any particular spot?"

"I'll figure it out when I get there."

"Right, 'cause you're so good at winging it. Why don't you come inside and drink some blood from the fridge, just to take the edge off? The way you look, you might go all Black Out Boy any minute and—"

"'Bye," I said brusquely. I slid into my Mustang and started her up, gunning the V-8 before peeling out toward North Side. I don't normally hunt over there, but I craved a change of pace and it was the first place that had come to mind when Roger asked.

A vampire can get tired of eating the same old people. Tonight I wanted to eat someone upscale who worked out every day and smelled like expensive perfume. By the time I reached the tony neighborhood, my head had cleared a little. I parked my car on the street and began prowling the specialty coffee shops.

I passed up two college students and a cop before I started to get desperate. I had to pick a victim soon or I might not have much of a choice—sheer need would make me grab whoever was closest. Just then a woman in a Jag pulled up and parked in front of the hydrant across from Starbucks, then got out of the car. Her perfume smelled like heaven, and her skin looked soft and supple. Finally. The street was empty for a moment and I dashed out from my spot in the shadows.

Everything dropped into slow motion. I was glad now that I'd decided to hunt away from my normal territory. Basically all vampires are monsters and I'm no exception. I'm not proud of it, and I try to keep myself well fed so that most of the time my prey are spared the worst of it, but bad nights do happen. Feeding was going to be bad tonight and I knew it. Roger might have known it, too. Maybe he'd been trying to help in his own weird passive-aggressive way. I was too hungry to hunt carefully.

She barely knew what hit her. I had her back in the alley and on the ground in the twinkling of an eye. The perfume was expensive stuff: delicate, but arousing. She'd even dabbed a little down below, on the nape of her neck, and between her breasts. Someone called a woman's name, so I leapt to the fire escape, dragging her up to the roof in spite of her struggles. She bit me, which always pisses me off (I'm the biter, not the bitee), so I slapped her. I didn't want to, but it happened. The worse the hunger is, the less time there is for thinking, and the more primal those few thoughts become. The slap dazed her, but she still tried to scream when she saw my fangs. Fingernails clawed at my face, hard and lacquered. I threw her down on the roof and unwrapped her like a Christmas present, shreds of fabric scattering as I ripped and tore.

Her lingerie told me I was screwing up someone else's evening. It was a lacy purple number, expensive and luxurious. She'd shaved her legs for someone who would never know. Some vampires like the jugular, but I prefer the vein at the inner thigh when I'm drinking a woman. Another hunger stirred and I fought it like a drowning man. *No*, I told myself. *Finish it.*

Normally I would have broken her neck first, but right now I wanted the blood hot and alive. She screamed so loud my eyes crossed. I wish I could say she tasted special, but the truth is all blood tastes the same. She bled out in little under a minute. When I was sated, I ripped her head off to make sure she wouldn't rise as a wampyre.

My memory's not great, but I did remember reading about wampyres—they're what happens when a human dies from a vampire bite. Wampyres are mindless rotting corpses that drink blood. They're kind of the black sheep of the undead family, just above zombies.

I dropped her body down a city drain and left her car illegally parked. It wasn't smart, but then again this wasn't my week for smart. In the end, all I'd done was kill her. I'd roughed her up some, too, but as hungry as I'd been, not doing more was a victory. A hungry vampire is capable of anything.

I was willing to forgive myself a little carelessness. Besides, in a town like Void City, you can get away with being careless if you've got the money. Despite the enchantment over the city, most of us take additional precautions. Various flesh-eating types can be brought in for corpse disposal.

Some pay to have the norms' memories professionally rearranged, just in case. We can even get a mage or shaman to come in and move along any angry spirits we leave behind. It's a hassle and it costs more than I like to think about. In my case, it would also result in a few hours of listening to Roger bitch and moan about the expense.

No wonder I prefer to eat in.

On the way home, my cell phone rang and I nearly wrecked the Mustang trying to find the damn thing. It was in the car charger. As I answered it, it occurred to me that it would have really pissed me off to wreck the Mustang.

"What?" I spat into the phone.

"Hey, buddy," Roger oozed.

"Yeah?"

"Did Brian tell you where he was headed last night?" He sounded concerned and more than a little weird.

"Fuck Brian," I snarled. "I don't even know why you keep bringing him out with us. If he doesn't learn to keep his mouth shut about the Void City Howlers I'm going to wind up shutting it for"—oh, shit. That was how I knew the headless vampire in the alley's face. It was fucking Brian. Damn it!— "him."

I swerved around on the road for a minute and slammed my fist into the console.

Roger's voice sounded even more distant, and I could hear faint music in the background. "Okay, well, just let me know if you hear from him. He was supposed to meet me here at the Artiste Unknown."

"Fine."

"What?" he asked incredulously. "You wanted to come?"

How the hell had Roger gotten that from "fine"?

"Um, have I even heard of that place?" I asked, trying to figure out how the hell I was going to tell Roger that I'd offed his buddy.

"It's Ebon Winter's club, very exclusive. Vampires have to bring a human date." He paused. "The only place more exclusive than the Irons Club?"

Have I mentioned that my memory is shit? "Doesn't ring a bell, but you and Brian have fun."

"I was supposed to meet him at eight. It is now eight thirty."

"Then I guess he's late." In the corner of my mind, an alarm was going off. I eyed the spotless white truck behind me, but didn't see anything strange about it. I checked all my mirrors, but still saw nothing suspicious. The hairs on the back of my neck stood up anyway and a cold shiver went down my spine. My body thinks it knows better than me whether I'm in trouble or not. It's usually right.

"I don't think so," Roger said, sounding pissed. "You're the only one who ever keeps me waiting."

"Get over yourself." I laughed. Roger certainly had an ego. If I hadn't known him from my living days, there was no way I would have put up with his crap.

I've always thought it was kind of weird that we both became vampires at about the same time. Roger's never given me a good answer about it either. If we'd had the same sire it would have been less confusing to me, but Roger's sire was from Atlanta and we have no idea who sired me. He told me not to worry about it, but I do. Marilyn tried to explain it away once. She had this whole sob story about Roger being distraught over my death and arranging his own; she seemed to believe it, but I didn't.

In my rearview mirror, the same spotless white truck was pacing me. A red truck pulled up beside it. Same make, same model, same year . . . my alarm kept going off. I shifted my attention from Roger's past to the present. "Look, he's probably just running late. I'm sure he'll show up. Why don't you go on in and have a good time. I've gotta go."

"Why? Have some other important werewolves to piss off tonight? Watch out for William, by the way. I hear he's not your average fare."

"What do you mean?" I asked, trying to sound nonchalant while keeping an eye on the trucks in my rearview mirror.

"He's supposed to be a real badass, one heck of an Alpha." Roger covered the phone for three or four seconds and then continued talking. "He's probably as hard to kill as you are. You'll have to use blessed silver, the whole nine yards."

I told him to go screw himself and hung up before I meant to, but he deserved it. This wasn't really my fault. If the werewolf from last night was so damn important then he should have been wearing a doggie collar and a tag. And he should have been warned not to hunt vampires so close to my club.

Before I could decide what to do about my suspicious tailgaters, my cell phone rang again. As soon as I said, "Hello?" the shit hit the fan. Another truck, a black one, pulled off of a side street and swerved to a sideways halt in front of me. The other two trucks sped up and rammed me from behind, knocking my Mustang into a skid.

I spun sideways, smashing into the truck in front of me. My Mustang flipped up and over. Metal scraped on concrete as it cartwheeled down the street. Loud music was coming from the cell phone. As the car rolled, I was dumped uncere-moniously onto the concrete (seat belt anyone?) and the cell phone flew out of my hand. Through the crunching death knell of my Mustang, I still managed to hear Sheena's whiny voice. "Boss, did Veruca say anything to you about coming in late, or taking the night off? Oh, and Talbot said to warn you . . ."

4

TABITHA:

MIDWIFE

When I awoke in Eric's bed, the first thing I felt was hunger. I was also cold, colder than I'd ever been. Nothing felt right. Noises were too loud, my skin felt too tight, and there was a really strong odor. It smelled like crotch. I realized Talbot was standing over in the corner. I snarled at him without meaning to, and suddenly my gums felt like they were on fire. The sensation was a cutting, jabbing, tearing feeling. I fell off the bed and smacked my head against the floor. That hurt, too.

I was on my feet again in an instant. The pain left, but my mouth still felt strange. Frightened, but excited, I ran my fingers along the inside of my mouth and there they were—

fangs! Oh my God! He had really done it. I was a vampire! I looked back in Talbot's direction; he was still there, silently watching.

Low, thumping, and filled with what I needed, Talbot's heart called to me. All other sounds faded into the background, a distant buzz. Talbot's features blurred until I recognized him only by his scent. I'd always thought Talbot was human, but no human could have a scent like his, tangy and wild. His skin grew semitranslucent and I don't know if it was an illusion or not, but I seemed to be able to see the blood coursing through his body. It wanted out. I wanted in.

So I charged him. Surely Eric wouldn't mind if I ate Talbot. Eric loved me and I was hungry. Thoughts that were not mine warred in my brain. Thinking rationally hurt. I didn't need to think, I needed to feed.

I can't eat Talbot, I told myself unconvincingly.

Of course you can, I disagreed. *He's food.*

No . . . he's . . . I wasn't even sure it really was Talbot now; his scent was gone, replaced with an odor that I couldn't describe. It was what food smells like, what blood smells like.

Talbot lashed out with his right hand and knocked me to the floor. I reacted instinctively, trying to scratch him, bite him, anything that would draw blood. He just laughed. God, how that pissed me off! Faster than I could understand, he was on top of me, straddling my thighs. One hand was on my throat and the other was on my chest pushing me down. He was so warm. My emotions went wild. Images passed through my head that would have made me retch the night before. I wanted him. I wanted him inside me and at the same time I wanted to rip his throat out. I wondered if I could have both if I was on top.

I don't know how long it took me to recognize the sound of my own name, but from the look on Talbot's face he'd been using it for a while. I opened my eyes, not realizing that I had closed them, and saw fresh scratches on his face. He was holding both of my wrists in one hand above my head while he squeezed my throat with the other. I was writhing and bucking under him trying to get free. He was surprisingly strong. I could smell his excitement; the scent mingled with that of the blood pumping through his veins . . . so close, just under the skin. I think I started screaming then, because he tightened his grip on my throat and told me to stop.

"One more scream out of you, Tabitha, and I don't care how put out Eric will be, I'll abort this little experiment. Now please try to be quiet. My hearing is better than yours and you're hurting my head. I'm going to feed you."

I went still, but I was keening. I think that's the word for what I was doing. I couldn't help it. I was so hungry. "I need it," I gasped. It was hard to speak with him choking me.

"I know you do." He sounded almost sympathetic. "But you have to be a good girl, or I really will kill you."

Staring at the slight trickle of blood running down his cheek, I strained to try and reach it with my tongue, even though his face was a foot or more from mine. I was vaguely conscious of a stream of babble coming from somewhere, as I stared at the blood. Someone was offering to perform a string of sexual acts ranging from simple to wild to outright depraved. Then I realized I was doing the offering. I would do anything for blood, or at least promise anything. I made myself stop. I hadn't expected it to be like this.

Talbot's light brown eyes turned green; the pupils became slits again. I remembered walking outside the lion cages at the zoo, the smell of the great cats. That was the smell of him. Shock flooded me at the realization he wasn't human, but then I was overcome by new images, dead lions, me crawling naked in their blood, lapping it up on all fours.

I shuddered in revulsion. "What's happening to me?"

"You're a vampire, princess, just like you wanted. You ever read 'The Monkey's Paw'?"

I shook my head. My books were about vampires, not monkeys. My sister had been the bookish type, not me.

"Why am I not surprised?" He laughed. I kept expecting his eyes to change back. They didn't. Instead, I watched fangs grow in his mouth, uppers and lowers, different than Eric's and mine. Ours were uppers only. Talbot's fangs looked like an animal's teeth had grown in, replacing his canines. It was hard not to keep staring at the blood on his cheek.

"Here's how this is going to work," Talbot said. "I'm not going to release you until I can trust you not to go into a feeding frenzy. . . ."

His voice faded away as I turned my attention to the door. Outside I could smell more blood. I could hear it calling me. There was a heartbeat to go with it and another smell, a bathroom smell that was dreadful. It reminded me of the women's restroom when I'd worked retail. Those women had been real skanks, but this smell was worse. My nostrils flared and I curled my upper lip. Another delicious heart-beat joined the first, but it brought with it even more yucky smells: age, smoke, and something else, something that reminded me of a hospital . . . some kind of sickness.

Talbot slapped me. I tried to bite him, but his hand was off my throat and back on it before I could react.

"Smell bad?" he purred. I nodded. I started keening again in spite of myself. So hungry. "I bet I smell pretty good, don't I?" I nodded again. I was having thoughts about Talbot that I'd never had before. If I could have put those thoughts on film I was pretty sure a whole lot of horny guys would have ordered it on pay-per-view. Talbot shifted his grip from my throat to the top of my head and slammed it into the floor two quick hard times. I saw stars, but I tried to bite him anyway, so he did it again. Dazed, I simply lay back and waited for what would happen next. I'd be damned before I let myself cry in front of him.

"It's simple, Tabitha. Marilyn and Desiree are each outside with a pint of blood. They are going to come in one at a time and feed it to you. It will be cold."

I began to shake my head violently. "No. Hot! I need it hot! I want it from the vein. Let me rip their throats open. We can share. I can drink them and you can fuck them—or me if you want. You can take me from behind and—"

"Shut! Up!" Talbot screamed and I tried to cover my ears. It was as if a gun had been fired next to my head. My ears rang. I thought he'd deafened me. I realized I was crying. The tears came rushing out and I couldn't stop them. As I cried, I could smell more blood, and I knew it was coming from me.

"Where's Eric?" I whined. "I want Eric! He'd feed me. He wouldn't let you do this to me. Let me go! When he finds out what you're doing—"

Talbot shouted again and all I could do was cry harder. Bastard. Didn't he know how it hurt? Couldn't he feel how I needed warmth as badly as I needed blood?

"Eric knows what I'm doing. He sent me in here to feed you because all it would take is one slipup from him and you'd be one short-lived little vampire. You get two pints of blood and you get them cold because if you had it warm you'd lose control of yourself and I might have to kill you in self-defense. Two pints ought to dull the pain and clear your head. Then I can educate you a little and answer your questions, but here's the thing. You have to keep the blood down and you have to drink both pints. Once the hunger starts to fade you're going to want to stop drinking, but you can't. I need you to have both pints in you so that you'll have a little self-control. Okay?"

I nodded. Two pints? God! Give me three pints. Give me a gallon! Let me drink the whole bar, every patron. Two pints. Ha!

Talbot called for Desiree and she came in. The smell of her grew stronger. She really did smell like a bathroom stall that needed cleaning. I realized that she must have just finished a set, because a sickening sweet smell of sweat and deodorant rolled off of her in waves, but as she drew near, the scent of the blood overwhelmed all of that. It wasn't that it smelled good or bad, it was just blood and blood was what I needed more than any junkie has ever needed any drug.

My muscles strained as I tried to pull free of Talbot to get to the blood.

Desiree kept walking. In her hands, she held a blood bag. It moved back and forth, almost hypnotizing me as it bounced gently from side to side with the rocking motion of her strides. Talbot must have been giving her instructions, but I couldn't hear them. Everything, my entire being, was centered on that pint of fluid. She knelt next to Talbot and opened one end of the bag before placing it over my open, eager mouth. I barely even tasted it. It didn't matter that it was cold or what type it was, all that mattered was that I needed it.

Before I knew it, I was finished with the bag and Marilyn was walking in while Desiree was hurrying out the door past her. Marilyn looked even more fragile than she had when I had last seen her. Her skin was wrinkled, her gray hair was unkempt, and she was wearing the same old-woman clothes she always wore. Her glasses made her eyes look huge and I could hear her labored breathing and the not quite steady beat of her heart. She smelled like smoke and I coughed as she came near. She gave me a disapproving look.

"You were so afraid of dying that you had him do this to you?" She shook her head, then attached one end of some IV tubing to the blood bag. Unlike Desiree, Marilyn seemed practiced at this. She knelt next to me and gently slid the tube between my lips like a drinking straw. She wasn't afraid at all, but I did notice that she was careful to keep her fingers out of reach. As I sucked greedily at the tube, she took a handkerchief from her pocket and began to wipe the bloody tears from my face. "Are you in love with him?"

A growing calm spread out from the center of my body, slowly moving through each limb, filling me, sating my thirst. It had nothing to do with Marilyn's words and everything to do with the blood. My senses seemed to dim slightly. Smells were still strong, but more bearable. I could still hear the beating of Talbot's heart, but it was a faint rhythm, reassuring in its presence.

Slowly, I began to notice the taste and texture of the blood. Before, I'd needed it and it wouldn't have mattered if it had tasted like battery acid. It wasn't bad, but it wasn't good, either; it reminded me of milk, but with a strong copper taste, sort of like sucking on a penny—a cold penny. It certainly wasn't the grossest thing I'd ever put in my mouth, and it definitely wasn't my first taste of the stuff. Vampire boyfriend, remember? I kept drinking and Talbot smiled at me from behind friendly brown eyes. Whatever he'd been expecting, I'd proved him wrong.

When I was done, Marilyn stood back. Talbot was still on top of me and I finally noticed that I was naked, on the floor, being straddled by a large man who was noticeably excited. Oh my God. I tried to cover myself and Talbot laughed as he let me up. "Oh, so now we're modest," he said jovially. "After all the things you were just offering to do to me?"

I expected myself to blush, but nothing happened. I rushed over to the closet, grabbed one of Eric's shirts, and ran into the bathroom. I looked into the mirror and saw nothing. I gasped. I should have expected this; I knew it would happen. But somehow it's different when it's you.

Marilyn opened the door behind me, carrying my underwear and one of my dresses. "You look better than ever, Tabitha," she said sadly. "You'll just never be able to look in the mirror for reassurance. You might find your clothes are a little loose."

I got dressed under her watchful eye. The silence was uncomfortable. "I'll just have to watch Eric's reaction to see how good I look now, I guess. It won't be so bad."

Marilyn shook her head and left the room. Dressed but shoeless, I followed her. "What? Is there something I don't know? Did something happen to him?"

Marilyn ignored me, walking out of the bedroom and shutting the door behind her. Talbot was leaning against the door frame with his arms crossed over his chest. "What's her problem?" I asked him.

"One thing you need to know about Eric, Tabitha. I've known him a long time and I know you think that this is going to be some wonderful eternal love thing, but I've seen this happen before and odds are—"

"Odds are?" I asked.

He let out a long breath before continuing. "Odds are he'll ask you to leave."

What? That wasn't possible. Talbot was playing some sort of sick game with me. My fangs came out and so did his. They didn't hurt as much the second time. The sensation was more of an uncomfortable distension combined with a jaw-popping feeling that was nowhere near my jaw.

"I love him," I said. "I would do anything for him. I did this for him, so that we could be together."

Talbot's voice was calm and steady like a judge delivering a death sentence. "I've only ever known Eric to love one woman, Tabitha, and she just walked out that door."

"Marilyn? But he can't even sleep with her," I argued. "She's old! She's nothing. I'm forever young. Look at me. I've got the body of a goddess. I can do things to him now that no human woman could ever imagine."

Talbot just stared at me. I tried to convince myself that he was lying, but there was a look in his eyes that wounded me. It wasn't sadness, but a look of familiarity, like he'd heard it all before and some of it twice.

"Did Eric ever say he loved you?" Talbot asked finally.

"No," I whispered.

"What did he tell you when you asked?"

"He . . . he would . . ." I could feel my lower lip begin to tremble. Whether it was rage, sadness, or despair, I didn't know. Maybe all three. "He would say I was a moist warm tightness with all the necessary parts." I was crying again. Talbot turned away.

"One thing about Eric, he doesn't hide his feelings. If he loved you, he'd have told you." As he opened the door, Talbot looked back. "I'll be right outside when you're ready to learn the ropes."

He left me alone and all I felt was the cold.

5

ERIC:

DEAD CAR

They'd killed my Mustang. It lay on its back in the road, a dead metal cockroach leaking oil and antifreeze onto the asphalt. One of the wheel covers rolled across the road, the three-pronged center of the simulated knockoff hub blurring like a propeller until it hit the base of a streetlight with an insulting clang.

The trucks skidded into a circle around the Mustang, completely blocking off the intersection. Two men stepped out of each truck. As I watched, long lupine claws pushed out through their fingernails and their human teeth dropped to the ground. The werewolves' muzzles flowed forward, fangs bared. I'm sure they meant the display to be impressive, but it still looked to me more like bad special effects. At least they weren't all the same generic brown as Wolfy from the alley. These six must have come out of the variety pack; there were two gray, two black, and two that looked more like werehuskies than werewolves.

"So which two are the Cool Ranch?" I asked. They charged at me, and I fought for control. The red tinge to my vision faded even as I popped my fangs. This was important. I wanted to remember killing the bastards that had murdered my Mustang.

The two gray wolves were a little faster than the others, so they reached me first. I caught one by the muzzle, flinging him across the intersection and through the glass front of an antique shop. The shop's burglar alarm sounded as the other guy sank his fangs into my shoulder. I wondered if there was a little werewolf handbook that insisted the shoulder was the best place to bite a vampire. It hurt like an old wound, a remembered pain.

The werewolf I'd thrown into the storefront recovered quickly and raced back to help his partner. When he ripped my belly open I definitely felt it, but I know what it's like to be engulfed in flame and staked through the heart. In comparison, this was nothing. Pain is fleeting for the undead. Our nerve endings don't work the same as those of the living. The initial damage registers, but unless the weapons are blessed or something, the ache doesn't last.

As the fight went on, I gained a little more respect for their methods. They worked well together, a real team. It made me miss fighting alongside Greta.

"You assholes know you can't kill me, right?" I tightened my grip on the muzzle of the gray that had gutted me and listened to his teeth crack. He kept right on tearing into me with his claws and his buddy kept chewing on my shoulder.

They wanted me to scream or beg for mercy, but it wasn't going to happen. The injuries didn't annoy me that much. Vlads heal quickly and I heal quicker than most, but healing is hungry work and it did mean that I would need to feed again before dawn.

I planted a foot on each of the grays' chests, but before I could try to push off, the two black werewolves joined the fray and grabbed my legs. Still, I was winning, not the fight against the werewolves, but the fight against myself. The more I reined in my anger, bit it back, choked on it, the more I realized that I needed to talk to these guys, to see if I could stop this before it got even more out of hand and I was facing down twenty or thirty of them.

Just then two more werewolves showed up in another matching truck. The werewolves that got out of it were brown. "You two must be the corn chips," I told the newcomers. They didn't get the joke, but one of the huskies hovering on the sidelines chuckled. I guess the huskies were the Cool Ranch.

"Do you have anything to say for yourself, vampire?" asked one of the black-furred pair.

I considered trying to bite the gray to get him off of my shoulder, but I answered the question instead. "Yeah, take me to your leader." Once again only the huskies seemed to get the joke. Maybe my humor was too old. "Seriously, I want to talk to your Alpha . . . Willard or whatever his name is." I sighed. "Why else do you think I'm not turning to mist right now?"

Actually the real reason I wasn't turning to mist is that I couldn't, didn't know anyone who could. Animals, yes. Mist, no. I'd tried it once and instead of turning into a cloud, I'd gone translucent blue like Obi-Wan Kenobi in *The Empire Strikes Back*. It had felt like dying, all the life-force draining out of me, the world changing colors, blurring. Turning back had been hard, too. It had taken the better part of an hour, and once my body finally re-formed, I promised myself never to screw around with it again.

Roger was the only one who'd seen me do it and we'd both agreed that I shouldn't try it again. "It looked like you almost died, Eric," Roger had told me. "I'd be scared of getting stuck that way."

I shuddered at the memory and came back to the present. Eight pairs of eyes stared at me from unconvincing giant Harryhausen-esque wolf heads.

I tried talking again, but this time I spoke slowly and clearly. "Will you take me to your Alpha? Maybe we can work something out." I felt a sharp blow to the back of my head.

"What the hell are you doing back there?" I asked angrily.

Two more whacks and my vision blurred; out of the corner of my eye, I saw the stake. It wasn't one of those fancy things with a real weapon grip like proper vampire hunters use. A long jagged splinter jutted out from a mahogany spindle with a dark finish, like someone had snapped the stretcher off of an old rocking chair. Either these guys didn't usually hunt vampires, or they weren't used to taking prisoners. As the stake arced toward my chest, I tried to transform.

I didn't care what I turned into: bat, cat, snake, rat, frog, wolf, or raven. I can do them all, which is unusual. I even managed a flea once. The problem is that changing into anything takes concentration, and I didn't have any to spare.

My other option was to just give in to my anger and let myself go berserk. But going berserk would mean more dead werewolves and I needed to keep the body count down if I was going to find a way to make peace with the Alpha.

Before I could think up Plan C, someone hit me again. My vision stretched and the lights went out as I felt the stake slide home. You learn something new every day. My lesson for today was: If you knock a vampire out before you stake him, you can drag him around in the back of your new pickup truck and he won't know what's happening.

Even in my unconscious state, letting them beat me grated on my nerves. I should have been able to take them. It's not like there was a full moon or anything. I know myths and legends talk about werewolves going crazy and eating people during the full moon, but as far as I can tell all the full moon does is make them bigger and meaner. I can't ever remember which one is waxing or waning, but the moon looked like a sideways grin, so I figured these boys were at about half power.

I decided to enjoy the nap. My night was fucked anyway. I'd already lost my Mustang. I didn't want to lose anything else. Fighting werewolves isn't like dealing with vampires. They travel in packs. The idea of two dozen werewolves tearing through the Demon Heart wasn't pretty. If they had me, then they'd leave the club alone; they'd leave Marilyn and Roger and Tabitha alone.

If I was lucky, they'd do what I was hoping and actually take me to their Alpha. Maybe we could work this out. I'd probably killed his son; he'd definitely killed my Mustang. It was an even trade from my perspective.

I don't know how long I was out, but my world came back in a sudden rush of pain. I swear stakes hurt worse coming out than they do going in. I was in a bag that smelled kind of like feathers, but there was flannel and something synthetic there, too. A sleeping bag. Cute. A ragged hole gaped in the bag over my chest where someone, one of my captors, I guessed, had ripped it open to remove the stake. I wasn't on fire, which meant it was either still night out or I was in a covered area someplace.

I fumbled with my watch, finally managing to hit the right button. A soft blue glow showed the time as 03:03, just after three in the morning. Still dark.

Fangs and claws at the ready, I ripped my way out of the sleeping bag and looked around. Pickup truck. Parking lot. Woods. The smell of water filled my nostrils. It smelled clean . . . untainted . . . no chlorine. There was no sign of whoever had unstaked me.

It was extremely dark . . . a real look-out-behind-you kind of dark, perfect for vampire vision. I took a few minutes to explore my surroundings. Crickets chirped loudly, a dis-

tant frog splashed down into lake water, and somewhere out
in the night an owl hooted. The gravel lot was almost full
of cars and trucks. A small building off to one side smelled
like it contained a couple of poorly maintained restrooms. A
concrete boat launch sloped gently down to the lake, and a
set of concrete steps led down to a little marina where thirty
or forty boat slips served as a waterside parking lot. There
were only a few boats parked at the moment: a couple of
pontoon boats, a speedboat, and a rickety-looking fishing
boat made of aluminum.

Dense woods covered the lakeshore opposite the marina
and I could only make out one house, old but in good repair,
its short wooden dock poking out into the lake, a moored
pontoon boat bobbing gently with the natural rise and fall
of the water.

I remembered this place. It was called Orchard Lake. My
family used to come out here when I was a kid. It was part of
the county water supply, not exactly a state park, but a public lake. The homes were only accessible from the water; the
absence of boats at the marina meant most of the residents
were home.

Far to the left of the marina, Orchard Dam kept the lake
fat and happy. It also kept all that water from destroying the
expensive developments that had sprung up downstream.
Below the dam, only a little creek tumbled away through
the woods, while the lake itself ran some fifteen miles in the
other direction.

Orchard Lake was old, a sprawling gem tucked away in
a pocket of forest and mountains, slowly being encroached

upon by overpriced suburbia. Sable Oaks, Greymont, and Harvest Estates bordered the Orchard Lake area, but none of them came within a mile of the lake itself. The lake homes were older houses, passed down through the families of blue collar workers, real salt of the earth folks.

Back when we were alive, every time we'd get a little plastered, Roger would talk about how he was going to be rich one day and buy up Orchard Lake. He wanted to turn it into a hoity-toity community for rich old farts and politicians. A lot of people had the same idea. Over the years, countless developers had tried to purchase the land, but nobody would sell. The news always seemed to show the same old guy claiming, "My grandpa built this house with his own two hands," and refusing to give in even at outlandish prices.

I shook my head to clear it, wondering where the werewolf variety pack had gone. It was three in the morning. I'd been out for six hours or more, and Orchard Lake was only an hour or so from town.

"Hello?" I called out. Silence.

Why go through all the trouble of ambushing me only to unstake me in an abandoned marina and run away? Clearly, I did not understand the modern werewolf. All four trucks could be accounted for amid the other vehicles. Gravel crunching under my feet, I scouted the place a little more.

As I followed the drive down to the boat launch, the scent of gunpowder and blood drifted over to me from the nearby woods. Werewolf blood. I followed the smell up and over the half of the mountain that the parking lot hadn't claimed and found the werewolves easily enough.

They'd been cut to ribbons, dead for at least an hour. It was worse than what I'd done to the werewolf in the alley the night before. I was pretty sure there were enough pieces to make most of eight werewolves.

Just to check, I sifted through the bodies, stacking the heads in a neat little row. Two of them had obvious bullet holes. One shot had been close range to the temple; the fur was badly powder burned. Not the most pleasant of smells. The second one had been shot through the back of the head, and I didn't see an exit wound.

Morbid curiosity got the better of me and I cracked the skull open. The bullet wasn't hard to find; I just followed the trail of blackened gray matter from the back of the skull to where the bullet had lodged in the side of the frontal bone, above the nasal cavity and between the eyes.

I'm not a big gun person, but the bullet looked weird even to me. On *CSI* when they pull the bullet out of a dead guy it looks like a little metal rock, but this one looked whole, casing included.

My brain was fuzzy and my head hurt. *Concentrate*, I told myself. Each werewolf's body had long jagged claw marks, and one had had his heart ripped out. Aside from the bullet wounds, the werewolves looked like they'd been torn apart by a vampire. It would look even more gruesome in daylight, when the remains reverted from wolf form to human.

I leaned in closer, examining the wounds. They looked familiar. Damn. Resting my hand atop one of the ragged cuts, I extended my claws. They weren't quite a match, but they were close, and now the whole area probably smelled like me, too.

If not for the bullet holes, someone might have convinced me that I'd blacked out and done it, but I don't own a pistol and these boys hadn't been killed with vampire claws. Now that I was suspicious, I could find bullet holes in several other body parts. No more bullets, though.

I'd been framed.

Unable to discern anything more from the bodies, I walked back down to the boat launch. Brains and blood washed off of the single silver bullet I'd retrieved, leaving it looking bright and new. It was warm to the touch even after I cleaned it off in the cool lake water. Little markings glowed faintly in the dark.

Magic bullet. Bodies cut up to look like I did it. . . . But why go through all the trouble to dig out the other bullets and leave this one behind—unless I was supposed to find it? I put the bullet in the pocket of my jeans and knelt by the water. *Somebody doesn't want me and the Alpha werewolf to kiss and make up, but they don't have the nerve to kill me themselves.*

It didn't particularly bother me that the variety pack had been killed, but something in the back of my head (my brain, maybe) was telling me that I'd been outsmarted. Someone had figured out that I would go with them to try to see Willard or Wilbur, or whatever his name was, and had arranged this mess to ensure that didn't happen, taking a fucked-up set of circumstances and boosting them to a whole new level of suckage.

That meant it was political and possibly out of my league.

But I did know a guy who might know a guy. Roger knew all the bigwigs in town, the annoying seedy little assholes who pretended to be royalty.

I reached for my cell phone before I remembered it was littering the street back in Void City. By my watch, I'd wasted forty minutes wandering around the parking lot. For once, I remembered the sun. I did not want to be caught hiding in the restrooms here if the pack managed to locate their buddies, and it was over an hour's drive back to Void City.

There were no keys in the truck and I've never learned how to hot-wire a vehicle. Unless I absolutely had to do it, I didn't relish the idea of breaking into one of the lake homes; too many windows, no basements. There had to be a gas station around here somewhere. I might be able to make it to a pay phone. Maybe Talbot could drive out here and pick me up before dawn. It wasn't a good plan, but it was the best I had.

I made it halfway up the mountain before I realized I'd make better time flying than I would on foot. Orchard Dam Road was a winding curving thing and the shortest distance between two points . . . I concentrated on what it was like to be a bat. To the observer, it's pretty quick, but to the vampire doing it, transforming into something that small is painful. It's like having cold-water shrinkage so bad your testicles retract, taking refuge in the pelvis.

Some vampires leave their clothes behind when they change. My daughter is one of them. I'm not. My clothes folded in with me as I sprouted leathery wings and launched skyward.

Bat radar gives me headaches, so I rely mostly on my bat vision. Bats have good eyesight at long distances, so it wasn't too bad. I felt very cold, though. A smaller body meant the cold went to my core faster, and even though it was a sultry summer evening at ground level, it's always colder in the air.

The trees stretched out below me as I flew, heading south to avoid crossing too close to Sable Oaks. County Road 58 was hard to miss, but every time I tried to cross it, something interfered with my senses, making everything hazy and wavering. I don't know if it was residual heat from the asphalt or what, but it was bad enough that I stuck to the forest edge.

A few miles down the road, I had a thought, and if I'd had a human throat, I'd have cursed. As it was, I made a little squeaky irate bat sound. Who the hell had unstaked me and where had he gone? How had he gotten far enough away to escape my notice in the time it took me to rip my way out of a sleeping bag? It didn't seem to make sense.

6

TABITHA:

VAMPIRE 101

Halfway through the lesson, I was having a hard time listening to Talbot. We were over in the Pollux Theater across from the club, alone. I loved every inch of its elaborately detailed elegance, from the real velvet of the curtains to the leather-covered seats to the sweeping balconies and carved balustrades.

There was no orchestra pit. I sat in the front row only a few feet from the wooden stage, a massive structure that appeared to be about three feet high, though I knew there was a whole basement underneath, still filled with props and pieces of scenery, and a little room where the pipe organ was stored when it wasn't onstage.

It wasn't that I didn't want to know how the whole vampire thing worked; it was more that I couldn't get a handle on Talbot and it was driving me crazy. I'm a focused girl. I set a goal for myself, a man I want or a dress or whatever, and I go out and do what it takes to get it.

Talbot was driving me nuts by refusing to do one simple thing. He was leaning casually against the stage in front of me, and I knew he must have had a good view from there, but no matter what I did, I could not get him to stare at my breasts. I'd never tried when I was alive because I didn't want to lead him on, but now that I was a vampire, it was like my brain had been restructured. My thoughts were still mine, I hadn't exactly stopped being me, but there was a predatory urge coloring everything.

I'd assumed it would be hard getting used to people as food, but it wasn't. The best way I can describe it is that it's like dreaming. You're in the center of a little make-believe universe. Everything around you is for your amusement, pleasure, or dismay. Nothing you do in a dream has any real consequences. For me, that was how being undead felt.

The red tones in the Pollux's velvet curtains were vibrant even though I knew there was a layer of dust covering them. The wind blew through the air ducts with a musical tone so distinct that I would recognize it anywhere. Talbot droned on, but his words weren't important. I watched his eyes, his skin, his pulse, and inhaled his scent.

Finally, he stopped trying to explain whatever it was he had been talking about, stalked up to my seat, and put his big hands right over my breasts. "If I stare at these will it make you pay attention to what I'm saying?" He jiggled them briefly as he spoke and then let go.

I was mortified. Had I really been that obvious? "Because," he continued, "I could do that, but I want you to know right now that neither you nor any other human is of any interest to me in that way."

So he was a pervert, a real pervert. I wondered what exactly he did like. Sheep? "Wait a minute," I protested. "You were really excited back in the bedroom. That wasn't fake. I could smell it, not to mention the way you were poking me with that thing."

Talbot laughed. It wasn't a mean laugh, more like he'd just heard a hilarious joke, but it felt mean anyway. I don't like to be laughed at. My fangs came out. It was only the third time, but it already felt natural. There was the same stretching jaw-popping feeling, but it was a good sort of hurt. I hissed at him, and he grinned crookedly at me. "Let's just say that it's a dominance thing. You were trying to get away and you couldn't. I like that. It's perfectly natural for one of my kind."

"Are you a were-something?" I asked. It was hard to believe he wasn't human. Then again, it wasn't like I paid close attention to any of the guys here, other than Eric.

"No," he answered. "Now listen; we aren't here to learn about me. We are here to learn about your new lifestyle. Your unlifestyle. You with me?"

I nodded. I knew that I could get him to tell me what he was eventually, or maybe get Eric to tell me. It was simply a matter of time.

"What," asked Talbot, "is the last thing you remember?"

"You told me about the whole mirror thing, which I'd pretty much figured out. You said I should stay out of sunlight, which I already knew. You covered the garlic thing and holy symbols, blessed weapons, and not getting my heart or head ripped out, off, destroyed, or whatever. That pretty much covers what I heard. I don't remember what was last. It all ran together."

"Okay," Talbot said. He slipped back into lecture mode, and I tried to pay attention this time. "The number one thing to remember about being a vampire is that the biggest threat that you have is yourself. When you feed, try not to kill anyone. The best way to do that is to eat before you get too hungry. The more ravenous you are, the harder it will be for you to control yourself. If you don't want to act like you did earlier, when you were totally out of control, don't skip meals.

"If you do kill someone, then remove the head or the heart to keep them from rising as bloodsucking zombies. Eric calls them wampyres because he's read too much crap on the Internet, but they're just zombies.

"Don't get sloppy. When you kill a human, you have to dispose of the body or have it done for you. It costs twice as much if the city has to take care of it."

"Costs more?"

"Void City is vampire owned and operated. The Council of High Magic makes them use guild mages for most disposal services, so they get a nice tidy kickback every month. It drives the prices up.

"What else? Oh, if one of your snacks comes back as a ghost, tell me or Eric about it. We'll get Magbidion to move them along. He's cheaper than a guild mage and he's pretty good at keeping under their radar. In addition, ghosts are less likely if you destroy the corpse completely. Don't get caught and don't leave any evidence behind.

"Eric does a piss-poor job of getting rid of bodies, which is one of the reasons that he likes to eat in and one of the reasons he keeps Magbidion around. Eric tends to eat a little bit from several different people and he tends to prefer his employees. You already know that, but what you don't know is that once you start feeding directly from the vein, it gets hard not to drink it all at once.

"Blood bags are good, if you don't mind it being cold or room temp. Eric usually feeds that way once or twice a week. Most vampires loathe cold blood. Eric doesn't and you don't seem to have that issue either, which puts you one up on a lot of them.

"You can even try animal blood. Eric can't drink it, his body rejects it rather violently, but most vampires can and some do so exclusively. If you choose to feed by killing people, Eric will be likely to make you leave sooner than he might otherwise. You may notice that he breaks his own rules. I wouldn't suggest pointing the double standard out to him. He already knows.

"For the first few months you may feel like you have to go to the bathroom. Don't. The phantom sensations will fade more quickly if you don't indulge them. Some vampires do continue those functions because it makes them feel more normal, but all that comes out is blood and it's better not to waste it that way. You may also have bouts of panic when you feel like you're suffocating. You don't have to breathe anymore, but your mind can and will play tricks on you. After all, you're used to breathing automatically and it can be disquieting once it sinks in that you only breathe when you consciously think about it."

Feeling a little bit like I was back in high school, I raised my hand. "When do you get to the powers part?" I asked when he acknowledged me. "I mean, I know I still need to know all this other stuff, but I should be able to do cool stuff, too. What can I do?"

I don't know how to describe Talbot's look. He clearly disapproved, but there was something else in his eyes that made me feel there was more to it. "That kind of attitude can get you killed, but to answer your question: I don't know. Eric has a lot of powers, real Dracula-type stuff. He's a Vlad."

"Vlad?"

"Vamps come in four flavors: Drones, Soldiers, Masters, and Vlads. They used to be called Serfs, Knights, Barons, and Kings." He hopped up onto the stage, pacing back and forth along the very edge. "Remind you of anything?"

"Should it?"

"It should remind you of the feudal system. Vampire society is slow to change, but as time goes by the names get updated by the new recruits."

"So Eric is like a king?"

"It's not literal. It's a classification of power levels. Vlads have all the powers in the book and tend to keep coming back no matter what you do to them, just like Dracula."

I knew my Eric was special . . . and as the offspring of a King, I should be special, too. "So that makes me a Queen, right?"

"It has nothing to do with bloodline, and everything to do with personality, the strength of an individual's character. I've always thought of it as a supernatural Rorschach test."

"Then what am I?"

"I don't know," Talbot said, hopping off the stage and landing adroitly on his feet in front of me. "You'll find out, in time, through experimentation. Roger could tell you for sure. He's a Master."

"A master of what?" I smirked.

"A Master vampire. Masters and Vlads can sense each other, tell who is who. Vlads can also announce themselves to other vampires, kind of like a psychic challenge, but it's rude, so even if you are a Vlad, you don't want to go around announcing yourself."

"Can't Eric just tell me what I am when he gets back?"

"You'd think so," Talbot said, "but a sire can't usually sense his offspring's power level."

"Why not?"

"I don't know. I didn't make the rules. What I know mostly comes from what I've observed with Eric. In some areas, I'm just as uninformed as he is. Thralls are a good example. I know very little about them other than that they are humans that serve vampires and that Eric refuses to make one or to allow his offspring to make them. For now, though, let's only worry about the basics."

I looked him in the eye to show I was paying attention, but I think he took it the wrong way.

"Don't try to mesmerize me either. Vampires can't entrance c—my kind."

"I wasn't," I protested.

"No harm done, but be careful looking other vampires in the eyes unless you trust them. As Melville said, 'The eyes are the gateway to the soul.' With vampires, he wasn't kidding."

"So I can take over people's minds?" I giggled.

"You can," Talbot replied, "but a human with strong will can resist you and a vampire with a stronger will than yours can take you over instead."

I yawned. I didn't care about Talbot, didn't want to be with him, didn't need to know this stuff. I wanted Eric. I did try to listen as Talbot began to lecture on what he called "the second biggest threat to vampires," but visions of Eric filled my mind. Despite what Talbot and Marilyn had told me, I had to see him. Even more so, I needed him to see me.

Marilyn had been right about my clothes feeling loose. After I'd been fed the cold blood and Talbot had left the bedroom, I had wound up borrowing clothes out of Amanda's trunk. Amanda was a charity case who'd overdosed on crack about a week before I'd moved in with Eric, and no one had ever come to claim her things.

She'd had this whole black leather temptress thing going on and she'd been frighteningly thin. I dug through her outfits and put together an ensemble I thought Eric would go for. It wasn't all that revealing, but it was what I call a highlighter outfit. What it didn't show, it highlighted and underlined. I was wearing it now. Since it was made for the stage, it came off in sections and I could barely wait to see which parts Eric would want to take off and which ones he would want to leave on. Kelly and Desiree had both assured me I looked sexy beyond belief. They had also helped me with my hair and makeup; I already missed mirrors.

Even the thought of Eric made me tremble in a way I hadn't been sure that I would be able to as an undead. I ached for him. He could say all of the terrible things he wanted about me and claim I was nothing more to him than a sex toy, but I knew the passion he showed when we were together, the way he needed me, the way he sometimes just held me close for hours.

If Eric didn't love me, then why was I the only one he took into his bed? Candice wanted him and I knew he wanted her, but he had never been with her. He was faithful. Sure, sometimes he would have me dress up as other women, now and then even call me by their names, but that was just his way of spicing up the bedroom.

All guys have fantasies, and Eric held none of them back from me. He trusted me with all of his darkest urges and most of them I was happy to fulfill, even if a few of them were a little nasty. Eric loved me, he had to love me, and what he'd said didn't matter.

"Anyone who says otherwise is a liar!"

It dawned on me that I had spoken that last sentence aloud. Color was slowly bleeding back into my vision, replacing the red tint that I hadn't even noticed until it started to fade. My fangs were out and as I looked down at my hands, I could see that my fingernails were longer than they had been. They were sharp and a little curved at the ends, like claws or talons. My skin had grown even paler than before, virtually a true white. Someone was growling. It was me. A rapid drumbeat pounded in my ears, throbbing.

Talbot clapped. "Well, now we know that you have claws, you can make your eyes glow red, and you haven't been listening to a word I've been saying unless you really do agree so vehemently about the third biggest threat to vampires."

I nodded. "Yes . . . I mean, no, I wasn't listening." As I calmed down, I noticed that I was standing up and that the pounding in my head was Talbot's heartbeat. My claws retracted into fingernails again. It felt much weirder than the fangs had, the physical equivalent of the sound fingernails make on a chalkboard. My vision returned to normal, too, although my skin tone didn't. Interesting. "I'm sorry, Talbot. It's just that I want to see him. I need him."

"I know you do," he said softly.

"He does love me," I insisted.

"I hope you're right, little girl." In an unexpected move, Talbot put his arms around me and gave me a hug. The warmth of him encompassed me as if his heart beat inside my own chest. I fought the urge to sink my teeth into his flesh, but it was one of the hardest things I'd ever done. The hug must have lasted less than a second, but when he stepped away I was trembling. He looked into my eyes and I saw what I thought was compassion.

"Very good. You pass."

"Pass?" I asked, confused.

"Do I look like a touchy-feely guy to you?" His eyes went slit-pupiled again and he roared at me, his bestial fangs looming large and dangerous between his jaws. This time he flashed claws, too, curved feline things, sharper than mine, with needle-thin points. His other smell resurfaced, too: jungle cat musk. "If you'd bitten me, I'd have ended you and told Eric you were too stupid to keep around."

"I'd like to see you try," I shot back with more defiance than confidence.

"I'd succeed." He chuckled and let his features become human again. "I don't know why I'm trying to impress you. I've been humanoid too long." He sighed abruptly. "We'll pick this up a little later. Why don't we see if we can round you up another couple pints of blood and then you can experiment with your powers."

I nodded and followed him back across the street to the club. Powers. I'd show him powers.

7

ERIC:

LITTLE SISTER

Dawn was beautiful. The fiery tendrils of morning crimson bathed me in their warm glow. The sun, with typical brilliance, cast its loving gaze in my direction. Had I been alive, I would have turned to face it with joy, or more likely put on my shades to prevent my usual hangover from getting worse. Either way, I wouldn't have fallen out of the sky and into the woods on account of it. I told you my time sense sucked. Admittedly, being ignited two mornings in a row was a bit unusual for me. It wasn't my record—there had been a really strange week in El Segundo—but it was unusual.

Flailing my fiery bat wings wasn't helping the situation, so I turned human again as I fell. Strictly speaking, I suppose

I should have been naked since I'd certainly been a naked bat, but it never works that way for me. I re-formed with all my clothes on just before I hit the root system of an oak tree. Fortunately for me, the trees would keep me shaded from the sun until it rose higher . . . a couple of hours, at least. My eyes started to close and I shook myself awake.

Shit like this never seemed to happen to vampires in the movies. Where were my vampire groupies, my loyal hench-lings? Where was fucking Renfield? I didn't want to break into anyone's house, but I didn't want to be burned to ash, either.

There were other options. I could hide under a car, or in a doghouse, or in a mailbox. I could dig a hole and bury myself, technically, but what I really wanted was for Talbot to somehow sense that I needed him and to come pick my burnt ass up and take me home.

I walked through the woods, grateful that I lived in the South, where civilization and forest intermingle from the mountains to the beach. Lots of subdivisions extended right into the woods. Through the trees up ahead, I could see a long line of houses, the leading edge of suburbia.

It had recently become highly fashionable to cut down as few trees as possible; in some areas, contractors built side-walks and even porches right around existing trees. This subdivision was older, but at least the contractor had let the trees run right up to the property line of the houses, espe-cially where the natural slope of the terrain made building a little more difficult.

One guy was starting his car on my side of the street

in the shadows while a woman was doing the same thing on the other side of the street in full sunlight. There were people in the houses. I could sense them. Some were asleep and others were waking, showering, getting ready, brushing their teeth. There were two people still in the nearest house, the one the man had just left. Both of them sounded female, one younger than the other: a mother and daughter.

I moved from house to house along the shady side of the street, concealed by the trees. The houses were all two stories, most with vinyl siding, and each house had somebody home.

I looked at my watch. It was 6:50 on a nice Sunday morning. Didn't any of these assholes go to church? Back when I was alive, it had seemed like I was the only one who didn't go to church on Sunday. How long had this been going on? What time did church service start now? Eight o'clock? Nine? I couldn't wait that long; the sun would be really most sincerely up and this whole stupid subdivision would be bathed in light.

I started toward the closest house, even though it had a family of four inside, but the same strange vibe I'd gotten last night, the odd discomfort that kept me from flying across the county road, repulsed me. It wasn't the same feeling a blessed house gives off, it was something else, and it almost had a smell, like badly burned toast. It could have been anything, an amateur mage, a botched breakfast attempt . . . I was too tired to figure it out.

Through the haze, one of the houses suddenly looked perfect. It smelled like freshly baked cinnamon rolls, and the aroma drew me closer nearly against my will. I'd never liked cinnamon rolls in life, but this was intoxicating, almost as much as pizza. If I'd been a cartoon, the scent might have lifted me off of my feet and carried me along.

The wooden privacy fence was short enough to jump and there was an obliging shade tree that completely bridged the gap from fence to garage; only one person was home, plus the house had blacked-out windows in one of the second-story rooms. An amateur photographer would have just the sort of room I could use as shelter until Talbot could come pick me up.

The door to the garage was locked. Rather than force it, I turned into a mouse and crawled under the space between the garage door and the concrete. I turned human again on the other side and looked around for a light switch. The garage smelled of old gasoline and bagged grass. Despite the noxiousness of the smell, I felt a twinge in the back of my throat. I was getting hungry. In the warmth and humidity of the garage, I caught myself falling asleep again. Being exposed to the sun by a goofball with a garage-door opener didn't sound like fun to me, though, so I shook myself awake again.

I usually go to sleep a few hours after dawn, but I can make it to early afternoon if necessary. Once or twice I'd managed to stay up all day, but each time, I'd passed out at sunset and slept clear through to the next one.

The bulb blew when I tried to turn the lights on. I had almost been expecting it. It was the way things had been going since Friday night: one big fuckup after another. The inside door was locked. My foot did a pretty good job of opening it before I remembered that I was trying to be sneaky. Upstairs I heard a girl sit up in bed. It sounded like she was grabbing something off of the floor. "Mom?" she cried out. "Dad?"

"Nope," I said under my breath. "Not quite."

I heard footsteps. Hungry though I was, I didn't want to eat this teenage kid, home alone on a Sunday morning. Wasn't she supposed to be watching cartoons? Or was that Saturday? The door from the garage opened up into a little eating space adjoining the kitchen. I sped across the linoleum and into a sitting room that had been converted into a home office. Hanging blinds over the bay window were all that stood between me and an instant sunburn. A small stream of sunlight scorched my leg where one of the blinds was askew.

Where to hide? I considered my options quickly, racing the footsteps overhead. There were no good hiding places. I could smell her now. Her scent was familiar, somehow, and afraid. She also smelled a little excited, which got me a little excited, too, but if I wasn't going to kill her, it was unlikely that I was going to force myself on her either.

I'd always thought vampires turned into black cats, but it never seemed to work that way for me. Slowly but surely she came down the stairs. A white long-furred kitty waited for her. Of the various creatures I could turn into, it was usually a good bet that the cat would get the most sympathetic reaction. She came around the corner, saw me, and shrieked. Now, what kind of person is afraid of cats?

She was a beautiful girl, dark haired, with smooth skin

and bright green eyes. She looked like a younger, more attractive Tabitha. She was wearing a white tank top and panties. Despite the baseball bat in her hands, I was noticing things that I shouldn't have been. And then I recognized her. She was the girl in the battered photo Tabitha carried in her purse. I cursed in whatever language it is that cats speak and turned into myself again.

She froze, midscream. "So," I said casually, "you must be Rachel."

She cocked her head to one side and began slowly backing away from me. "I'm Eric," I offered lamely. "Your sister's boyfriend?"

She stopped and looked at me. Her fear was subsiding and I smelled something that it would have been better if I hadn't. Was Tabitha's whole family a big mob of vampire junkies? I wondered what would happen if I got Tabitha, Rachel, and their mother all in a room together. It was yet another image to be added to my internal wall of shame. Did all men have thoughts like these? If so, why wasn't I smart enough to keep them to my subconscious?

Roger had once told me that all I had to do if I wanted to rule the world was keep my mouth shut, my pants on, and my temper under control. "What about sunlight?" I'd asked him. He'd laughed at me and said that if I was strong enough to rein in the first three things, he was pretty sure even sunlight wouldn't be a problem for me.

"Holy shit! And you really are a vampire? What are you doing here? Is Tab with you?" Rachel asked. She'd gotten closer to me in the brief moment I'd been lost in thought. I shook my head, backing toward the door.

She continued to walk toward me and I considered running out the front door and into the sunlight. She had the same look in her eye that Tabitha had had when she'd first approached me at the club. Maybe one of the other houses had a pack of werewolves in it or a few vampire hunters . . . something safe. Anything but this. My eyes were glowing against my will and my fangs had dropped down in full-on vampire munch mode. She should have been running away at this point. Instead, she was taking off her tank top. She was certainly pierced in interesting places.

Closing my eyes, I fought back either a yawn or a snarl. I could not eat, sleep with, or otherwise enact upon Tabitha's sister. Even though I couldn't see her anymore, her scent still plagued me. There hadn't been any cinnamon rolls in the oven when I'd passed, yet their tantalizing aroma mingled with hers. What was I doing here?

With supreme effort, I mustered enough concentration to turn back into a cat. Lower to the ground, I struggled to keep my gaze on her ankles. A low rumbling echoed from my chest. I was purring at her. Damn it.

Sunlight was beginning to reach the side windows of the house, so I darted past her and up the stairs. She yelped as I brushed by her in transit, and if cats could smile, I would have. Now all I had to do was figure out a way to call Talbot and explain my situation without being the jumper or the jumpee with regard to Rachel.

My memory really sucks, but even so, I knew that I had never encountered this kind of problem in my living years. What was it about vampires that attracted these women? Surely they couldn't all be necrophiliacs. When I'd died I had been in my thirties. I didn't remember much, but I did recall that I hadn't been particularly handsome. I wasn't Quasimodo either, but . . .

Focus, Eric. Drowsiness was making me punchy. I skidded on the hardwood flooring at the top of the stairs and slid into the wall. Rachel sprinted up the stairs behind me. A phone and a door, that's what I needed.

Mom must have been a great housekeeper, because I couldn't smell anyone but Rachel. Everything else smelled new. Maybe they'd just redecorated?

Photographs of Rachel, Tabitha, and their parents lined the hallway in cheap frames, plastic that was meant to imitate wood. I passed the bathroom in my mad feline dash down the hall. There were two bedrooms upstairs, one with a "No cats!" warning symbol and the other with a two-drink-minimum sign.

I surmised that the second room might have been Tabitha's and darted toward it. Changing back to human form felt like coughing up the world's largest hairball, but without thumbs, I couldn't turn the doorknob. I vaguely remembered Tabitha having told me once that she spray-painted her windows black when she was a teenager. They must have been the windows I'd noticed from outside.

"Thanks for not scraping the paint off the windows, Mom," I muttered. Rachel reached the top of the stairs as

I closed the door behind me and locked the dead bolt. I hoped she didn't have the key. Why had Tabitha needed a dead bolt on her bedroom door? Rachel slapped the door with a perturbed grunt, then her footsteps disappeared back in the direction of the stairs.

Tabitha's room was done in black and crimson. No wonder she liked the color scheme at the Demon Heart. She had crosses mounted to the walls and a blacklight bulb hung in the overhead lamp. Little Goth dolls lined a shelf on her wall where I still laughably expected a teenage girl to have wooden horses, old Barbies, and pretty glass knick-knacks.

It looked like Tabitha had cleared out all of the stuff she really wanted and left the junk she didn't want for her parents to throw away. That sounded like the Tabitha I knew. When I saw her queen-size bed, piled with fluffy black pillows, I almost went to sleep on it. Instead, I slapped myself a few times. I heard Rachel's footsteps pounding back up the stairs. Either she was quicker than I thought, or I'd just spent a minute or two staring into space.

Phone! There didn't seem to be a phone. In one corner, I saw a huge pile of books and an empty cordless phone charger. All the books appeared to be about vampires. That explained a lot. I heard a key in the exterior lock on the dead bolt and leapt for the door. It was impossible that Rachel could have been fast enough to open it before I could reach her, but it happened anyway. There was probably a fancy psychological term for it, but the only way she could have been faster than me was if I subconsciously wanted her to be faster. Then again, maybe it was just sleep slowing me down.

She was still topless and determined. I tried to ignore her body heat. The warmth of her as she entered the room called to me almost as much as the blood coursing through her veins. I had just healed from major injuries and I needed blood. I needed a phone. I needed Talbot. He could make things simple. He could handle things. That was his job. I needed Marilyn to slap my face for me and tell me to control myself, to act like the man she'd agreed to marry. Every time she told me that I wasn't a monster, for a few minutes, a few hours, I wouldn't be.

I grabbed Rachel by both arms and pulled her against me. She was afraid, but willing, just like her sister. I threw her down on the bed and straddled her thighs. Shifting my grip, I trapped her arms above her head. She leaned up and we kissed. Her tongue was pierced. Roger once told me that it's always the younger sister that you have to watch out for. He must have been talking about girls like Rachel.

"I need . . ." I struggled to find the words.

"I need you too, baby. It's okay. I want you." It was her turn to purr.

I pictured Rachel lying cold and dead on her sister's bed or worse, rising the next night, like her sister had, only eighteen instead of twenty-three. It was enough.

"What I need is a telephone," I managed.

"After," she whispered. She turned her head to one side. "Drink first. I want to feel it. I want to feel the pleasure and the pain."

"I need to use the telephone. I need to call the Demon Heart and have someone come pick me up." I was proud of myself. Total control was mine. I could resist the young woman underneath me. She started kissing me again. Her breath smelled like those cinnamon buns they sell in the mall. Her heartbeat filled my ears and then I did the only thing that I could think of that would keep me from doing exactly what she wanted me to do. I fell asleep.

8

ERIC:

PRICE TAGS

When I woke up, I was in the back of the party van. The party van had two seats up front and two benches along the sides in the back, with heavy shutters separating the driver from the people in back. It had originally been a paddy wagon, but I'd bought it a few years ago and had it fixed up to suit my needs.

The shutters were adorned with crosses. It wasn't anything that would keep a vampire at bay for long, more of an attention-getter to help jar me back to my senses in case I was ever out of control. Talbot had also replaced the rear doors with windowless ones. The other additions we'd made included a good air conditioner and a stereo system.

I realized belatedly that I was not alone. Rachel was in the back with me; my head was resting on her lap. I don't know what it is about the hour or two of sleep that I get each day, but I wake up hungry, much hungrier than I am after twenty some-odd waking hours. Combined with the hunger from before, I didn't stand a chance against it. Rachel was going to get bitten whether I wanted it or not.

Faster than humanly possible, she found herself on the floor of the van as I spread her legs and bit into her femoral artery. As soon as I started drinking, I was trying to stop. Rachel's fear was real. It made things harder to control. It was obvious to the thinking part of me that she had expected it to feel good. Why anyone would expect puncture wounds to feel good is beyond me, but I'd been around long enough to know that the pain often takes humans by surprise.

Fighting the hunger is like being in a wrestling match with a bigger, badder version of yourself; like getting a starving man to slowly sip broth a little bit at a time, only the starving man is ten times stronger than you and at least twice as mean.

I tried to hear Marilyn's voice in my head. *You are not a monster. You are the strongest man I know. When you rose for the first time, I was standing right there and you didn't touch me. Roger himself told you that a newly risen vampire has no self-control. If you could control yourself then, you can control yourself at any time.* Over and over, I repeated it in my head like a mantra.

I still don't remember rising. Marilyn has told me the story, but I don't remember doing any of it. According to her, I rose in full daylight. She was standing over my grave, but I did not attack her. I stood there for a minute in the sunlight, thick black smoke pouring off my exposed skin. Then, I took refuge in the cemetery's chapel. When she followed me inside, I supposedly said, "Am I late for something?" and passed out.

My memory has been like Swiss cheese ever since. I've always blamed it on having been embalmed. Sometimes I forget what happened yesterday, or five minutes ago, but just then, for a moment, I remembered what it was like to control myself. I remembered the calm and ease of my early days as a vampire. I remembered a different me, just long enough to take my teeth out of Rachel and hold her close.

"That was so fucking incredible," she gasped weakly, "and it hurt so fucking much! Holy shit!" She laughed as I held her. The danger was lost on her. She wouldn't believe how close she had come to death, or maybe she didn't care. I shouldn't have cared, but I did. I knew Rachel. I had a connection to her, through our kisses, through her sister. If I murdered her, she wouldn't be a faceless woman who died in the night, soon forgotten. Knowing the victim makes it more real, makes it harder to forget, and I damn sure don't want to remember.

By the time we got to the club, Rachel was sleeping. Talbot gave me the hairy eyeball as I carried her out of the van, under the awning into the club's rear entrance. Marilyn met me at the door. She looked and smelled old, but if I half closed my eyes, let my vision blur, I could almost see her like she used to be, the red-haired vixen on the motorcycle.

My Marilyn stared at me from behind a mask of age, her hair cut short and grown gray, the once luscious lips dry and stern. Her eyes were the same, though, blue as an ocean and every bit as tempest tossed. Old as she had become, I still wanted her as badly as I had on the day I'd died, but she wouldn't have anything to do with me, not like that, not since my death, not once.

She studied the girl I was carrying. Rachel looked like a trollop in her hip huggers and white tank top. There was a bloody rip where I'd bitten through her jeans. The blood was making the material stick to her leg. "Who is that?" Marilyn asked.

"It's Tabitha's little sister," I said, handing her to Talbot. That was all I got out before Marilyn slapped me hard across the face. "She . . ." I let my voice trail off as she slapped me again.

"For heaven's sake, what is the matter with you?" she yelled. The pain was nice. It was nice to receive any physical sensation from Marilyn. Not only had she refused to sleep with me since I'd become a vampire, she rarely touched me. A psychologist could have probably written volumes regarding what that said about my getting into trouble. They'd say I was like a child who did bad things to get my mama's attention. Maybe they'd be right.

I caught Marilyn's arm when she tried to slap me a third time. It was something I'd never done before. "The third slap is foreplay, M," I said. It didn't even sound like me. It was half growl, half scorn. "Unless you're up for it, I suggest you leave it to the younger ones." I let go of her arm. She winced.

Talbot stepped between us and inwardly I thanked some higher power for small favors. "Where's Tabitha?" I asked.

"She's in your bedroom," Talbot answered. "She's a late riser. Most vamps rise early on their first night and she didn't get up until eight. She went to bed a full hour before sunrise. She's looking at maybe eight or nine hours of wakefulness a night; more if she manages to break schedule."

My short daytime sleep requirement often got me twenty hours or more out of a day-and-night cycle. Maybe I could put up with her for eight hours a night. Maybe not. I checked my watch. It was nine in the morning. I walked back toward the rear entrance and gestured with my head for Talbot to follow me. As we moved past Marilyn again, I could feel anger coming off of her in waves. No fear, though, just anger. When I knew she couldn't see my face, I grinned. "That's my girl," I whispered.

"We're going to spend the day over at the Pollux," I told no one in particular. "Have someone bring Rachel orange juice and a big breakfast."

"I'll take care of it," Talbot said gruffly. As he fell into step behind me, carrying Rachel, he mumbled something else under his breath. "In for a penny . . ."

No shit, I told myself. No shit.

If Tabitha was going to sleep until eight this evening then I had eleven hours to figure out what to do about Rachel, not to mention the damn werewolves. The notion that I was forgetting something rolled around in my head. Talbot helped me get Rachel back into the van and across to the Pollux without incident.

Of the two movie palaces that had once been in Void City, the Pollux was the only one still standing. The Freemont may have been a little more stylish, but it had been turned into a parking deck twenty years ago, so I guess the Pollux won. The projector still works and I own a large collection of old films.

I'd kept the original glass entryway, even the old-fashioned central ticket booth, but beyond that, the new doors were reinforced steel, well-decorated, but secure. Beyond the doors, the foyer was still brightly lit by the original crystal chandelier, its glow magnified by the mirrors lining both walls. Rachel took in my absence of reflection without comment, paying more attention to the chandelier.

I'd moved several of the couches and tables from the downstairs lounges to the lobby, creating a sitting area for guests. Rachel plopped down on a burgundy velvet sofa and stared up at the painted art nouveau ceiling. A grand marble stair led up to the mezzanine and my offices. There were more offices and some dressing rooms behind the stage, but I only used them for storage.

"You like it?" I asked.

She nodded. "It's awesome. How do you afford it?"

"I get by," I told her gruffly. "Guys like nudity and I don't waste much money on groceries." How long would it take Talbot to get breakfast? If he went to Jackie's on the corner, he could be back in ten minutes. I didn't want to be alone with Rachel for much longer than that.

"If you're thirsty, the soda fountain still works. I only keep the Coke and the lemonade refilled, though. Everything else will get you water. I tried to put in a blood dispenser, but it clogs the machine."

Rachel watched me with smug contentment. She had just opened her mouth to speak when my rescue arrived. I could smell the food before Talbot opened the door. He was early. I don't pay him enough.

Muscling past the steel doors, Talbot backed into the foyer, carrying two covered breakfast plates. The scent pulled at my stomach. I craved breakfast only slightly less than pizza. One plate had scrambled eggs, crispy bacon, and a side of hash browns. The other had two fried eggs (sunny-side up), link sausage, and cheese grits.

"Rachel, isn't it? Do you like your eggs scrambled or fried?" Talbot asked.

"Which does he like?" She asked the question with purpose. To a vampire, that question is a signal, a sign that the woman he's with knows a little about vampires. Talbot remained valiantly smirkless, but he noticed.

"You'll want this plate." Talbot sat the tray before her, poured some orange juice in a glass, and laid a straw across the top. "I think I'll take my breakfast at the club," he said, walking right back out the door with the other tray of food. *Bon apéritif.*

Bon apéritif. Happy before-dinner drink. Fucking Talbot. I pay him too much. I wanted to protest, but the words stuck in my throat. In the split second I'd been distracted by Talbot, Rachel had taken the lid off of her tray, picked up one of the sausage links and commenced licking the grease off of the underside. For lack of a better word, she nearly fellated it.

"Less sexual, more sensual," I corrected. A rookie mistake most women make is equating eating to sex. For a living, breathing man, that would be correct, but for vampires it isn't about sex, it's about the food . . . about what we can't have and watching someone else have it. In polite circles, they call it voyeuristic dining, but food porn is more honest.

Criticism made her nervous. Each bite came a bit too quickly and her *mmmms* and *ahs* sounded forced. She had raw talent, though, and unlike Tabitha, she didn't forget that I was watching her. She purposefully let little beads of egg yolk gather at the corner of her mouth, then asked me to wipe it away. When I did, she seized my wrist, sucking the egg yolk from my finger, peering up into my eyes for approval. Long after the yolk was gone, her tongue danced along the bottom of my index finger, the curious stud on her tongue providing an erotic counterpoint to the softness of her flesh. It felt strange and wonderful. I approved.

After breakfast, Talbot sauntered back in and cleared away the dishes. For me, the next quarter hour passed like time-lapse photography. I didn't think there'd been cinnamon in any of the food, but I certainly smelled it. Maybe it was a breath mint or a new perfume. Talbot and Rachel blurred around me, politely avoiding each other in an elaborate dance, while I sat perfectly still, trying to remember whatever it was I'd forgotten. The image of Rachel sucking a little drop of golden egg yolk from my finger haunted my thoughts, making it harder than usual to think straight.

"I killed Brian," I said suddenly.

"What?" Talbot and Rachel spoke in unison.

"Brian. You know; the guy Roger met through that real estate thing, the one who was always talking crap about the Void City Howlers, trying to start a fight. I don't remember exactly what happened, but I think I ripped his head off."

"Rage blackout, huh?" Rachel asked.

Talbot and I both looked at her funny. "How the hell do you know about my rage blackouts?" I asked.

She laughed and rolled her eyes. "Sorry. I guess everyone who knows anything about vampires in this city knows about your rage blackouts." Her pulse quickened, but I couldn't decide whether she was lying or nervous.

"She's got you there." Talbot walked over to the door. "I just want to know how you're going to break it to Roger. He and Brian seemed pretty tight."

"Yeah, well, Roger isn't renowned for his choice of acquaintances," I said, "present company included."

"Depends on what you're looking for in a friend," Talbot countered. "He certainly attracts the powerful, wealthy, and influential. Present company included." He added that last bit with a mocking nod. Talbot had a smirk on his lips and he cut his eyes toward Rachel as he left. "I'll be across the street. Call me if you need anything."

Rachel squirmed under his gaze. As the door closed, she seemed comfortable again. Too comfortable. "What are you going to do about the werewolves?" She slunk toward me and the vibe was suddenly very different than it had been with Tabitha. This wasn't about sex. I could smell that sex was an option, but this was something different. She was teasing me, flirting with me, manipulating me.

"So . . . you know about the rage blackouts and the werewolf fiasco. You're pretty well informed."

"I'm just lucky." She moved close to me. I couldn't help but notice that her breasts were nearly touching my chest. "I heard some of your employees talking about it." She closed the gap between us. "That's okay, isn't it?"

It was more than okay, but more because of how she was touching me than the answers she was giving. She could read me better than Tabitha ever could and we'd known each other less than a day. She was extremely dangerous, a very good liar. She hadn't heard my employees talking about the werewolves; she couldn't have. I reminded myself to be careful.

"You're standing a little closer than I think your sister would approve." I took a step back, mentally applauding my fortitude.

She put a hand on my chest and I found myself staring down her tank top.

"You like it," she said, following my gaze.

"She wouldn't." I pushed her hand away.

"No, Tab would be mortified. If she even knows what mortified means," Rachel said.

"Look, what's going on between me and your sister is complicated and I'm not sure I want to complicate it any further than it—"

"I know," she said, "you're trying to be a good boy, but if you want a girl who really gets the whole vampire thing, who can give a vampire everything he wants and make him go all weak and kitteny . . ."

"That would be you?"

She nodded again.

"Not interested." Now I was lying. I decided to give Rachel the benefit of the doubt. We all lie sometimes. Maybe if I were a eunuch, I mused, things would be easier.

I left the seating area, passing the old refreshment stand as I crossed the lobby. At the top of the stairs, to the left of the mezzanine access, a long hall led to a row of offices. She followed me to the stairs. I held out a hand behind me to stop her. "No one comes up to my offices uninvited."

"Can I send somebody home to get my clothes?" Rachel asked. "Do you have any movies?"

"Why don't I just get Talbot to take you home, period?" That was my first good idea of the night. "Won't your parents be looking for you?"

She laughed. "Not likely."

I turned to face her. "If I were your dad, I'd be worried sick."

Rachel moved in close, too close, and kissed me. "Don't stress over it." I wasn't supposed to be kissing her back, but I was. Maybe it was the perfume she was wearing. Something about the cinnamon smell made me want to keep her around. Sure that was it. It was the cinnamon. It had nothing to do with my desire to throw her on the ground and tear her clothes off.

"Let me worry about my parents," she said, pulling away briefly and rubbing at her thigh where I'd bitten her. "I'm still kind of sore. You should at least let me hang out for the rest of the day."

"Fine," I said. "Get one of the girls to take you shopping. Tell Talbot I said it was okay. I don't care what you spend. I just don't want one of my employees having to explain to your dad why they need to pick up a change of clothes."

She squealed; I turned into a bat and flew up the stairs. I was showing off for her. It was not a good sign.

9

ERIC:

DAMAGE REPORT

Sitting at my desk with a small stack of notes, I looked at the bricked-up windows and shook my head. The first two notes were from Talbot. One said that Carl needed to know what to do about the Mustang. He hadn't done a complete assessment yet, but most of the interior looked salvageable. The rest of the car was a mess and Carl's best guess was that repairing it wasn't worth the effort or the money. Talbot noted that he'd told Carl to protect the interior of the car, and to start looking for replacement parts, but to do nothing further without calling first.

His second note was attached to a clipping from that morning's *Void City Echo*. The headline read "Local News Anchor Found Dead in Sewer." I *would* have had to drop my victim down a drain someone was going to start working on in the morning. Her name had been Evelyn Courtney-Barnes. Lots of people were going to miss her, blah blah blah.

The third note was from Roger telling me that he'd given Veruca the night off again and asking me to get Tabitha to cover. Veruca. Veruca. It took me a moment to recognize the name, because I always called her Froggy. She was Roger's girlfriend. She could only transform into one creature: a frog. Her other vampire powers were fine, but it seemed to piss her off that all she could change into was an amphibian. According to Roger's note, she might need the next several nights off. I wondered if this was some kind of payback for me having turned Tabitha . . . making my vampire girlfriend work so his wouldn't have to.

The last note was an invitation to a hockey game, though, also from Roger. For the last decade or so Roger and I hadn't exactly been bosom buddies. We didn't hang out much anymore, and when we did, he almost always brought some new friend or other along. Lately, it'd been Brian.

Our business relationship hadn't been much better. Roger had been big in real estate when he was alive. Now that he had more time, I think he aspired to be an undead Donald Trump. Roger always picked what stocks we would buy and how much of each we needed. He'd made us both rich men. He had also been the one who'd figured out how to transfer our wealth back to ourselves once we'd officially died.

But time changes things, and it had certainly changed Roger. I knew he didn't like the way I was running the club, though I'd noticed it didn't stop him from taking payouts from the register whenever he needed petty cash. My guess was that the whole operation made him look bad to his high society buddies. I kind of missed the way things had been between us. Maybe he did, too. On the other hand, I'd just whacked his buddy Brian . . . and it was probably Brian's ticket to the hockey game that Roger was offering me.

Stacking the notes to one side of my desk, I looked around my office. Except for the modern conveniences, it looked like it had jumped fully formed out of *The Maltese Falcon*. The door in the outer office had my name stenciled on it in nice black letters. The secretary's desk was vacant. Sometimes when I was working I'd have Tabitha come up and sit at that desk. I'd have her run errands for me to and from the Demon Heart. I could have used the telephone, or even e-mail, but I liked the illusion that it created. For a time it let me pretend that the world was still the same place where I'd once walked in sunshine, a world in which area codes were new and there were some numbers that you just couldn't dial without operator assistance.

"What the hell am I going to do?" I asked the room. I put my head down on my desk like I was a little boy in school and the teacher was mad at me. I wasted an hour or more that way before I noticed the burning sensation in my pocket and remembered the bullet.

"Son of a bitch." I picked up the phone and the number for the Demon Heart went right out of my head. I could remember the first three digits, but the last four . . . well,

I knew it had a six in it. One quick flip through the phone book later, I called over to the Demon Heart.

Roger answered, but I wasn't in the mood to talk to him. Having ripped his friend's head off and lied to him about it made me a little uncomfortable.

"Get Marilyn on the phone," I said brusquely.

"She's kinda busy, Eric," Roger snapped. Why was he being so bitchy lately? Was all this really over the damn Froggy crack? Was this my fault? Maybe I should go to the hockey game after all.

"Look, just get her on the phone," I answered.

"She's not here because you broke her arm, tough guy." He sounded so smug about it that if he hadn't just invited me to a hockey game, I'd have walked across the street and wiped the accompanying look off of his face. "She's old and fragile. You can't just push her around like that. She didn't want you to know, but she's gone to the emergency room."

Cursing, I hung up on Roger. Sometimes it seemed like Roger was closer to Marilyn than I was. Then again, maybe that was a good thing. Why did she even stay around a guy like me? Couldn't she see I was dangerous? I told myself that what happened was her fault, that she shouldn't have slapped me. I was lying to myself again. I wondered if I'd ever get any better at it.

If I concentrated, I could hear Rachel talking to Sally downstairs, their words vibrating along the air ducts and the building's central vacuum system. I went downstairs and found them in one of the dressing rooms behind the stage.

Tabitha had a tendency to dress like a sex doll. Her sister had better taste. She was wearing a floor-length backless evening gown. The green set off her eyes beautifully. Her hair was up and she'd replaced her nose ring with a small silver stud that was barely noticeable. Even her makeup was right. Have I mentioned how dangerous I thought she was? I had no idea where she had gotten the dress, but it was beautiful. She was beautiful.

"Goldman's opens at ten and it's not that far from here," she explained. "Sally went down with me and we picked up a few options." Rachel twirled and the dress rose off the floor a little, enough for me to see her matching shoes and a glimpse of ankle. Sally looked proud of herself. I was proud of her, too.

"We spent almost five thousand dollars," Sally told me.

"Why the hell did you buy a prom dress?"

"Because we all know what happens after prom," Rachel whispered.

"Yeah." Sally giggled with amusement. "You kids have fun." She winked at me on her way out the door. What the hell had Rachel told her?

Rachel smiled. I checked my fucked-o-meter. The gauge was set firmly on "Seven ways from Sunday." That seemed about right.

Rachel pulled up her dress and showed me her thigh. The wound was gone.

"It's already healed," she said.

"Mine always do," I told her. "I don't know why. Roger's bites don't heal like mine. Talbot tells me it's an unusual ability for a vampire."

She looked at me quizzically, dropping her dress back into place. "Talbot tells me that about most of my abilities, though," I added.

She walked over to me casually. "Have you asked him about it?"

"No," I answered. She was leaning close to me again. Her smell was different, less musky, and I couldn't smell cinnamon anymore. I decided it wasn't a perfume that she'd been wearing; it was something else, something that came and went. I didn't ask, for the same reason I didn't ask a lot of things. I was afraid that she might tell me, or worse, lift up her dress and show me.

"Why not?"

"Because I was worried that he might tell me." I backed away from her, pausing at the doorway.

"You want to know about that bullet, don't you?" She was just full of surprises.

"What bullet?" I asked.

"The magic one you're holding in your hand." Rachel pointed. "Or is it just a party favor?"

I looked down and sighed. The bullet glowed even more brightly now, like it was charging back up, replenishing itself.

"I was going to call Magbidion. He's kind of my mage on retainer."

"Can I see it?" She held out her hand. Since I had no reason other than blatant paranoia not to hand it over, I gave her the bullet. She held it up to her eye and put a hand on my shoulder. We both got popped by static electricity. "Ow.

Yep, it's magic. I'm no expert on magic bullets, but it's made of silver. My guess is that it's enchanted to kill lycanthropes. One of those swirly symbols kind of looks like a rune I've seen used to represent them."

"How do you know all this?"

There was mischief in her eyes. "Because, unlike some people, I ask questions."

"Yeah, but I'm a vampire. How come you know more about it than me?"

"I don't jump blindly into anything. I do research. There's a place called the Irons Club. It's really exclusive and a lot of vampire thralls meet down there and play golf when their Masters are asleep."

"And they just told you all this stuff?"

"It took a little doing," she said, leaning in close to nuzzle my neck, "but you know how persuasive I can be and how curious I am."

"Remember what curiosity did to the cat."

"I'm not a cat," she answered. "I hate cats."

"I'd noticed. You know, your sister is going to wake up about an hour after sunset. I should talk to her about things." Rachel opened her mouth, but I shushed her. "Not about us, if there is an us . . . which there isn't." Shit. "I need to explain. I have to break up with her. She's dead now and I don't date corpses. I've tried it and it doesn't work."

"She talked you into it, huh? What an idiot. There is no quicker way to lose your undead boyfriend than turning off the body heat." Rachel turned her back to me and looked over her shoulder in my direction. "Unzip me? I want to change out of this before I get it dirty." Reluctantly, I did as she asked. She was wearing a strange-looking bra underneath it.

"What is that?"

She looked down. "A backless bra," she said with a smirk. "I can't go braless all the time, silly. I'd sag."

"What was I just talking about?" I sighed.

"My sister," Rachel answered. She bit her bottom lip thoughtfully and then stepped out of the dress. I watched her put it on a hanger and pull a plastic bag over it. I was still staring at her when she took off her shoes. She had a small frog tattoo just above her ankle. It was cute and dainty and I seemed to remember it from somewhere, as if I had previously seen one just like it.

"You like frogs?" I asked.

"Better than cats," she answered mysteriously. She glanced at me as if waiting to see if I had any other questions, then pulled on a new pair of jeans and a silk blouse.

"You were talking about my sister," she repeated. "She's going to be really pissed off when you dump her. Does she have any idea that it's coming?"

"It's what happened to the one before her," I answered defensively. "Look, I think she knows, but either way I'm sure Talbot will have told her that it's likely."

Rachel shook her head as she pulled a pair of socks out of a shopping bag. They were followed by a pair of new tennis shoes. "So in other words, she's probably in denial. You're not one of those guys who tosses 'I love you' grenades around, are you?"

"I told her she was a moist warm tightness with the right attachments."

Rachel looked exceedingly amused. "Holy shit! You did not tell my sister that." She stopped laughing and looked up at me. "You did tell her that? Oh my God!" She sat down on the dressing chair and tried to catch her breath. Amusement was not the reaction I had been expecting. Anger would have been my bet, maybe a little dash of outrage, but not this. It was a clear sign that I did not understand the modern teenager.

"What does she expect?" Rachel continued. "You're a fucking vampire. You eat people." Her comments weren't accusations. I might have felt better about it if they had been.

"I have to go across to the club and talk to Roger," I said, changing the subject. I needed to ask him about the hockey game, maybe find some way to mention Brian. I also wanted to be there whenever Tabitha woke up. "Look, just hang out here. Watch a movie, listen to CDs, just . . . whatever. I'll be back." Applauding my mental fortitude, I left, walking up the stairs, out through the lobby, and across to the Demon Heart without a backward glance.

Since it was a few minutes before noon, I caught fire again on the way. Catching fire always reminds me of that one horrible week in California, a week full of demons and hellfire. "Fricking El Segundo," I griped.

◆ 10 ◆

RELATIONSHIP ISSUES

When I awoke, I was in Eric's bed again and he was standing over me. "You're up early," he remarked.

"Hello to you too," I said with a smile. I expected him to kiss me. Instead he pointed at the shower. "You smell," he said bluntly. "Go take a shower."

There was an odor in the air, like natural gas or methane mixed with pee. I sniffed my forearm. "That's me?"

Eric pulled me off of the bed by my arm and dragged me to the shower. Too stunned to react, I just lay there while he turned the shower on and pushed me inside. I was still wearing my leather outfit. He didn't notice. Instead, he stripped off his shoes and stepped into the shower. The cold water slowly became warmer as he removed my clothing. I closed my eyes and imagined him delicately unsnapping each snap and kissing the soft white flesh underneath.

"My darling," my imaginary Eric said. "I love you. Now we can be together, creatures of the night, unstoppable, unquenchable; the world is ours."

I opened my eyes and looked at the real Eric as he roughly undressed me.

He met my gaze. "These clothes are ruined. You won't be able to get the smell out."

I closed my eyes again and resumed my fantasy. In my mind, we made love passionately, more passionately than ever before and as we reached climax, Eric said he loved me again and again. He whispered it in my ear and then we both sank our fangs into each other, our minds touched, we were one.

In reality, I could feel him rubbing a bar of soap over me. It might have been sensuous except that his touch was coarse and businesslike. His hands did not linger and no gentle kisses were forthcoming. He washed my hair three times and I began to smell blood. I'd started crying without realizing it. I was getting tired of crying.

"Stop crying," Eric ordered. Out of reflex, I did. "It's called corpse sweat," he continued. "Did it happen last night? I mean, last day . . ." Frustration filled his voice. "I mean when you woke up last night did you stink?"

At first I didn't answer. Talbot's voice was playing in my head repeating all the things he had said the night before and I didn't like what he was saying. I must have started moving my head from side to side, because Eric took it as a response and continued talking.

"Good. Then it might not happen again. You were probably playing with your powers. Most vampires only get the sweats when they discover new talents. Some get them every night. I don't get them at all. Anybody I've ever heard of that had corpse sweat on the first night has to deal with it every night. Still, it's too early to tell. You probably ought to sleep naked on a plastic sheet or get one of the girls to move you once you fall asleep. Otherwise you might get corpse sweat on your sheets and whatever you're wearing."

He picked me up in his arms and carried me to the bed. Thankfully, someone had already changed the sheets. The Eric behind my closed eyelids made love to me again on that bed and promised to never leave me. In reality, though, I felt myself being toweled off and opened my eyes. The look on Eric's face said everything I needed to know. There I was, naked, in all my glory. According to the other girls, I looked better than I ever had, and he looked at me like I was a chore. There was no hunger there at all. He turned away from me and dropped the towel on the floor, then began to remove his shirt, peeling the wet cloth from his body. I guess that was a chore too.

Rage came over me. He'd treated me and the shirt with equal disdain, as if I were no more than an article of clothing to be tossed away and forgotten. Nobody forgets me! I leapt at him, my vision tinting red, claws and fangs at the ready.

One moment he was there and the next he wasn't. I had no idea where he had gone until I felt him behind me. Both his arms went underneath mine and he locked his fingers behind my neck. Smiling, I popped my claws and scratched his face, opening four short furrows in his cheek. He released me more out of shock than surprise and I snarled at him.

The wounds on his cheek healed as he began to do his little fast-moving trick, only this time I did it too. He was still faster than me, but I was quick enough to keep him from getting a good grip.

"You do look nice," he told me.

"What?"

"You look very pretty." He looked deep into my eyes, and suddenly I couldn't move; I couldn't react. I was frozen, staring into his eyes, mesmerized like any number of Dracula's victims in the movies. Had Talbot told me vampires could do that? I couldn't remember. I pushed back, tried to grab Eric the way he had me, but either I was too inexperienced or he was too strong. Those beautiful blue eyes sucked at my mind, pulling me deeper. They seemed to glow and flash, not a red glow, but a strange warm blue overwhelming color. I struggled, but his hold on me felt like a vise. He moved with casual menace and the look was back . . . that look that said I was no more important than ruined bedsheets, possibly less.

He wrapped his hands around my throat and squeezed. I couldn't move. He forced me down onto the clean silk sheets, never breaking eye contact. Inside I was screaming at myself, trying to move a finger, a toe, anything.

"In case you have forgotten," he began in a calm and steady voice far more frightening than any time he'd ever yelled, "I am the biggest, baddest motherfucking vampire that you will ever meet. Nothing has changed just because you have claws. Any stupid crap you think up has already been tried. I created you. I made you undead and I can make you 'dead' dead, too. I am your vampiric father or sire or whatever lame-ass little tagline you wannabes use. Any vampire power you can think of, I have it and I either use it better than you or I don't need to use it because I have a better way of doing the same thing. Do you understand me?"

At first I couldn't speak, and then it was like a ghostly force had relaxed its hold on my body, but just enough for me to answer the question. "Let me go, you . . . you bastard!"

"Say, 'Yes, Eric.' "

"Yes, Eric." I replied. What was I doing? I felt my jaws lock again, but I tried to scream anyway. Nothing happened.

"Now I want you to pay attention to what I'm going to tell you." His words trailed off; sadness suddenly filled his eyes. As quickly as he had evaded my claws, he was on the other side of the room. He leaned up against the dresser, cursing. After testing myself gingerly to make sure I could move, I sat up slowly, confused.

"This is not how I want to do this, Tabitha."

I got up and walked toward him. He tensed, but I kept coming. When I reached him, he glared at me.

"Look, Tabitha, just back off."

"You're standing between me and my underwear, Eric. Do I have to be naked the whole time I listen to you? If I am, will this end differently?" I tried to keep calm, but I was certain he could hear the anger in my voice. That sorry son of a bitch was going to dump me. What the hell was wrong with him? Hadn't I performed every sick act that his dirty little mind could think of? Did I do too much, too little? It was beyond me. The idea of it was too much for me to wrap my brain around. I felt like this all had to be happening to another person.

Eric slid away from the dresser and I opened the top drawer, my panty drawer. The smell of lilacs hit me as I opened it. I kept lilac-scented sachets in my underwear drawers to keep my underwear smelling nice. With my heightened senses most of them now smelled too strongly of lilacs for me to put on.

I stopped, taking a good look at the open drawer. It was filled with panties that were exactly what a man would like to see me wear. None of them were comfortable. They were lingerie, not real underwear. Digging through them, I found one pair of white panties that weren't crotchless, lacy, or a thong. I put them on. The next drawer down had my bras in it. It was like déjà vu. I had the same problem with the bras. They all seemed to have snap-off cups, too much lace, or no support whatsoever. A little digging revealed one plain beige bra. I put that on too.

"Your underwear doesn't match."

I glared at Eric; my expression must have spoken volumes because he literally flinched. "What the hell did you just say?"

He flinched again and walked to the far side of the room. I suddenly realized this was no different from all the times he'd insisted he wouldn't turn me, sworn that he didn't make vampires anymore. I knew exactly how to handle him. I grabbed a see-through bra out of the second drawer and threw it on the bed. I grabbed the matching pair of panties out of the top drawer and threw them on the bed too. I added a pair of black high-heeled shoes and a little leather choker the same color. "Is that what you want me to put on? What you'd like to see me in? Is that what you want?"

Eric shrugged.

"Because all you have to do is say it. You don't even have to tell me you're sorry. You just have to tell me what to do!"

I started crying again, this time on purpose, though the smell made me hungry. Streaks of red ran down my face and onto the bra. I took it off and threw it down on the floor. His eyes went involuntarily to my breasts. Poor Eric.

"Tell me you want me to wear something sexy tonight! Tell me you want to screw me, to sink your fangs into my jugular and drink my blood when you come. Tell me why we can't do that anymore. The only thing that's changed is I'm like you now. I'm a vampire. I'm not warm and alive, but I am still here. If you want a living girl to join us so that there will be some body heat, tell me and I'll go out and find one. You can pick one, it doesn't matter . . . just tell me . . ."

I threw myself into his arms, half worried he would push me away, but some emotion, some feeling of shame or guilt, possibly even some strange version of love kept him from doing so. He closed his arms around me.

His chest was damp and cold against my skin, but I didn't care. The world was a cold place anyway now that I was a vampire. I had thought it would be the other way around despite what Eric had always said, that I'd feel hot because I was at room temperature, but it definitely didn't work that way and I didn't know or care why. After a long moment, he kissed me on the forehead.

"Wear the lacy black set with fishnet stockings and a garter belt. Wear white over the top of it. I know it will show through; that's okay. Wear those strappy high-heeled shoes you have and that little white jacket thing with the short sleeves. Roger and I are going out tonight. You can't come. It's a guy thing, so don't freak out on me."

I didn't smile, because he might have thought I was laughing at him, at the way he'd given in, but I was definitely smiling on the inside. Talbot could say whatever he wanted, but Eric loved me. He just needed to talk tough, make demands, and be in control . . . typical male.

"You may be asleep again before I get back, but if so," he paused, "if so you'll wake up next to me tomorrow."

Eric could be as macho as he wanted, but when it came down to it, he'd give in. He wanted to give in; he was just afraid . . . and he loved me. I wanted him to say it, but I knew he wouldn't. Not yet. He kissed me again. This time he kissed my cheeks where the blood had begun to dry.

"I want you to help Talbot keep an eye on things tonight. I broke Marilyn's arm earlier and I need you to help out. You might have to dance tonight because Roger's happy ass keeps giving Froggy the night off. Can you handle that?"

I nodded. I wasn't sure if I could or not, but for him I would try almost anything that might give him time to realize what I already knew. It might take longer than it had to convince him to turn me, but I had time, buckets of time. When I was human, time had been the enemy; now, time was on my side.

He held my arms and pushed me slowly away from him, as far as he could without letting go. "Maybe this will work out, Tabitha. It probably won't. It never has before, but . . . but I suppose that it might be possible. We can try a human in the bed with us, but it will have to be a girl. I don't like to feed on guys."

"Fine," I agreed eagerly. I'm not afraid of other women; the only girl who ever managed to steal a boyfriend from me was my sister Rachel, before she got sick. I felt a pang of grief when I thought of her. If only I'd been a vampire then, I could have brought her over, but it had taken too long.

"And I get to feed off of the girl. You will have to eat before or after."

"Okay," I said. If he needed to feel like he was in control that was okay with me. He began taking off his wet things and I toweled him off with the driest parts of the towel he'd used on me. "And you don't get to bite me," he added. "Ever. Not unless I explicitly say so. I don't like to be bitten."

I helped Eric dress in jeans and one of those *Welcome to the Void* T-shirts he usually wore; then he kissed me one more time. "Don't leave the room until you've eaten."

I nodded. As the door closed behind him, I could hear him muttering, "I bet Dracula never had to put up with this shit."

I laughed. "Dracula had three wives, honey," I whispered. "It was probably much worse."

11

ERIC:

THE VOID CITY HOWLERS

My to-do list was a mile long. I needed to look up Magbidion's number and get him to take a look at the silver bullet I'd dug out of the werewolf skull over at Orchard Lake. Roger might appreciate it if I found a way to tell him I'd accidentally whacked his buddy Brian. Werewolves were apparently out for my blood. If I had half a brain, I would be out there now, looking for a way to get them off my ass.

With that same half a brain, I should have turned around, walked back into my bedroom, and told Tabitha that it was over. Since I apparently wasn't going to do that, I needed to put Rachel in a cab and send her home. Yes, there were a lot of things I should have been doing.

Instead, I was going to a hockey game. C'mon—front row, center ice. Who could turn that down? Believe me when I say that, up to the last minute, I tried.

"I can't go to the game, Roger."

"What are you even talking about? You know you're going. Brian already stood me up. I'm not getting stood up by you too."

Ah, guilt. "Yeah, sorry about Brian."

"It's not your fault the guy turned out to be a flake," Roger spat. "Screw him."

He trailed after me from the front door of the Demon Heart to the Pollux. Rachel was waiting just inside the door. She'd changed into hip huggers and a crop top. When I was born, seeing a girl in her bloomers was indecent. Now, my girlfriend and most of the women I knew were strippers. You might say that I've changed with the times. Even so, I stared at Rachel's pelvic bone. A hint of her thong peeked out over her hip huggers and the only thing that stopped me from attacking her on the spot was Roger's hand on my shoulder.

"If she's why you can't go to the hockey game, you have my blessing," Roger whispered.

"Hockey?" Rachel perked up. "I love hockey."

Roger bit his lip. "Brian's a no-show, so we do have an extra ticket." He'd bought one for Brian and one for me, so he wasn't just giving me Brian's unused seat. I suddenly felt better about having accepted.

"I thought you liked high society gals," I teased.

"Just because you like orchids," Roger said, taking Rachel's hand, "doesn't mean you ignore the wildflowers." She blushed when he kissed her hand. The light in the room took on a crimson tinge and Roger backed off.

"Don't go all flashy-eyes at me, buddy." He held up both hands in supplication. "I was just being friendly."

I counted to ten in my head and reminded myself that Roger was my best friend. Slowly, the red receded. Rachel looked on with a bemused pout. I didn't like the look of accomplishment that I saw blazing in her eyes. At least with Roger, we'd have a chaperone along.

I *should* have sent Rachel home and invited Tabitha to the hockey game, but there just wasn't time. We'd miss the whole first half arguing. So I went to the hockey game with Roger and Rachel.

The Void City Howlers weren't all that good, but they were the home team and they could usually be counted on for a fight. They didn't win very often, but when they took to the ice someone always got hurt, and that's all I wanted to see anyway. My favorite player was Sparky Parker, the Howlers' power forward. Without fail, he always started a fight in the last seven minutes of the game. He used to do it at five minutes until the NHL screwed it up with all those crappy penalties. Even so, he was the king of the Gordie Howe hat trick, pulling off the goal, assist, fight trio in most matches to the exclusion of all else, even winning.

Roger led us down to the front row, where the cold from the rink seeps up through the floor. Rachel was already freezing when we got to our seats, and the souvenir jersey that I'd bought her wasn't helping much. I took off the jacket I always wore to hockey games and hung it on her shoulders.

"Thanks." She touched my hand and the world went black, white, and red. It can happen when the bloodlust gets bad. Thing is, I didn't think I was hungry enough to justify it. Before I had time to give it much thought, Rachel whispered, "Later," in my ear and snuggled up under my arm, a warm little cinnamon-scented angel. Her proximity, the sheer physical closeness, should have made things worse, but color slowly bled back into my vision. That was weird.

"How did you—" I began to ask, but Roger cut me off.

"So, does Tabitha know about your new girlfriend yet?" asked Roger.

"No." I looked down at Rachel. "She's not my . . . look, just drop it."

Roger just smiled and scanned the crowd.

"Looking for someone?" I asked.

"Something like that." He waved at a blond guy who was dressed to the nines. He couldn't have been much older than twenty. The blond came over, carrying two boxes carefully in his arms. He handed the boxes to Roger with a curt nod.

"With Lady Gabriella's compliments, Lord Roger."

"New boyfriend?" I asked Roger.

"Yeah, yeah. Go screw yourself." Roger slipped him five one-hundred-dollar bills, holding on to his hand when the boy accepted. Five hundred dollars and Roger didn't even flinch. Must not have been his own money. I wondered if I checked the receipts back at work, whether I'd find a five-hundred-dollar payout with Roger's name on it. "And, Dennis, the other thing?"

"It's been arranged, Lord Roger," Dennis responded. "If there will be nothing else?"

Roger barely noticed him. He had released Dennis's hand and was busy opening one of the boxes. "Huh? Oh, yeah, we're good. Run on."

"Seriously," I continued, "you pitching or catching, Rodge? I bet you're catching."

"Shut up." Roger pulled a dark bottle out of the box and handed it to me. It said *Horace Gibson—1922—AB negative* on the label. "If you keep giving me the business, I won't share."

"Giving you the business? Who the hell says that anymore?"

"I'm serious, Eric."

"Fine." I handed the bottle back. "I can get my own blood. I don't need to have it delivered."

"Yeah, but can you ferment yours?" He broke the seal and popped the cork.

"What?"

"Blood booze." He took a swig from the bottle, shuddered, and then coughed. "Smooth."

"How does it taste?" I asked.

"Like blood," he admitted, "but with a serious kick."

"Can I try it?" asked Rachel.

Roger agreed and I disagreed in unison.

"She doesn't need to start drinking blood, Roger."

"Oh, like that won't be part of this evening's festivities for you two." Roger handed the bottle back to me. "Blood is the only bodily fluid we've got."

Rachel raised an eyebrow. "Come on, Eric. What do you think it tastes like when I kiss you?"

"Fine." I handed her the bottle. She took two small sips and passed it back to me.

"Not bad," Roger told her, "but save the rest for the vampires, if you please. It cost me more than you know. They don't just sell this stuff at the local liquor store."

"Where'd your boyfriend get it?" I asked. Roger's eyes lit up from within, a dull orange pinpoint encompassed by his pupils. The fading brown pigment in his irises set it off nicely. He normally wore contacts to conceal the fade. Plenty of vamps do. Vamp irises typically lose their hue with age, resulting in a washed-out shade of the original color.

Talbot once told me that truly ancient vampires have red irises, and sometimes even the whites of their eyes go permanently crimson. Mine hadn't faded at all, but most Vlads have weird traits that set them apart, like my ability to turn into a white cat instead of a black one. My guess was that my blue eyes were like that. I once heard a rumor about a Vlad who can eat hamburgers. I'd have rather had the hamburgers and worn contacts.

"Well?" asked Roger.

"I drifted off there for a second," I told him. "I was thinking about hamburgers."

He tossed his head back and laughed. "You could drive a saint to murder, you know that?"

"Game's starting," I answered. "Are we going to fight or watch the game?"

The row behind us was enthralled by our conversation. I

looked at the fat guy behind me and bared my fangs. "Don't mind us," I told him. "We're vampires."

"My son plays that game," he replied. "Aren't you guys a little old?"

I turned my attention to the start of the game without answering him. Halfway through the first period I took a swig of the fermented blood. My taste buds couldn't tell the difference. Maybe they had all died, or perhaps my palate is unrefined. I enjoyed the kick, though. It burned going down my throat and every swallow sent a dagger of heat into my heart, like heartburn would feel if it involved real fire.

"Good?" Roger asked.

"It's different," I shrugged. "Anything different . . ." I yawned. "When are they going to start playing?" I asked.

"They are playing," said Roger.

"Not that I can see."

"It's not that bad," Roger said.

"Which game are you watching?" I took another pull off of the bottle and realized that it was empty. Roger opened the other box and handed me a second bottle.

"This is total crap. Sparky hasn't even cross-checked any-body."

"You can tell him about it after the game." Roger smirked. "I have a friend who knows the owner. We've got permission to go and talk with the team."

"Cool." I offered Roger a drink from bottle number two. It had a red label on it with *Unidentified Female—1982—O positive* written on it in bold black letters. If anything, the burn was worse with the second bottle, but there was a taste to it, acidic and bitter.

Sparky Parker played like he was more intent on ice skating than cross-checking anybody. In the second period, Fordman, the Howlers' left winger, had about as much chance of scoring as a hippo in a full-body condom. They weren't even trying. Halfway through the third period, I finished the bottle.

"Let's just go," I told Roger.

"What about meeting the team?"

"Screw 'em." My tongue felt heavy and things were a little blurry. I was completely wasted.

"Please, can we stay and meet the team?" Rachel asked.

"Fine." I cupped her breast. She didn't seem to mind. "Anything you want." We kissed and time rolled away. She moved onto my lap, grinding against me. Some parts of my body became more engorged with blood than others. The little voice in my head that normally would have thought twice and worried about consequences had passed out in the middle of that first bottle of blood booze. In his place was a horny little voice that I hadn't heard since college. He didn't care if we got caught or if security threw us out. All that mattered to him was getting inside Rachel's jeans.

The world blurred around us like time-lapse photography. Only Rachel and I were still, cocooned in cinnamon bliss. I wondered if it was some kind of magic or just the booze, but I couldn't bring myself to care.

"Guys?" Roger whistled in my ear, then thumped me in the forehead.

The game was over, the crowd all gone. It was just the three of us. Rachel got to her feet, blushing sweetly as she straightened her outfit. What the hell had happened? Without her to hold on to, I fell backward and began sliding off the bleachers. Maybe blood booze had been a bad idea. Roger pulled me to my feet.

"Jesus, you are totally crocked," Roger told me. "Let's go meet the team."

Resting one arm on Rachel and the other on Roger, I stumbled in the direction that they led me. "You're my best friend, Roger," I slurred. He didn't answer.

12

ERIC:

BISCUIT IN THE BASKET

Arm in arm, Roger, Rachel, and I stumbled down a long hallway behind the bleachers. I vaguely remember singing at one point. Then, suddenly we were in the locker room, meeting the Void City Howlers.

My vision cleared long enough for me to see Sparky Parker, my former hero, the king of the ten-minute penalty, transform into a werewolf. A snarl started at the base of his toes and ran up his entire body, leaving hair, fur, and muscle in its wake. The only signs of his human form were the green and white Howlers jersey he was wearing and the hockey stick gripped tightly in his left paw.

You'd think I'd have put it all together. After all, the

team was called the Void City Howlers. In my own defense, though, the Mighty Ducks had never turned into mallards on ice. So the deductive reasoning wasn't as intuitive as it might seem. Plus, I was totally wasted for the first time in forty years.

Autograph book in hand, I looked around the room. It was just me, Sparky, and the other Howlers . . . no sign of Roger or Rachel. "Where did they go?" I asked.

"Your friends just ditched you, vampire," Sparky growled. "They ran."

"That's good." I blinked. "Did I run away too?"

"You shouldn't have done it, vamp," he growled.

"You've got spots." He did have spots. Wolf Sparky looked sillier than any werewolf I'd ever seen. Coarse white fur covered most of his body, but it was speckled with dark black spots. He blurred. A large Dalmatian-spotted blob hit me in the face with something long and thin with a curved end: a hockey stick. I was grateful, because when the world stopped spinning everything was a little clearer.

He grabbed me by the face, palming my head like a basketball, and tossed me through the double doors that led out to the rink.

Other blobs expanded. They were angry fuzzy blobs with white and green middles, kind of cute, really. My vision cleared a little and a very wavery Wolf Sparky loomed over me. A long trail of drool dangled from his muzzle and pooled on the souvenir jersey I was wearing. I wondered if it was the one I'd bought for Rachel, and if so, how I'd ended up in it.

"You have a droopy ear," I observed. "Did you know that you had . . . have a droopy ear? I think your mom got a little drunk one night and . . . oof."

That time he grabbed my leg and tossed me out onto the ice. I felt kind of bad about mentioning the whole parentage thing. I'm kind of a happy chatty drunk and my mouth gets away from me. Cold hard ice broke my fall and I slid along the freshly resurfaced rink. The top layer hadn't quite refrozen and the glacial water soaked into my clothes.

No crowd cheered the Howlers when they took to the ice this time, but I was impressed. "You guys just skate around me, okay?" I told them. "I don't think I can get up."

I don't know who took the next several shots at me, but they must have been pissed off about something, or maybe . . . "I'm starting to think you guys don't like me," I complained.

"He's totally hosed," growled a dark black one with a bobbed tail and brown highlights like a Doberman's. "Just stake him and get it over with."

Trying to roll over, I lost my balance and fell to the ground with a loud crack.

"Lookit. One of his eyes is blinking." Strobelike red light flashed rapidly on and off, upsetting my stomach.

"I think I'm going to be sick," I said to no one in particular.

"He's gonna yack," one of them said, gliding past me.

"Vampires can't yack," called number 45 from one side. Each of them moved as easily on the ice bare-pawed as they had with skates, but in wolf form their strides were more confident, their reflexes better.

"You guys ought to skate like this all the time," I said. "Then you might win a game or two." That didn't come out the way I had meant it.

A sharp pain in my side sent me spinning along the ice quickly. Sparky was driving me down the rink, a human-size hockey puck, across the blue line, straight through center ice, and toward the goal.

"Yeah, Sparky!" someone shouted.

Two of the other Howlers, Fordman and Hartaff judging by the jerseys, skated in to try and steal me from Sparky with more resounding thuds. One of my arms gave way with a crack and pain lanced up to my shoulder; my blood was smeared all over the ice.

"Okay, fellas," I said. "That's enough."

Sparky brought me in, shoving me across the goal line and into the boards. About that time, I realized they weren't just playing, they were fighting. My growl was louder than Sparky's.

"Stake him!" Fordman shouted. Sparky's custom stick plunged into my back and out through the front of my souvenir jersey. I didn't want to think about how much strength it took to jam a blunt handle completely through a man's torso. Red illumination flashed on the boards in spurts. Off. On. Off. On. Blood wine erupted violently from my throat. It ran down the stick and onto the ice. The glow from my eyes blinked twice more and stayed on.

"Biscuit in the basket, baby!" several of them roared.

"Get the cooler." The hockey stick wasn't made of real

wood, but I was still moving far too slowly. Two of them ran off of the ice and then came back toward me with a cooler.

"This ain't football," I complained. "What the hell are you guys—" They dumped the cooler over my head. It burned like acid. Holy water. I think they thought it would kill me. It was a good try. It would have worked on a Soldier, or possibly on a Master, but as I keep trying to remind everyone, I'm a Vlad and we are damn near indestructible.

"I am so fucking killing you guys," I said as my skin peeled away and caught fire. Holy water is powerful stuff. It ate right through my clothes, my skin, through the bone, mixing with my liquid remains and flowing out onto the ice like gruesome pancake batter.

The blood wine I'd spewed mixed with the puddle of water and with, well, me, turning the mixture into a bubbling red mess, with smoke pouring off the top as I sizzled and popped like a fried egg. I knew I was going to survive, but a vampire who has been melted is in bad shape even if it doesn't send him to the great beyond. We need blood to re-form. Fortunately for me, I was lying in a puddle of it.

As the holy water boiled away, the smoke stopped and bit by bit the grotesque liquefied mass developed solid chunks, drawing in on itself. I floated above the ice, looking down on my body, detached and clearheaded, glowing that same ghostly blue I'd been the one time I tried to turn to mist.

Being melted was pretty damn low on my list of sobriety quick fixes, but it did the job. My bones re-formed first. One of the werewolves rammed another hockey stick through my ribs where my heart was going to be. I guess he thought the stick was made of wood, but it was some high-tech plastic. Plastic doesn't do dick.

My body lay naked on the ice and I found myself drawn back into it, momentarily disoriented, but regaining my senses just fast enough to pull the stick out of my chest before my clothes came back.

It's good to be a badass. Using my anger as a focus, I turned into a bat. It took longer than usual and felt different, like when your dick falls asleep because your underwear is too tight and there is that long agonizing wait followed by a pins and needles sensation exactly where you never want one. I flew out over the rink and landed in the stands. When I changed shape again, my clothes were back. I'd instinctively regenerated my usual outfit, but at the high price of what felt like every last drop of blood in my body.

I missed the Howlers jersey, but it was okay. I was over them. Now these assholes had it coming. They'd lured me back to the locker room with Roger's unwitting help, used me as a hockey puck, and been the first group of people to ever melt me down with holy water. Worst of all, they'd made me sit through a piss-poor game of hockey. There is no excuse for bad hockey.

They'd make it up to me though. I was hungry.

This time, I wouldn't make the mistake of holding back like I had with the guys who'd wrecked my Mustang. I was tired of talking, and at this point the hunger wouldn't have let me hold back anyway. I felt the blackout coming, bitter and cold like winter rain. Yep, these jerks had it coming. They had it coming Dracula style.

As my vision started to blur, I hovered at the edge of awareness just long enough to make one last taunt. "So are you motherfuckers going to come and get me or do I have to hang a steak around my neck?"

13

HIDDEN DEPTHS

The whole no-reflection thing was really starting to grate on my nerves. I needed mirrors. There is only so much a girl can tell about how she looks by craning her neck and bending over backward. The other girls were busy, so I did the best I could on my own and then called up front to ask Talbot if he had a few minutes to come to the back.

"Why?"

"I need someone to check my makeup and stuff; the other girls were busy, so I tried to do it myself, but—"

"Ten minutes." He laughed and hung up.

While I waited, I finished up the second pint of blood he'd brought me earlier. It tasted a little funny, but I didn't want to have to argue with Talbot over it when he came back to check me out. I was tired of being cooped up in the club and I wanted to go outside for a while after my set. After I finished the blood, I still had five minutes to wait, so I practiced popping my claws and making my eyes glow. It was cool and all, but I wanted to know more about what I could do. I wondered what would happen if I used a power that I didn't know how to undo. What if I turned into a bat and got stuck that way?

When Talbot came into the bedroom, I retracted my claws and let my eyes turn back to normal.

His smell wasn't human and it was thrilling to be near him, to not know what he was. He looked me up and down and I studied him in return.

"You look fine," he said. He turned and started to leave again.

"Wait. Talbot, do you have a few minutes?"

He looked at me over his shoulder. "Why?"

"I wanted to try and figure out what other powers I have." I walked over to the dresser and fiddled with my hairbrush. He showed up clearly in the mirror even though my reflection would have been blocking his.

He closed the door and turned back to me. "You don't need me to do that."

I looked down at the brush in my hand. It was silver. For a moment, I was lost in the shiny surface. My grandmother had left it to me when she'd died. She had always intended it for Rachel, but cancer had taken my sister away from us earlier than anyone could have expected. She was so angry at the end, she blamed me for not finding a way to save her.

"I'm afraid," I admitted.

Talbot came closer, put his hand near my shoulder, and then pulled it away. I could feel the heat of him behind me. It was like standing with my back to the fire on a cold winter day. I leaned into him involuntarily and closed my eyes. "You feel so warm."

Gentle, but firm, he pushed me away from him. I was off balance and I almost didn't catch myself. Something was wrong. "You don't want to play the kind of games I like, Tabitha," he told me softly.

How embarrassing! Did I have to throw myself at every warm-bodied man that crossed my path? I shivered. "I'm sorry. It just feels so cold."

"You'll get used to it." He sat down on the edge of the bed and I realized that it was the first time that I had ever seen Talbot sit down. He was always leaning on things, but never actually sitting.

"So how do I do it?" I asked.

"Do what?"

I put down the brush and threw my hands up in the air. "Do anything! I've read lots of books, but it isn't something that Eric ever talked about. I could ask Roger, but—"

"You don't want Eric to get jealous." He nodded. "I get you. Which do you like best: bats, cats, fleas, wolves, frogs, or do you want to try for something funky, like a virus?"

I turned around and leaned up against the dresser. "What?"

"You don't know yet how powerful you are. If you're a Soldier or a Drone, you might only be able to do the first one you try, or you might not be able to do any of them. You might not get a choice, but if you do get a choice and you can only do one . . ." He shrugged. "Well, they say that's what happened to Froggy."

"So, it'd better be one that I like," I mused. "Okay. Wait, a virus?"

He laughed. When he did, I could tell that even with his fangs retracted, his canines were a little longer than normal. "It's been done. I guess it was a good way to avoid hunters back in the day, but it sounds kind of gross to me."

"Can I try something else weird? Is there a bird, like a raven or something?"

"Try it and see," he urged.

"Do I need to take my clothes off?"

"Some do, but why don't you just go ahead and try it with clothes for now." He got up and walked around the room, arms outstretched like a big kid playing airplanes. "Close your eyes and think of yourself as a bird. See yourself flying over the city, like in a helicopter ride only the wind is underneath your wings. You aren't in some metal cockpit. There is no glass between you and the air, no metal. It's you, just you."

I spread my arms like he had done. At first I felt silly, but gradually, I really could see it. My body tightened, wrenching painfully in on itself, my skin an overfilled balloon that might pop any second, and then the wind was beneath my wings; I was free! It was so sudden that I screamed in surprise, but no human sound escaped my lips. It was a bird's cry. I had done it! Of course, I didn't know how to fly, so I fluttered to the ground. When I landed, I felt dizzy and confused, sick to my stomach. Talbot pounced, catching me between his hands and eyeing me closely with his fangs out and his cat eyes flashing. "Gotcha!"

Willing myself back to human size didn't work. I flapped my wings ineffectually and started pecking at his fingers with my beak. If I'd had fangs I would have bitten him. As it was, I tried for his eyes, but he was too far away.

"If you're a Master vampire," he gloated, "you'll be able to turn back even though I have you trapped. Just concentrate. Think about being humanoid. Picture yourself biting my hand or something."

It didn't work. I couldn't focus.

"Try it. Picture yourself dancing onstage."

Nope.

"All right," he said as he set me down on the bed. "Try it now."

Instantly, I was myself again. "You bastard!"

"The test isn't definitive, but you're probably a Soldier." He stood up and grinned. "Care to try for a mouse?"

I did not care to try for a mouse. Instead I tried for a cat. I pictured myself as a large gray kitty I'd had as a little girl. I loved that cat more than anybody in my family. I used to sit and pet him for hours and listen to him purr. He was the only thing that was mine and mine alone. He never let anyone else touch him, especially not Rachel. It was almost as if Mr. Fuzzy Bottom had some kind of never-ending feud with her. Cats in general didn't like her; maybe they knew something I didn't.

The change was not as sudden as before; quick, but not instant, like a slow collapse into a nice warm ball of fur. It was a relief to be warm again. Talbot took a step away from the bed, his eyes wider than usual and his mouth open. I looked down at my paws. They were gray, just like Mr. Fuzzy Bottom's. I preened myself at Talbot and gazed at him haughtily.

"Okay, so maybe you are a Master vampire," he allowed. "You could have been too panicked to make the change before."

Master vampire or not, I could turn into a bird and I could turn into a cat. My chest felt funny, though. It sort of vibrated. "Meow," I told Talbot. "My chest feels funny," is what I had meant to say. My heart was beating! I was breathing! I stumbled and accidentally sat down.

"I'll just bet it does," Talbot whispered. He reached over and grabbed me, holding up my kitty-cat self to the mirror so that I could see my reflection.

I could see my reflection!

"Meow!" I said, meaning "Holy shit!"

"Holy shit, indeed," he said as he put me down on the dresser, in front of the mirror. I put a paw against the mirror and stared at myself. Even though it wasn't the human me, just being able to show up in a mirror, to see a reflection that belonged to me, made me feel safe and warm inside. I rubbed up against the mirror and purred at myself.

"Meow," I said to myself, meaning "Hello, me."

Veruca opened the door and glanced around the room.

Her makeup was sloppy and her shoes didn't go with her dress. I could tell that she wasn't happy.

"What's a cat doing in here?" Veruca asked. Talbot just looked at her. Veruca's lip curled. "Tell Tabitha not to get too full of herself, Talbot. Just because she's been turned, she's nothing special. She's supposed to go on in half an hour. Then it's serving drinks and doing lap dances just like everybody else. I'm taking the night off."

"A little hard on your new sister in undeath, aren't you?" Talbot asked. "As a matter of fact, since you're here, she doesn't have to go onstage at all. . . ."

Veruca flipped Talbot off and pulled up her shirt. Claw marks crisscrossed her stomach and from the look of them, they went around to the back.

"What happened?" I meowed.

"What happened?" Talbot repeated for me. Interesting. Talbot understood cat speak and Veruca didn't. Was he a werecat? A weretiger? What else could he be?

"None of your business, asshole!" Veruca slammed the door and stalked off down the hall. The sound echoed in my head. My vision blurred and for a moment there were two furry "me"s in the mirror.

"Meow?" I said, and I had no idea what I meant. Something was definitely wrong.

I rolled over on my back and swatted at the pretty rainbows and the colored lights that had appeared in the air. There was that same funny taste in my mouth, like the second pint of blood. In the distance I heard Talbot's voice calling my name.

The rainbows started moving faster and I tried harder to catch them. Then, I heard someone barfing. I wondered if it was me. At some point, I fell off of the dresser. Talbot caught me. The psychedelic swirling stopped, replaced by a vibration deep in my skull. There was a sound like when a monitor blinks out. My skin went numb all at once and little sparks danced in front of my eyes. Talbot blurred in hazy motion lines, faded, and then was gone completely.

14

TABITHA:

THE SHOW MUST GO ON

When I woke up, Talbot was snapping his fingers in front of my eyes and calling my name. I was wet and I was still a cat. The lights were too bright and my heart was beating in my ears. Was I drunk? Did vampires get drunk? Did cats get drunk? For that matter, why was my heart beating? I was breathing too fast and my skin was all tingly.

"C'mon, Tabitha. Get up!" Talbot told me. I sneezed a pitiful cat sneeze at him and it made my head pound.

"Meow," I said, meaning, "God, I feel awful."

"It's probably just transformation sickness," Talbot explained. "Try turning back to normal and see if that helps."

It was hard to concentrate with my head pounding, but I

managed it. It was even slower than before, my body chilling and expanding like a balloon slowly being filled with cold water. After a few minutes, I was myself again, panting on the floor. I even had clothes on. The dull ache in my head eased up and the world stopped spinning in circles.

I blinked a few times, steadied myself, and stood up. "Okay. That was both awesome and shitty at the same time. So, what? I can turn into a cat, but only if I want to start tripping and then barf?"

Talbot looked at my eyes closely. "Your eyes are dilated." He held my right eye open with his fingers. "Okay, better. They're normal now."

I started to rub my eye, but stopped myself when I remembered my eye shadow. I touched my cheek and looked reflexively to the mirror to check my makeup. No reflection. An inexplicable rage welled up inside of me and I turned on Talbot.

"You better not have fucked up my makeup, asshole!" My claws were out before I even thought about extending them. I wanted to tear him apart, drink his blood, drain him dry, and then tear the pieces up when I was done. I knew my reaction was over the top, but I couldn't explain what was happening. Talbot seemed just as surprised as I was, even more so because I had actually slashed his forearm with my claws, moving too fast for even Talbot to avoid. We both looked down at the blood.

"I—" I didn't know what I was going to say, but I opened my mouth to say it. Talbot wasn't interesting in listening.

"Your makeup is fine. Get your ass out there and do your

job." He walked into the bathroom and began washing the cuts out with soap and water.

"Talbot?" I followed him into the bathroom, reaching out to him.

"Just go, Tabitha!" he yelled. Closing his eyes, he let out a sigh. "Just go out and dance. We'll talk about this later. I probably pushed you too hard."

Of course it was his fault, I cursed inwardly. Talbot was the one with experience. Talbot was supposed to know better, to teach me. I left the room and headed toward the stage. "Dumb, fucking asshole," I said aloud.

My emotions were a mess. Edginess does not even begin to describe what I was feeling. Imagine that someone ran over your cat, and then backed into your new car trying to get away. Imagine that when the police came, the officer laughed and told you to buy a new cat. Picture how angry that would make you. I was that mad at everyone and everything, and I could not understand why.

In the dressing room behind the stage, Candice and Sharon were getting ready to go serve drinks and sell lap dances. Sharon said hello and I flipped her off in response. She shrugged it off, but I could smell her anger.

Candice looked up at me with that stupid innocent look she always gave to Eric. "Did somebody wake up on the wrong side of the grave this morning?"

I don't even remember hitting her. She just seemed to lift up out of her chair and fly backward through the air of her own accord. One of the mirrors shattered as she hit it and there was a blinding flash as the lights around it exploded. Bouncing off of the wall, she landed facedown on the floor. Shards of glass landed all around and over her, like glittery sprinkles. It was pretty in a violent, deadly sort of way. It was too much trouble to get to her throat with all the glass in the floor, so I leapt over her and landed on the steps leading up to the stage.

I smiled back at Sharon and she froze, evidently hoping that if she stayed still, I'd leave her alone. "One word and I'll put you right fucking next to her." She was used to being around vampires and it probably saved her life. I'm sure she was terrified, but she knew better than to show it. It was one of the first things Eric told new girls. I'd been with him long enough to know how true it was: Fear was like a good marinade to a vampire. Running could get you killed. Hold still, submit, and you might have a chance.

A weird taste played across my tongue, bitter and sweet at the same time. I knew I had tasted it before, but I couldn't think clearly enough to figure out where. By the time I hit the stage I had all but forgotten about Candice. Jasmine was out there doing her Little Red Riding Hood routine, managing to look innocent and sexy all at once. Her long brown hair trailed behind her, down over the hood and cape. The light creamy texture of her skin stood out in perfect contrast to the bright red cape, a thin layer of baby oil glistening on her skin, her pink nipples hard and erect.

I decided to play the Big Bad Wolf. When I walked out from behind the stage, I could hear the emcee asking Marilyn what was going on. I couldn't remember what his name was; only that he was a pig who always tried to get us to suck him off. Tonight, I decided, he would get his wish.

I hit the stage and Jasmine looked back at me, pretty brown eyes wide in surprise. She was down to her G-string and the little red cape. I strutted up to her and pulled the G-string off. It was what the guys really wanted to see anyway. Jasmine protested, but I was having fun. Excitement emanated from the audience. The scent filled my nostrils and made it even harder to think. I showed my fangs to the crowd and they cheered. As far as they knew, this was all part of the show. Jasmine's scent was the most thrilling of all: fear and uncertainty, combined with sweat and a hint of sex.

It woke the inner predator in me. I began a routine of my own. I danced around her, stripping; Jasmine relaxed and started to dance with me, closer than I would have normally found comfortable. When the tips started rolling in, she whispered her thanks into my ear.

But Jasmine's terror started to return when she realized that I wasn't going to let her leave the stage. By the time I was down to my own G-string, we had collected more money than I normally did in an entire night, but I didn't want money. Talbot had made his way to the edge of the stage and was whispering just loudly enough for me to hear him.

"Let her off the stage, Tabitha! Let Jasmine go backstage and then follow her. Something is very wrong here and we'll figure it out. Just don't hurt her."

I wanted, no, needed, Jasmine to run, but she wouldn't do it; she'd been trained too well. Like Sharon, she knew running from a vampire would get you killed for sure. If you didn't run, then you had a chance. I pulled her close to me, pressing her back to my chest, and whispered in her ear, "Let me taste you and you can leave."

She nodded slightly and I sank my teeth into her neck. Fresh blood touched my tongue and it felt hot enough to burn. It was more than a taste. The liquid warmth ran down my throat, into my core, spreading like traces of fire along my veins. She sagged in my arms, another trick, designed to cue a vampire that she'd had enough. The audience went wild.

Somehow, I let her go. She stumbled toward the rear of the stage and into someone's waiting arms. I didn't care who. That one taste of fresh blood unleashed a monster inside me. I hesitated momentarily in the calm before the storm. Sounds grew even louder than before. I could hear people all around the club, both voices I knew and those I did not know.

"Didn't I tell you this was an awesome club?"

"Fake blood, you can tell by the way . . ."

"Lap dance . . ."

"What the hell is she doing, Marilyn . . ."

"Get off the stage, Tabitha."

"Don't know, boss. I haven't seen him, but his ex is going nuts . . ."

Music flickered brightly above the speakers, wave after wave of electric blue. I heard rather than felt the terror of those around me, high-pitched and frantic like a mad guitar solo. Sensory confusion. In a detached way, I realized I was tripping again.

One sound flashed red, more enticing than the others, a

sensual pulse: a summons, pulsing faster. Heartbeats. I was the monster and the monster was me. It felt like I was gaining control over myself, like I was winning. All sense of right and wrong flowed away to be replaced by the new morality: drinking blood, good; not drinking blood, bad.

I remember shoving Talbot to one side, leaping for the emcee. People screamed as I bit through the emcee's pants into his femoral artery.

"How's that for a suck job, asshole?"

Claws raked down my back and I kicked in my vampire speed without having to concentrate, fluidly, as easy as sneezing. I remember laughing, long purple streams of laughter rising over my shoulder. Power over life and death was mine. Killing led to drinking blood. Not killing led to not drinking blood. Killing became a virtuous act.

Even Talbot was too slow to stop me. I moved like a whirlwind, dancing through the crowd. His attempts to stop me were like cheap scares in a haunted house. He could jump out at me, growl at me, but he couldn't touch me any more than a dancing plastic skeleton with glowing eyes could. A series of bleeding lines on backs, faces, necks, and chests slid beneath my claws and it was fun, like finger-painting.

I felt warm inside and out. These stupid perverts didn't need their lives. I did. I needed all that they had to give and more. I deserved it. They were cattle, little more than fast-food wrappers. And I . . . I faltered. The new morality flickered, replaced by my former sense of right and wrong. I saw what I had done and it sickened me. I staggered backward.

Twang.

Pain lanced through my chest as I fell to the floor. In the distance, across the club, I saw Marilyn. She had taken her arm out of its sling so she'd have both hands for the crossbow. Beyond her, people were pounding on the doors, but they wouldn't open. Talbot was beside me, picking me up, charging through the crowd to get me out of there.

"Use the crystal, Marilyn!" he yelled behind him, and instantly there was silence. Then, I heard the unmistakable sound of bodies hitting the floor.

I blacked out, not comprehending exactly what had happened.

When I came to, I couldn't see. Someone had closed my eyes, but I could hear voices. It sounded like they were in another room. Unable to move, I listened carefully. Bugs skittered inside the walls and what sounded like a larger thing, a mouse, probably, thumped its leg against the floor as it scratched at a flea. There were birds on the roof. A man was chanting over the speaker system in the main club. His words were nonsense mixed with what might have been Latin. I also heard Marilyn.

"I want you to have Magbidion check her out as soon as he's done with the mind job on the customers, Talbot. I want him to check her and everything she's touched. She's a stupid girl, but I looked into her eyes after she'd turned. She's still too human inside to do something like that."

Liquid splashed against the sides of a mug. I couldn't smell what it was. They were too far away. "Thanks," said Marilyn.

"Look, he's just going to have to put her down," Veruca

said. "There is something wrong with him. Whenever he turns a new slut, she winds up defective."

"No," Marilyn disagreed. "It isn't that. Something happened to her." She stopped talking abruptly.

Talbot paced back and forth across the floor. It sounded like he was walking on wood. They had to be in the office, since I doubted they were on the stage. "Do you think it was a spell?" he asked. "You know Eric pissed off the local Alpha. I wouldn't think a religious type like William would stoop to this, though."

Marilyn sipped her drink carefully. The aroma of coffee, strong and bitter, reached my nostrils.

"I couldn't say, Talbot, but you tell Magbidion that I'm not paying his fee until he finds out what on God's green earth happened." She fiddled with a package that crackled and when she next spoke she sounded like she had a cigarette in her mouth. "Could you?"

A mechanical lighter clicked and Marilyn inhaled deeply. "Thanks," she told him.

"I think I'll spare myself the secondhand smoke, Marilyn." Talbot coughed. "I'll get back to you when Magbidion has more information."

I heard the door open and close and then open again.

"Talbot," Marilyn called down the hallway.

"Yes?"

"She didn't drink a junkie or anything tonight, did she?"

"No," he answered. "I brought her some of Eric's stash from the fridge in the break room. I meant to ask you to check your ledger and see whose turn it is to give more this week so that I could replace it."

"Not from here in the office?" Marilyn asked.

"No," Talbot answered. "According to Veruca, Roger pitched a shit fit when you fed Tabitha some of his stock last night, said for us to stay out of the office fridge . . ."

"Like he ever drinks cold blood," Marilyn snapped.

"And that Tabitha should have to hunt, like Veruca," Talbot finished.

"Well," Veruca interjected defensively, "that's what he said."

"The stash in the break room is all Eric's, though," Talbot continued, "so I thought that'd be okay."

Marilyn took a long drag off her cigarette and blew smoke into the hallway. "Have Magbidion check the blood. All of it."

"Will do," Talbot replied.

I knew that blood had tasted funny.

15

ERIC:

SPIKED

It was a warm August night so I didn't mind flying home. Roger had been right to get Rachel out of there, but I was still a little pissed that he hadn't come back to give me a ride. He did know I was going to win, right?

It didn't take as long as I thought it would for me to fly back to the Pollux. I landed on the old theater's roof. Across the street, the Demon Heart's large neon sign was off and a *Closed* sign hung on the front doors. My watch had stopped, but I didn't think it was closing time yet.

The scent of blood hit me before I had made it halfway across the street. The smell wasn't quite as strong at the back door, but when I walked in I had to pause, allow myself to adjust. Whatever had happened, I was relatively certain that going into a feeding frenzy wouldn't help. Down the hall, in the business office, Marilyn and Talbot were talking. They looked my way when I opened the door.

Marilyn looked stressed, puffing away at a cigarette, her arm in a sling. Talbot was pretty well banged up. His shirt was shredded, and I could see scratches on his arms, chest, and back. The ones on his back looked particularly deep. The sorcerer Magbidion was with them. Sometimes I call him Mag because it gets on his nerves. He wasn't with the local mages' guild, so he was free to work for vampires; I'd used him before. In fact, I'd been meaning to call him. I made a mental note to have Mag look at the silver bullet while he was here.

"I was just telling them they did the right thing when they used the Somnolence Crystal," Magbidion told me. "I was able to fix all the humans out there, but you'll need a new Somnolence Crystal. I can have it ready tomorrow for fifteen grand."

"Fifteen thousand?" I asked incredulously. I seemed to recall the last one costing less than that.

"Pay it," Marilyn snapped. "And I don't want to hear any complaints about the fifty thousand we owe him for cleaning up the mess tonight. It was worth every penny."

"What the hell happened?" I walked past them into the office and slid the company checkbook out of the drawer. The carbon copy above the check I was writing caught my attention.

"Who the fuck is Fergus Jenkins and why did we write him a check for thirty thousand dollars?"

Talbot shrugged. Marilyn's eyes narrowed, but her mouth stayed firmly shut. "Anyone?" I asked again.

"Who wrote the check?" Veruca asked innocently.

I looked closely at the signature. Roger had signed my name. He never dots his *i*'s. He also he made the *e* in *Eric* look more like a *c* and connected it to the *r*. When I write my name the *e* stands alone.

"Roger," I said flatly, "I'll ask him about it." I sniffed the air. It was hard to tell over the carnage, but I didn't smell him. "Isn't he back yet?"

Veruca shook her head. "I don't think so. I'm headed out, though. If I see him, I'll ask him to call you."

"Fine." Someone was going to have to explain this to me eventually, but in the meantime I wrote Magbidion a check. He reached for it, but I held back.

"What am I paying sixty-five thousand dollars for?" I asked.

"Fifteen thousand for the new crystal. I could do it for five, but then it wouldn't put paranormals to sleep. It costs ten to cover werewolves, ogres, those kinds of things, and another five to make sure that it doesn't put any of the Demon Heart staff to sleep along with the riffraff. I have to key them in individually."

"I know that. I mean the rest of it."

"Ask them." Mag pointed at Talbot and Marilyn. "You don't want to pay me to explain it to you." I held the check back out to him. He took it, shook my hand, and started to leave. "You know," he called over his shoulder, "you'd save a lot of money if you just agreed to be my champion."

Ever since Mag had seen me fight that demon in El Segundo he'd been after me to champion his cause when the time came. Magbidion hadn't been born with magic; he'd cut a deal to get it. He was going to lose his soul unless he had a champion who could kill whatever demon it was that he'd made the deal with. Mag lived in fear of repo day, and I wanted no part of it.

"Let's keep it cash and carry for now," I told him. He headed for the exit and then I remembered the silver bullet in my pocket.

"Mag," I said, following him out to the hallway, "Let me ask you something."

He stopped and peered at me from beneath bushy brown eyebrows. As far as I knew, it was the only hair on his body and that was why he let them grow a little wild. "What is it?" Mag asked.

"I found this bullet out at Orchard Lake in the skull of a werewolf. You ever see anything like it?" I handed him the bullet. He promptly dropped it.

"You can't just hand somebody a thing like that!" Mag wiped his hands off on his pants. "It's a soul stealer."

I knelt next to it. "I've been carrying it around in my pocket."

"You can hold it safely." He emphasized the *you*. "You're a dead thing."

"Sorry." I picked it up and held it out in my palm. He bent over to examine it more closely. Lines of blue shone on his face, cast by the runes carved into the bullet. "If death wasn't enough to pull your soul out of your body," Magbidion continued, "then this won't be a problem for you."

He took a ratty-looking pair of wire-framed reading glasses out of his shirt pocket and put them on. Magbidion traced his finger over one of the symbols, the same symbol Rachel had recognized. "It only kills werewolves." He sighed. "You want to be careful, though. It's not made to kill vampires, but it shape-locks anything supernatural that it hits. You get hit with one of these and there'll be no turning to a bat and flying back to the crypt until you get the bullet out. The silver would probably set you on fire too. Hell, I didn't have anything to worry about."

"Then you hold it." I handed it to him. The way I dumped the bullet into his hand made me remember having handed it to Rachel. Good thing it only worked on werewolves.

"It has souls inside of it, too." He crossed his eyes. "Two, four, six . . . hold still . . . eight . . . nine . . . Lot of 'em in there. Fella could make some impressive wards with these guys."

"Wards?"

"Are you kidding me?" Magbidion tapped the bullet. "Werewolf souls are perfect for wards. They're supernatural and mundane at the same time. . . . Human, yet not human. Perfect for keeping normals and paranormals at bay. I hear it took about thirty to erect the wards over at the Highland Towers and they're damn near impregnable."

He made a series of motions in the air.

"Looks like you're trying to adjust the focus on an invisible camera," I told him.

"I am." Mag paused. "Well, kind of."

He kept motioning and my stomach turned. The sound

of fingernails on a chalkboard rose from the bullet. "It's a tricky artifact," Mag explained. "I nearly missed it, but this bullet is linked to something . . . some things. More bullets, maybe? I could tell for sure if I saw the gun."

With each adjustment he made, the sound got worse until with a final twist it stopped. Seven little blue cables of light extended three feet from the bullet's base. Magbidion touched one of them and bit his lip. "It's no good. Someone would have to follow the trail and you don't have enough money to pay me to do that." He perked up. "Unless, of course, you want to be my champion."

"I'll think about it." I took the bullet back. "For now, why don't you tell me what you can."

"This bullet is connected . . . it has five little brother bullets, and all of them are tied to one another and more importantly, to one hell of a gun." He took off his glasses and put them away. "It's powerful magic. I couldn't make something like that. Whoever made it is either real bad juju or had a demon to help them."

"Now I just have to find a tracker, right?" I put the bullet back in my pocket. "How much do I owe you for the info?"

"I'll put it on your tab."

"I'd rather write you another check."

"Just let me know if you decide to make any wards with that stuff. I've always wanted to work with the real thing."

"It's a deal," I agreed.

He started to leave, then stopped himself. "Can I park my RV in the Pollux parking deck tonight? The first floor is tall enough."

"Anytime," I told him, meaning it. I followed him out the back door and watched as he walked over to a ragtag RV with what looked like a decade's worth of dust and grime on it. He unlocked it and looked over his shoulder at me.

"You know Talbot could probably follow the bullet's trail back to the gun if he knew to look for it." He tapped his temple. "Cat's eyes." He climbed in and the vehicular behemoth came to life, spewing a cloud of black smoke from the tailpipe.

I walked back inside and returned to the office. Marilyn hopped out of my chair as I approached, moving to a folding chair across the room. Talbot loomed near the door as usual. They gave me a rundown on what had happened and it didn't make me the happiest boy in the world to find out that my newly turned girlfriend had gone batshit and tried to kill every human in my club. "How's Candice?"

"They're keeping her overnight for observation," Talbot said matter-of-factly. "Broken clavicle, cracked sternum, a pretty good concussion, and a fair assortment of cuts and bruises; I wouldn't expect her to work for a while even if she does decide to come back. We had six girls working when it happened. Jasmine will be okay in a day or two. She's weak from the blood loss. Kaylee got off with bumps and bruises, and Sharon and Desiree were just scared half to death. Lil's dead, though, and that emcee you were trying out, Rick . . . we'll need to find a replacement. He's dead too."

"Fuck! That stupid bitch!" I stood up, brushing past Talbot to stick my head out into the hall. Tabitha's new scent drifted toward me from the dressing room.

"It wasn't her fault, Eric." Marilyn sighed. I turned to look at her, my hand still on the door. "Magbidion was surprised that she lasted as long as she did before exploding."

The question I was about to ask must have been betrayed by my expression, because Talbot answered it. "I fed her cold blood again tonight. I got it out of your emergency stash in the break room fridge because I didn't have much time."

"And?"

"And Magbidion said somebody spiked your blood," he concluded. "Not the blood in the office fridge that you and Roger share. Just the stuff in the break room . . . just yours."

"It's easier to get to," I said. "Anybody can get into that break room.

"Call the girls and tell them that the Demon Heart is closed until I get this all sorted out. Everyone still gets paid," I told Marilyn.

It's not like I need the money anyway, which I've tried to explain to Roger more than once. It doesn't matter if we turn a profit. The Demon Heart's all about food supply, not money. Managed properly, the club could lose twenty grand a month and we'd still be fine. As it was, we usually made money anyway, assuming we didn't have to shell out for a lot of high-priced magical stuff. Maybe it would have been cheaper to be Magbidion's champion. I just didn't know exactly what it entailed, aside from killing the demon, and as usual, I didn't want to know.

"Damn werewolves," I griped. "Do you think they could be behind this? I mean I get the attack at the hockey game, but—"

"You got attacked at a hockey game?" Marilyn wheezed. She'd walked around behind the desk and started dialing, receiver in hand.

"Yeah. I killed the Void City Howlers." I shrugged. "They were werewolves. Didn't Roger and Rachel tell you about it?"

"Veruca told you they aren't back yet," Talbot reminded me.

"Shit. They left first. They really should have gotten back first." Marilyn hung up the phone and the three of us walked back to the fridge in the break room. Talbot slid past me and opened it. I kept five pints of blood in there for emergencies and weekends, in addition to the supply Roger and I share in the office mini-fridge. There was generally at least one night each week when I wound up drinking blood out of the fridge, usually when all the girls were busy and I just didn't feel like going out. There were two left, pushed to the back behind various salad dressings, bottled water, diet sodas, and the remains of Candice's pizza; Magbidion had marked both bags with a big red X. Marilyn reached past me for a bottle of water with a large M etched into the cap.

I picked up one of the blood bags and shook it at Talbot. "What the hell did he say is in these things?"

Marilyn set her water on top of the fridge, took the bag from me, put it back in the fridge, and closed the door. She stood facing me, but her eyes were on the floor. "Someone tried to slip you the be-all-end-all of Mickey Finns, Eric. Magbidion did two thousand dollars worth of mojo over it and said it was something mixed with werewolf blood. He took one with him to study it, but we already know it makes the vampire who drinks it go berserk. He thinks that at the beginning it gives the victim a mild euphoria and erodes their self-control, but when the drinker next tastes human blood, warm blood, from the source—"

"They go apeshit," Talbot concluded. "We're just lucky that it wasn't you."

"I'd have killed everyone," I said softly. "Is there any way to know who did it?"

"No." Marilyn shook her head. "All of the girls use this room, and our security's not all that tight to start with." She grabbed her water bottle and took a drink. There was a bruise on her right arm, like it had been grabbed too hard, but it was her left arm in the sling. I thought back to the slap. Had I grabbed both arms? I didn't think so, not that I could ask. "Hey, did I do that, too?" seemed a little insensitive.

Talbot seemed to be considering something.

"Spit it out," I said.

"Well, Veruca was back here even though she had the night off. That struck me as a little odd."

"I think that blood's been in there all week. Could have been anyone. Go make your calls, and if you get any leads from the girls, let me know," I told Marilyn. "I'll check on Tabitha." Pushing past both of them, I headed down the hall toward the dressing room. Tabitha was inside lying on the floor. A crossbow bolt protruded from the side of her left breast. Dried blood covered her from knee to earlobe. Combined with the unnatural pallor, she looked like a murder victim.

I sniffed. Most of the blood was human, though some

of it smelled like Talbot's. She was also naked except for a G-string. The whole scene reminded me of a little kid looking at his favorite toy broken on the floor, but I knew that Tabitha was more than a plaything, whether I wanted to believe it or not.

Scooping her up, I carried her into the bedroom and kicked the door shut behind me. I sat down on the bed and held her tight against me. She was limp, cold, and lifeless, but not "dead" dead. A piece of wood through the heart kills Drones, Soldiers, and some of the wimpier Masters, but it only paralyzes the rest of us.

I kissed her forehead and silently thanked anybody that was listening for letting her be powerful enough to survive. For a few more minutes I just sat there with her, holding her, then I laid her on the bed and straddled her. Her eyes were closed. I pushed them open so that I could see them.

Any vampire can use telepathy if they have eye-to-eye contact with someone, but it opens you up to being mesmerized by the other vampire . . . unless you're their sire, or have a stronger psychic fortitude than they do. Using my power over her as her sire, I reached into her mind. She was awake and aware. She could feel everything, hear everything, but she couldn't move.

I'm going to pull the bolt out, I thought to her. *If you can't keep control of yourself, I'll have to put it back in.*

Okay, she thought at me, weakly.

I tried pulling the bolt out backward, tearing muscle, but in the end, I rolled her up on her side and slowly pushed the bolt through far enough to snap off the bloodied head. I let her fall back, locking eyes with her again, and extracted the bolt, a foot-long shaft of thin wood covered in blood.

She cried out and grabbed my shoulders. "Ow! Fuck!" She clutched at the gaping hole in her chest. "That really hurts! Shit!"

She seemed fine. The wound was already closing; her healing worked about as quickly as mine, which was a good thing. I tossed the bolt aside and kissed her, happy she was alive, undestroyed, whatever. I wanted to lick the blood from her breasts, but stopped myself, afraid it might be tainted with whatever had drugged her. It was then, as I leaned down, tongue hovering over Tabitha's breast, that Marilyn walked in.

"I've called all the girls," she said in a disapproving tone. "If you're going to lick that blood off, let me reload the crossbow first, just in case."

Why did I feel like my wife had walked in on me and the other woman? "No, that's okay," I told her. "We'd both better get cleaned up."

Tabitha and I headed into the bathroom and two minutes later, Marilyn joined us with the crossbow. "Just in case."

✦ 16 ✦

ERIC:

BUYING A CLUE

Talbot, Marilyn, and Tabitha sat across the table from me back in Marilyn's office. The tableau reminded me of a bunch of escaped prisoners trying to decide how to get out of the country. Everyone expected me to have the answers, but my think tank was running low.

"Okay, so we've got Willard's werewolf pack," I said.

Talbot coughed. "William."

"What?"

"William, not Willard. I found out a little more about him, too. He's trouble."

"So am I."

"I know, but not this kind of trouble. He's not just any werewolf."

"Yeah, Roger told me. He's an Alpha. It takes blessed silver to kill him."

"Roger said that?" Talbot cracked his knuckles. "Did he tell you that silver doesn't always work? You might need a specific type of blessed silver, something that's also magic, or maybe inherited. In rare cases, silver doesn't work at all and you have to make them drink mercury."

"Oh for Christ's sake," said Tabitha. "How is he supposed to find out something like that?"

I tossed the bullet to Talbot. He sniffed it gently, then popped it in his mouth and rolled it around. A few seconds later, he spat it back into his hand and studied it with all the intensity that a cat might give a mouse.

"Blessed, magic, and silver," Talbot said. He held it next to my hand. "Hold still."

His pupils changed from round to oblong. He whistled appreciatively. "Your auras are similar. It might even be inherited."

"My aura and the bullet's?"

"Yes," he said, serious despite my incredulous tone. I wanted to throw a flag on that play and give him a fifteen-yard bullshit penalty, but Talbot doesn't lie about things like that.

"One of my ancestors owned a magic gun custom-made for killing werewolves? You'd think Dad would have mentioned something."

"Like you even remember your father's name," Marilyn muttered under her breath.

"Sure, I do." I paused. "It was . . . Dad."

Marilyn laughed.

"John Albert Courtney," she said in bittersweet tones. "It's okay, Eric, that's why you have me." I wanted to kiss her for that, but I knew she wouldn't let me. She'd made that abundantly clear, time and again.

Talbot leaned forward, breaking the uncomfortable silence as Marilyn and I looked at each other. "It's news to me too."

"It's almost like somebody wants me in a fight with Willard. I mean William," I said. "Who would want me to kill him?"

"Why do you say that?" Tabitha asked.

"I don't know." I ran my hand along the desk and stared at my lack of reflection in the computer monitor. "I . . . I think . . . the day they murdered my Mustang . . . I was out hunting and I didn't stumble on one werewolf or two, I got jumped by eight of them while I was hunting in a part of town I don't even usually go to." I felt close to figuring it out and then it tumbled away from me, a lost thought.

"Who would want William dead?" I asked again.

"Who wouldn't?" Tabitha tossed up her hands. "He's a werewolf."

"Most werewolves have learned to stay out of the public eye," Talbot told her. "They form large packs, stick together in groups or communities. Some of them hunt vampires or humans, but those are mostly outcasts. William's group is a little different."

"How so?"

"Well . . . his pack believes they have been given lycanthropy for a reason."

"What reason is that?"

"Whatever William tells them it is, but basically it's to defeat the servants of Satan. Fight fire with fire. Use their unnatural powers for good."

"Oh, give me a break," I put in.

"William himself is a fanatic, or so I've heard," Talbot assured me. "His wolves tend to pick off lone vamps and leave groups alone, but when you get him on the warpath, everything turns into a crusade. He also has connections to the Lycan Diocese."

I held my head. See, this is why you leave werewolves alone.

"Diocese?" Tabitha snorted with laughter. "What, like the Furry Roman Catholic Church or something?" The laughter died on her lips when no one joined in.

"If by Rome, you mean Rome, Georgia," Talbot answered, "then yes. They aren't part of any human church, though; they don't exactly report to the pope."

"Why spike my blood?" I asked. "If William's a real in-your-face kind of guy and he has access to heavy hitters like the Lycan Diocese—"

"If the Diocese pissed off the high society vamps they might run the risk of starting a turf war. Maybe they wanted to make you look out of control . . . so that no one would take it badly if they vanished you," Talbot said. That made sense. "Or maybe the blood spiking was done by someone else entirely."

"I don't like it being someone else," I said.

"Why?" Talbot held the silver bullet out to me, but I didn't accept it.

"Because it complicates things." According to the clock, it was just past midnight, meaning today was technically to-morrow . . . a Monday. "How do I find this Will guy?"

"I can ask around, but if you're thinking about buying him off, I doubt you'll get anywhere. Last time I heard, he had ninety werewolves running with him, but it could be more. And like I said, he's a real power, not just in the city, but in the whole state, Eric. He could be a problem even for you . . . and he has no reason to make a deal."

"Okay. Talbot, I want you to get out there and try to find the magic gun that belongs to that." I pointed at the bul-let. "Magbidion says the bullet will lead you to the gun and the other bullets. They're connected. Tabitha, I want you to back him up in case he runs into any vamps that have issues with . . . his kind."

Talbot nodded and Tabitha's eyes widened.

"Marilyn, I want you to forward the calls from here to your apartment in case Mag calls back with any informa-tion." She nodded. I like it when everyone agrees with me.

"What are you going to do?" asked Tabitha.

"I'm going to see if I can't clear up the damn werewolf mess. See if I can set up a meeting with Wilbur . . . I mean

William. Maybe we can just get a tape measure and settle it. I'm also going to try to look up Greta to see if she'll help hold down the fort for a few nights."

The only one of them who didn't seem to immediately dislike that idea was Tabitha. I guessed that was only because she didn't know who Greta was.

"I don't think that's such a good idea, boss," Talbot said.

Marilyn shook her head. It didn't take vampiric senses to feel her anger. "You just keep reeling her back into this, don't you?" She snatched up her purse and headed toward the hall. At the door she stopped and looked back at me. Her arm was still in a sling, but she looked fierce, not frail, challenging me with what I had done to her. I tended to forget how long it takes humans to heal. I tried not to look at it. My avoidance amused her. "You can't tell her to stay away from you and then expect her to come running whenever you need her." Head held high, Marilyn stalked out of the room.

"Who's Greta?" Tabitha asked.

"Vampirically speaking," I told her, "she's your older sister. She and her brother are the only children I've made that I haven't . . . that are still with us."

"So your old girlfriend and boyfriend?" Tabitha looked scandalized. "I had no idea you were so broad-minded."

"No, it's not like that. They're my son and daughter. I tried to start a family. It didn't work, or maybe it worked too well."

"What went wrong?" she asked.

"See," I said to Talbot. "This is why it's better just to kill them. It saves on aggravation." I regretted it immediately. "I didn't mean that," I said hastily to Tabitha, "or I did, but not about you."

"How many have you killed?" she asked quietly.

"More than you'd like to know about." Tabitha looked a little sickened by that, but she pushed it down deep and plastered on a smile even I could tell she didn't feel inside.

I looked over at Talbot. His body language was tight and coiled underneath a stony exterior. As he headed for the door, I said, "Before you go, is there a way to check my cell phone voice mail on a regular phone? I want to know if Roger left a message."

Talbot walked over to Marilyn's desk and grabbed a blank piece of computer paper out of her printer. He wrote the instructions down and left them on the desk. "Anything else?"

I shook my head. "Head on out. You know what I need you to do." There was more that I wanted to tell Tabitha, but it wasn't the time, especially not with the possibility that she might still be experiencing a few side effects from the blood. Hell, it was probably a bad idea to send her with Talbot, but I definitely didn't want her there with me. Besides, I wasn't ready to tell her about Rachel, and I couldn't risk Tabitha popping over to the Pollux and finding her.

Tabitha nodded and left with Talbot, but the look on his face let me know that I'd be hearing about this later. He didn't like Greta or Kyle, he never had, but he also knew what they meant to me.

Maybe I knew too. I had their damn pictures in my wallet, right behind Marilyn's: family photos from the night I'd turned them; their last moments among the living. It was almost like carrying around an ultrasound in an odd sort of way. After all, you can't take pictures of a vampire, not without more magical assistance than I could easily pay for, and carrying around an artist's representation just didn't seem right. I picked up Talbot's calling instructions, folded them and put them in my pocket.

Feeling conflicted, I walked over to the Pollux. Rachel was waiting for me in a white bustier with lacy white panties, stockings, garters, and high heels. She wore a little black choker with a cameo on it. Dressed that way, she looked even more like Tabitha. Rachel pouted when she saw me, beckoning me with one finger.

I knew why I wanted her. She was young and alive. I could only guess about her desire for me. Maybe it was an adrenaline rush, the thrill of near-death, the danger that I might lose control. Maybe she just liked pain and knew from her sister's experiences that a relationship with me was a good way to get hurt. Either way, her passion and eagerness rubbed off on me. Vampires are like that.

Her excitement fed mine as we kissed. It was a bad idea.

My kisses moved from her lips across her jaw and down the side of her neck. She tensed slightly when I kissed her throat, afraid perhaps that I was going to dispense with the pleasantries and feed. She needn't have worried; I knew it wasn't time for the fangs yet. It hadn't taken me long to discover that women like it best if I feed right as they climax. The pleasure deadens the pain and the pain enhances the pleasure. Sex with a vampire is a monumentally bad idea, but I try to make sure it has its benefits.

Of course, having sex with Rachel was somewhere around a nine out of ten on the stupid scale, which was actually surprisingly low for me based on the evening's events.

Maybe, if I had actually broken up with Tabitha, I would have felt better about it, less guilty. I wondered if I really loved Tabitha. If I loved her, then wouldn't I be faithful? Yet, there I was. . . .

My jacket fell to the floor and I grinned as Rachel tugged at my shirt. Grabbing her by the shoulders, I pushed her down onto the rich red-and-gold carpet of the Pollux and knelt between her legs.

We kissed again, nipping at each other playfully and not so playfully, before she tore my shirt off and ran her hands over my chest. I had been in good shape when I died; I supposed I would remain that way until I died again. Just as she knew I could smell the scent of her excitement, I knew she could feel mine. She undid my belt while I kicked my shoes off onto the floor behind me. For an awkward moment, I was off balance and thought I might fall on top of her, but it didn't happen. I regained my center, but not my composure, and rolled the top of her bra down. Her piercings were simple but fascinating, two golden hoops. I couldn't help but think how painful they must have been. Even so, the effect was quite appealing and I lingered there in my affections before continuing downward.

A single diamond stud pierced her belly button, and she giggled involuntarily when I kissed it. "I'm sorry," she laughed, "but that tickles."

I moved lower, removing barriers and discovering yet

another piercing. There were no giggles accompanying my kisses there. "Does that tickle?" I asked.

"Don't stop," was her answer, "that's amazing."

Of course it was; I had been doing this for over fifty years. The difference in our ages surfaced briefly in my mind and I did my best to put it aside. Her heartbeat sped up; oddly it did not encourage my bite, but rekindled a lower passion instead.

She rolled me over on my back and straddled me. I could smell her blood; it surprised me that I didn't feel its pull as strongly as usual. Her body heat flowed over me, strong and vibrant, but it didn't call to me the way it usually did. I wasn't ungrateful for the extra restraint, but at the same time, it felt controlled, artificial. Why couldn't I stop this? It almost felt like magic.

I chalked it up to all the fresh blood I'd been drinking over the last few days, but that didn't fully explain it. Rachel crawled backward over my legs, pulling my pants with her and forcing me to lift my hips to accommodate her motion.

"Socks, off or on?" she asked.

"Off."

She pulled them off and kissed her way up my legs. I don't know why women get their tongues pierced, but why men like it became self-evident. Before I had a chance to think, I was on top of her, our movements urgent and impassioned. I'm not necessarily quiet in bed, but Rachel was very vocal. As we moved together she began a steady stream of soft little nonsense words, a rhythmic chant that sounded almost like another language, and dug her fingernails into my back, drawing blood. Our pace increased and she put both hands on the sides of my head turning it to face hers. We locked eyes and the smell of cinnamon filled my nostrils.

"Bite me!" she commanded. "Bite me, now!"

We both climaxed as I bit into her neck. For the first time in my unlife, the blood had a taste beyond that monotonous sameness to which I had become accustomed. Sweet and bitter all at once, it burned my throat as I swallowed. With each mouthful, the sensation grew. My mind was on fire and my skin was awash with heat. I felt the sun on my face, but there was no sun.

Then, all at once, I was full, completely sated even though I couldn't have had more than a few ounces of her blood. Inside my chest, my heart stirred once, twice, three times before growing cold and still once more. Collapsing on top of her, I panted like a human, as if I actually had to catch my breath.

"What . . . what was that? How?" Sex had never been that way for me before, and neither had feeding. I'd never experienced the easy fullness, the beating heart, such complete satisfaction.

Rachel kissed my forehead and rolled me onto my back before resting her head on my chest. My heart beat one last time and I could see her smile. "How many times did it beat?"

"Four," I answered. My panting slowed and my skin began to cool.

Laughing, Rachel bent her neck back and kissed me once more. "How long has it been since you felt your heartbeat?"

"The day I died," I said softly.

"I can't believe Tabitha hasn't done that for you, baby." Her voice held a note of reproach in it, but she didn't say anything else. Instead, she laid her head back on my chest and sighed. "You wore me out."

"How did you do that?" I asked again.

"It's easy," she said sleepily. "It's a thrall thing. The thralls at the Irons Club told me. If I was your thrall . . ."

I didn't know how to make a thrall. I only vaguely understood what they were, and from Roger's explanation, it sounded too much like slavery to me. I used humans for a little while and let them go. Okay, so sometimes I killed them, but I didn't *enslave* them, had no interest in even knowing how to do so. In my opinion, thralldom was more high society vampire bullcrap to make the wannabe Dracula types feel like kings and queens of the universe. I pictured Rachel eating insects like Renfield in the movies and shuddered. "No."

"Maybe I can do better next time, but I've never actually done it before and it took more out of me than I thought it would. Can we try again in the morning?"

"Maybe. Let's get you to bed."

She muttered a soft assent and slowly started to get up. I stood more quickly, swept her off her feet and carried her into the next room. I'd had the office next to mine converted into a bedroom for when I wanted to spend time away from the club and my employees. It wasn't much, but the windows had been bricked up and the sound system was excellent. There was no bathroom, but there was a sink in the corner with a towel rack next to it. I laid Rachel down on the bed and walked over to the sink. She fell asleep the second her head hit the pillow.

It took a while for the water to heat up, but once it was warm I wet a washcloth and went over to the bed. There was blood caked on her thighs and I gently wiped it away before drying her off with the towel that had been hanging next to the sink. She didn't stir.

"What have you gotten yourself into, Eric?" I asked myself aloud.

I watched her sleep for a while then climbed into bed next to her, feeling like one of those old kings in the Bible who'd been given young girls to warm their beds, except that I was making love to my human bed warmer and drinking her blood.

Guilt wasn't what I was feeling. It was more a sense of profound stupidity. There was more to Rachel than there appeared to be, but I couldn't bring myself to care. I wanted to bite her again, to taste anything other than the coppery taste of blood, to feel my heart beating, to feel alive for even a matter of seconds.

It was selfish and dumb and any number of things, but none of that mattered. I needed her. She made me feel like I was in control, or at least in control of being out of control.

And yet, if I was very still, I could sense an inner conflict. Deep down, I knew that being with Rachel was a *loss* of control, even if it did seem to bring momentary calming of my inner storm.

A little voice inside me told me otherwise. It argued that

if I could maintain control of my emotions, even if I lost control to Rachel in the process, then I had an advantage. That didn't make any sense, but the harder I tried to think about it, to analyze it, the murkier it became, as if my thoughts were being deliberately clouded.

The only reason I could come up with for the werewolves spiking the blood supply in the Demon Heart was that they wanted me out of my mind, needed me to go berserk.

If I wanted to stop them, then I not only had to maintain control, I also needed the help of a human who could handle herself when it came to the supernatural, someone who could walk around in the sunshine. Rachel certainly seemed like the best woman for the job. I was going to have to be careful not to feed off of her for the next few days, though. I normally had a once-a-week rule for feeding on my girls, to help them stave off anemia, and I'd already violated that with Rachel.

Before I let myself fall asleep, I checked the time on the wall clock. It was a quarter to four. I shook my head and rolled out of bed. Time was getting away from me and I hadn't even checked my messages yet.

I went into my office, took the paper out of my pocket, and followed Talbot's instructions. I had five voice mails. The first was from Talbot and dealt with the Mustang. There was a message from Carl that told me how long fixing the Mustang would take and how much it would cost. He wanted me to call him on Monday and let him know what to do. I fast-forwarded through the details. The cost didn't matter. Fixing the Mustang was imperative.

Message number three was from Roger. "Hey, pal. Sorry about ditching you back at the game, but I'm betting you had it handled. I dropped Rachel off at the Pollux, but listen: a pack of werewolves jumped Veruca and she's all freaked out. I'm going over there now to see if she's okay. She's a slow healer, so I'm going to give her another few nights off. She can't dance with claw marks all over her. I'll catch you tomorrow."

The last two messages took me by surprise. I listened to them one after the other and then sat down at my desk and listened to them again. The first one was from Kyle.

"No one answered at the club, Pops, so I guess something is going down. Just had a weird feeling and thought I should check in. You didn't close the club, did you? I think Greta would have let me know, but you know how she is when she's mad, so if it happened, you know, recently or something, then I understand why she wouldn't tell me, because you know, she's busy and everything, being mad and all, but if it isn't that maybe you could call me back, because I've been getting these freaky phone calls from a guy named William. He said he's coming for me and I kinda want to know what it's about because—"

Crashing sounds and shattering glass interrupted him; I could hear a scuffle and growling. Werewolves. Kyle never screamed, but I heard him die. It was a whooshing rush of air. Drones always turn to dust when they die. It sounds just like that. Soldiers usually turn to dust as well, but beyond that it's all based on power level, as if a vamp's extra power bought better special effects. Kyle had been a Drone; no special effects for him.

As I listened to the recording, I could tell when one of the werewolves picked up the phone. "You and your vampire whore have a lot to answer for, dead boy," he said. "You killed my son. You and your bitch killed eight more out at the lake. Did you think I wouldn't be able to smell your stench through hers? I was willing to negotiate, but you don't get that chance anymore. I'm coming for you. I'm going to tear down your unholy family and wipe your allies from the face of the earth. You, your unholy spawn, your den of immorality, even the humans that you've tainted with your presence will be wiped clean. Amen." Damn werewolves.

The last message was from Greta wanting to know why she'd just had to kill three werewolves. She gave me her new cell number and asked me to call her soon. Greta was a Vlad, like me. Three werewolves were no problem for her.

Kyle's death was more of a relief than anything else. Just because I hadn't killed him myself didn't mean that I was a big fan. He had just been too stupid to bother killing. What irked me was the part about my "bitch" killing people out at the lake. It couldn't have been Greta because she'd said three werewolves, not eight; and anyway, she'd have let me out of the sleeping bag. It couldn't have been Tabitha, because she had been with Talbot, and, well, the werewolves would've won that fight.

I slapped my palm into my forehead. "I am so fucking stupid!"

Froggy. Veruca didn't have an alibi for last night or for the night before. She had constant access to the break room fridge, and could easily have spiked my blood supply. Veruca wouldn't have been fast enough to unstake me and run, but—an image of a frog hopping away from the driver's side door of the truck flashed up in my mind's eye—she was definitely fast enough to unstake me, turn into a frog, and slowly hop away while I wandered around like a jackass trying to figure out what the hell was going on. It had to be her, but how had she managed to kill eight werewolves by herself?

The silver bullets. They certainly would have evened the odds. If Magbidion had been right (and I had no reason to doubt him) all it took was a single bullet to kill a normal werewolf, to steal its soul. With six bullets, she could have killed six werewolves and only had to fight the other two. I may make fun of her for only being able to turn into a frog, but she's a mean little fighter. She's fast for a Soldier, and she has claws. She could believably have taken on two werewolves.

She'd covered up her scent or maybe I'd missed it, but werewolves have a better sense of smell than vampires. William's phone call meant that he hadn't been fooled, which put him one up on me. The only thing that bothered me was why she'd left one of the bullets behind for me to find. Had she been in a hurry? Had trouble finding the last bullet? It didn't seem that way. It felt purposeful.

I picked up the phone and called Talbot on his cell. When I told him about Veruca, he agreed that it was possible, even likely. I told him about Kyle, too.

"Sure sounds like he's dead," Talbot allowed.

"Par for the course, I guess."

"Are you going to call Roger?" Talbot asked the question carefully, not wanting to imply anything. He knew how long we'd been friends. Just because Roger's girlfriend was mixed up in all this didn't mean Roger'd been in on it too. He'd been with me at the hockey rink when the werewolves had attacked. Sure, he had run away, but he'd just been taking care of Rachel. I still hadn't told him about Brian . . . how was I going to tell him my suspicions about Froggy?

"Not yet. Look, I gotta go. Be careful, Talbot."

Grunting his assent, he hung up.

I still needed to call Greta, but couldn't think of what to say. She hadn't done anything wrong, exactly, but I had sent her away. It had seemed like the right thing to do at the time, even though she thought of me as her father. She also called me Dad; one more reason I had come to find her presence disturbing. Greta looked up to me and genuinely cared about me, which always makes me want to push people away. There was also her eating problem. Compulsive eaters make bad vampires.

I played back her message and scribbled the number down on a piece of paper. The number stared at me. I stared back. My finger finally punched in the digits and to my relief, my call went straight to voice mail. "This is . . . this is Dad. Head over to the Pollux. I'll explain about the werewolves and then we can go kill their boss . . . or talk things over with him . . . or whatever. Oh, and you may know about your brother already, but they got him. Fuck. I don't know. Just come to the Pollux." I carried the handset into the bedroom and set it on the floor by the bed before climbing under the covers and snuggling up with Rachel.

Maybe Tabitha and Talbot would end Froggy, tell Roger about Brian, and make peace with William while I slept. That would be nice.

✦ 17 ✦

TABITHA:

FINDING FROGGY

Moving on four legs had been uncomfortable at first, but now that I was getting used to it, the warmth and the heartbeat were addictive. I changed into a cat as soon as we got into Talbot's Jag XKR and stayed that way for the whole trip to West Side.

West Side is all high-end apartment buildings and high-rise businesses. Roger's apartment was in the Highland Towers. You couldn't even get near the parking garage without an ID and a pass card. Talbot parked on the street and I forced myself to get out of the car, abandoning the comfort of the soft leather seats.

"This is it," Talbot said. "The trail leads right to the front door."

"How can you tell?" I meowed.

"The eyes of a cat see things the eyes of a human can't," he answered mysteriously. "Can't you see it? It'll be easier to spot when we get closer."

With Talbot leading the way, we walked over to the security gate. Actually, I sauntered. If I squinted and held my head just right, I could see the thin blue line from the bullet, brighter now that we were close to the source.

The Highland Towers loomed before us. I'd never been to the high-rise before, never even driven past it. Close up, it looked huge and imposing, a building that would have been more at home in Gotham City, very noir.

"Somebody's compensating," I meowed.

"Most of these people don't need to compensate. It's a status symbol to live here. That's probably one of the reasons Roger picked this place. Roger is conscious of appearances; it's why he keeps trying to get Eric to close the Demon Heart. His pals in the upper crust probably bust his balls on a regular basis about being a partner in a strip club."

I could smell the security guard even before we reached his booth. A few steps later, I paused in the street. Three faces leapt into my brain, and I yowled, hackles rising. No one had warned me about seeing things in my head. At least, I think they were in my head. They hovered like phantoms, or effects in a 3-D movie, right in front of my nose, but when I swatted at the images, my paw passed through them.

There were two men and a woman. The woman was gorgeous, blond hair hanging down to the middle of her back. Her body was soft and curvy like Marilyn Monroe's. She dressed like one of those old-school movie starlets and she felt old, lots older than me, like she'd seen the passing of centuries, even though we appeared to be physically the same age. She noticed me, and I got the feeling that my presence irked her. I knew why, too. She was less powerful than me. I can't describe how I knew; I could just feel it in my gut.

As my attention shifted, the woman vanished and the first man came into better focus. He was good-looking, but he was dressed more than a decade out of style. It looked good on him, but still, his friends ought to tell him to update his wardrobe. He was old, vampirically, but not as ancient as the actress. I was more powerful than him, too. He seemed startled by my age and power. I actually caught a glimpse of myself in his mind. He saw me as a cat and he couldn't quite tell whether I was a boy or a girl. It unnerved him, and he seemed relieved when my attention moved on to the third and final image.

The other man was short, fat, and balding. He felt just as powerful as me. Physically, I guessed he had been in his fifties when he had been turned, but he hadn't been a vampire very long—maybe thirty years or so. He smiled at me when I sensed him, spread his arms and gave a short bow. "A pleasure," he whispered in my mind and then vanished from the air as the others had, but before I was done examining him. It was less like I had dismissed him and more like he'd dismissed me.

I blinked rapidly, clearing my head. I was still standing in my cat form in the middle of the street. Looking up, I saw Talbot, arms outstretched, blocking traffic, so I darted up onto the sidewalk. He followed me and the cars moved on, their drivers cursing angrily.

"Next time, I might let you get run over," Talbot muttered.

"What the hell was that?" I meowed. "Who were those people? What where they doing in my head? What was I doing in their heads?"

I turned human and grabbed Talbot by his jacket. "Talbot, what the hell is going on here?"

"What people in your head?" he asked. "Tell me exactly what happened." Concern filled his voice, but he looked more amused than worried.

"I saw three people: two men and a woman. They were floating right in front of my face, Talbot, like holograms or something!" I shook him once and then let go of him. "Sorry. I . . . It's just . . . I could feel how old they were and whether they were more or less powerful than me . . ."

Talbot looked down his nose at me. "Less powerful?"

"Well, yes. Two of them were less powerful and one of them was the same as me." That stopped him for a second and then he grinned. I liked the way his teeth seemed to shine in the dark. It wasn't anything supernatural, just the contrast between his oh-so-white teeth and his dark skin.

Both of us were too distracted to notice the approaching guard until he announced himself. I didn't like him. He was too plain. Even though he was a vampire, he had a semi-vacant look, like he wasn't awake.

Talbot turned to respond, but I brushed past him. "What?" I said icily.

He recoiled from my question like it had been a slap. I wondered if he would rub his cheek. He didn't, but he did take a step back. Outraged. I was *outraged* that he had dared to speak to me. That wasn't like me. Was it spiked blood again? Or transformation sickness? Was I about to lose it? I didn't feel like I was losing it. . . .

Talbot started to speak again but I gestured for him to be quiet. "You wanted something," I said to the guard. "I know you did, because you walked over in the middle of my conversation." My voice came out louder than I'd meant it to. "So now that you've interrupted me, you might as well tell me what you wanted! What is it?"

He bowed. "My deepest apologies, Lady Bathory. Lord Phillip wishes to invite you and your servant to join him for a drink, if it pleases you. If you are not inclined to join him, then I am to tell you that it is his great hope that you will accept his offer at a later date. I am to await a response." The words were nice enough, but his delivery was off. He might as well have been reading from a cue card.

"Why did he call me Lady Bathory?" I asked Talbot.

"It's a polite name older vampires use for the female equivalent of a Vlad. Nowadays most vamps use Vlad, regardless of gender, but you might still run into a few vamps who will call you a queen vampire, or Lady Bathory."

"Holy shit!" I looked at the security goober. He was waiting patiently, eyes looking at the sidewalk. "Holy shit."

Leaning in closer to Talbot, I whispered, "But I thought you said I was a Soldier or at best a Master."

"I thought you were," he answered softly. "It's not an exact science."

"How does this guy know when you didn't?"

"I'm not a vampire." Talbot touched my arm and the contact surprised me, my skin oversensitive to his. "Phillip is a very influential Vlad."

"How influential is very?"

"This is his city."

"So, with a capital 'V' then."

"All caps," Talbot confirmed.

"Right." The guard was still waiting patiently, gaze politely averted. "Which one is Lord Phillip?" I asked the guard.

"I'm sorry, Mistress, but I don't know how to answer that."

I sighed. "Is he the tall good-looking one or the little balding fat one?"

That time I got an incredulous look from the guard, but he covered it up quickly. "What Lord Phillip lacks in height, he makes up for in stature. He is—"

Talbot took two steps backward.

"Impressed that you made the effort, Hollister, but it isn't strictly necessary." The light tenor voice seemed to come from all directions at once. Mist flowed through the security gate and the little man who had bowed to me in my mind coalesced before us. "I am indeed the little balding fat one."

"I am *so* sorry about that," I told him.

"Think nothing of it, Lady—?"

"Tabitha," I answered. He took my hand and brought it to his lips.

"A beautiful name; it has its roots in Hebrew, meaning gazelle. How appropriate." He released my hand and offered me his arm. I placed my hand on the crook of his elbow so that I wouldn't have to stoop. Hollister opened the gates for us as Phillip led me toward the building.

"My name is actually Phillipus," he continued. "It means friend of horses, though I've never much liked them. In recent days, it has behooved me to accept the name Phillip, which both shortens my name and also strengthens, by meaning, my relationship with horses . . . from friend to lover."

"I guess it had to happen eventually," I offered, not quite knowing what to say.

Phillip looked at me questioningly. "Well, you know," I continued, "sometimes when you've been friends with someone for a long time, it's only natural for the relationship to blossom . . ."

"Yes, exactly," my host said with a chuckle, "exactly so."

Two glass doors slid open before us. A tingle spread across my skin as I crossed the threshold. Turning my head, I watched Talbot step through the field without incident. "Pay no attention to that annoying ward," Phillip explained with mild embarrassment. "The less supernaturally adept tenants insist on it for protection. It's paranoia, if you ask me, but then again, most are not as capable of defending themselves as we are. Are they, my dear?"

I said something that I hoped didn't sound impolite, but it was hard to concentrate on what Phillip was saying. I didn't have the words to describe what I was seeing. The building was beautiful, all stone, marble, wood, and stained glass. I can't tell Frank Lloyd Wright from Andrew Lloyd Webber, but this place was perfect. Paintings hung on the walls in just the right light, while sculptures graced the alcoves and hallways.

The elevator was manned by a human attendant, who smiled and spoke to us as if we were royalty. He knew Phillip on sight and pressed an elevator button marked with a strange symbol. "Don't forget that sunrise will be at six eighteen, Lord Phillip," the young man said cheerfully.

"Thank you, Dennis," Phillip answered. "This charming young woman is Lady Tabitha. I'd like you to treat her and her escort as my guests." His lip curled briefly as he said *escort;* he'd come close to being less polite. As he continued, I wondered what he'd almost said. "They are welcome without chaperone in the common areas, the lounge, the elevator, on the roof, and of course, in the waiting area outside my own quarters. See to it and let me know immediately upon completion."

"Of course, sir." Dennis smiled at Talbot and me. "I'm pleased to make your acquaintance, Lady Tabitha. Could I trouble you for a drop of blood?"

"It's for the security system only, I assure you," Phillip explained. I held out my finger and Dennis produced a tiny golden needle with a small crystal on one end. He pricked my finger and the crystal turned red. It flashed once then faded to white again. Dennis repeated the procedure for Talbot. As the crystal turned white for the second time, the doors opened and Dennis ushered us politely out of the elevator.

"It shouldn't be longer than ten minutes, Lord Phillip," Dennis called after us.

When the elevator closed, Phillip led us toward a large wooden door. The wood looked like it had been stained purple. Outside the door was a large sitting area that I mistook for a library at first. To one side of the elevator stood a midsize wine rack filled with bottles labeled with dates, ethnicities, and blood types. Phillip must have noticed my interest.

"Oh, this is my waiting area. I'm an erratic sleeper, so one can never be sure if I'll be receiving guests or snoring the morning, evening, or afternoon away. This is just my little way of apologizing to guests for the inconvenience. Of course, Dennis can arrange for food to be brought up to the more broad-dieted, the humans, werewolves, and whatnot"—he glanced at Talbot as he said the last—"but since I understand firsthand how quickly the thirst can come upon our kind, I like to keep a wide selection of appropriate vintages at hand."

The grand door opened as we approached it and Phillip welcomed us inside. "Enter of your own free will."

"Isn't that what Dracula says?" I asked, pausing in the doorway.

"My apologies," he said, shaking his head. "I thought I was being clever. Please, do come in. I promise my intentions are not malevolent."

"It's okay," Talbot said softly.

I went in. There were even more books inside than in the waiting area. Lovely oak bookshelves lined the walls and wrapped around the oddly shaped room. The interior of Phillip's apartment was humongous; he seemed to have the floor to himself. Glass cases contained displays that ranged from a suit of samurai armor to an actual vampire with a wooden stake through his heart. Startled, I backed away from the glass case and bumped into Talbot.

"Talbot, that's—"

"You mustn't mind Percy." Phillip ran his hand along the glass as he passed, without ever actually touching it. "He's being punished."

For what? I thought. Percy was supported by a metal stand extending up from the bottom of the case and passing concealed under the rear of his jacket. He wore a tweed suit, gold-rimmed spectacles with round lenses, and a thin little mustache. The expression on his face reminded me of the Mona Lisa, a smirk perhaps, or bemused disapproval.

Age hadn't worn away his good looks; in fact, vampirism had frozen him at the magic moment before men stop looking distinguished and become simply old. He was the first vampire I'd seen with eyes so thoroughly faded, the irises gone from whatever color they had once been to the slightly gray off-white of recycled paper. He was trapped in there, frozen by the stake that had entered at an angle, piercing his tie neatly through the middle several inches above a diamond tie tack. I gave myself a quick mental biology lesson—the stake had pierced Percy's heart.

The plaque at his feet read "My dear Percy, who serves as

a remembrance to all that I do not bluff, I do not make empty threats, and there are indeed worse fates than death."

"He was such a naughty vampire." Phillip chuckled.

"He's dead, then? Or he's a Soldier or whatever?" I couldn't imagine him being anything less than a Vlad or a Master, but I hadn't sensed him. "I thought a stake would dust a Soldier."

"Oh, no, my dear," Phillip answered merrily. "Percy's no mere Knight. The stake masks his presence. He can see everything, hear, feel, smell, but he cannot move. He cannot reach beyond his body, even if you stare him in the eye."

I shuddered. Phillip raised a finger in a just-a-moment gesture and vanished around a corner of the room. I wandered about, admiring his collection of miniature antique statues, vases, and expensive knickknacks until he returned with two glasses and a bottle of what looked like wine.

"Care to join me?" he asked.

"Yes," I answered, smiling.

❖ 18 ❖

TABITHA:

AN AUDIENCE WITH INFAMY

It kind of bothered me that Phillip hadn't offered Talbot anything, but once I tasted the "wine" I knew why. It wasn't exactly wine. The texture, taste, and smell of it were like wine, but my body knew that it was blood. Surely if Eric knew about this, he would have had some at the club, especially with all the bitching he did about not being able to taste anything.

"This is nice," I told Phillip. "Is it a family secret? Because I've never heard of it before."

"Begging your pardon, Lady Tabitha, but you *were* born yesterday."

I must have blushed because he almost dropped his wine-glass and I felt a familiar warmth in my checks.

"Extraordinary! A blush response. You have no idea what a priceless jewel you are."

My cheeks grew warmer and I looked away. Part of it was real and the other part was a test. I wanted to know how he would react. He touched my cheek briefly and then withdrew his hand.

"To answer your question, it is not a family secret, at least, not my family. Most of my stock is made up of gifts from other creatures, tokens of respect or appreciation . . . an occasional peace offering. What we're drinking, for example, was made from the blood of Carmella Goshaunt's late lover, Emil. She interfered with my most recent attempt at ascension. The poor dear failed, obviously, but her machinations did prove a distinct inconvenience. . . ."

"Ascension?" I asked, taking another sip of the blood wine.

"Of course, my dear . . . from Master to King, or Vlad, if you prefer."

Talbot pretended not to react, but I could see him stiffen.

"I didn't know that you could do that."

"One can do many things with the correct ingredients. Why, I was commenting on a similar subject some months ago to a young Master vampire who has rather amusing ideas regarding werewolf souls. I think perhaps you may know him." Phillip smiled a genteel smile and put the cork back in the bottle. He hurried off again and Talbot and I shared a look.

"Roger?" I mouthed.

Talbot nodded, but before he could say anything Phillip

returned with a small black container roughly the size and shape of a cigar box, made of some kind of stone. "Volcanic glass," he informed me. "Percy made it for me when we were . . . on better terms."

He offered me the box and I handed my wineglass to Talbot. The box itself felt warm to the touch, but it wasn't real heat. It felt more like what I imagined magic might feel like. Inside the box, six items were carefully arranged on black velvet: a thumbnail-size red crystal, possibly a ruby, with a crack in it; a silver ring molded in the shape of a snake; a golden amulet; a pair of yellowish dice; and a small black stone.

"Each of these items was a part of a ritual or ceremony that allowed me to become a vampire or to grow in power."

"Become a vampire? Didn't you have a sire?"

"Not everyone travels an identical path to immortality," Phillip explained. "Vampires have always been reluctant to embrace wizards. As I could locate none to aid me willingly, I was forced to improvise." Trapped by a memory or an old thought, he looked off into space, sighing wistfully before his attention returned to the box.

"The Stone of Aeternum is the only one I haven't used, but it requires a vampire so rare that even a *helluo librorum*, a bookworm, such as myself has read of only a few. It's not as if one meets such a creature every day."

He held his hand out for the box and I handed it back to him. He looked fondly at its contents and then shut the lid. "It's of no true consequence, however; I must wait at least another seventy years before I can attempt an additional ascension. And I'd have to contact the right demons. . . ."

He walked off around the corner of his room again and called back over his shoulder. "That is a lesson worth remembering, my dear. Never try to ascend more than once a century or you may undo the work you've done. None of those soul-thirsty power brokers will tell you that either, so take my word for it."

He returned quickly, his glass in one hand and a necklace case in the other. "Now, this," he said with a smile, "you will appreciate."

He handed the case to me and took a sip of his wine. "Open it," he said eagerly. "It won't bite."

I did as he requested. Inside was a diamond necklace. I could tell it was real just by the way it sparkled in the light. A double ring of round-cut diamonds set in platinum formed the base of the necklace and alternating strands of one or two smaller pear-cut diamonds dangled like priceless teardrops at regular intervals. Queen Elizabeth might have worn such a necklace, or maybe the real Lady Bathory, but I had never seen anything like it, not up close.

"Try it on," he said. Suddenly self-conscious, I looked down at my clothes. I'd changed into a sequined black tank top, a pair of black knit leggings, and running shoes after Eric had unstaked me back at the club. I'd worn it to be comfortable, but it didn't go with a necklace like this. This necklace deserved to be worn with a gown.

"Do try it on," he urged. "It will look gorgeous on you."

"Okay." Just holding the necklace in my hand made me feel beautiful and extravagant. Trying it on was better and worse at the same time. From the look on Phillip's face, I knew that it must have looked wonderful, but not being able to see it for myself was unbearable.

"Oh, you simply must look at yourself. It's astonishing!" He toddled off again, mumbling to himself, then glanced back at me. "Oh, by all means, follow me. I never move the mirror, it's too delicate."

Around the corner he'd so frequently darted past was a large ornate desk with a gold reading lamp shaped like a dragon. Light poured out of the dragon's open mouth, illuminating an old book with pretty little pictures around the words. A leather case containing an assortment of pens lay open on the desk and a slim silver laptop rested in an overstuffed reading chair directly across from the desk.

Phillip brushed past the desk and over to a pair of doors set back between two bookcases. He opened them to reveal a full-length mirror held by a crystal frame that was decorated with fanciful flowers and artful designs. In the mirror I could see not just Phillip's reflection, but my own. I looked better than I ever had in life.

Everything about being a vampire rushed in on me at once—the rampage in the Demon Heart, the blood, Eric, Lillian's terrified face as I struck her down, all of it, my mind seared like bacon in a hot frying pan.

Then, almost as if the mirror had a will of its own, I sensed that it wasn't satisfied with what it had made me feel. I guess I hadn't been dead long enough to truly horrify myself with what I had done, so the mirror rummaged through my life for ammunition. The last conversation I'd had with Rachel had been a fight. Our words rang out in my ears. Each mistake I'd made, each humiliation I'd ever endured, the mirror latched onto, multiplied, and distilled. All the times I'd ever been hurt, by Rachel, by my parents, by Eric, crashed back on me as one exaggerated assault.

You want to see how pretty you look? the mirror's whispering not-quite voice wheedled in my thoughts. *I'll show you what you look like on the outside, but only if you can endure what you are on the inside.*

Turning into a vampire had made my emotions more volatile than they'd been when I was alive. I'd been crying right and left since the change, like having PMS all the time. I was easy prey for the mirror: the tears came quickly, pouring red down my cheeks, a deluge of self-loathing, self-pity, and remorse. I turned away.

Doors clicked shut behind me as Phillip covered the glass. The mirror's taunting voice slowly faded, but having once peered into it, I could feel it there, behind the thin paneled doors, watching me, waiting for me to take another look.

Talbot rushed to my side, but I waved him away. I didn't want to be comforted; I was too busy being mad at myself for crying. I was tired of crying. I hadn't cried when my grandmother had passed away or when Rachel had died, and the mirror had exploited that, thrown it back at me in a horrible way. Phillip offered me his handkerchief and I took it, soaking the red silk with my blood as I tried to stop the tears.

"Damn it," I said between sobs.

"It's my fault," Phillip said, sounding genuinely angry with himself. "The mirror allows a vampire to see his reflection, but it takes its toll in other ways. We who gaze within that mirror must face the things we've done as vampires, our hidden sins, the things that would make us cringe and weep were we still human. I'm so used to it that I had forgotten the effect it can have. I shan't show it to you again without giving you time to prepare."

"Is it alive?" I asked.

"There is a demon trapped inside to power it," Phillip answered, "if that's what you mean. It's only a small one."

Talbot took my arm and we walked out of Phillip's study and back into the main room of his chambers. "If there is anything I can do to make it up to you," Phillip offered, "I would be most pleased if you would tell me. You may keep the necklace, of course. I knew at once that you should have it."

"No, I can't, it's too much."

"Bah," Phillip protested. "It was a gift from so long ago that I no longer remember who gave it to me. It's yours whether you take it or leave it, though I'd rather you took it. I have collected so many things over the years that I could give half of it away and never notice."

I smiled, and my tears began to subside. "How long have you been alive—I mean, how old are you? You seemed—that is, you felt kind of young, you know, outside."

"Oh, not quite a thousand . . . each time I ascend it makes other vampires sense me as though I were younger, but my mind has not forgotten the truth that the magic conceals."

"And you really used those things in the box to become a vampire—to ascend?"

"You will, in time, learn not to question my veracity, my dear." Phillip's eyes hardened briefly before softening once again. "But you are new and I can't bring myself to hold it against you, so yes. Oh, yes. Vampires have always been reluctant to grant immortality to wizards, are strictly forbidden to do so now, unless it is done via a thralldom, which is a capricious immortality at best. So, yes, I had to find alternatives.

"I used those 'things in the box' along with rituals, demons, and of course, vampires of the required power level. . . . Does it concern you? I'm already a Vlad; you have nothing to worry about from me on that account. I've no further need for sacrifices from those of our rank; my final ascension will be much more difficult to arrange. Besides, I've made it a habit to expend only those I found distasteful, and I find you anything but." He waved a hand. "Enough talk of me, though, I am still waiting to know how to make it up to you—my faux pas with the mirror."

"But the necklace—"

"The necklace is a gift, my dear, not an apology. I gave it to you because I wanted you to have it." He gestured around the room. "Excepting the Stone of Aeturnum and my own existence, you may choose from anything I have. Even Percy. Please, take your pick. I insist."

His eyes sparkled mischievously. "I could dispel the enchantment on the city. I used a Veil of Scrythax, you know. Have you seen one? Oh, they're ghastly-looking things, but incredibly effective and oh, so delicate. There are nights when I'm gripped with the urge to rush to the vault, seize the hideous thing and smash it to pieces, to let the humans see us for what we really are and remember all the things I've hidden from them. Think of the panic! It would be impossible for the Council of High Magic to contain it. Another war with the humans would be such . . . fun. It's always so interesting to see how the human rulers choose to conceal it from their constituents."

Uh . . . no. There was nothing that I saw in Phillip's house that I really wanted and a war was not my idea of fun. There were plenty of things that it might be nice to have, but . . . I wondered what Percy had done and whether I ought to ask for him and let him go. Then Talbot mouthed *werewolves* at me and I remembered that I was supposed to be finding out about the magic gun thing.

I held my hand out to Talbot and he handed me the silver bullet. Phillip's eyes lit up when I showed it to him. He delicately took it from my outstretched palm and held it up to one eye.

"A bullet from *El Alma Perdida*, meaning in Spanish 'the Lost Soul.' I wonder where he found it."

"I was . . . we were looking for the rest of it, the other bullets, and the gun. Talbot tracked it here for me."

"Ah," Phillip said excitedly, "information, the most valuable gift of all! Do you realize how rare it is for one of my new acquaintances to ask me for information? They all ask for money or power—"

A knock at the door interrupted him. "That should be Dennis," Phillip said as he walked to the door. "He is one of my applicants, you know. An intern . . . as it were." Phillip looked through a small eyehole, midway up the door and smiled. "It is he."

He opened the door and invited Dennis inside, but the man declined. "I just wanted to let you know that the lady and her companion have been added to the ward matrix, sir. I apologize for taking so long, but Mistress Gabriella was quite interested in your new guest."

"What did you tell her?" Phillip asked eagerly. He seemed giddy, childlike in his delight.

"As per your standard request, sir, I told her only that the lady and her companion were your guests and that they were to be given access to all of the common areas."

"Was she vexed?"

"Quite vexed," Dennis replied.

"Excellent as always, Dennis," said Phillip. "You may go."

He closed the door and walked back over to me. "Please, excuse the interruption. Gabriella has been a bit wroth with me for the last few decades. She recently relocated from Atlanta in hopes that she might be the agent of my eventual demise. How quickly my offspring turn against me. But you wanted to know about *El Alma Perdida;* you thought you might find it here?"

"Yes. We think a female vampire, a Soldier, has it and we think she's in the building. Her name is Veruca."

"Meaning wart . . . such an unpleasant name for a lady."

I'd been taking one last sip of blood wine when he said that and it shot out my nose as I tried to stifle my laughter. I caught the blood with the handkerchief I was still holding, but I continued to cough and sputter. My nose and sinuses started burning and I would have dropped to my knees if Talbot hadn't caught me.

"I'm sorry," I said, coughing, "that's just too funny. Her name means wart? Eric calls her Froggy."

More blood tears formed in the corners of my eyes and even Phillip chuckled. "That is indeed an unfortunate nickname for one whose name comes from the Latin *verruca*, meaning wart. At least he doesn't call her *acuminata*. *Verruca accuminata* would be just too terrible. . . ."

Only Phillip laughed that time. He quickly controlled himself and sat down in one of the armchairs. They were slightly undersize for a person of average height, but they suited Phillip quite well. He smiled in my direction and motioned for me to sit. Instead, I walked over and knelt next to him. It let us look at each other eye-to-eye and I was tired of looming over him.

"And you believe her to be in possession of *El Alma Perdida?*" he asked.

"I do."

He caressed the air about the bullet with his fingertips, but his eyes did not leave mine. "No one by the name of Veruca lives here, I'm afraid, but that doesn't mean she isn't staying here with someone else. Did she have any other acquaintances who might have a residence here?"

I nodded. "Her boyfriend, Roger."

"Ah, yes, Germanic, meaning quiet . . . or famous spearman. And this Roger, would he be a Master vampire?"

I nodded again.

"I spoke with him several months ago," Phillip said as he

stroked his chin with his left hand. "Utterly ignorable. He tried to engage me in no less than three business transactions. He wanted to buy the Stone of Aeternum from me. I didn't sell it to him, of course. You don't sell those sorts of things; they are given or sought. I am not in retail. I think I suggested that he talk to one of the local demons, though. It's in my log." He raised both hands in a dismissive gesture. "I can always check it later."

"Do you remember the other transactions?" I asked.

"Oh, he had some foolish notion about my backing him in the Orchard Lake acquisition. Naturally, I declined. Vampires like him will be the ruin of us." He trailed off and his eyes focused on someplace far away and probably long ago. Eric has that look sometimes. "Let's see if your Wart is sleeping over, shall we?" He walked over to an old-fashioned wall phone, lifted the earpiece, and held it at arm's length. "Dennis?"

I could hear Dennis easily, one of the benefits of being a vampire. "Yes, my lord?"

"I want you to check on a Master vampire named Roger. See what suite he is in and find out whether or not he has another vampire by the name of Veruca visiting him. Ring me back as soon as you know anything, would you?"

"Of course, sir," Dennis answered.

A barely audible click signaled the end of the connection on Dennis's end.

"He's going to find out and get back to us," Phillip explained. "He's such a clever boy; he's the current leader amongst the male applicants."

"Applicants?" I asked.

He laughed. "I do hope you will excuse me for not ex-plaining earlier. Every decade I have a contest to determine my next two children: one boy and one girl. It keeps me busy, and some of them make wonderfully entertaining op-ponents after a few centuries.

"But enough of that. Dennis should be back soon and I don't like to let them hear too much about who is in the lead. It makes them insufferable. While we wait, could I get you another glass of wine? Perhaps your mouser is hungry? I'm certain Dennis could scrounge up a rodent or two."

I stared at him blankly. "I'm fine, Lady Tabitha," Talbot told me.

"He's fine, thank you," I said with a puzzled look on my face.

Phillip nodded absentmindedly, then snapped his fingers. "I could play the violin for you. I've only been playing for a century, though, so I haven't mastered it yet."

Talbot cleared his throat. "Maybe you could tell Lady Tabitha about the Lost Soul? What's it for?"

Phillip set the bullet down on a table and dashed off. It sounded like he was wrestling with a box of Christmas lights. When he returned, it was with a beautifully crafted violin case. "Perhaps I shall do both?"

I nodded and he opened the case.

◆ 19 ◆

ERIC:
GRETA

I woke to a cacophonous mix of werewolf howls and trucks revving their engines outside the Demon Heart. I was getting tired of fucking around with these stupid werewolves. The door to my bedroom in the Pollux swung open and Greta stepped inside. She'd cut her hair. It was short now, but still blonde. Dressed in running shoes, jogging shorts, and a sports top, she looked none the worse for wear. The only sign of her recent conflict with the werewolves outside was the remains of a tiny media player still clipped to her shorts; there wasn't much left of it.

"Up and at 'em, Dad. There are werewo—" She paused in midsentence as she spotted Rachel. "So that's Tabitha," she said awkwardly. "She's certainly . . . um, pierced, isn't she? Those cannot have felt good."

"Her name's Rachel," I muttered as I rolled out of bed. "I turned Tabitha. This is her little sister."

"Jesus, Dad," Greta complained. "That's screwed up even for you." Greta blanched at her own sentence, worried that she'd criticized me too harshly, that I might have taken her seriously, missed the teasing tone in her voice. She looked purposefully away from Rachel's nakedness and cocked a thumb toward the door, hiding her dismay behind a jaunty smile. "Let's kill the werewolves across the street and then you can tell me all about it." She looked back at Rachel and sighed. "Or better yet, you could just not."

I rolled my eyes and headed for the door. "Did you have a nice trip?"

"Oh, yes," Greta quipped. "It's been great. Those werewolves have been chasing me all night. I probably could take them, except they've got crosses and stuff. How's Mom?"

We headed out of my room and down the stairs.

"I think she suspects that the Demon Heart is really a strip joint," I joked.

Greta jumped over the rail and landed next to the door. Why hadn't I thought of that? "That whole 'interpretive dance school for nudists' story couldn't hold up forever," she tossed back at me.

That, in a nutshell, was my problem with Greta. I liked her too much and we got along too well. She fell into the father-daughter role easily and could make it seem so normal when it definitely isn't. She accepted me. Even when she snarked about my lifestyle, her complaints were usually voiced as lighthearted teasing.

If we were a real family, when I grew old, Greta would have never sent me to an old folks' home; she would have kept me close and taken care of me. That kind of devotion was scary, especially coming from a cold-blooded killer even more amoral than me. Greta viewed me as a hero growing up, justified my every mistake, and lionized my flaws. She took my dislike of other vampires to another level, too; sometimes, she even hunted them.

Greta opened the front door and one of those fake-looking werewolves was there waiting for us. His hair could have been badly dyed rabbit fur glued over latex rubber skin, and his smooth tan teeth reminded me of a botched resin model kit. He snarled, snapping at Greta.

"Bad dog!" she admonished. "No biscuit!" Greta caught him by the muzzle, snapping his jaws shut with a pop and giggling when he whined. "Can I keep him, Dad?"

Roger likes to tell me I don't think before I act. Compared to Greta, I'm well-reasoned, insightful, and reserved. The werewolf swiped at Greta with his claws and she laughed, popping him twice in the forehead with her right fist. While he was stunned, she grabbed his neck and pulled the beast down into a headlock.

"Well, can I?" Greta asked insistently.

"I don't care if he did follow you home," I said as I grabbed either side of his head and twisted. "You're not keeping him."

The wolf's neck broke and Greta let him drop to the floor. He wasn't dead, but the broken neck would keep him out of the fight.

Behind him, I could see about a dozen of his companions strutting across the street like some kind of inner-city gang, clearly confident that we'd be no problem for them. The four in the middle of the pack seemed to be the ones in charge. Two of those wore cross-studded collars around their hulking necks, their fur a uniform dark brown. The third was larger than the rest, a mottled gray werewolf with a pug-nose muzzle more befitting a bulldog than any wolf I'd ever seen. He hefted a large wooden cross made from two interlocking railroad ties. Next to him, a black wolf with a priest's collar stared directly at me, rosary beads wrapped around his right paw.

"William?" I asked.

"The flock calls me Reverend." His voice was light and airy, a complete contrast to the wolf's hulking black form. The sound didn't even synch up with his lips, like a badly dubbed kung fu movie or spaghetti western. Maybe he was using some big magic mojo to translate snarls and growls into English for the wolf-speech-impaired. Quite possibly I should have been impressed, but it only served to enhance the goofy unreality that I experience whenever I run into a werewolf.

I glanced at Greta. She had a hungry look in her eyes. I imagined it was the same look that I had in mine when I woke up each morning, ready for my next drink of the red stuff. That's the other problem with Greta. She's always hungry.

"What about one of these?" she asked with mock sincerity.

We walked out into the street side by side. I stopped to lock the door behind me, casually, as if there was no rush.

"Sorry, honey. You know the rules. No pets."

We were both smiling; it seemed to confuse the werewolves. They outnumbered us five to one and they expected trepidation at the least, outright terror at the most. Cocksure bravado was not in their list of likely prey responses. Unfortunately for them, we weren't prey.

A wave of holy power hit me as they crossed the center lane. The four in the middle were true believers; no wonder they felt confident. I realized immediately why Greta hadn't wanted to fight them on her own. She doesn't heal from holy wounds easily. The more powerful the vampire, the more quirks he or she has. That was one of hers.

The true believers were going to be the real problem. Most werewolves just charge in without thinking, but these guys held back, waiting, I supposed, on the good reverend's word.

"Let's not do this, Reverend," I said. "I'm not a bad guy. Ask Jackie, down at the—"

Reverend made the sign of the cross with his rosary-clad paw and spoke Latin: "*In nòmine Patris, et Filii, et Spìritus Sancti.*"

"Amen," the other werewolves said in unison. My teeth went numb, my fangs retracted, and I took two involuntary steps backward. You only feel power like that every once in a while, and generally not from locals. These guys were from the Lycan Diocese, or the one with the rosary was; he had to be. What the Inquisition was to witches the Lycan Diocese is to vampires and other things that might threaten the therianthropic flock. Your average skinchanger can't go to them for help, but William obviously had some pull.

This was exactly the sort of attention I'd wanted to avoid.

"William was right to call us," said the big one with the giant cross. He unlimbered the heavy thing as he spoke and swung it like a giant hammer. Greta screamed, but I couldn't move, as if a spell were fixing me in place. The cross hit me midchest, igniting the front of my *Welcome to the Void* T-shirt and hurling me back into the brick next to the *Casablanca* poster at the side of the Pollux's main entrance.

"I was kind of disappointed when Deacon sent you instead of coming himself. I see that I was wrong," one of the other werewolves told him. Three werewolves on the left teamed up on Greta, grabbing her as the one called Reverend advanced. He placed his rosary-wrapped paw at her throat. The sizzle and pop of her flesh was all I could hear, the smell of the rosary charring her flesh.

She screamed out one word, "Daddy," and then, suddenly, I was free. I could move again.

Speed. Most vampires have it all the time. Mine comes and goes. Sometimes I can control it, but usually it just kicks in and out. This time, it kicked in. Each sizzling pop of Greta's flesh resounded like a gunshot. My whole body began to vibrate. I felt like I was going to lose control, go into one of my rage blackouts, but then, somehow, I didn't. In a wave of remembered cinnamon scents, my proximity to Rachel, even asleep upstairs in the Pollux, gave me reins for my rage. I took a deep breath and charged.

In an instant I was on the three werewolves holding Greta, bypassing the two werewolves with the cross-studded collars that were headed toward me. I cocked my hands back and plunged my claws through the backs of two of Greta's captors. My hands closed around their hearts and I let them each beat a single time before I tore them out.

It must have broken Reverend's concentration or something, because suddenly Greta could move, too. Greta's claws were out and I couldn't stifle my laughter when she gave Reverend a knuckle-deep two-finger eye poke, Three Stooges style, accompanied by an imitation of Curly's famous "Nyuk nyuk."

I tossed the two hearts I was holding down onto the pavement. The remaining werewolf with a grip on Greta let her go and threw up. Weak stomach, I guessed.

Reverend drew back howling, clutching at his ruined eyes, blood matting the fur around them. The sight distracted me, and the two collared werewolves took the opportunity to sink their fangs into either shoulder. The shoulder bite I'd gotten on Friday had hurt; two hurt more than twice as bad. The added sizzle of their collars against my cheeks didn't help either. I grabbed them both by the scruffs of their necks like oversize puppies and flung them across the street. The movement didn't do my shoulders any good, but I didn't have much choice.

"Don't fucking bite me," I snarled furiously. "I'm the vampire! I bite you. You do not get to fucking bite me!"

I pointed my finger at the remaining combatants. "You can claw me. You can hit me. Hell, run me over with a truck, but no biting or I'm going to stop dicking around here and you won't even have time to run away."

Everybody stopped.

"And another thing, your fight is with me and me alone. You touch my little girl again and when I'm done with you, I'll get your scent from the pieces, I'll track it back to your home and I'll bring the fight to your kids, your family. Does that sound fucking fair to you, assholes?"

They seemed to suddenly shrink before me, or maybe I was expanding. I could feel a familiar burning in my chest. I wasn't just standing on the brink of a blackout, I had jumped off the cliff and now everyone was waiting to see if I would catch the rope dangling behind me.

"Oh, great!" Greta sighed. "You guys went and pissed him off! Now he's going to go all uber vamp and I'm not going to get to play anymore."

"Okay," Reverend said softly, his paws still pressed to his eyes.

"Okay what?"

"Just let us leave. We heard what happened to the Howlers, but we assumed you'd had help. Lots of help. We couldn't believe that you'd done it alone. I can see we were wrong. So just let us take Jim and leave."

"Who the hell is Jim?" I asked.

He pointed blindly in the direction of the werewolf with the broken neck.

"Okay, Reverend." I smiled. "You have a deal. You grab your boy Jim and get the hell out of here. Anybody that wants to go can go, but if I see you around here again, you die. Oh, and I want you to tell your boss something for me."

"You can't do that, Reverend!" one of the collar-wearing fuzzies protested. "They've killed Bruce and Annie. We can't just walk away. They are unholy monsters. We have to kill them, now!" One of them had been a girl? I glanced down at the bodies, but they were too furry for me to tell. Dead werewolves do change back to human form, but only when the sun hits them.

The Reverend seemed to think it over before answering his packmate. He didn't take long. "I'm sorry, Paul, but William is going to have to come out here with us if he's going to send us up against something like this. That isn't a normal vampire. It can't be. A normal vampire could not have broken free of my spell like that. You can stay here if you want, but the rest of us are going." Eyes still covered, he turned blindly back toward me. "What is it you wanted me to tell William?"

"Tell him I know who killed the werewolves out at the lake and it wasn't me or any of my people. I'll admit to having killed his son, but he killed my son, not to mention my car, so I'm willing to call it even and let things blow over. If Willy Boy won't go for that, then I'm even willing to find the ones responsible for what happened out at the lake and gift wrap them for your boss. You got all that?"

Reverend nodded.

"One more thing. Tell him I'll need an answer by tomorrow night." I pulled Greta back to the sidewalk, trying not to pay attention to how badly burned her neck had gotten.

I shouldn't have spent so much time talking. Reverend pulled his hands away from freshly healed peepers, a bit bloodshot but clearly functional. This time my speed didn't kick in. Damn it. Before I could react, the two werewolves next to him grabbed me, one furry bastard on each arm. Reverend reached up and put the paw with the rosary over my eyes. An eye for an eye. It was even less fun than El Segundo, but this time I had Greta at my side. I heard the slight jingle of werewolf collars as they ran for her, but she was already in motion.

I heard the swoosh of Pug Nose's big hammer-cross thing, and felt the displacement of air brush past my face as it just missed me, connecting with Reverend instead. His skull caved in with the sound of a smashing watermelon, music to my ears.

"You missed," Greta taunted.

Two sets of claws I couldn't see tore into my belly, spilling my guts onto the concrete about the same time I heard the sickening tear of a werewolf's head being torn from his neck.

"Grow that back, Rev." Greta laughed again, but the laugh turned into a shriek and a sizzle. Damn it. Not sure of what to do, I jumped backward, carrying my two captors with me, shattering the glass doors at the front of the Pollux and landing with a crash in what used to be the ticket booth.

The werewolf on my left arm relaxed his grip and I used the moment to tear free of him; then I pulled in the one on my right and sank my fangs into his throat. Werewolf blood doesn't taste much different than human blood. The tricky part is not getting any fur stuck in your teeth.

I didn't have time for a prolonged snack, just enough to speed my healing. Blood is both food and medicine for us. I tore out enough of his throat to put him out of the fight, and rubbed my eyes against the wound. Gross, but effective. My vision returned, but it was still cloudy, like viewing the world through a sheet of wax paper. Lucky for me, werewolf silhouettes are easy to recognize.

I turned on the second werewolf just in time to get a claw slash to the chest as he extricated himself from the ruined ticket booth. Cuts and scrapes from the glass dotted his hide. Behind him, I could see Greta going toe to toe with pug-face and the others in the middle of the street.

A minivan sped by, swerving to avoid the melee, and I could only imagine what the driver would remember. Greta used the distraction to snatch the railroad-tie cross away from Bulldog and concuss him with it, her hands igniting even as she touched the wood. She sank her flaming claws into Bulldog, using his blood to extinguish the flames, and then latched onto his neck with her fangs.

I pulled myself upright and boxed my opponent's ears. He howled in pain and I did it again. The second time, I heard the pops I was waiting for and he dropped to his knees.

I saw that Greta was now on her own against the collared werewolves that had been helping Bulldog, so I simply wrenched my opponent's jaws apart, taking the top half of his skull with me as I turned away, hastily stuffing guts into my rapidly healing torso.

I charged toward Greta only to get pulled off my feet by Jim, the werewolf with the no-longer-broken neck. He had the same fighting style as the wolf from the alleyway, and I had terrible déjà vu as he battered my head first into the concrete, then the brick, then the bench in front of the Pollux.

I caught a *fwoosh* of flame out of the corner of my eye as Wolfboy kept swinging, applying the tiger by the tail principle. One of the werewolves had removed his collar and strapped it around Greta's neck. He and his companions were holding her down as she burned.

So much for keeping my temper. My vision blurred, and then everything went dark, but I could still hear the screaming. Usually, a rage blackout was a hole in time that I could never get back, but this time was different. I heard flesh rending and tearing. I heard bones break and smelled fur charring. Underneath it all, there was another noise, like wings flapping in the night. Finally, when everything was silent, I could see again. Greta was in my arms and the fuzzies were scattered in piles across the street. One of them was impaled on the massive railroad-tie cross, his ribs splayed open by the massive wooden center beam protruding from his chest. The rosary beads and cross-studded collars were nowhere to be seen. I was pretty sure I didn't want to know what had happened to them.

I took Greta inside the Pollux and called Tiko. He's an oni—sort of a Japanese ogre. His kind are body-disposal specialists. They eat them. Sometimes they play with them first. I don't ask any questions as long as the corpses go away and don't show up again.

"I need you to get out here," I said when he answered. "I've got a bunch of dead werewolves for you . . . and the good news is that some of them had shiny new trucks."

Tiko said he'd get there as quickly as he could, but that he was going to have to charge extra. "I have a few cousins over in Georgia who could help," he offered, "if you're going to keep killing off werewolves left and right. We can only eat so much."

"Yeah. Call 'em," I said, sighing. "There may be seventy more where those came from and who knows what else."

I hung up before he said anything else and carried Greta up to my office. She was pretty badly burned. There would be no talking to William now. Son for son, I was willing to accept. I was even close to overlooking the Mustang. But now he'd fucked with my little girl and there was going to be hell to pay.

◆ 20 ◆

ERIC:

EYE OF THE . . . ?

One of the things Roger taught me was that a sire, if he or she is powerful enough, can heal their offspring with their blood. Not that he'd meant to teach me on purpose, but near the end of the whole El Segundo thing, the only way we found to heal the cross-shaped burns Roger received was to take him home to mommy. He, like Greta, had difficulty healing wounds inflicted with holy implements. I'd thought the burns were pretty darn funny, myself. Anyway, we'd looked up Roger's sire in Atlanta and she had taken care of his wounds.

I didn't get to meet her; Roger made me wait outside. For weeks afterward, I had to hear how she'd had this whole ritual that I thought was her way of making sure Roger knew what a pain in the ass it was to do the healing for him. Roger had been impressed, but I was pretty sure that it was little more than the strategically placed flour women get on their faces in the movies. You know, so the audience can tell they've been toiling for hours to bake those instant cookies?

As far as I could tell, the ritual was like that, all pomp and circumstance, and highly unnecessary. Fortunately for Greta, she had me for a sire; trust me, I'm powerful enough, and I have no use for ritualistic ass kissing.

I tore my wrist open with my fangs and bled directly onto her ruined face, working the blood into the remaining skin, smearing it across bare bone where necessary. Skin bubbled back into place, like burning in reverse. Greta's hair grew back long and blonde, the same as when I had embraced her. My blood bubbled like thick red hydrogen peroxide over the marks on her neck, only when the bubbling was over, the wounds weren't just disinfected, they were gone.

I moved on to her injured hands, withered stick fingers crackling as I doused them liberally with blood. It started to work immediately. The claw marks on her side and a nasty bite she had taken to the left calf healed just as quickly after a similar treatment.

When I was done with the front, I rolled her over and checked her back. There were a few claw marks, but they had already started healing, so I left them alone. My own wounds were gone by the time I finished with hers, but I didn't feel the hunger I thought I should. Between my own

healing and bleeding all over Greta, I should have been ravenous. Instead, I felt nothing.

I washed myself off using the sink in my Pollux bedroom
and changed into jeans, tennis shoes, and a fresh *Welcome to
the Void* T-shirt. By the time I was done Greta was waking
up. The clock in my office read four o'clock. That meant I'd
slept for a good hour before the fight, maybe more. I should
have been feeling the daily hunger as well, but I wasn't. True,
I'd ingested a little werewolf blood, but that didn't account
for everything.

"Dad?"

Greta stood up, covered in blood, and looked down at
what was left of her clothes. The running shoes were okay
and her panties had survived (they were soaked with blood,
but technically intact); the rest was in a desperate state.
"Okay, either you healed me or you thought it would be fun
to blood wrestle your unconscious naked daughter."

I averted my eyes. My first thought was to send her down
to the dressing room Rachel had appropriated, but Greta
was taller than Rachel and more endowed. "You can probably find some clothes across the street in the club, but if
Tiko is out there, I'm going to want to walk over with you.
Oni have two favorite pastimes: eating people and raping
them. Tiko is a good guy as far as oni go, but—"

"Seeing me naked and covered in blood might stretch his
self-control a little?"

"Yeah, something like that. And you can't kill him. . . . I
need him right now."

She walked out and I waited, listening. I heard her footsteps on the stairs, the door opening and closing, but I didn't hear her go outside. I couldn't hear Tiko working, but I assumed that was why she had stopped. Finally her footsteps echoed on the stairs again, then down the hall to my office door.

"Is he out there?"

"Yep."

"So you came back to get me." She nodded and I headed out with her. "Good girl."

"Dad?" she asked on the stairs.

"Yes?"

"Is there something wrong?" She bit her lip nervously. "Did I do something wrong? Are you mad at me?"

"What? Where the hell did that come from?" We stopped midway down the stairs and she put a hand on my shoulder. She looked genuinely concerned.

"No, nothing, it's okay, it's just, you know, your eyes . . ."

I didn't know. "No. What about my eyes?"

"They're still . . . doing the thing."

The thing? I held a hand up in front of my eyes, but there was no red light shining on them. "What thing?"

She exhaled and I was a little taken back. Greta never breathed unless she was talking; even then, she took only the necessary breaths. Breathing was like pacing for her; she only did it when she got nervous. "You know . . . your angry eyes."

"My angry eyes? Am I supposed to be Mr. Potato Head all of a sudden? They aren't glowing red. I just checked."

She looked away and removed her hand from my shoulder. "I'm sorry. It's nothing. I shouldn't have brought it up."

"No," I said quickly. "It's okay; I just don't know what you're talking about. Seems like everyone mentions it but no one will talk about it. You act like I'm going to chomp you or something. Can we please talk about it?"

"Okay," she said, "but let me shower and dress first. This blood is starting to congeal on me."

I took off my shirt, right there on the stairs and slipped it over her head. Why hadn't I thought of that before? The hem of the T-shirt only came down to mid-hip on her, but it concealed most of her nudity. We crossed the street to the club uneventfully. Tiko stared at her, hunger in his eye, but looked away when he realized I was with her.

Greta showered and dressed quickly. The clothes came from a stash Marilyn had been keeping for her, but hiding from me. She walked straight to Marilyn's office and pulled them out of a small travel bag stored in the bottom drawer of the filing cabinet. I wondered absently what other secrets Marilyn was keeping from me.

When she was finished, Greta met me back in Marilyn's office. She was wearing jeans and a black T-shirt that read *Welcome to the Void*. It was similar to mine, only hers showed a fair amount of midriff and had pink lettering.

"Are they still doing it?" I asked.

"Your eyes?"

"Yes, my eyes."

She sighed. "Yes, Dad, they're still doing it."

"Describe it to me."

She got up and crossed the room, knelt in front of me and rested her arms across my lap as she stared into my face.

One thing that I find unnerving about other vamps is the lack of heartbeat. If she had been human, there would have been all sorts of signs to give me insight into what she was feeling, whether she was scared and trying to look calm, or vice versa.

"I've never gotten a good close look like this before," she said, sounding fascinated, "but it's actually kind of cool. The whites have turned black and the veins in your eyes . . . from a distance I couldn't see it, but up close they're dark, dark purple. Your irises are purple too, but sort of crimson at the same time. They're shifting back and forth slowly from one color to the other, with a kind of subtle glow. When you get totally furious they glow more and more brightly until there are actual beams of light shining out of them. I've only seen that once, but I didn't stick around. I've never been too sure about how safe you are when you're like that."

"Like what? Angry?" I asked. Greta scooted back away from me across the floor and climbed backward up into her chair.

"No, Dad," she said quietly. "I mean when you go all uber vamp, with the wings and all."

I stood up so quickly my feet nearly left the floor. "What do you mean 'wings'?"

❖ 21 ❖

TABITHA:

WAYS AND MEANS

Phillip's violin was made of a beautiful dark-colored wood and so was his bow. I could tell it was old and probably expensive. The light dimmed as he began to play, and underneath the music, outside the range of human hearing, disembodied voices moaned along with the song. I didn't like classical music; pissed-off girl rock was more my style. But Phillip's music, indescribably beautiful and sad, captured even my attention, although it was still a little too loud for my enhanced hearing.

Talbot listened with rapt attention. His eyes were half lidded and subtle movements of his chest and head suggested that he was in full-blown musical bliss. Finally, Phillip put down his bow and bowed to us. Talbot and I clapped with an appreciation that wasn't feigned on my part. I was glad that Phillip wanted to spend time with me. It was very flattering, and I had to admit that the whole violin playing deal was pretty romantic.

"That was beautiful," I told him.

"Too shrill for your ears, though, I fear," Phillip said sadly. "I forget how sound-sensitive newborns can be."

I blushed again. "I'm sorry, Phillip. It truly was beautiful, my ears just aren't"—I struggled to find the right word—"refined enough to really appreciate it yet."

"The fault is mine," he said as he put his instrument away. Even the case was lovely. It also looked expensive. Everything around Phillip looked expensive.

Phillip glanced at the wall clock and frowned. "It's after four and I promised to tell you about *El Alma Perdida*." The fire in the fireplace turned blue, then green, and the lights dimmed even further. Phillip either had the coolest dynamic lighting setup I'd ever heard of, or he was using magic.

"The Lost Soul is the Colt Peacemaker used by John Paul Courtney in his misguided quest not only to kill werewolves, but to save their souls. Oh, it's such a remarkable story. No one knows how Courtney came by the weapon, but many know its description. *El Alma Perdida* is a pearl-handled six-shooter with silver crosses worked into the grip to help ensure that his enemies, vampires and werewolves, could not use it against him."

Phillip flicked his wrist and a translucent image of the gun appeared in front of him. It just looked like any old gun to me, but Talbot leaned in closely. Must be a guy thing. "Made in 1873, it was lost when Courtney died in 1925 at the ripe old age of one hundred and two. Few knew he was that old. You wouldn't have suspected that he was a day over fifty." Phillip's expression became dark and mysterious. "Some say his soul was bound to his weapon and resides there to this day." He smiled. "If one is inclined to believe in ghost stories."

Another gesture from Phillip caused the gun to transform into the shape of a man. He wasn't handsome, but something about his eyes, the confidence there, reminded me of a lion. They were a startling shade of blue. "He looks familiar."

"You might find he resembles your sire. I tried to turn Courtney," Phillip mentioned casually. "Do you know his blood actually burned my mouth? I had to snap his neck— twice. Such a waste. He would have made a most interesting foil for those long boring nights. I had such hopes. . . ." Phillip must have noticed my confusion, because he smiled sweetly. "You're so young, Lady Tabitha, but trust this wizened old vampire when I tell you that eternity, after a time, begins to wear on one's nerves."

"What would a vampire want with his gun, though?" I asked.

"Guns are generally used for two purposes: one is display, the other killing. It's the motive that always interests me. How did you come by the bullet?"

"It was found."

"By whom?"

"Eric."

"Eric. Hmmm. Scandinavian, I think, meaning kingly,

honorable ruler, or even ever-powerful. How interesting. Did you know that in the hands of Eric, your sire, this gun could be used to kill nearly any werewolf?"

"Because its bullets are blessed——" I started.

"Magical, silver, and, in his case, inherited," Phillip completed. "It's made for lycanthropes, but it will work on any type of therianthrope that walks this mortal earth excepting one."

"Which one?"

"Snakes," Talbot answered too quickly. "Reptilian skin-changers are vulnerable to gold, not silver."

Phillip wrinkled his nose. "Yes, snakes. These bullets would still hurt them, though, lock their form."

"Magbidion already told us about that part." I clapped my hands over my mouth. Lord Phillip didn't appreciate interruptions and Talbot and I had both managed to cut him short, back to back.

"Then I won't bore you further." Phillip snapped his fingers and the room brightened so swiftly that spots danced in front of my eyes. "Surely Dennis won't be much longer," he added.

I looked at the clock and suppressed a yawn. It was only 04:17 and I was already starting to feel tired. Shit! What was going to happen to me when the sun came up? Would I just pass out? I gave Talbot a concerned look, but he gave a slight shake of his head. Did he mean I shouldn't mention it or that it was okay and he'd take care of everything? I stared at him for a few more seconds until he finally nodded toward Phillip. Not knowing what to do, I turned my attention back to the elder vampire.

"So," I began, "based on what you said earlier, you're kind of your own sire? How does that work?"

Phillip stiffened for a moment, but then chuckled and relaxed. "After a fashion, you could say that, yes. I was a wizard during my human days, but as I grew older, I became obsessed with immortality. The prospect of what lay waiting for me in the great beyond was a bit too chilling. At first, I sought out a true immortal, one of those lucky souls who walk the earth born to immortality: human, but unending. I spent decades searching, but never found one. I had a ritual, you see, that would have allowed me to steal his immortality. Along the way, I made certain discoveries about vampirism and as time grew shorter for me, I decided that vampiric immortality was better than none at all and so, here I am."

"That's interesting," I said. I stilled another yawn as I stretched.

"How about you?" Phillip asked gently. "I assume you were sired in the more conventional manner?"

"Yes, by Eric," I answered.

"Oh, yes. If I'm not being too bold, are the two of you involved?"

"I'm in love with him," I blurted. I hadn't meant to say that, but it came out anyway.

Phillip didn't look surprised. He smiled warmly and closed his eyes. He stood and waltzed himself in a little circle. "Ah, young love." He put his hand to his heart. "I hope it lasts. Lady Gabriella and I were in love once. Now we are waging a merry little war of intrigue against each other."

There was a knock at the door and Phillip rushed over

to it. "That should be Dennis," he pronounced. Checking the little peephole, he clapped his hands together excitedly. "It is!"

He opened the door and invited the man in. As he had the last time, Dennis declined.

"What do you have for me?" Phillip asked.

"It seems that the Gryphon Suite houses a Master vampire named Roger. According to security, Master Roger hasn't been home since Friday, but his girlfriend, who answers to the name Veruca, has been in and out of the apartment at odd hours for several days."

"How interesting," Phillip said gleefully.

"She returned Friday in the early evening with an assortment of bites and scratches that prompted the security guard to ask if she needed help. According to his report she responded with a rude gesture. She went out again on Saturday. On both days she carried a pistol Master Roger had registered with security."

Outrage washed over me. That bitch! She was a part of it. And Roger . . . what an asshole! How could he do something like this to his best friend?

"And why, may I ask, did security not alert me to the presence of *El Alma Perdida?*" Phillip asked.

"Greed, milord."

"Greed?" I asked.

"He was bribed," Dennis explained.

"His name wasn't Fergus Jenkins, by any chance?" Talbot asked.

"No, sir. Salvadore Belino," the man replied. Shifting his

attention back to Lord Phillip, Dennis smiled. "He awaits your pleasure in the lower galleries, milord. I've also taken the liberty of sending a car around to collect his family."

Thinking about Veruca, the spiked blood, and the way I'd had to cover her set made me really mad. My eyes flashed red, but I shut them down quickly. Dennis was a little taken aback, but Phillip just laughed it off. "Ah, the impetuousness of the young."

"I'm sorry; it's Veruca . . . not you." I looked at Dennis. "Did she come back here?"

Dennis looked questioningly at Phillip before answering my question. When Phillip nodded, he proceeded. "She returned just after dawn looking much worse for the wear. More scratches, I'm told, and some burns."

"Is she still here?" I asked.

The same series of looks was exchanged between man and vampire, and then Dennis hesitantly answered my question. I guess he didn't want to ruin his chances of being Phillip's newest son. "As a matter of fact, she is still here. She hasn't left Master Roger's apartments since she returned this . . . that is, yesterday morning."

"How do I get to the Gryphon Suite?"

"Not so fast, milady," Phillip said, holding up his hand. "Everything in its own time." He walked around to his desk, opened a drawer and came back holding five one-hundred-dollar bills. He folded them carefully and handed them to Dennis. "Thank you, Dennis; that will be all."

Phillip closed the door, turned and leaned against it with a tired look on his face. "I'm afraid I can't allow you to go rampaging through my building, knocking down doors and dragging people from their apartments, my dear. Neither you nor your mouser will be allowed to behave that way within these walls without earning my most sincere reproach, as did my dear friend Percy." He gestured to the vampire in the glass case, the one with the stake through his heart.

"Then why even bother to tell us she's here?" I complained, stomping my foot. "God, that's infuriating!"

Phillip clasped his hands. "Anyone who has been granted access to the common areas of the Highland Towers may call upon any resident by simply approaching their rooms, wings, apartments, or floors, whichever is appropriate, and knocking upon the door in a polite manner.

"It is forbidden for one of my guests to physically assault a resident." He acted like I was supposed to be going "A-ha!" From his tone, I knew he was trying to give me a hint, but I sure as hell didn't know what it was.

Talbot walked over to me and put his hands on my shoulders. "We've taken enough of Lord Phillip's time, milady. Perhaps you could assure him that we wouldn't dream of physically assaulting any residents of the Highland Towers, but would be quite happy to pay a call on a good friend of ours by the name of Veruca. Perhaps we'll find we see eye-to-eye on a few things."

Talbot stressed the word *residents* and the phrase *eye-to-eye* when he spoke, but I still didn't get it. Still, Phillip seemed to understand and he carefully explained how to go about getting an elevator to the Gryphon Suite. I gave Phillip a kiss on the cheek and, by virtue of our comparative heights,

a really good look down my top, and walked out wearing
the diamond necklace he had given me. As the door closed,
I stifled a yawn and started to ask Talbot what was going
on, but he shushed me and walked over to the elevators.
We waited a few seconds for the doors to open. Dennis was
not inside. Talbot pressed the correct button and when the
doors closed he winked at me.

"Not bad, Tab. I think he wants to go steady."

"Whatever!" I liked Phillip, but I wasn't going to date a
balding little short dude no matter how much money he had,
not unless I was in love with him; and since I was currently in
love with an attractive, not to mention quite wealthy in his
own right, vampire, things didn't look good for Phillip.

"He told you everything you need to know to get Veruca
out of this place and wherever you want her."

The elevator slowed and we walked out into one of the
building's elegant waiting rooms, crossed to a set of elevators
that served the correct floors, and waited for another elevator to show up. After the doors closed and the button was
pushed, I asked Talbot what the hell he was talking about.

"You're a Vlad and she's a Soldier. All you have to do is
lock eyes with her and you can make her leave with us."

"Oh. If you wanted to make me feel stupid, you succeeded,"
I told him.

Now all I had to do was get Veruca to answer the door,
lock eyes with her, get her into the car, and restrain her
somehow before I passed out from vampiric sleep depriva-
tion. Great.

So there I was, a few minutes later, in front of Roger's door, doing my impersonation of Mr. Fuzzy Bottom. It was a silly plan, but I didn't have a better one. If Veruca hadn't eaten, then a cat might seem like a tasty treat to take the edge off. On the other hand, if she didn't want to eat a cat, she might want to cuddle with one and enjoy the body heat. Heck, she might even like cats for all I knew. It was worth a shot.

Talbot was waiting down the hall next to the television playing in Roger's waiting area. Which, incidentally, was nothing compared to Phillip's. There were no comfy chairs, no stashes of bottled blood. It looked like a waiting room in a doctor's office, right down to the magazines that nobody interesting would want to read. They were all about money, or people who have money, or what was happening to other people's money. Even the station the television was turned to was all about money. I wondered what Eric's waiting room would have looked like if he'd decided to live here. Lots of strippers, maybe, or a giant neon sign that said, *Go away!*

Stifling a yawn, I meowed at the door and rubbed up against it. Pacing in little circles, I rubbed against the door eight or nine times, meowing, before the sounds of someone stirring in the apartment reached the doorway. Footsteps started for the door, followed by cursing and the sound of something clattering down to tile and shattering. Yet more cursing and then the handle on the door began to turn. I stopped and sat in front of the door flipping my tail back and forth. No wonder cats do that; it's fun. The doorknob stopped turning.

"Meow," I complained, by which I meant, "Open the door, you stupid bitch!"

Veruca stood on the other side of the door and waited. "I know it's you, Tabitha," she gloated. "And tell Talbot that I can smell him, too."

I turned human and looked incredulously at Talbot. "Any other bright ideas, Sensei?"

"Just one. She's not really a resident." He grinned and walked closer to the door. "Here, Froggy, Froggy, Froggy. Here, Froggy!"

"Stop it, Talbot!" Veruca snarled.

"I've got a hundred-dollar bill out here if you'll give me a lap dance, Froggy. Here, Froggy, Froggy, Froggy!" With each "Froggy" Talbot grew incrementally louder.

"I'm serious, Talbot," Veruca shouted. "I'll call security."

"You know, Froggy," Talbot continued. "I was just talking to Lord Phillip about you. Did you know Veruca means wart? I thought warts were what you got from frogs and toads, not—"

That did it. She charged out at us in a rage.

22

TABITHA:

CAT FIGHT

I expected Talbot to do all of the fighting, so I hung back, watching as he and Veruca tore at each other. Talbot's claws popped right out of the tips of his fingers like a cat's. Veruca's were scarier; her fingers curved and hardened, like talons. Talbot tore a chunk out of her side and smoke billowed up from the wounds. He tried to pull her in close, using the leverage to bite her, but she spun free, slashing open his forehead.

"What the hell?" Veruca yelled. She fell back into a crouch, gripping her side. "You burned me!"

"My claws are holy." Talbot took a step closer. "I'm a noble hunter, a sacred guardian. You're just a damn vampire."

"Hey, watch it," I blurted, slightly offended. "I'm just a damn vampire, too."

"It's just an expre—" His attention left his opponent for only a second, eyes flickering in my direction, but Veruca took advantage. She dove between his legs, rolling to her feet on the other side and flaying open his back with her claws. Talbot stumbled forward away from the door, cursing loudly. I stood in front of Veruca, hands out in front of me to ward her off.

"Stop her," Talbot ordered. "Don't let her back in the apartment."

"Look, uh . . . Froggy—" I shouldn't have said that. It slipped out. Naturally, it pissed her off even more.

"You think it's fucking funny, huh? That you can do a kitty cat and I can't?" She barreled into me, face contorted with rage, literally tackling me through the apartment door.

"Look out, damn it!" Talbot reached for my arm, but we fell, entangled, into the apartment and down on a throw rug in the center of what seemed to be a sitting room, with tacky chairs and a coffee table. Veruca kicked the door shut with her foot.

"Lock!" she shouted, and the door flashed blue for an instant. Talbot hit it from the outside and the wall shook, but it didn't give. "Tabitha! The rooms are warded; I can't get in."

"Unlock! Unlock!" I shouted at the door, but it didn't want to take orders from me.

"Talbot may be too much for me to handle," Veruca snarled, baring her fangs, "but I can still end you!" Time slowed as she stalked toward me, claws at the ready. I slid across the floor, got to my feet and tried to force the door from the inside. It wouldn't budge.

"It won't open!" I yelled.

"Not until she or Roger opens it." Talbot's voice sounded like he was leaning against the door. "Just fight."

I turned in time to see Veruca's claws slashing my way again. I dodged in the nick of time, but only because I don't think she expected me to have time to react. Her claws slashed the door, leaving large furrows in the dark wood.

Veruca growled, then spun with terrible speed and lunged at me again. Her claws were larger than mine and the tips were hooked. Brawling wasn't my thing; I misjudged her range. Both sets struck home. Getting hurt felt weird: an initial shock of pain that immediately faded, as though the nerve endings registered it once, then forgot about it.

"Get off of me," I screamed. My own claws came out and I used them as best I could, scratching at her eyes with one hand and her neck with the other. She might know how to kill, but I knew how to hurt a woman like her. She'd always been vain and petty. If she didn't have her looks, then, at least as far as she was concerned, she had nothing. Flesh ripped away from her face in jagged ribbons.

Veruca rolled away from me as we both howled in agony. Vampires aren't supposed to bleed much, but the chunks of flesh she ripped from my sides as her claws pulled free sent a shower of bloody spray across the living room, dappling the ceiling and the walls. This time the pain was jagged, raw and angry, pulsing.

"My face!" she screamed, launching herself back at me.

I moved with vampiric alacrity. Heartbeats faster than she could strike, I rolled backward and to my feet with a grace I hadn't had since ballet class, pressing my back against the door.

"Your claws may be bigger, but the wounds mine make don't heal," I lied. "When I'm done with you, you'll be lucky if you can pay a man to look at you, much less touch you."

I took a step forward, claws raised to strike. She reared back, feinting with her right hand. I dodged to the left to avoid her deadly claws, and fell right into her trap. As I moved, she dropped into a low crouch, knocking my feet out from under me with a leg sweep. She got in two more slashes before I landed. The first slash caught me in the belly and wasn't too deep, but the second dug into my left breast and I heard her claws scratching against my breastbone.

I hit the floor right on top of the broken vase and then rolled up into a ball, clutching my breast. Veruca slashed at my back, cutting easily through my sequined top and flaying me open to the spine. I knew Eric could take injuries like this and laugh them off, but I wasn't Eric and it hurt more than anything I had ever felt.

"How do you like that, pussycat?" Veruca taunted.

I didn't like it at all, not that I could have replied anyway. Pain was my world and I wallowed in it. Veruca continued to slash at my exposed back, but the more she hurt me, the more I began to drift away from the pain. It was there, but it was being replaced with another feeling. Outrage, maybe? I was a queen, after all, and she was merely a Soldier.

Then a funny new sensation rose in my chest, the outrage mixed with something else: disdain. Before, when I had lashed out verbally at the Drone, I had felt the same thing. I lashed out with it again, now, but not verbally; more than voice and yet less. My mental voice screamed, not in terror, but in utter fury that a lesser vampire would dare to treat me this way. Me—her better! *I may be only two days old*, my mental voice proclaimed, *but a queen is still a queen!*

She paused for three seconds and three seconds only, but three seconds can be an eternity when you're fighting a vampire. It was more than enough time for me to roll over and lock eyes with her. "Who's the badass now?" I shouted.

My vision tinged with red and I knew my eyes were glowing. I pushed my will right in through her eyes and down into her little brain, just like Eric had done to me the night before. In my mind's eye, tiny invisible strings affixed themselves to her arms, legs, and head. She fought back, but she had no depth. There was hardly anything to fight.

We stayed there, eyes locked, while my wounds healed. I don't know how long it took, a minute, two minutes, five, but once I felt whole again, I stood slowly, making sure to keep eye contact with Veruca the entire time. I grabbed the sides of her head and pulled her to her feet, willing her to stand. I walked us over to a large framed photograph of a marina that hung on one wall, feeling like a puppeteer working a life-size marionette.

Talbot was saying something outside, but I didn't have time to answer. I could feel Veruca fighting me, trying to buy a second or two of freedom so she could tear out my throat. Smashing the picture with my left hand, I snapped the bottom of the wooden frame loose and thrust it through Veruca's heart to immobilize her. Or at least, that was the plan.

It didn't work like in the movies, though, and my first thrust hadn't been hard enough to penetrate all the way to her heart. I glanced down at the stake, remembering Percy and mentally checking biology. I'd rammed it against her sternum, splintering the shard of wood and deflecting it into the side of her breast. I instantly realized my mistake. Stake jutting through the ripped front of her shirt, Veruca head-butted me and shoved me away from her. I grabbed for her shirt to steady myself, but it ripped, coming free in my hand, and I landed on my ass.

"You are so dead, bitch!" Veruca yelled. She kicked at my face and I twisted away, catching a glancing blow to my cheek. I threw her tattered shirt back in her face as she stumbled, put off balance by the kick. I got a good look at the cute little frog tattoo she had above her pelvis when I grabbed her leg and hurled her across the room.

Vampire strength is fun for the whole family. She flew over the coffee table and crashed through a pressed-wood closet door, bringing coats and jackets down on top of her. I glanced around the room for something wood, something sturdier than the picture frame. The coffee table was glass and the chair legs looked like metal. Damn it.

In the closet, Veruca roared, clawing at the jackets as she got to her feet. Her head bumped the top shelf in the closet, sending a shoe box tumbling and spilling its contents—a pair of leather gloves with scorched palms and an unmistakable pearl-handled six-shooter—onto the floor.

Veruca grabbed for the gun, wincing as the crosses on the butt smoked against her skin. I launched myself over the coffee table at her, grabbing for the stake, but she pulled away from me and it popped free of her chest.

She fired once, twice, missing both times either because the pain in her hands threw off her aim, or because I was moving too quickly. I darted in low, under the gun, thrusting the stake in at an angle under her ribs. The gun barked again, pain lanced through my shoulder, and she froze, hands flaming as *El Alma Perdida* tumbled from her limp fingers. The little frog tattoo flashed bright white and vanished. I was afraid that she might do the same. Her skin began to melt away, followed by the muscle underneath. Her skull opened its mouth in a silent scream and then her entire skeleton exploded into ashes with a loud *fwoosh*. I'd killed her. I felt sick to my stomach.

At least I'd found the gun. Eric would be pleased with me. Smoke poured out of a nice neat hole in my shoulder where the third bullet had passed clean through. Talbot and I were going to have to dig three bullets out of the wall.

Dropping the stake, I walked over to the door. "Unlock?" I asked it tentatively, wondering how the hell we were going to get the door open if Veruca's death hadn't reset it. I guessed killing her had broken the spell, or maybe it was that I still had her dust on my hands, but when I touched the doorknob, the door pulsed blue and opened easily.

Talbot stepped inside and looked at the pile of ash, the broken bit of picture frame, and the blood covering the floor. Finally he looked at me, my clothes in shreds and covered in blood, most of it mine.

"A stake through the heart kills Soldiers and Drones," he observed. "Bet she wishes she'd made Master."

"Yeah," I agreed numbly. I kept expecting her to re-form like Dracula did in the movies, and while I knew that was possible for me, since I was a Vlad, for her *poof* seemed to pretty much mean *poof*. "I wonder when security's going to get here."

"They won't." Talbot smirked. "Veruca swung first, and she's not a resident." He picked up *El Alma Perdida*. "Eric will be glad to see this." Gun in hand, he walked across the room and dug three perfectly preserved bullets, casings and all, out of the wall. "That's just weird," he said after reloading the gun and returning it to the shoe box.

I sat down in one of the chairs, the bullet wound still throbbing. It was healing very slowly, not like the other wounds, where I could literally feel them closing. Talbot looked down at me, his eyes softening. "You did good. Are you hungry?"

I noticed his heart speeding up as he asked me. Sexual excitement rolled off of him in waves. Talbot ripped open his already ruined shirt, exposing his muscular, chocolate-colored chest. Watching me intently, he popped a claw, drawing it lazily down his body, blood welling up along the wound.

His blood smelled strong and powerful, but more importantly, it was warm and so was he. My hunger awoke with a need almost as overwhelming as when I'd first risen. "I thought I didn't have anything you were interested in," I said coyly.

Three magic words left his mouth, almost as strong and powerful as *I love you.* "I was wrong."

The need for blood permeates everything when you're hungry, gets confused with other hungers. At that moment there was no difference between the hunger for blood and the hunger for sex. I leapt on him with animal glee, licking the long line of blood off his chest. He shivered and his excitement ignited mine. I wanted him inside me and he didn't resist as I fumbled with his belt, lapping at his bloody chest while I pushed down his pants.

He slipped off my pants and panties, awkwardly because I wouldn't lift my lips from his chest. I dove for the artery pulsing in his thigh, but he caught my head and forced me up to his neck. I pushed him back onto the coffee table, following him down, and it shattered, but I didn't care. Talbot began to protest, but I sank down onto him and he snarled with pleasure.

His hands cupped my breasts and he seemed only slightly startled when I sank my fangs into his neck, penetrating him in my own way.

When he tired, I made him keep going and he did everything I asked and more, like a dying man following the orders of the one person who can give him water. Sex with a warm, breathing person was more than I could have explained. No wonder Eric liked to sleep with the living. They are so alive, so hot, and so full of blood. When I was finally sated, I lay sprawled on his chest, wearing nothing but my diamond necklace, and listened to him breathe, wondering when we'd left the remains of the glass table and found our way to Roger's bed. Tiny wisps of smoke rose from the little scratches Talbot had given me.

"I bet you've never done that with Eric," I teased.

"Definitely not," he laughed. "He's even less my type than I thought you were."

"Why do you stay with him?" I asked.

Talbot's beautifully massive chest rose and fell deeply. "He's a unique individual—worth protecting. You could say he awakens in me an infinite curiosity."

"And me?"

He blinked and smiled, showing me his fangs. "You're unique, too. I find you almost as curious as I find Eric."

"I still love Eric, you know," I told him seriously.

His eyes flashed and the pupils became slits. "I'm glad. If you fell in love with me, it would end badly for one of us. Eric would kill me or perhaps eventually you would kill me. After all, my kind is incapable of the kind of love you more human types feel for each other. Our bonds are based on dominance, mutual need, and, at most, a deep and abiding fondness."

I still didn't understand what Talbot was, but I felt I understood him. Maybe he was some strange cat-human hybrid, or perhaps he had lied about not being a lycanthrope. The romantic in me liked to think it was a spell. Anything was possible. I'd met a wizard, become a vampire. Perhaps Lord Phillip himself had trapped Talbot in the body of a man, as punishment, like with Percy. No, that didn't sound right. Talbot had described himself as a sacred guardian, a noble hunter. To me, that said: cat. Obviously not a normal cat, but a magic one. I wondered absently if it counted as bestiality if you had sex with an animal that had been turned humanoid.

I lay there, trying to bask in his warmth, in the after-glow of our intimacy, but the moment was gone. A final curl of smoke drifted up from the shallow scratches around my breasts and my pale skin was whole once more, as if the act itself had not taken place, leaving me empty and restless. Talbot had been a nice substitute, but I craved Eric.

I got up, found Roger's shower and washed the last traces of combat from my body. Once I was dry, I started going through Veruca's clothes. She'd been smaller than me, in every way, and her clothes tended to be one size too small for her already. Not having to breathe enhances a vampire's ability to dress for effect, but it also meant that there wasn't anything in her closet that fit me. Which left me my panties, my shoes, and my diamond necklace. The pants had long rents in them and I didn't want to put back on what was left of the sequined top.

"What the hell am I supposed to wear?" I asked, hold-ing the remains of my clothes and shaking them in Talbot's general direction.

"I think that outfit suits you just fine," Talbot murmured throatily from where he was sprawled on the bed.

I rolled my eyes and changed into a cat.

"That suits you even more." He wasn't teasing.

I changed back, in further exasperation. *Poof* . . . clothes. Yay me! The clothes I'd been wearing were new again and I wasn't holding them in my hands anymore, I was wearing them. The magic that had repaired them left them feeling right-out-of-the-dryer warm.

"Now, that's something I've seen only Eric do." Talbot rolled out of the bed, naked. He stretched and yawned, his fangs and claws popping out midway through and retracting at the end. He flexed at me and I admired him openly. He was taller than Eric and more heavily muscled. His dark skin was sleek, almost glossy, and stood out in perfect contrast to the red satin sheets. The picture he made was incredibly alluring, and I considered taking off my newly created clothes. Just because I was in love with Eric didn't mean I couldn't enjoy a little companionship from the living. What was good for the goose . . .

"How does it work?" I asked softly, placing my hand on Talbot's shoulder.

"With Eric it seems to work automatically," he told me. "When he changes shape, unless he's paying close attention, it changes whatever he was wearing into the same jeans and T-shirt outfit he prefers. I mentioned it to him in El Segundo, but I'm sure he's forgotten by now. Not that it matters much since he wears the same damn thing every day."

"I think he looks nice," I said defensively.

Talbot laughed at that, and I couldn't help but join in.

✦ 23 ✦

ERIC:

NO GOOD NEWS

With no music playing in the Demon Heart, no crowd, not even Marilyn or one of the girls getting ready to open the club or shut it down, the silence ate at my nerves. I needed something to block out the sound of the oni out front jabbering back and forth at each other in Japanese in between mouthfuls of dead werewolf.

I thought about ordering a pizza—Italian sausage, black olives, mushrooms, and daikon—just so I could smell it, look at it, feel the warmth of the box.

I don't know what daikon tastes like, but I'm fond of the smell and I'm curious. Few things are more annoying than a curious vampire. If the smell of a particular food entices us, we want to make people eat it, so they can describe the taste to us. The best description I'd gotten of daikon was "kind of like a pickle, but not." How can something that looks like a big white carrot taste like a pickle, but not? Did they do something to it first? The question vexed me.

Greta sat across Marilyn's desk from me, playing with a staple remover, pretending it was a shark or a vampire, something with fangs. The phone rang in my office across the street and Rachel stirred in her sleep, but didn't wake. On the third ring, Greta heard it too.

"Phone's ringing," she told me.

"I know."

"You want me to go and—"

"No," I said too quickly. "Just wait a minute." My brain wouldn't process what she'd told me about my "uber vamp" form. How could I have been turning into a giant, black-skinned, leather-winged beast thing off and on since 1965 and not know it, not even have had an inkling beyond the understanding that I blacked out when I got really mad? It was like Bruce Banner not knowing about the Hulk.

I didn't want to think about who was setting me up, either. If I'd known where the investigation had been likely to lead, I never would have looked into it. I would have taken on the werewolves without question. A wise man once said "Ignorance is bliss," and he was right. I wanted Veruca to be behind everything, needed it. I wanted to forget about the check I'd seen where Roger had forged my name. I wished Roger had dotted his damn i's.

So I concentrated on the pizza. If I gave up on the daikon, I could call one of the big pizza chains, but if I wanted the daikon, I had to wait until Jackie's opened at six. I could get Jackie to put anything I wanted on a pizza, even if he had to run down to the Asian market. Jackie knows about vampires, and if you let him know that your order is for eating in front of one of us, he tacks on an extra 50 percent surcharge and makes it look like it does in the pictures on the menu.

I remembered sitting in his diner with Roger watching Froggy, still Veruca then, eat a Reuben. It's a big deal for vampires to share their food porn like that, proof of our long friendship.

The phone rang in Marilyn's office and I jumped, startled. It wasn't supposed to do that. I glanced at it suspiciously. For all I knew the phone was undergoing a demonic transformation. It certainly seemed like the week for it. It rang a second and a third time before I answered it. It was Talbot; I recognized his breathing.

"How did you get through to this phone?" I asked. "Didn't Marilyn transfer the calls to her home number?"

"Star six eight," he answered.

"Huh?"

"It forwards the call, but only if the number dialed is busy or there's no answer. . . . Look, don't worry about it. I tried you at the Pollux first."

He sounded upset. Tough shit, it wasn't all blow jobs and balloons for me either. "Did you know that I turn into some sort of rampaging berserker flying vampire thing when I lose my temper?"

Talbot scoffed. "Of course."

"Even Talbot knows! Am I the only fucking person around who doesn't know I've got go-go gadget bat wings?" I yelled, holding the receiver about a foot from my face. I hung up the phone and threw up my hands.

Greta acted sympathetic, but I could tell that she was trying to hold back her laughter.

"Who else knows?" I asked her. Before she could respond, the phone rang again. It was Talbot. "Does Marilyn know?" I asked him.

"I . . . I think so," Talbot answered. I hung up on him again and cast a disparaging look at Greta.

"Even Marilyn knows! Why does nobody tell me these things?" Greta watched me as I paced the room angrily. Small snorts of nasal laughter escaped despite her best attempts to hold them back. "It's not funny, damn it!"

Greta couldn't even speak. Tears of blood rolled down the sides of her face and she burst out laughing. Loud obnoxious guffaws filled the room punctuated by a periodic "I'm so sorry" or "I know it's not funny." She clutched her sides, sliding farther down in her chair, leaving me staring at her in impotent rage and disbelief.

The phone rang and I picked it up before the first ring finished. "I swear to God, Talbot, if Tabitha knows, I am going to fucking kill somebody!"

"I don't think she d—" Talbot began.

I hung up the phone again and put my hands on my hips. "Well, at least there is one person who is as clueless as me. Of course it's frickin' Tabitha."

More laughter erupted from Greta and she began to gasp for air in a way that looked absolutely human.

"It's not that funny!" I yelled, standing over her.

She nodded her head. "Yes, it is," she gasped. "Hello, Talbot? Blah blah blah. Click."

I didn't get it. Maybe that was funny in a women-are-from-Venus way, but here on Mars, it didn't make a whole lot of sense. The phone rang again and I picked it up. "Talbot, I think Greta has gone loopy. She's over here laughing her head off like it's some big joke. I've been a vampire for over forty years and nobody bothered to—"

"You have a collect call from 'Talbot,'" interrupted a mechanical voice. "Will you accept the charges?"

"Yes," I answered. Why was Talbot calling collect?

"Talbot?" I asked.

"Yes," he answered, drawing out the word. He sounded pretty ticked off.

"Why the hell are you calling collect?"

"Because, if you'll pardon my language, some asshole keeps hanging up on me and I thought that if you had to listen to the operator first, you might actually stop and pay attention!"

Talbot didn't usually yell. Greta stopped laughing and climbed back into her chair. Her chest was still heaving a little, but she had control of herself. I breathed in and out deeply a few times to calm myself. I don't need oxygen, but the act of breathing triggered a physical memory, giving it much the same effect. "Okay, sorry. I'm ready to pay attention now; it's just a big shock to find out something like that."

"I'm sure it was," he interrupted, enunciating slowly and clearly. "I'm sorry none of us knew how to tell you, but I need you to listen right now. Okay?"

"Sure."

"If you hang up on me again, I'm going to come over there while you're asleep and put a big 'jackass' tattoo on your forehead. Do you understand?"

I rolled my eyes. "Yes."

"Okay. Good. The good news is that we found the gun."

I slapped Marilyn's desk. "Hot damn!"

"Veruca had it."

"What did she have to say for herself?"

"Not much, but it's pretty clear she's the one who shot the werewolves you found at Orchard Lake."

"Did you get her to tell you why she left one of the bullets behind?"

"No, and I don't quite know how to tell you this, Eric, but we found her at Roger's place."

"Was he all right?" I asked.

"He wasn't there," Talbot answered. "But you have to consider the possibility that he is wrapped up in all of this."

"That's crap, Talbot," I said, determined to deny it.

"He's been covering for her," Talbot said patiently. "He took you to a hockey game, got you drunk, and let eighteen werewolves try to kill you."

"Yeah, but—"

"Eric," Talbot said. "Where is he right now? Did you call him?"

"No, I haven't called him yet. Greta and I ran into some werewolves here at the club. Real Lycan Diocese types that William called in."

"You both okay?" he asked.

"Yeah, no problems here. Tiko and some of his cousins are taking care of the bodies for us."

"Good. Now listen. I want you to go back to the alley where you fought the Alpha's son. He was killed at Thirteenth Street and Eleventh Avenue. I want you to go there and see if you recognize it."

"Why?"

"Because I don't trust Roger, damn it!" he snapped. I heard him take a deep breath and his next words were calmer. "He gave Veruca that night off and she had the gun with her. We can't ask Lillian where she picked you up, because Tabitha killed her when she went loco."

"Talbot, I did kill a werewolf in an alley."

"I believe you, boss." He sighed. "I just want to make sure you killed the werewolf that you think you killed."

"Ask Froggy," I said. "Make her tell you."

"I would if I could, Eric, but Tabitha put a stake through her heart."

"*Poof*, huh?"

"*Poof*," he confirmed. "We found the gun before Tabitha fell asleep. It looks like Veruca was wearing leather gloves in order to fire it. They're scorched through on the palms. The silver crosses on the grip must have burned her even through the leather."

"It can happen," I said noncommittally.

"I think I'll hole up here with Tabitha until she wakes up tomorrow."

"And what if Roger comes home?"

"I don't think he will," Talbot said. "The sun will be up too soon. Roger takes a lot more sleep than you do and he'd never cut it this close. Wherever he is, I think he'll stay there until sunset. Besides, he hasn't been here since Friday. I don't think he's going to come back until this whole thing is over."

"Why?"

"Because he's setting you up. Veruca was the fall guy in case anything went wrong."

"I don't believe that," I said flatly.

"If you don't believe it, then check the alley."

"I—"

"Eric, please. Will you check the damn alley?"

No, Talbot, I can't, I wanted to say. I don't want to look in the damn alley. If Roger set me up, I don't want to frickin' know about it.

"Fine," I answered, "and thanks."

Greta and I walked back across to the Pollux. The bodies and trucks were all gone. Tiko and his crew had worked fast. "So, who else knows?" I asked her as we walked.

"About the alley?"

"No," I said. "About the super vamp thing."

"Dad, I don't know." She put her arm around my shoulders, emphasizing the fact that she was over two inches taller than me. "But look on the bright side. Most of the people who knew got killed before they could tell anyone. I'll bet Roger doesn't even know, with the way he runs away from fights so fast."

Reminded of Roger, I plopped down onto the sofa in the Pollux's lobby and punched buttons on my cell phone until it decided to dial his number for me.

"Hello?" The voice on the other end sounded strange, like he was whispering into the receiver from the bottom of a giant tin bucket.

"Roger?"

"Yeah. Dude. I've been trying to call you. Why the hell did you close the club? Marilyn says you sent everyone home with pay."

"You talked to Marilyn?"

"I'm at her place now. She needed a little help. Seems some asshole broke her arm."

"Yeah," I mumbled. It was a classic Roger deflection. Question: Roger, why are you trying to put my club out of bussiness? Answer: Hey, do you remember that time you broke Marilyn's arm?

"Same asshole killed Brian," I blurted.

"What?" he demanded. "You killed Brian? Why?"

Why? What an interesting question. I didn't know why. Another good question was why Roger didn't seem more upset about it.

"Because he annoyed me, I guess," I said vaguely. "I don't remember."

"It's all right, man. He was always picking fights with you and it wasn't like he hadn't been warned."

"He was your friend, though. I'm sorry."

"Don't worry about it," Roger assured me. "He was just a Soldier."

Huh. I wonder if he would've responded the same way if he'd known Tabitha had killed Froggy. Besides, Brian hadn't been a Soldier, he'd been a Master. What the fuck?

I tried another tack. "Do you know anything about a check for thirty thousand dollars to some guy named Fergus?" I asked.

"I'd been meaning to ask you about it," Roger countered. "You can't just spend money like that without clearing it first. We're flush and it's not a problem this time, but what if I hadn't had enough money in that account to cover it? The money moves around, man. I gotta keep it working for us, not just sitting in an account in case you overspend."

You fucking liar, I wanted to scream, *you're behind everything!* Then, again, this was Roger and he could have been covering up for something else, maybe just some run-of-the-mill embezzlement. If that was the case, I didn't care. He'd always taken a little without asking. When an investment deal paid off later, he'd slip it back in and tell me I'd okayed everything. It usually worked out.

"Yeah," I whispered, "my mistake." *Please just be embezzling money,* I thought at him.

"Gotta let you go, pal," he said. "I want to hunt before I turn in."

"Which gives you what," I said, checking the clock, "fifteen minutes?" Roger had to be lying to me. He always hunts first thing. "You're going to hunt and make it back to your place in fifteen minutes from Marilyn's?" I willed him to say yes. If he said yes then—

"No," he answered. "Not that it's any of your business, but I have a place nearby. Look, don't worry about it, Mom. I'll be fine, but I've got to go if I'm going to hunt. Like you said, fifteen minutes."

"How close by?" I asked, but he was already off the line.

Rachel was up and moving; I could hear her rummaging around downstairs in the dressing room she'd confiscated. "Sounds like the Pierced Princess is awake," Greta said snidely.

I shushed her and walked upstairs to my office, opened my desk drawer, and pulled out a pair of sunglasses to conceal my eyes, since I didn't want to scare anyone without meaning to do so. Eyes safely covered, I went back down to the dressing room and checked on Rachel.

She was naked except for a pair of lacy white panties. Her scent filled my nostrils and I pulled her into my arms. God, she was warm. She kissed me and I caught a faint hint of cinnamon.

"You smell nice," I told her. "I keep smelling cinnamon around you, but only sometimes."

"It's a special trick for girls with vampire boyfriends."

I let her step back and playfully tugged one of her piercings. "More fun facts from the Irons Club?"

She let out a little sigh followed by a wicked grin. "Do we have any plans or do we get to play all day?"

It was tempting, but I walked away from her, toward the door. "As much as I'd like to, I need you to take me for a walk."

"Does it have to be right now?" Rachel ran her hands suggestively over her breasts.

"Yes," I insisted, ignoring the part of my anatomy that disagreed. "You can get a shower over at the Demon Heart if you need one."

She raised an eyebrow. "Do I?"

I shook my head. "No, but I thought I'd offer."

She smiled. "Are we taking a cab?"

"It's only three blocks," I answered. "Get dressed and bring your purse."

I walked out past Greta, who was leaning against the wall in the hallway.

"Do I need a shower, Dad? Can I use the one over at the Demon Heart? Can I? Please?"

Ignoring her as best I could, I went back to my office to wait for Rachel. Soon I heard a loud thump, the sound a body makes when it hits the floor. "Sun's up," I muttered to myself. Out in the hall, Greta lay in a heap. Dawn always hits her hard and like me, she never seems to remember that it's coming. I don't know if she does it on purpose to be more like me or not, but I find it endearing in a dysfunctional sire sort of way. Unlike me, she's impossible to wake up during the day. At least when she wakes each evening she's cheerful and well rested. Some days I envy her. I picked her up in my arms and carried her back to my Pollux bedroom, tucked her in, and kissed her on the forehead.

"You ready?" Rachel called from the doorway. "How am I walking with you somewhere, anyway? You're not going to turn into a virus and infect me are you?" Her heart rate sped up. "I mean, it's okay if you are, I guess. It's just that . . ."

I turned into a mouse and back again, the rapid transition feeling only slightly more comfortable than a shot to the nuts. I really needed to stop showing off for this girl. "I want you to jog up to the intersection of Thirteenth Street and Eleventh Avenue with me in your purse."

She knelt down and opened her purse on the floor. It was smaller than I was happy with, but it was leather and I doubted enough sun would get through the material to be a problem. I admired the view down Rachel's top before transforming. Rachel zipped me up in her purse and away we went.

I really wanted Talbot to be wrong, but in the back of my furry little undead mind, I already knew that he wasn't. Roger had betrayed me. Froggy was too stupid to come up with a plan so complex on her own. I don't know if he wanted me dead—I hoped he didn't—but he definitely wanted me at odds with William. Maybe that's all there was to it. Maybe he wanted me to kill William and knew that I wouldn't do it just for shits and giggles, so he'd arranged for William to come after me, knowing that I'd be able to defend myself.

But why?

Deep down, it didn't matter why he'd done what he'd done. He'd betrayed me and I'd found out about it. I silently hated him for not being clever enough to slip it all past me. *Dot your damn i's*, I thought again. If only he'd done a better job of forging the check. If only he hadn't lied about it. If only we could go back to being best friends, like none of this had ever happened. . . .

24

ERIC:

THE OTHER SHOE

Checking out the alley took about an hour, but only because I made Rachel investigate all four intersections that were three blocks from the club. If Talbot's suspicions were correct, then two werewolves had been killed three blocks from the Demon Heart at the same time. I'd killed one and Froggy had killed the other.

We found the place where I'd killed Brian first. I knew it was the right alley because long scratches in the concrete showed where I'd dragged the Dumpster to the sidewalk. I examined the scene from the safety of the shadows. That alley, at Thirteenth Street and Fifth Avenue, had been completely cleaned. The Dumpster wasn't there anymore, but the wall still bore a scorch mark from where I'd beat my head out when I'd caught fire.

We checked Thirteenth Street and Eleventh Avenue last. The odor of gunpowder and werewolf permeated the site. It wasn't the scent of the werewolf I'd killed. This one smelled stronger, more primal. I smelled Veruca in the alley, too, and sex. What pissed me off the most, though, was the smell of my own blood. Someone had siphoned some off of me and sprayed it on the walls. Werewolves have a better sense of smell than vampires; I wondered momentarily if William thought I'd slept with Froggy there, rolling around in his son's remains.

"Son of a bitch," I said, standing in a shadow. "Talbot was right. Roger played me. Why the fuck would he do that?"

"Maybe it isn't what it looks like," Rachel offered. "Maybe he didn't know what to do. Maybe he knew that the werewolves were after his girlfriend. He could have been scared."

"So he set them on my trail because he knew they couldn't kill me?" I asked.

"Maybe," Rachel said with a shrug.

"Nah, I don't think so. He sent Veruca out here to kill Willie Junior so that Willie Senior would come after me. He sent Veruca to kill the werewolves at Orchard Lake because he wanted to make sure I didn't talk it over with William and make peace. He's behind everything. I wonder if he's still over at Marilyn's."

Cars whizzed past dangerously on Eleventh Street heading for the interstate on-ramp one block down. I stood along the edge of the shadows and watched the people inside. Were any of their best friends trying to screw them over? Fucking their spouses, cheating on them, framing them for murder? What would Roger say if I confronted him? And why did the thought of him having a place close to Marilyn's apartment suddenly make me queasy? *She'll be fine*, I told myself. Besides, like a lot of vampires, Roger slept all day, every day.

I was going to ask Rachel to drive me over there when horns honked on the street outside the mouth of the alley and two identical trucks, one black and the other blue, peeled past on the wrong side of the road, within ten feet of me. In the back of one of the trucks, I saw a big metal box studded with crosses, secured to the bed of the truck with elastic cords. I thought I heard a scream.

Instinctively, I took off after them, running right out of the shadows into the sun.

"Shit!" I jumped back into the shadows, on fire again. "Fuck!"

"We need to get back to the Pollux," I growled after I'd dropped and rolled to put out the flames. "Run."

The Pollux felt wrong. I knew it the moment Rachel panted across the threshold and let me out of her purse. Old buildings have moods, especially those full of personality, like the Pollux. She had once been a grand affair, a celebrated showplace, and the center of attention. Now she had been reduced to a quaint old memory of better days. She was distressed about something; a palpable sense of anxiety resonated through her. Something was out of place. Something was wrong. Rachel seemed to feel it too. It was as if, while we were away, the proverbial other shoe had dropped.

"Greta," I said under my breath. Rachel and I both hit the stairs running, but I was in full-on combat mode and had already thrown open the door to my bedroom by the time Rachel was clearing the fifth step. My bed had been made and the sink had been cleaned. It even looked like my towel had been washed and dried. Maybe Greta had woken up early and headed out, but it wasn't like her to clean stuff up and she'd only been asleep for an hour, tops. She had to have been taken.

I went into my office, and noticed some stuff had been moved around. The light on my answering machine was blinking. I pushed PLAY as Rachel walked in and closed the door behind her.

"I have your whore," growled a voice. It was the same voice I'd heard on the answering machine when Kyle died: William. "Your Jezebel is with me. Is it true that you make her call you Daddy? How can you compare this twisted unholy family you have created to the son you stole from me? The brethren you killed? Their souls cry out for vengeance. 'Vengeance is mine,' sayeth the Lord, but I am his instrument. Through me you will be returned unto the dust from which you came.

"This time you will come to me, vampire. You will walk into the sunlight and face us in a place of our own choosing. Come for your so-called daughter to Bald Mountain State Park, Campground B. If you are not here by five p.m., I will end her miserable sinful existence once and for all, freeing her soul from its cage so that God may judge her and she may receive her eternal damnation."

Rachel hugged me from behind and cinnamon filled the air. I didn't even feel angry, just empty. She whispered her sweet nonsense words into my ear and told me everything was going to be okay. I turned to her and before I knew it we were kissing. My daughter needed me. I didn't have time for this, but I couldn't stop myself. Rachel helped me out of my clothes, undressing herself in the process. I was lost in her warmth, her need, and the beating of her heart. Her own natural smell blended with the cinnamon on her breath and I couldn't stop myself.

As we neared climax, writhing on top of my desk, she put both hands on my chest to support herself and looked deep into my eyes. "Bite me, Eric. I need it and you need it."

I held back. She seemed okay, but I had never fed on the same person so many times in succession, not even Tabitha. "It'll be okay, baby," she said. She ran her left hand across the top of my head. "You'll know when to stop." Her hand moved over my forehead. "I trust you." She touched my throat. Her hands wandered lower, touching lightly over my heart and on my belly. She reached between us to cup the base of my testicles.

It wasn't right. It felt completely wrong. A line of heat shot through my body from the crown of my head to my groin where she still moved, grinding against me. Internal alarms were going off in my head, but I couldn't interpret them properly. She kept moving on top of me, but slowed her rhythm, prolonging the inevitable. "Please," she whis-

pered. The smell of cinnamon replaced everything; it was
the only odor in the room, overwhelming all else. I bit into
her neck, white pinpricks of light searing my vision. My
teeth went numb, fangs retracting, and my taste buds awoke,
assaulted by stimuli to all their receptors, as if I'd bitten into
a jalapeño rather than an eighteen-year-old girl.

My heart spurred to life, beating as if it might burst from
my chest. I couldn't breathe properly; each breath came fast
and furious, too short and too quick. Heat spread across my
body from the core outward. I stopped drinking and we both
cried out in unison, reaching completion.

In Rachel's eyes, I could see a vague reflection of myself.
Hazy, but me. I didn't want to look at myself, not in her
eyes, not in a mirror. Purple light flickered from my eyes and
the reflection faded. An urge to hurl her against the wall, to
break her in half, to fight her, fight something, came out of
nowhere, but I suppressed it. Cinnamon was replaced by the
smell of sweat and sex. She looked down at me, her wide
eyes torn between terror and exhilaration.

"Are you going to eat me, baby?" she cooed.

"What are you doing to me?" I asked breathlessly.

"Making you feel alive," she said as she collapsed on my
chest. Her heart was racing too. Mine began to slow to a
stop. "It's what I'm supposed to do. I want to be your thrall.
A thrall does her best to make her master forget the things
he has lost in order to gain immortality. A good thrall is supposed to train several replacements and then join the master
in unlife, but I don't want to be a vampire, Eric. I just want
to be yours."

"Bullshit," I mouthed.

We lay there for a while without moving and I felt my body grow cold once more. The clock said 09:43. We had wasted over an hour, basking in the aftermath of my inability to resist Rachel's advances. This wasn't like me and I knew it.

Well, *inappropriate sex* was all me, but usually, when things need killing or my friends are in danger, sex takes a backseat. I told myself that I had hours to spare and that was why I went ahead with it, but I was lying to myself.

My little cinnamon girl was more than she appeared to be and the whole "it's a thrall thing" excuse was wearing thin. If all thralls could do what Rachel could do, then Roger would have had one. Hell, it had been Roger who'd told me that thralls were little more than slaves, that any human who became a thrall descended into madness, like Renfield. I wondered if he'd lied, and why.

"Thralls." I gently pushed her up and she rolled off of me. "Is there a way to tell who is a thrall and who isn't?"

"Sure," Rachel answered, surprised. "You should be able to tell just by looking at them and thinking about it."

I started putting my clothes back on and Rachel did the same. "Really? How? Do they have big glowing signs over their heads that say 'I belong to X,' or what?"

Rachel looked puzzled as she slipped her bra back on. She put it on backward, fastened up the hooks, and then slid them around to the back. She flipped the cups up to cover her breasts and put her arms through the straps before pulling them up onto her shoulders. I'd never paid attention to how women got dressed. I wondered if Tabitha did it the same way. I'd probably seen her get dressed a thousand times and I didn't know how she did it.

"I think it's supposed to be similar to the way Vlads and Masters sense each other, except that even Soldiers can have thralls. Only Drones can't."

Which was not what Roger had told me. "I thought only Vlads could make thralls."

"Who told you that?" She looked like it was the dumbest thing she'd ever heard.

"Roger." Rachel's heart skipped a beat when I answered. She continued getting dressed, but I stood there in my underwear, watching her. "So I should get a sense of age and power, but it would be the thrall's master I was sensing?"

"Yes, you should get a sense of the vampire, probably a mental image of the master overlaid on an image of the thrall."

For forty years, I'd gotten all that I knew about vampires from talking to Roger. Big mistake. "So do a lot of high society vampires have thralls?"

"Sure," she said. "They're a status symbol. Who has the most attractive, the most talented, that sort of thing."

So Roger would have known. He hadn't just been mistaken; his had been a deliberate deception.

"You've really never sensed a thrall before?" Rachel asked.

My attitude toward other vampires meant that I didn't know many of them, but Roger knew all the most important ones around. I had steered clear of vampire society . . . or had Roger steered me clear of it? I had trouble remembering which way it had been. But how had I never sensed even one thrall before? "No, I haven't. Not that I've noticed."

She shrugged and slipped her blouse on. "Maybe you have to make one before you can sense them."

"No," I said immediately, stepping into my jeans.

"No what?" she asked innocently.

"I'm not making you my thrall. You seem to be doing just fine with what you've learned from those friends of yours at the Irons Club." I looked around for my shirt, found it in the wastebin next to my desk. I shook the little bits of paper off of it and slid it over my head.

"You need me, Eric," she said as she put a hand on my chest. I brushed her hand away and finished pulling my shirt on. She took a step away, but I could still feel the warmth where she'd touched me. "What if it would help you find Greta? You might be able to sense vampires better, too . . . those that are yours, anyway."

"How does that follow?"

"You know how sires don't sense their children?"

"Uh-huh."

"Well, that's not strictly true. When you sense another vampire, you don't sense them all the time, right?"

"Just until you've acknowledged each other," I agreed.

"Yep, and then when you get out of each other's range and come back into contact . . ."

"You sense each other again."

"Well, the reason sire and offspring don't sense each other is that they're always linked."

"But if that's true, then I should be able to sense something, shouldn't I? Because I can't sense Greta or Tabitha."

"You need to practice. Which is why you need to make me your thrall. Thralls help focus a vampire's mental abilities. In time, the most powerful vampires can learn to see, hear, and in rare occasions even taste through their thralls."

"No," I insisted. She sat down on the edge of my desk, crestfallen.

"Not even if it can help you find Greta?"

"I know where Greta is! She's in Bald Mountain State Park, Campground B, like the man said."

"He could have been lying," Rachel argued. "What werewolves always tell the truth? What if Greta is already dead and—"

I put my hand over her mouth. "Be quiet and let me think."

She nodded, eyes wide.

Rachel had been right about everything so far and she seemed to genuinely want to help, but no one dates a vampire unless they want something. It was possible she was just in it for the danger and the thrill, but I doubted it. She had to have an ulterior motive. Or was I just being paranoid? It wouldn't be the first time.

And yet—when we'd had sex, why had I suddenly viewed her as a threat? And what was that feeling that made me want her incessantly? It was something more than lust, but much less natural than love. It probably had something to do with cinnamon.

Still—I didn't see how it could hurt to bind her to me. And, most importantly, I'd do anything for Greta. Even this.

I took my hand away from her mouth. "Okay."

Rachel let out an exhilarated yip and began bouncing up and down. If it was an act, it was a good one. She seemed genuinely excited. Then again, bouncing up and down like she was doing would accelerate her heart rate. I looked at Rachel in a whole new light and waited to smell cinnamon. "Can we do it now?" she said, rushing into my arms.

"How do we do it?" I kissed her neck. "Does it involve sex?" I tugged at her blouse and she removed it with a laugh. Still no cinnamon.

"No, but I'm ready any time you are, lover." Damn.

I lifted her off the desk and kissed her breasts through her bra. She wrapped her legs around me and I smelled her desire. Double damn. "How do we do it?" I asked again.

"You smear your blood on my head and over my heart, then put a single drop on my tongue and we kiss. You look into my eyes and push your mind into mine, like when you control other vampires. We'll both feel it when it happens. I've been told that it hurts a little for you and a lot for me, but when we're done, I'll be able to do even more for you."

She pulled at my shirt. "Of course, there's no reason we can't do it while we have sex."

"I don't know," I said. "Maybe I should just—"

"Oh, please, baby." Still no cinnamon. Maybe I *was* being paranoid.

"Fine," I relented, telling myself it was for Greta. "Let's do it."

❖ 25 ❖

ERIC:

THIRD EYE OPEN AND READY FOR BUSINESS

Rachel hadn't been kidding. It hurt like a motherfucker, but when it was done, I could feel her with my mind. Without looking, I could sense where she was and how she was doing. It wasn't telepathy, in that her thoughts were closed to me, but her general mood was clear.

She wasn't the only new presence in my mind, either. I felt them all, my "children," including three who were supposed to be dead. To be honest, it was kind of nice to see them.

I don't stay mad long. Usually, I'd rather wish someone a long happy life the hell away from me. It's just that so often, they won't oblige. I'd staked the first two and left them to greet the dawn. I'd taken care of Irene in El Segundo; her survival proved she really was a heartless bitch.

They felt me too.

My oldest, Lisa, squirmed in her sleep, long blonde hair cascading over her breasts. She'd fallen asleep with her jeans on, the flared bottoms finally back in style. Lisa had been my rebound girl, once I'd given up on Marilyn ever taking me back. It felt like she was in the back of a plane. Someone was playing acoustic guitar softly in the background; they stopped and I felt a presence near her, a human. He wanted to know if she was okay.

Nancy was Lisa's replacement. She was sleeping not far away, no farther than Sable Oaks. She still slept in a coffin with dirt in the bottom, the interior lit with blacklight bulbs. She'd always been superstitious. Nancy wore a white silk teddy, her supple chestnut-colored skin standing out in sensuous contrast.

In the quasiviolet light, her eyes flashed open briefly, the once-black irises now faded close to gray, flaring red before she surrendered again to the sleep of the dead. Nancy and I had had a falling out over Greta. Nancy believed that teenage girls shouldn't talk back to vampires. I didn't disagree, but held an even firmer conviction that nobody got to slap my little girl around.

Irene was awake, smiling, and in the act. She still got me hot. Irene had been wild, too wild, and she'd dyed her hair red, really red, like a Porsche. She climbed off of her lover and gripped his member, smiling at me. "It's longer," she mouthed, before beginning to fellate the lucky bastard.

Irene was the farthest away of all, miles and miles across the ocean.

I gestured to Rachel. "She's younger," I mouthed, but Irene was gone, replaced by Tabitha, asleep in a bed in the Highland Towers. Talbot was curled up next to her on the bed, in his natural form, a little black ball of fur, purring. He'd never curled up to me that way.

Last came Greta. She was immobilized, but not by a stake. A metal box enclosed her, the sides lined with little crosses. Even if she'd been one of the chosen few who can turn to mist, the box was airtight. She twisted and turned, trying to position herself so that the crosses no longer burned her skin. Each time she found a moment's peace, sleep claimed her, and she fell back against the sizzling signs of faith.

I waited to feel angry, but the most I could manage was irritation. The werewolves were dead either way, but it would be trickier if I couldn't go berserk on them. Just hours ago, seeing Greta in agony had been enough to send me directly over the edge. I was in control, but I shouldn't have been. I should have been a raging black-winged terror, tearing ass across the country to save my little girl.

"Shit." I rolled off of Rachel and sat on the edge of the bed. We'd moved the whole thing to the bedroom because she'd asked nicely and I hadn't cared.

"Are you okay?" she asked. There was a slight tremor in her voice. "Did something go wrong? It's supposed to hurt me more."

"It's not that," I said. "Just some unfinished business. A

few of my children, ones I thought I'd disposed of, are still around. It worked; I can sense them."

I walked over to the sink and started sponging off, thinking about Irene, Lisa, and Nancy.

Irene might try to start a fight eventually, but none of this current mess was hers. She wasn't very subtle. She would have just blown up the Demon Heart with me in it. Lisa wasn't a threat; she was big, beautiful, and about as smart as Kyle had been. Roger had assured me once that she wasn't a Drone, but she certainly acted like one. Nancy could have come up with a plan like this, but she never would have been able to execute it. Besides, she would have been up in my face gloating by now.

Tabitha was safe, but asleep. Greta was my only real concern.

I went back into my office and dialed Marilyn's number.

"Hello?" she answered.

"Any messages?" I asked.

"I got a call from our friend Captain Stacey with the VCPD. He says that he hopes you can afford to keep paying for the cover-up. He wanted to make sure you knew that you have had him, two folks in dispatch, and six other officers working double duty to cover up your—and I'm quoting—'bullshit shenanigans' this weekend."

"Can I afford it?" I asked.

"For a while." Marilyn sounded like she was speaking to a delinquent teenager. Rachel walked in wearing tennis shoes, short shorts, and a baby-doll T-shirt that said *Boy Toy*. She approached the desk, pointing happily to a new necklace she was wearing; it was a black choker with a tiny golden padlock.

"I've also been meaning to talk to you about the money that you've been spending on clothes. I assume that Sally told me the truth about your little shopping spree?" Marilyn choked out the words.

"She did."

"Were those clothes for your new little trollop? Will I be meeting that one again or do you already have a different one?"

I wanted to tell her she was wrong about me, but I didn't know whether that was true anymore. There had been a line that I had been trying not to cross, the line between being a man who was monstrous and an actual monster. Now I couldn't even see the line. I had passed it without realizing it some time ago.

"I have a couple of things to do tonight," I said, ignoring her questions and my own guilt. "So I might be late. I have to go rescue Greta. Then I might have to kill Roger."

"Serves him right." Her voice was acid.

That took me by surprise. "Is he still over there? Stake him for me."

"No, he wouldn't be that stupid, although I imagine he isn't far. I'm sorry I can't stake him for you."

"I was kidding." I wasn't kidding.

"Me, too." And the funniest thing was that for the first time in the half century or so I'd known Marilyn, I could tell that she was lying to me.

"No," I said in stunned amazement. "You weren't."

"Leave it alone, Eric. Please."

"Marilyn, if something's going on—"

"It's nothing. I'm just tired. You said something happened to Greta?" She sounded more concerned about Greta than she usually did about me. "What happened?"

"Werewolf trouble. I'm going to take care of it now."

"But it isn't even noon, yet. What about the sun?"

I played with the lock on Rachel's necklace. "Hey," I spoke into the phone. "This is Greta we're talking about here. Fuck the sun. Me and my new thrall are going to get creative."

I hung up the phone and Rachel put her arms around me. She was nervous and curious at the same time. "Creative?"

"Yeah," I told her as I walked back to the bedroom. "Creative."

I emerged from the bedroom a few minutes later with my clothes on. "How do my eyes look?"

"They're back to normal," she said. "I guess a little blood was all you needed."

"I need you to go shopping for me," I told her. "I need a jumpsuit that covers up as much skin as possible and a full-face motorcycle helmet with one of those little thingies that covers up the neck. Get the helmet visor as dark as you can. I have boots, but I need a pair of gloves in my size. Call a cab. Get the stuff and meet me back here by two o'clock. I want to be up on Bald Mountain by four."

"Okay," Rachel said. "What's the rest of the plan?"

"Leave that to me." I kissed her. "Oh, and buy a bigger purse, it might need to hold two."

I gave her the money from the safe and she laughed at

the amount. "When I get back from Vegas, will you still love me?"

"You head anywhere near Vegas," I said, tapping my temple, "and I'll know, remember?"

"Only if you think to check," she teased.

We kissed a long, lingering kiss. She let her hands wander across my chest and lower still. It was then that I smelled the cinnamon. I was ready for it this time. Thoughts and feelings that were not quite mine danced gently through my brain like little puffs of cotton candy. "Trust Rachel," a sweet tender voice ordered my mind. "Love Rachel. Need Rachel." Riding the wave of sensation, I let my hands drift across her breasts and down her back. I grabbed her butt and started kissing her harder. She pushed gently away from me and I didn't let her go, kissing my way down her neck instead.

"Not that I'm complaining, Eric, but if you want me to get everything done in time to leave . . ."

I let her go reluctantly.

I had Magbidion's phone number written down on a blue sticky note stuck to the bottom of my desk drawer. It came free easily and I stuck it on the desk. Did I care if Rachel was trying to use magic on me to enhance our sex, to calm me down, to make my heart beat? The sad and sorry answer is that I didn't.

Roger was in the same category as Rachel. I didn't really care that he had set me up. I wanted to know why he'd done it and if we could resolve things, but basically, he was my best friend. Sure, he was an asshole, but so was I. He was also the only person still around, other than Marilyn, that I'd known when I was alive. Like my Mustang, I wouldn't give up on him unless I had no choice.

So what if Roger had sicced some werewolves on me. I could kill the werewolves. I would rescue Greta. Hell, if he wanted the Demon Heart shut down bad enough to spike my blood supply, maybe I ought to just shut it down. I knew that it embarrassed him, that he was afraid his upper-crust pals would look down on him. What if this all could have been avoided by my buying out his interest in the Demon Heart? I hate questions like that—what-ifs. They can drive you crazy.

I wasn't proud of it, but it all boiled down to the bliss of ignorance. If I knew for sure what was going on with Rachel, or with Roger, then I might have to take action and the truth was that I just didn't want to do that. Why would I? Let's say your spouse is good to you, treats you right, and you have a long happy life together. Do you really want to find out fifty years down the road that she hated your guts the whole time or that for thirty of those years she'd been banging the milkman every Monday and Wednesday? If it were me, I wouldn't. Does that make me a bad person?

A little voice in my head told me that I was a bad person regardless. Everything else was just a bonus.

26

ERIC:
AGORANAUT

Bald Mountain wasn't much of a mountain compared to the Rockies or the Smokies, but it was big enough to count. Oak, dogwood, and pine trees made up most of the surrounding forest. The bulk of the land had been designated a state park in the late thirties or early forties. For two dollars, anyone could get a day pass to visit the park from about seven a.m. until sunset. They also had overnight passes for campers and areas set aside for RV parking. I hadn't been out to Bald Mountain since Marilyn and I had been dating. The picnic area was different and there was a conservation center, but the park itself looked surprisingly familiar.

Rachel looked beautiful in the light that poured between

the trees and in through the windshield. If I squinted just right, I could pretend she was Marilyn. It took me back to my last picnic. Roger, Marilyn, and I had gone to the park in my Mustang, top down, the wind blowing through our hair. Marilyn drove that day and I'd let Roger ride up front. The ice chest sat next to me on the bench seat. Back then, the grilling stations in the picnic area had been new. All we had to supply was the food, the charcoal, and the fire.

The fire. I'd caught Marilyn looking at me in the rearview mirror. I'd forgotten it on purpose, that look . . . a sad look with I-don't-know-how-to-tell-you eyes. I buried it again.

Rachel looked over at me, the way you look at an angry dog who's cornered you. Her hand touched my leg tentatively. "Is there something wrong?"

"Why?"

"You just . . . um, the link, it goes both ways a little and, I don't know, you felt lost."

I turned my head. Outside the window, the leaves were rich and green. "Only for the last forty-three years," I whispered.

It had never occurred to me before, but I'd now been undead longer than I'd been alive. My vampiric existence had eclipsed my human life, and it seemed like each year beyond that balance eroded me more. Forty-three years of undeath. It seemed longer. My watch was still broken. "What month is it?" I asked.

"It's August, Eric," Rachel told me.

The leather outfit she'd brought me would have looked more natural on a rock star like Marilyn Manson. It did cover my whole body, though, and it was real leather, so it could probably take a beating. The mask had zippers where I thought it ought to have holes, but it wasn't noticeable with the helmet on. Over the suit's gloves, I wore a pair of work gloves secured with duct tape. I had the legs of the jumpsuit tucked into a pair of steel-toed work boots, secured like the gloves. Between the tinted goggles and the tinted visor, the sun didn't hurt my eyes that much, but my vision was restricted to whatever was directly in front of me.

"What day?" I asked.

"Monday," she answered.

"Monday the what?"

"Monday the ninth," she answered, looking over at me. "Why so interested?"

I watched the trees go by, noting each hiking trail we passed. Rachel was doing a good job playing chauffeur. After I'd hung up with Magbidion, I'd had Carl drive a loaner out to me. It was a rusted-out hunk of junk with no air conditioner, but that just showed Carl's intelligence.

It was always a crapshoot when it came to me and loaners. He knew that I would pay for damages, but we both felt better about it if he loaned me cheap cars . . . just in case. No sense in throwing money away. The heat didn't bother me, but Rachel was covered in a thin sheen of sweat and her deodorant wasn't keeping pace with demand.

"Roger will have something big planned for tomorrow. Something drastic . . . probably his big finale."

She looked confused. "How do you figure that?"

"It's my birthday," I told her.

"That's great! How old will you be?"

My sense of Greta grew stronger as we passed a turn and then started to grow fainter. "Turn around and go back," I ordered. "She's down that road." Rachel made a three-point turn and headed down the road I had indicated.

"This way?" she asked.

I nodded. "Yeah, we're getting close."

"How old are you going to be?" she asked again.

"I don't remember," I said distractedly. I was turning forty again. I turn forty every year, but it never sticks.

Greta was screaming in a metal box. Rage reached up into my chest. I could see the box clearly. Men—werewolves in human form—were taking turns rolling the box over and shaking it back and forth. Greta's cries were louder than my thoughts. Something inside me roared, but made no sound.

"Sweet Jesus!" Rachel swore. I guessed she'd felt that one along our link.

"Stop the car," I commanded.

Brakes squealed as Rachel slammed her foot to the floor and the car turned sideways, sliding as it went. We came to a halt at the edge of a drainage ditch that directed the camping area's runoff under the road as it ran downhill. The car had rotated one hundred and eighty degrees from where we had started, facing back down the way we'd come. I stepped out of the car and looked back at Rachel. "If I'm not back in fifteen minutes, go home."

I didn't wait for an answer. Instead, I ran down the slope into the drainage ditch and started scrambling up the rise in front of me. Greta was on the other side of the hill.

My mental picture of the campground grew clearer and clearer the closer I got. As I topped the hill, I saw the first werewolf, a lookout. He looked human, but even through the visor of my helmet, I could smell him. He'd been a wolf recently. We both froze, momentarily stunned. He couldn't have been more than sixteen, an inexperienced fighter, so it was no surprise that I recovered first. I put my fist through his chest and it came out on the other side holding his heart. Young or old, these werewolves were my enemies and anyone who wanted to live had better change sides quickly.

His body rolled halfway down the hill and stopped when it hit the base of a pine tree. His pack would smell the blood soon. I broke into a run and hit the campsite as soon as I cleared the tree line. A group of tents was arranged in a circle around one large tent. Garlic cloves hung on ropes over the entrances and each tent had a cross painted on all four sides. It was definitely not a vampire-friendly zone.

On the far side of the camping area, RVs with out-of-state tags were parked in double rows. Not a good sign. I'd already seen the kind of help William was rounding up and I didn't want to get in a fight with more fun-loving representatives of the Lycan Diocese.

Two men—werewolves—saw me walk into the camp. I staggered like I'd been injured and they rushed toward me. Before they reached me, the taller one slowed down, his eyes widening. "Chuck, no! It's a—" I grabbed Chuck by the shoulder blades, hooking my fingers into his collarbone for leverage, and tore him open at the chest, his sternum popping, ribs gaping apart. His buddy staggered away from me.

It was probably the sunlight that confused him. Even though I was expected, vampires are creatures of the night. The werewolves were used to hunting us inside houses, sewers, crypts, or apartments during the day. Was it possible that I was more frightening in the light? I wiped my visor with the back of Chuck's shirt and charged his pal.

"Vampire!" he yelled at the top of his lungs. We ran at each other full tilt. He transformed as he ran, shedding teeth. He swiped at me with his claws and the blow caught me just right, turning my leaping dodge into an out-of-control tumble through the air. I cannonballed into one of the tents, crumpling it, tent poles snapping. The fabric wrapped around me completely, blocking my vision of all but bright blue tent flap. I'd landed within a few feet of the metal box; I could feel Greta inside.

I struggled out from under the tent as the werewolf landed next to me. Reaching out, I grabbed him by the muzzle and threw him hard and high into the bough of a nearby oak.

The box. I spun quickly, searching, and saw it. They had welded the box shut, and it looked like a professional job. I also found the folks who had been rolling it around. Six men and two women were gathered around the metal container, taking turns rocking it from side to side. A handful of children stopped playing and ran for the big tent. The adults started to change and more werewolves began pouring out of the other tents and the RVs. I counted at least forty. There was no way I could outfight them all, not in the daytime. I grabbed a little boy and a little girl by the scruffs of their necks and I felt like scum when I did it.

They both screamed for their mommy and one of the female werewolves turned human again. "Please, no!" It was a standoff. The males started circling, but kept their distance as I walked toward the box. The females who were still in werewolf mode backed slowly away from me, but the one in human form stayed put. I heard the tent flaps flutter behind me and I spun around.

"Don't make me hurt them!" I shouted.

I hoped they would buy it, because I already knew I wouldn't do anything to the kids. The little boy might have been as old as eight, and the little girl was only four or five. I couldn't have killed either of them.

A tall man stepped out of the tent. He was six foot five and had dusty blond hair. I couldn't tell the color of his eyes, but he looked like a real mountain man. A foot-long wooden cross hung from his belt, the base sharpened to a point. A smaller metal cross hung from his neck over a flannel shirt.

"What in God's name is going on here?" he spat.

"You called," I said acidly. "I came."

William didn't look fake when he transformed. No weird latex-looking skin, no fur turned all the wrong way, and when he moved, it was smooth, not the jerky stop-motion effect I'd seen so often. That alone would have earned him the Alpha title in my book. Pure white fur covered him from head to toe, and he stared at me angrily from behind ice-blue eyes. "How dare you threaten children?" The voice rang more in my head than in my ears and it was angry.

"Fuck you, pal," I shouted back. "You see, believe it or not, I haven't done a damn thing to you. Your son got lured into an alleyway by a vampire stripper and, as weird as it sounds, she used a magic gun to kill him. I wound up playing the scapegoat. I think her boss wants me to kill you, but I'm still working on why.

"As for the stripper who killed your son, not to mention your packmates out at Orchard Lake—she's dead now. I had my girlfriend track her down and kill her. If you want, you can have her ashes. All I want is my daughter back and for you guys to back off."

"Liar!" William's huge clawed hands shook with rage as he bared his fangs at me. "My son was pure. He would never consort with some vampire whore."

"Have you ever gotten a blow job from a woman who doesn't have to breathe? Trust me, he'd consort."

"No more of your lies, vampire. I know what you want and we will never surrender our land to one of your kind. No matter how many dead you lay on our doorstep, we will not give in."

"Land? What do you think this is, the Louisiana fucking Purchase? Let's try it this way. I don't want to kill you. I didn't even bring any silver with me. Hell, I didn't even bring the magic gun with me." Which, by the way, I was already regretting. "I just want to be left alone. If you can't do that, then we have a problem and if we have a problem, I'm going to have to put you and your little wolf pack down."

"Those two children you hold in your hands are sinless, vampire. If you kill them, we shall not be sad, but shall rejoice. They will fly to their Heavenly Father and join him forever in paradise. We, unlike you, are living, breathing creatures of God. We worship in many ways, but we all worship, and he will send us more soldiers to fill our ranks and more pups to fill our hearts." He looked meaningfully at his pack when he spoke, trying, I thought, more to convince them than to persuade me.

I saw grim commitment in the eyes of the gathering pack, some of them wearing crosses, some clutching crucifixes, even a few wielding Stars of David. They didn't like it, but most of them would do whatever he told them.

"Kill it," he shouted.

I mouthed an obscenity as he struck. I wouldn't have had time to break the children's necks even if I'd been willing to do it. He was faster than anything I'd ever seen, faster than me, faster than Talbot. His huge white paws smacked my helmet with lightning speed and it shattered. The Beatles' "Here Comes the Sun" played through my mind. Now I had definitely beaten El Segundo.

◆ 27 ◆

ERIC:
POWERHOUSE

I'd been on fire before and it usually made me feel like an idiot. Often, when I ignited, it was a result of forgetting what time it was or watching an impending sunrise just a little too long. This time it made me angry. Claws tore at my clothes, and as each strip of fabric fell away, new pain erupted. But hey, at least I was warm.

Part of me wondered if it wasn't better this way, to die on Bald Mountain, in the sun on a breezy day in August. The other part of me told the suicidal part to shut the fuck up and fight.

It only took a few seconds for the flames to completely engulf me. I wondered if I looked anything like the Human Torch or if it was more like one of those movie stuntmen.

Several werewolves were laughing and the mama werewolf was fussing over her children. I was just as glad as she was that they were safe. Then I heard a single word that changed everything.

"Daddy!" It was Greta. She could feel me burning, even through her own pain. People say that monsters only come out at night. Mine came out right then. Rage doesn't even begin to cover it. Steel bands snapped inside my chest and chains pulled free of their wall mounts.

Suddenly, I could see. The flames were out and everyone looked a little shorter. Tendrils of smoke rose off dark black skin that I didn't recognize as mine. It didn't look charred. It was smooth and sizzled softly in the sun. I tried to move, but couldn't. My whole body had gone numb and useless, as if I'd been staked through the heart, but then it started moving of its own accord. I could see and hear, but something else was in the driver's seat.

The thing I had become held up its arm and high-pitched squealing filled the air, joined by the sound of a few thousand wings. Clouds of bats and birds swarmed overhead, blocking out the sun. My opponents looked on in silence as the sky turned black. My new skin stopped sizzling. William looked up at me and crossed himself. Several of the others presented their holy symbols and began to pray in Latin, Hebrew, Spanish, and English. The super vamp I had become roared and started toward them.

No! Wait! I started yelling inside my head. *Get Greta, jackass!*

There was no response from Ericzilla. It was more like

watching the demo for a first-person shooter video game than actually being me. Two werewolves jumped at me in slow motion. Uber vamp speed was unbelievable. I darted forward, plucking both werewolves from the air and tearing them into quarters, not just killing them, but mangling them with a purpose. If this was what happened when I blacked out, then I wished I would black out again, because I really didn't want to see this.

Blood jetted in lazy streams from the werewolves' remains as I struggled with all my might to regain control. If I could even just turn my head toward Greta . . . Instead, I was forced into the skies as the uber Eric darted down at another unlucky werewolf, pulling it up into the air and tearing off its head with talon-tipped fingers.

There was no doubt that I could destroy the entire pack this way, but if I did that and then suddenly found myself back at the wheel, standing over the bodies, the living curtain of wings would probably disperse, and Greta and I would both be fried. My death would have been fast, and right now I almost welcomed it, but hers would be prolonged and torturous. I couldn't abide that.

Stop screwing with the werewolves and get Greta out of the box, you dumb fucker! I yelled at Ericzilla. *She's going to die in there if you blow this! If you can even pick up a single thought, you cave-brained bastard, then open the damn box!*

Another werewolf entered the shredding zone and went from living thing to flesh-chunk confetti with bright red liquid streamers. Either I had slowed or the pack was speeding up. They were doing their best to fight against me, and so was I. Then, the two little kids wolfed out and my uber vamp body turned on them. I tried with every bit of mental strength to stay the death that awaited those children; *They're just kids,* I shouted mentally. *We are here to get Greta, shit-for-brains! So get Greta and get us the fuck out of here!*

I pictured myself standing in front of the uber Eric, blocking the children and pointing at the box. My mental image head-butted the black-skinned beast and kicked it in the groin. When that didn't work, I fought dirty. I showed him the night I'd first found Greta, lying bruised and bloody in her foster father's bed. She'd been nine. The uber vamp howled. *You remember that?* I shouted. *You want to be like that, like the human so evil I wouldn't even bite him?*

Greta is in that damn metal box right over there and she needs me! Comprendez? I had my mental image walk over to the box and rip it open. Greta was inside and I imagined myself ripping open a vein and spraying blood like my arm was a fire hose to heal her wounds.

Uber Eric paused and time returned to normal. Ten werewolves piled onto me, clawing and biting like mad to take my uber vamp body down. Had I gotten through? Did it, whatever was driving, understand? I began to suspect that it had, because it slowly turned, ignoring the wounds and the werewolves, looking for the box. Black blood flowed down one of my arms from a multitude of cuts and bites. I couldn't feel it, but it looked painful.

Uber me turned its head to look at the blood, swatting the werewolves away on autopilot, using both wings and the less-injured arm. Then, I got a look at the box with Greta inside and heard my own voice say, "Hold tight, sweetheart. We're getting the hell out of Dodge!"

I still wasn't in control, but that certainly sounded like a step in the right direction. The uber vamp grabbed the box and leapt into the air.

Gunshots sounded from below and the twang of arrows filled the air. The arrows made me laugh on the inside, but Supervamp must not have thought it was funny. Real wooden arrows are much more useful than bullets against a vampire, and William's werewolves knew it.

I wanted to see how many werewolves were down there, but uber me wasn't interested. A mass of bats poured out of the sky, diving toward the werewolves, and the uber vamp's black skin began to sizzle again in the now imperfect screen created by the remaining bats above.

I spotted Rachel in the loaner car. My uber vamp body made a beeline for the vehicle, landing a few feet from the front bumper. Rachel screamed, but she didn't hit the gas.

Crouching low over the box, shielding it with tenebrous wings as if afraid an arrow or stray beam of sunlight might strike Greta, the uber vamp and I punched through the seam of the metal box with one black talon. Metal screeched as the weld gave way, little curlicue strands falling to the grass as we peeled back the top. Tilting the box to the side, we let Greta roll out onto the ground. She looked pretty bad, like charred hamburger, but she was still with us.

As soon as I saw my girl, the whole transformation happened in reverse. My nerve endings woke up. It would have been just fine with me if they had waited a while. I had multiple gunshot wounds, cuts, scratches, bites, and two or three arrows in me. One of the arrows was close enough to my heart that I was afraid to move too quickly lest it wiggle those last few centimeters and leave me paralyzed midrescue.

"Rachel!" I shouted. "Get over here and pull these arrows out!"

She stared at me motionlessly for a moment before springing into action. "How did you do that?" she asked.

"Arrows. Out. Now!"

Rachel grabbed the first arrow and jerked it out of my shoulder with a loud grunt. It came free, red blood mixing with the black blood already covering the shaft. She grabbed the next and pulled with all her might. I gritted my teeth against the pain as the shaft came free. Rather than pulling out the arrow in my left side, she thrust it the rest of the way through. My legs buckled and I fell to one knee. But when she grabbed the last arrow I couldn't stand it anymore. It was too deep.

"Leave it," I said.

"I've almost got it." Rachel put her knee in my back for more leverage and I shouted as the arrow twisted in my chest.

"Just leave the damn thing in and start the car!"

More spots of sunlight appeared on the grass as she dove straight through the open window of the car and into the driver's seat. Overhead and back near the camp, the mass of winged minions was beginning to disperse. A core group of gray bats struggled to maintain formation, but was losing the battle. As Rachel kicked open the passenger's side door, dozens of werewolves, no longer blinded by the horde of bats, howled a battle cry and began loping toward us.

I gashed my wrist open with my fangs and bled into Greta's eyes. When they flickered open I pushed my thoughts into her head. "Turn into a mouse."

"Can't, Dad," she replied. "Too tired."

I latched hold of her thoughts, but they were hazy, jumbled, and confused. So were mine. I tried to block out the sound of the approaching werewolves and pushed harder, so hard she screamed. She managed the change, then went limp again.

She was a sad, burnt-looking mouse. Talbot would have thought her an hors d'oeuvre gone wrong, but she was still my Greta and she was still undead, which was all that mattered to me. I jumped into the car, holding her carefully in my fist, and yowled as sunlight hit the exposed flesh on my back where claws, bullets, and arrows had torn through the leather. Rachel gunned the engine and started pulling away.

As the first wolf cleared the hill I tucked Greta into Rachel's purse, turned into a mouse, and jumped in after her. Rachel reached over, closed the purse flap, and drove hellbent toward the park exit. Inside the bag, I cuddled against Greta and hoped William's pack didn't catch up with us.

I had no idea how the whole uber vamp thing actually worked, but I knew it was tied to my anger. If I got angry enough to have a rage blackout, then I did my own little version of the Incredible Hulk or Super Dracula, whatever you wanted to call it. Freud would have said that it was pure id, unleashed and given form, not unlike Dr. Jekyll and Mr.

Hyde, but that was a little too easy an answer for me. No one was lining up to explain why I'd been aware this time either, why I'd heard and seen what happened, though I'd never remembered any of it before.

Could it be that making Rachel my thrall had been responsible? If it allowed me to sense my offspring, and to supposedly recognize the thralls created by other vampires . . . who knew if it helped control the part of me that went berserk? Was it a good thing or a bad thing? I couldn't decide.

I'd been a vampire for over forty years, and all along I'd been turning into this thing right, left, and sideways, whenever people pissed me off. Why had nobody said anything? Talbot said he hadn't told me because he thought I knew. I believed that. How do you not know you turn into a giant vampire blender and puree things when you're mad? Maybe Marilyn had never seen it. No one ever had to tell me that I turned into a bat, a cat, or anything else. Why would they assume I didn't know? But Roger knew me better than that.

In fact, I'd bet Roger knew the most about it, and I couldn't ask him about it. Not right now. What if we'd already had that discussion before, or after one of my blackouts, and I'd forgotten? What if I'd "figured it out" any number of times, but, unable to control it, had forgotten?

What's your father's name? Marilyn's question from earlier rose, a disturbing specter in my thoughts. I'd already forgotten what she'd said. The last name started with a C, I thought.

Take it from me: If you're going to die in a car crash and miraculously rise as one of the living dead, don't let them embalm you. I was starting to think maybe it had screwed with my head. As I lay puzzling out the complexity of my life, the thrum of the motor and the exertion of the day lulled me gently to sleep.

28

TABITHA:

PMS

Void City was quiet and brooding that Monday night. Every traffic light glared bright red before allowing Talbot's Jaguar to weave its way homeward. Halfway there, the two of us realized that it was Eric's birthday, or at least, it would be after midnight, so we went shopping.

Talbot bought him a new cell phone and I made do with a selection from Victoria's Secret, Frederick's of Hollywood, and Sahid's Adult Books and Novelties. I spent too much money, but I felt guilty about sleeping with Talbot. Eric would have slept with a human and not called it cheating. Maybe he already had. I hoped he had. It would make me feel better about what I'd done.

I stood up on all fours, turned in a circle, and sat back down on the seat fitfully. I liked being a cat, feeling warm, having a heartbeat, breathing autonomically, things that my human body no longer provided. Even as a cat, though, I was increasingly on edge. "Damn him, that man has me wrapped around his little finger!" I hissed.

"I would hesitate to refute that," Talbot said as he glanced down at me.

"I have never cheated on him, not once! There is no telling how many times he's screwed around on me, but I'm the one who feels guilty."

Streetlamps and skyscrapers passed by the windows and Talbot did not comment. "Well?" I meowed.

"Well what?" he answered. Eyes on the road, he reached down and silenced the classical music on the radio. I hadn't even noticed there had been music until he turned it off. "Eric never made any pretense at being faithful. You did. Maybe you took pride in it? It kept you in the right as the long-suffering faithful member of the relationship. Now you're not the martyr anymore and it's eating away at you."

Turning human, I crossed my arms and stared out the side window. "That is so totally screwed up! I don't even know how you said it with a straight face."

"Oh, so now you're mad at me?" he said with a grin.

"I was vulnerable and hungry, and I'm still new to this. You're used to dealing with newborn vamps." I kept my eyes focused on the window, staring out at the city. "You should have stopped me. I wasn't in control of myself."

"Buckle your seat belt," he ordered. Outside the window,

a little boy in dirty jeans and a ratty T-shirt stood on the street corner. He smiled at someone across the street. I rolled down the window as we passed. Wind hit my face, tousling my hair. Craning my neck out of the window, I watched the woman the boy was smiling at cross the street. "What happened to your jeans?" she asked him.

The rest was lost to me as we sped past. Remorse struck me by surprise and I blinked back tears. "I can never have kids."

"And this didn't occur to you before you decided you wanted to be a vampire?"

"It did. I thought I didn't want kids, but now that I can't have them . . ."

"Buckle your seat belt if you're going to be in human form," he said patiently. "I don't want to have to pay my way out of a ticket."

"What do you mean? Couldn't you just flash your fangs or go all cat-eyed so they'd let you go?"

"And then I'd have to pay for the ticket in cash later when one of Lord Phil's cronies called me up to talk about the fang fee."

"Fang fee."

"Hey," Talbot said more cheerfully. "Now that you know Lord Phil, maybe you can get him to fix my tickets."

"What are you even talking about?" Rushing in on the end of my thoughts about children, I thought about my last sunset. Shouldn't I have looked at the sun one last time, to say good-bye?

"I'm talking about you buckling your seat belt so that I

don't get a ticket. Void City cops love to pull people over, particularly if they think you're undead."

Drops of blood flew off of my cheeks when I jerked around to face him. "I don't want to wear a fucking seat belt!" Fingernails elongated into claws at the end of my hands and my jaw popped to accommodate the fangs that slid out of their sheaths in my gums. Refusing to flinch, Talbot remained blasé.

"Turn back into a cat if you don't want to wear a seat belt. There is a cop up ahead."

"Would you shut up about the damn cop?" I yelled, not sure why I was reacting this way. "If he pulls us over I'll rip his fucking head off, okay? Just forget about it! I'm not wearing a damn seat belt, you stupid motherfucker, and you can't make me! I'm the boss here! I'm the vampire, not you. I'm a Lady Bathory and you're just some . . . some . . . mouser, whatever that is. A cat, or a human that used to be a cat, or whatever the fuck you are. You're not even human. You probably don't even have a soul. You probably never had one . . . and . . . and you raped me, you bastard!"

The officer in question eyed us warily as we passed, saw my fangs, and mouthed "Fuck that" to himself. Smarter than the rest of us, he knew when to mind his own business.

A twinge of pain squeezed my chest. With it came other thoughts, emotions, a flood of regret. If Rachel hadn't died, I'd never have become so obsessed with death. I never would have gotten wrapped up in the vampire scene. I'd have stayed in college like my parents had wanted instead of rebelling and deciding life was too short to waste.

I wouldn't have even met Eric, I wouldn't be in love with him, and I wouldn't have spent the last two years praying that he loved me back. I'd probably have been off somewhere, hopelessly in love with some asshole who just wanted my body, but he would have been a human asshole. Maybe I'd even be pregnant.

The tight ragged pain spread out from my chest, up into my skull, and down my arms and legs. My insides felt tight and shrunken. At the back of my eyes, the pain and pressure increased, as if my eyes were going to jerk through the sockets and become recessed in my braincase.

"It hurts," I yelled.

"What?" Talbot asked.

"It hurts!"

I grabbed the sides of my head with full vampiric acceleration. My elbow touched the window with what would have been a light bump, but the increased velocity magnified the force of the blow, shattering the passenger's side window. Glass cut into my elbow and I started to scream. I needed to get out of the car, to run; I felt trapped, as if the car were attacking me, or keeping me prisoner, or both. I attacked back.

Brakes squealed and the Jaguar swerved into an alley. The driver's side door flew open, and I lost sight of Talbot as I lashed out at the upholstery, leather shredding easily under my claws. Something was wrong with me again and it was worse than the drugged blood. Euphoric anger had detached me from my actions in the Demon Heart, but this was real.

Pain lanced through my hand as I punched through the

dash and into the glove compartment. Metal and plastic cut me, but I jerked my hand free, leaving blood and skin behind, before kicking away from the dash, breaking my seat, and flailing into the back of the car, my claws tearing at the ceiling and smashing out the rear window.

Suddenly my lungs started working and went into overdrive, pumping air in and out with such urgency it might have been trying to atone for all the breaths it had missed over the last couple of nights.

Once, in high school biology class, we'd had to dissect a frog. I had been so afraid I'd hyperventilated and passed out. This felt a lot like that. Rapid, shuddering booms shook my chest and I realized my heart was beating. Not only was it beating, it was beating far too fast. Gritting my teeth, I managed to stop actually screaming, but a high keening sound escaped my throat.

Talbot rounded the car, put his hand on the passenger's side door, and I hit it from the inside with both feet, ripping the door loose of its hinges and sending Talbot and the door flying into the concrete wall of the building. He was still holding on to the door when he hit the ground. "Get away from me," I screamed through chattering teeth. "Don't touch me!"

Color leached out of my vision, the world sliding to black and white, to grayscale, and then to shades of red. Waves of heat rushed over me and my entire body began to vibrate. Staggering out of the Jag, I pressed my head against the cool metal on the roof. Beating loudly in my ears, the sound of my heartbeat was joined by another sound, a loud *whooshing* sound, I realized it was the blood rushing through my veins once more. The pain left my chest, the inner tightening faded as blood flowed. Color vision came back, but the colors were too bright, blindingly kaleidoscopic. "What's happening to me?" I demanded.

"Turn back into a cat," Talbot choked out as he shoved the door off onto the sidewalk.

I tried. Desperately. I couldn't.

Panic continued to swell inside me. I felt like my heart was about to tear itself out of my chest like a baby alien from that space movie with Sigourney Weaver.

He got to his feet and took a deep breath. "It's probably autonomic function return brought on by postmortem stress, maybe even a panic attack. It's rarely this bad, but I've seen it before."

None of that made sense to me. My body was too loud. At the end of my fingers, claws extended and retracted, rhythmically gouging holes into the roof. "Don't touch me," I panted. "Get away from me." Bottom fangs pushed their way into my mouth from between the teeth in my lower jaw, blood filling my mouth as the gums ripped open, a long searing pain. I shouldn't even have bottom fangs. What was happening to me? "Your blood must have done this to me," I spat out, shaking so hard I could barely talk. "It's poisonous or something."

"It's not my blood, Tabitha, it's you. Your body is reacting to stress the only way it remembers how. Turn back into a cat," he urged, "and it will stop. You have a pulse as a cat. Your body will remember what it's supposed to be doing."

He didn't sound mad at all, but there was a tone in his voice that I didn't recognize, a tinge of concern or wonder. "Trust me, Tabitha. Turn into a cat."

Hugging my arms tightly around myself and closing my eyes, I finally managed to turn into a cat. The panic and anxiety were still there, but my body was calm and controlled. Normal heartbeat. Normal breath. Normal blood flow. Everything felt right, natural, as it should be.

Talbot leaned in through the passenger's side door, turned off the engine, and pulled his keys out of the ignition. Leaning up against his poor Jaguar, he asked, "Better now?"

I nodded.

He looked down at the keys in his hand and mumbled, "Ninety-three thousand dollars. Damn, you're high maintenance."

Angry, sad, and terrified all at once, I curled up into a ball of fur, pressing myself against the brick wall of the alley, not knowing what to say, what to do, or how to react. Why had I let Eric do this to me? No more sun. No more mirrors. No food but blood. How could I have wanted this? Liquid diets had never worked for me, and now I was on the ultimate liquid diet. Not just for six to eight months, either. No, I had signed up for the infinity plan. Immortality was all fun and games until you read the fine print.

"What's happening to me?" I meowed.

"PMS," he said, stone-faced.

I glared at him.

"Postmortem stress," he continued. "It happens to the newly undead. There comes a point when you stop thinking of yourself as human and accept your new self. You let go of who you were and become what you are. When it happens, your body freaks out. Your mind freaks out. So essentially, you're freaking out," he answered. "Eric is the only vampire I know of who never did it. I meant to tell you about it first thing. I guess it slipped my mind." It hadn't, though; I could tell from the smug cat grin on his face. He'd worn the same self-satisfied expression when he'd held me down at the Demon Heart while Marilyn and Desiree fed me cold blood.

"Bullshit," I meowed. "You guess it slipped your mind? You wanted to see me freak. You got off on it."

"Told you I wasn't human," Talbot said without remorse or shame.

I rose to all fours, pacing back and forth, my tail twitching furiously. "PMS when I'm alive and PMS when I'm dead. Retaining water may have made my ankles swell, but it never made me rip a sports car apart."

I turned human again and it no longer felt strange or otherworldly. The change was as natural as stepping out of one dress and into another: a momentary vulnerability, followed by comfort in my new outfit. My body was still warm and my heartbeat was steady. I was still breathing. Blood pumped through my veins, but the sound was muted. Now that I expected it, none of it was so alarming.

"One in a mill—" Talbot reached for my cheek and I slapped him so hard it knocked him across the alley. When he landed, I was there, claws out and waiting. It was a cheap shot and it left him too dazed to react.

"I told you not to touch me, Talbot!" I sank my right-hand

claws into his chest, just above the heart. Crouched on his chest, the claws of my left hand at his throat, I said, "I'm very grateful for all your help. I needed it. I needed your knowledge and experience. I really, really did, but I swear to God that if you ever touch me again I will rip your heart out with my bare hands, throw it in the street and back over it with Eric's Mustang! Do you understand?"

Fur puffed up under my fingertips as Talbot's ears slid upward and extended, pointed, like a cat's. I made a move to claw him with my left hand, as a threat rather than to rip his throat out, but he caught it with a hand covered in sable fur. His voice echoed in my head, his jaws unmoving as he spoke.

Tabitha, you do not want me as your enemy. Cat's eyes glared at me from his handsome face as his nose broadened and whiskers erupted from his cheeks. The first three buttons on his shirt popped loose as his chest expanded, the material drawing tight and ripping where my claws pierced it. *I can make your life a living hell.*

"Too late!" I spat. "Don't you understand that? Everything is totally fucked up now. Eric will never want me now that I've been with you and you should have known better, Talbot. You should have fucking stopped me. You're supposed to be my damn babysitter!"

"It had been a long time for me, Tabitha. A very long time, and if I took advantage of you, if you think I did, then I'm sorry." He took hold of my right hand and gently pulled my claws from his chest. I let him. Even with my hand poised to hurt him, possibly kill him, I was afraid. His claws were holy.

He was some kind of sacred hunter. I was just a vampire, a queen, sure, but . . .

His expression softened as my claws came free, the fur subsiding, his pantherlike features not quite melting into human ones, but fading, like an illusion. He stared at me with human eyes that were too cute, too endearing, and I let him up.

"My kind does not apologize, Tabitha. We don't have to, because we are never wrong. . . ." I bared my fangs, arms crossed, standing against the brick, away from him, as he continued, "Or we claim we aren't. I'm different." He straightened his clothes, brushing at the dirt, and the rips disappeared. I wondered if they were really gone or if it was an illusion. Did he really look human at all or did everyone simply see what he wanted them to see?

"I am willing to admit that it is remotely possible that I share part of the blame, but not all of it." He leaned in close, his lips a breath away from mine. Despite myself I wanted to kiss him. "You did not smell out of control," he continued. His left hand traced the outline of my body, almost, but not quite touching me. "You smelled like you knew exactly what was going on and I trusted that."

He looked me straight in the eyes, dared me to make contact, to pit my will against his.

"Now I'm going to smell like you," I said, looking away.

"Most people only get one chance with me, Tabitha. You've already had two; this makes it three. I let it go the first time you jumped me, because you didn't know any better. I let the second one go because you were drugged. I'm going to let this one go because of the postmortem stress and the extenuating circumstances, but don't try for a fourth chance. I'll tear you apart and swallow all the pieces. Unless you've made a pact with a demon that I don't know about, you won't be coming back from that."

Angry with myself and with Talbot, I brushed past him, stopping near the car. Little dots of light reflected up at me from the Jag's passenger's side mirror, which lay cracked in the alley. I picked it up and looked at my reflection. I was a mess. My new blouse was ruined, grime and blood spotted it in multiple places and there was even a small rip where glass had cut it. My hair—

I don't think I could have been more surprised if I went to my folks' house and Rachel answered the door. I dropped the mirror, stumbling away from it in denial. "My reflection. How . . ."

After a moment, I picked the mirror up again. I did look beautiful, even with the grime and dirt. Then, my image slowly faded, along with the body heat and my other renewed bodily functions. It was more depressing than the ruined blouse, like dying all over again, without the promise of immortality.

"Damn." I shivered, cold again, as my fingertips caressed the glass. "Come back." With unbearable slowness, my face reappeared in the glass. "How is this possible?" I whispered.

"I suspected it when you first turned into a cat, and appeared to be alive," Talbot said from across the alley. "Eric seems to draw vamps that defy the norm. Every one he creates comes prepackaged with pain and wonder. Maybe one in ten thousand, possibly one in a hundred thousand vam-

pires can turn their bodies back on, choose to cast a reflection in animal form or human form. The number of vamps
who can do both? I couldn't even begin to calculate. Maybe
one in a million? My guess? No more than five and possibly
just you."

"What?" I asked. I'd heard what he said, but it wasn't sink-
ing in.

"They're called Dolls. They are vampires that can seem
completely lifelike. You can stop worrying about whether
he'll want you or not. He'll probably fall head over heels for
you. You're immortal, you're beautiful, and you will never
change. You can have body heat, a heartbeat . . . even blood
coursing through your veins. You can even cast a reflection
when you wish. You'll probably even be able to have saliva
and, um, other appropriate fluids after a little practice." He
let out a long breath again.

"But I tried that earlier and it didn't work—"

"The first time you tried to transform into a bird it didn't
work either. It takes practice, like anything else." Talbot
reached out as if to touch my cheek again, but checked the
impulse before I swatted him, though I don't think I would
have.

"If you think Veruca was angry that you could turn into
a cat," he continued, "you should know that there will be
plenty of vampires that will hate you for what you can do.
Just stop worrying about your boyfriend. The only way
another girl could compete with you now is with magical
breasts and an enchanted crotch. He's yours for the taking,
if you still want him."

I smiled. "Oh, no; he'll have to earn it." If he wanted this Snow White, then first he was going to have to kiss my cold dead lips. I didn't want him to want me because I could be warm and lifelike, his precious little doll. First he had to want me for me.

And then . . . I forced blood to run through my veins, watched as my pale perfect skin grew pink and pretty. Mine for the taking. I liked the sound of that.

29

ERIC:

PICTURE PERFECT

Have you ever slept through an entire day and woken up at night thinking it was still the same day? That's kind of what happened to me. I woke in my own bed at the Pollux, with Rachel paying me some not unwanted attention below the waist. Disorienting—but nice. I don't know how it is for girls, but for guys, when something like that happens, you go with it. Everything else is immaterial. For instance, the rainbow wig completely escaped my attention at first. As did the *Happy Birthday* banner hung on the wall opposite the bed and the balloons tied to the bedposts.

"Are you wearing clown makeup?" I asked.

Rachel looked up. Though bereft of white paint, she wore

thick black mascara mixed with blue, strategically smudged at the corners of her eyes. The big red clown nose was obscene in contrast to her nakedness and the black choker around her neck. I wondered if the tiny gold padlock held some special meaning.

"Happy birthday!" Rachel straddled me and doffed the wig and nose, going from clown to Goth as easy as smiling. While I'd been asleep, she'd apparently highlighted her dark hair with streaks of reds and blondes.

I don't like clowns. I'm not afraid of them, but I've never found them amusing. This, the Goth thing, was more my style. We kissed, smearing her black lipstick. My heart began beating in time with our rhythm. As birthday surprises go, this was near the top of the chart.

It isn't hard to get up there though; my birthdays are usually a disaster. Or at least as far as I can remember. Ninety percent of the women who have ever dumped me chose my birthday as the magical day. When I was alive, two of the three wrecks I'd been in were birthday related. My mom died of a heart attack on my nineteenth birthday. You get the idea.

Maybe, I thought, maybe this will be one of the good ones. The knob on the bedroom door began turning, almost in slow motion. Have you ever had your girlfriend walk in on you while you were screwing her sister on your birthday? Yeah, I thought not.

Tabitha wore a midnight-blue dress that clung to her curves. A diamond necklace sparkled at her throat in the partial light from the hallway. The necklace accentuated her cleavage even more than the dress's plunging neckline. Her skin took on a golden tone, little bits of glitter catching the light. She was beautiful. She looked almost human. Her expression was exactly the sort of complex blend of shock and embarrassment I might expect her to have worn if she'd walked in on her parents having sex.

A package rested in the crook of her arm. It tumbled to the ground as she turned and ran. A gun I supposed to be *El Alma Perdida* was visible for a microsecond, flipping through the air.

It was a single-action pistol. They call them single-action because you cock the hammer back manually and all the trigger does is let the hammer fall. It can go off accidentally if the hammer strikes the round in the chamber hard enough to discharge the bullet. In the Old West, most folks would only put five rounds in the gun to keep accidents from happening. Tabitha must have put in all six.

I don't get shot very often. All the vampire hunters I'd ever met used arrows, holy water, and crosses. Bullets hurt, but they don't generally give any vamp but a Drone much trouble. The bullet went through the side of the mattress at an angle, lodging itself in my right butt cheek. It sizzled like fire. I yowled in pain. Rachel rolled off of me. I know I'm not a werewolf, but the bullet clearly did not like me.

"Get it out!" I shouted. "It's magic."

Just when I thought things couldn't get worse, my ass caught fire. Flames literally jetted out of the bullet hole in my butt. Rachel laughed uncontrollably while I fumbled with the sink. She laughed even harder when I sat in it. Cracks formed in the plaster around the corners. My ass still stung, but the lack of fire made things more bearable.

I tried to pop my claws to dig the bullet out, but nothing happened. Shapeshifting didn't work either. I even tried misting. I was that desperate, but I couldn't change. Rachel ran out of the room and came back with a letter opener. She dug the bullet out, periodically splashing water on the wound to keep it from reigniting. Several agonizing minutes later she handed me a perfect little bullet with no signs of damage, just like the one I'd found out at the lake.

"It's not funny." I dropped the bullet on the bed. She didn't stop laughing and I realized I wanted to snap her neck. The anger was so sudden, so visceral that had I been another vampire, one who had the speed all the time, who didn't have to hope it kicked in when he needed it, I think she would have been lying broken on the floor without my ever consciously deciding to act.

"Oh, it's funny all right," she said, sobering slightly. She was going to get herself killed acting that way around me. At least that's how I justified it in my head when I grabbed her left arm.

"If you thought that was funny, you're gonna love this."

"What are you doing?" she asked, a tinge of fear in her tone. Her heartbeat sped up. *Don't be mad,* said a voice in my head that wasn't mine. *Forgive Rachel. Love Rachel.* The smell of cinnamon hit me, enough to make blood tears well up around my eyes. I wasn't mad anymore, but I was still mean.

"Feeding," I answered. I sank my fangs into her inner elbow, hitting the ulnar artery. It's inefficient and painful for the donor, but it works. Rachel cried in short gasping sobs, but she didn't fight me. Instead, she wiggled her feet nervously.

"I'm sorry," she said. Taste hit my tongue, sweet and bitter like before. *Leave, damn it,* I thought at her. *Don't you understand, this is what I am? I'm a monster. You don't want this.*

"Yes, I do," Rachel whispered. "Yes, I do."

I let her go. She cupped her hand over the wound and her teeth dug into her bottom lip. Good one, Eric, I thought. Just beat the crap out of her next time, you fucking moron.

"Did you get enough?" she asked. "Do you need the other one?" She let go of the wound and held out her uninjured arm.

"No." My voice cracked when I spoke. "That was . . . Look, I'm sorry. Do you need a doctor?"

"I'm a thrall now," she said through gritted teeth and indicated the choker and the golden padlock with her uninjured arm. "I can take care of it. Just give me ten or fifteen minutes and I'll be good as new."

"Right." I pushed open the bedroom door and slunk away, grabbing my jeans off the floor as I went. I slipped them on in the hallway and rested my head against the door. You'd think there was a monster inside me, a creature that wanted to hurt people, a creature to whom violence was the most favorable answer to all of unlife's problems. Oh, right—a vampire!

But to be honest, I don't think just any vampire would have felt guilty about what I'd done, would have recognized the monstrosity. I did, and it didn't feel much different than it might have felt when I was alive. You do what you have to do to get by. You try to stay out of trouble, but when life or unlife throws you lemons, you don't make lemonade, you warm up your pitching arm and you throw them right back.

There were presents lined up along the concession counter, each wrapped in different paper and bows. It looked more like Christmas than a birthday. I looked down over the rail to see Tabitha waiting for me in the sitting area below. I'd half expected to find her sitting there with blood running down her cheeks, ruining her makeup, but her cheeks were dry. She was upset, but she wasn't crying. She was almost smiling, her lips pressed against each other in a thin severe line. I walked down the stairs, and sat down on the coffee table, my knees on either side of her.

"Sorry you walked in on that," I told her.

"It's your birthday," she said matter-of-factly. "Besides, I told you that you could sleep with whoever you wanted. I was just . . . surprised, that's all."

"I noticed that you found the gun." I leaned closer, resting my hand on her knee. She was wearing too much perfume and her skin smelled like two or three different types of soap. She was covering up an odor she didn't want me to notice. Probably corpse sweat again. She needn't have worried.

"I hope it didn't hit the girl when it went off." Tabitha's words were faint, less than whispers. She hadn't recognized Rachel. Thank God!

"Nah, it hit me in the ass." I laughed. "It was pretty funny."

"It didn't sound funny."

"It wasn't funny when it happened, but it's funny now."

"Oh." She looked left and right, anywhere but at me. "Do you want to open your presents?"

"If you want." I walked over to the concession stand with Tabitha in tow.

"You don't have to," she whispered. "I did tell you that I'd try, you know, it, with a human and you. We could go upstairs."

"No," I said too quickly. "No, let's . . . do you know what I really want to do?"

"What?" She had calmed down a bit, her body language more relaxed, more like the Tabitha I knew.

"I want to get Greta and go kill those fucking were-wolves." I pulled her close. "Wanna come?"

"You're joking." Her face lit up like New Year's Eve. "Can I?"

"You'll want to change clothes first, but I can help you with that." We exchanged a quick kiss. Her cold dead lips couldn't match her sister's heat, but I still cared for her.

"Sounds like a plan," she agreed with a slow smile.

"You run across to the Demon Heart and get changed," I said. "I'll find out where Greta went off to."

"I thought you were going to help me change clothes," Tabitha pouted.

"I will," I promised. "Just let me round up Greta and I'll be right over."

Her eyes lingered on the stairs. "Okay," she said slowly.

Upstairs, Rachel was curled under the covers. She didn't say anything when I walked in or when I slipped on the rest of my clothes. The silence was a relief.

Without thinking, I picked up *El Alma Perdida*. It didn't burn my hand. I took the barrel in my left hand and touched the cross on the grip to my forearm, and it didn't burn that either. It was hot, but not hot enough to burn. The bullets didn't like me, but the gun seemed to think I was okay. Weird. I put it back in the box and tucked the box under my arm.

"I'll be back later," I said.

"Okay." Rachel sounded tired and hurt. I fought the impulse to say anything else. Anything I said would have just made things worse. I'd never had a woman like her. She didn't want to be a vampire and she liked being hurt, wanted it. I was going to have to get used to that.

Thanks to the new thrall sense, I could feel Greta nearby, in the parking deck attached to the Pollux. When I reached her, she was sitting on the hood of a Pinto looking up at the moon. Dried blood clung to her chin and throat and the matted tangle of her hair was plastered to the side of her head. Two half-naked teenagers lay in the backseat; their disembodied heads stared with sightless eyes from the roof of the car.

"I was really hungry, Dad," Greta offered apologetically.

A cat, two pigeons, and a rat lay on the concrete next to the car. Greta's eating problem in a nutshell.

"It's fine. No lectures tonight." I took off my shirt and wiped gently at the blood on her neck. "It's my birthday."

"The girl was supposed to be your present," Greta sulked.

The blood wouldn't come off. She needed a shower and a change of clothes. "Why don't you get cleaned up and then

as part of my present you can help me do something important."

"Really?" Her expression was a mirror of Tabitha's. Why
do so many beautiful women think so highly of me? It's like
a kind of brain damage.

"Yeah." I dropped the shirt on the car hood and put an
arm around her. "I want to go kill those werewolves and put
an end to this whole mess. It'll be just the three of us: me,
you, and your new mom."

"Okay." Greta got up slowly, uncertainly. "Where are the
werewolves? I wouldn't think they'd still be hanging around
the park."

They wouldn't? No, I guessed not. The campground at
the State Park couldn't have been a long-term living arrange-
ment. They probably went there just to set up the confron-
tation with me.

"Why do you think they picked the park?" I asked myself
aloud.

"Because they like the woods?" Greta offered.

"No," I said, still rolling the idea around in my head.
"Because it's not the city. It's exposed. A vampire could
take cover from the sun, but not the same way he might in
the city. There are no sewers to hide in, no people to hide
among, no way to diffuse the scent."

We will never surrender our land to one of your kind. That's what
William had said. *No matter how many dead you lay on our doorstep, we will not give in.*

Our doorstep . . . the only place . . . no, damn it, I couldn't
remember. It was somewhere . . . somewhere . . . I'd been out

there. I found the bullet that went in the magic gun, the one that led to the Highland Towers . . . Yesterday I knew, I'd remembered it, known it.

"Son of a bitch," I shouted. "What the hell do you call it, the place with the big lake . . ." I barely noticed the smell of cinnamon and then I remembered. "Orchard Lake. William said I left dead werewolves at his doorstep. If he was talking about the ones Froggy killed, then he meant Orchard Lake. That's where they are," I finished triumphantly.

"Will there be fish?" Greta asked.

Will there be fish? What the hell kind of question was that? "Yes, sweetheart," I assured her. "There will be fish, but we'll be there for the wolves."

30

ERIC:

ORCHARD DAM ROAD

The drive out to Orchard Lake can take anywhere from an hour to ninety minutes, depending on traffic. The trip takes you from interstate to highway to County Road 58 where you wind through Keener and Tartarus, cutting through broad areas of wooded acreage and low mountains punctuated by small townships and the occasional empty strip mall.

I pulled off of 58 onto Orchard Dam Road and parked in the driveway of an abandoned house. I was still driving Carl's loaner. The car's rear bumper was somewhere back at Bald Mountain State Park, or maybe the werewolves kept it as a trophy.

There was a farm across the road, boasting a small herd

of cattle and horses, a hobby farm by the looks of it. The entrance to Sable Oaks was just beyond, a broad stone arch lit by ground lights so that it blazed formidably. Two vampires dressed like Secret Service men, in earpieces and black suits, stood on either side of the entrance to the gated community. I'd flown south when I'd left Orchard Lake the other night, partially to avoid the place. Sable Oaks was for high society fangs, not me.

I'd half expected to find two werewolves on this side, standing guard over Orchard Dam Road from the empty house where we'd parked. A weathered piece of cardboard announced that the house was for sale, but the number had been washed away by rain or bleached out by the sun. If it had really been for sale, then the same vampires who owned Sable Oaks would have undoubtedly snapped it up. I could easily imagine the reason the werewolf community had abandoned it. Too close to the undead.

I waved cheerily at the two vampires, but they stared straight ahead, ignoring me.

Greta unfolded out of the backseat and stretched her arms. "God, it's nice to be out of there," she said.

"You could have traveled as something smaller." I stepped out and closed the door, slamming it so it would catch. It bounced back open and fell off. Vampire strength: gotta love it.

"No thanks," Greta said. "I'll leave the shapeshifting to you."

"Why?" asked Tabitha. She still looked happy to have been invited. She'd even dressed appropriately. Her jeans, tennis shoes, and old T-shirt weren't as glamorous or sexy as the clothes she usually wore, but were much more sensible for fighting werewolves. I wondered if she would still be happy once the killing started. So far, she had killed only when under the influence of the doped blood Froggy had slipped into my reserve at the Demon Heart. As far as I knew, she hadn't ever killed to feed.

"I'm not an animal," Greta answered.

"So?" Tabitha walked around the car and stood next to me, her hand tucked possessively into the back pocket of my jeans.

"So, I don't like being anything I'm not," said Greta. "It feels weird." She rubbed her left arm, taking in her surroundings.

"Being a cat feels awesome," Tabitha said.

"Not to me."

"Are you two done?" I asked. "It's half past one and sunrise is at six eighteen."

"You checked?" Greta's hands flew to her cheeks in exaggerated shock.

"Ha. Ha," I replied dryly. "Yes, I checked." *El Alma Perdida* was in the glove compartment. I leaned across the interior of the car, flipped open the compartment, and pulled out the gun, measuring its heft in my hand. The gun hummed, its grip warm, but the crosses still didn't bother me.

"That is so odd," said Tabitha. "I barely touched the thing and it burned the crap out of me. Why doesn't it hurt you?"

"Talbot told me that my aura and the gun's looked the same, that the gun might be inherited. Did you find anything else out about it?" I asked.

"Just that it was used by a guy named John Paul Courtney back in the Wild West."

Greta laughed.

"What's so funny?" asked Tabitha.

"That's Dad's real last name, Mom," Greta told her.

"Could you not do that? Call me Tabitha."

Greta shook her head. "I can't do that, Mom. That would just be too weird."

Tabitha looked at me for assistance, but I couldn't help on this one. Anytime I turned a girlfriend, Greta started calling her "Mom" until we broke up. The only exception was Marilyn. She had always called her "Mom" or "old Mom." Maybe in Greta's head, even though we'd never married, Marilyn counted as my first wife and that made her Greta's real mother. Marilyn had certainly helped raise her, taken her to school, made her lunches, and picked her up at the end of the day.

Marilyn had been furious when I turned Greta at twenty-one, but I'd had my reasons. Most humans don't know what they're getting into if they become a vampire, but Greta had known better than most. She'd spent twelve years with a vampire for a dad, watching what I did, how I was.

I kept very little hidden from her, hoping that if she saw everything, if I took away the mystique, she'd change her mind. I'd expected her to grow to hate me, but she didn't. To Greta, I'd always be her knight in shining armor, the hero who came in through the window one night and killed the bad guy. She didn't care that if she'd been older, I might have also killed her.

"I thought your last name was Jones," said Tabitha, snapping me out of my fugue.

"Alias," I said. "Roger says we have to roll everything into a new identity every three or four decades so that no one at the federal level gets suspicious."

Courtney sounded familiar, but a lifetime away. "I used to be a Courtney, I guess. Marilyn would know."

What's your father's name? Marilyn asked again in my head. The truth was, I didn't want to remember. I knew Marilyn's name, though: Marilyn Amanda Robinson. It should have been Marilyn Robinson Courtney . . .

"How can you not remember your last name?" asked Tabitha in amazement. Her hand was no longer in my pocket. She stood beside me, gesturing as she spoke.

"I haven't used it in forty years," I replied defensively. I didn't have time for this conversation. Talking about the past wakes up all the ghosts in my head. My brother, my parents—they were all better half remembered. I hadn't made them proud when I'd been alive, hadn't been what they wanted me to be. Even if I still had nieces and nephews out there, I didn't want to know about them and they didn't need to know about me. We weren't part of the same world anymore.

I began to walk up the road toward the marina. Greta fell in step beside me, but Tabitha blocked my path, hand on my chest. "But it's your name," she insisted.

"So?" I stepped around her.

"What do you mean 'so'?" Tabitha moved to intercept me again. Her white T-shirt looked red in the sudden light from my eyes.

"Why is it important to you that I remember it?" Now that I was away from Rachel, I felt more like my old self, my anger closer to the surface, harder to control. Tabitha couldn't possibly understand the difference, but now that she had no heartbeat, it was difficult for me not to think of her as a thing, not a person, not a woman. She'd gone through the change, and she wasn't my Tabitha anymore, just a convincing fake. The urge to crush that impostor, to tear it apart, brought my claws out. But then a look of surprise in her eyes that reminded me of the Tabitha I had given in to pushed that urge away and dimmed the red light in my own eyes.

"It just is," Tabitha said. "You can't forget who you really are." But she already had. She didn't realize it, but she had. The Tabitha I knew would have screamed at me when she walked in on the birthday sex at the Pollux, or fled the room in tears.

"Are you hunting werewolves?" I asked, exasperated. "Because Greta and I are hunting werewolves."

"Yes, but—"

"Good," I interrupted. "Everyone who's hunting werewolves is walking this way." I pointed at the rough paved road that ran up the hill and down the other side to the marina.

Tabitha moved to my right side and walked with us in silence. The night was quiet, any sound absorbed by the stands of oak and pine that flanked the road. A half mile from the intersection, the road turned twice. I stopped next to the yellow sign warning drivers of the sharp curve and looked down the hill at the creek forty feet below.

"You okay?" Tabitha asked.

"No," I answered. I'd been thinking about Brian, the vampire I'd decapitated, wondering why we'd both been in the alleyway. If Roger was behind this, then it meant he'd talked Brian into it. Or had he scammed Brian too, knowing that we couldn't get along, that my losing my temper in a fatal way was inevitable? "But it doesn't matter."

We walked about another mile, the road continuing up a steep climb and then angling down at an equally steep incline toward the parking lot.

We walked carefully along the downward slope and stopped about fifty yards from the parking lot, where the pavement turned into an uncertain mixture of gravel and dirt. A large blue Dumpster hulked in the corner of the lot, obscuring the sight of us from the small brick utility building that housed the restrooms. The werewolves had posted a guard outside the building. I smelled him on the wind as it blew both his scent and that of the Dumpster our way.

Trucks, RVs, and all manner of off-road vehicles filled the parking lot, many more than when I'd last been here. The werewolves had regrouped.

I set *El Alma Perdida* on the lid of the Dumpster for safekeeping and turned into a white cat, then picked my way along the gravel quietly until I got a better look at the guard. He was sitting in a lawn chair on the sidewalk that ran across the water side of the parking lot, near the steps that led down to the long bridge connecting the marina's floating docks to the shore. His back was to the utility building, his eyes gazing out over the parking lot to the hillside where

Froggy had left the bodies of the werewolves she'd killed. Hard rock classics played on a small portable radio, Pink Floyd's "Hey You" suggesting ironically that the guard not give up without a fight.

A small gray cat settled next to me. "What do we do?" Tabitha meowed.

I looked back to where Greta crouched low and ready next to the Dumpster and gave her a nod. She darted across the parking lot, little more than a blur. The werewolf barely had time to blink before Greta picked him up by the feet and slammed his head against the wall of the utility building.

She was back at my side before he hit the ground, blood and brain matter splattering. Tabitha and I morphed back to our human bodies and I stepped out onto the concrete, looking down the long set of steps to the boat slips below. I couldn't smell or sense anyone down there. If anyone else was keeping watch, they were doing it from one of the lake houses.

"We're not allowed to eat until we find the werewolves," said Greta. She looked pointedly at Tabitha when she said it. "Then we can eat anyone we want. Dad just doesn't want us getting carried away."

"Oh, God." Tabitha sounded like she might be ill. I guess she'd never seen brains on brick before.

"Do you need to wait in the car?" I asked quietly.

"No," she forced out past clenched teeth.

"Try to remember what it feels like when you're hungry," I advised. "Think of them as food, just blood sources, not people."

"That makes it worse." Huh. Maybe there was more Tabitha still in there than I wanted to believe. What if I didn't *want* her to be Tabitha, wanted her to be a monster like me, because that made it easier not to feel guilty about being with Rachel?

"Then go back to the car," I said sharply. The Tabitha I knew was squeamish about killing a mouse in a trap. She'd killed Veruca, yes, but that had been self-defense more than anything else. A straightforward werewolf slaughter was another matter.

"It'll be all right, Mom." Greta tried to put her arm around Tabitha, but Tabitha pulled away. "Dad and I can handle it. We don't need you."

"I can do this," Tabitha insisted.

"Then stop acting like a prissy little bitch," I said as I walked back to the Dumpster and retrieved *El Alma Perdida*. I hadn't meant to say that, it just jumped out there.

"I said I can do it!"

"Fine." *If you can, then you really aren't my Tabitha anymore,* I thought. I tucked the gun into the back of my pants and tried to turn into a bat, but nothing happened except an angry hum from *El Alma Perdida*. The Lost Soul didn't seem to like vampire games. I couldn't leave it behind; I was going to need it if I had to kill William. Only in my hands was the gun blessed, magical, silver, and inherited. As a bonus, I liked the idea of trapping William's soul inside one of the bullets. For all I knew, death didn't hold anything scary for him and I certainly didn't wish him a happy afterlife.

"You want to be helpful?" I asked Tabitha.

"Yes. I said I could do this and I—"

"Can you turn into a bat or a bird, mist, maybe?"

"Yes."

"Which?" I asked with a slightly impatient sigh.

"I can do a bird. I can probably do a bat."

"Good, then turn into a bat and go find the werewolves," I said. "Don't fight them, just find them and come back."

"Why?" she asked.

"Just do it," I said.

She shifted into a bat just fine, but fluttered to the ground and flapped weakly. Greta giggled, but I kept a straight face. It isn't easy to fly the first time out. Tabitha got the hang of it after the radio played through two more songs and finally took off over the gentle waves of Orchard Lake, three bars into "Magic Carpet Ride."

I waited until I knew she was out of earshot, but still spoke quietly. "There are some kids with the werewolves."

"Kids or puppies?" Greta asked.

"They're werewolves, too."

She kissed me fondly on the cheek. "You old softy. Don't worry, Daddy; I'll kill them for you." I let the music from the portable radio fill in the silence. I told you that there are other reasons Greta makes me uncomfortable.

I don't like hurting children. Hell, even though this whole outing had been my idea, I would have preferred not to have to kill *any* werewolves. I much preferred just beating them up enough so that they knew they couldn't take me and then letting them go. Unless I went into a rage blackout, of course.

Even the werewolf I had killed in the alley when all this

crap started might have survived if I hadn't been trapped by the sun. Killing werewolves tended to be more trouble than it was worth. As the last few days had shown, once you start killing werewolves, your wolf problems multiply. The pack gets angry. The pack comes after you. There's more killing. The pack calls in reinforcements, maybe from the Lycan Diocese, maybe from one of the other freaky-ass skinchanger cults out there, but either way there's even more killing. If you leave the cubs alive, then all you've done is buy yourself a brief respite, because cubs grow up and when they do, they remember the vampire who slaughtered their pack and the process starts all over again.

I picked up the guard's lawn chair that lay half-folded on its side. Underneath it on the concrete was a sheet of paper, a list of names, all checked off. The lake houses didn't have addresses per se. Mail was delivered in a drop box at the utility building. The local paper got left in an old vending machine with a note on it that said "For Subscribers Only."

On the sheet, each werewolf residence was recorded by family name and dock number. It looked like the guard had tracked who had come and gone and the license plates of the vehicles that had been driven in or out of the lot. For some of them, he'd listed their driver's license number too.

William's name wasn't on the list, but I was pretty sure that if I started killing whole families of werewolves, he was bound to show up sooner or later.

31

TABITHA:

BAT GIRL

Prissy little bitch, huh? Well excuse me for not being used to seeing some guy's brains splattered on the wall! I should have told him about Talbot and me. I should have turned on the bodyworks and shown him what I could do, that I could have body heat, a heartbeat, even a reflection. I bet that would have wiped the smile off of his face. *Prissy little bitch* would turn into *honey, baby, sweetie pie* pretty damn quick then. At this point I didn't know why I'd been so excited to come out to Orchard Lake in the first place.

Most of the houses I saw looked run-down or cobbled together, built along the slanted lakeside with boat docks sticking out into the lake, and irregular steps leading from the docks to the houses. I flew a quick loop around the inlet closest to the marina. There were three houses there, one on the same side of the water as the marina, the other two staring at it across the inlet.

There were no numbers on the docks and I wondered how they got their mail. I saw power lines but no phone lines, and the only air conditioners were window units. At the far side of the lake, where it narrowed, continuing in a wide ribbon upstream, two fishermen sat on an old wooden dock, kept afloat by what looked like white plastic barrels under the water. They each dangled their feet off the edge of the dock, beer and fishing poles close at hand.

One of them let a flashlight shine out over the lake. It cut a blue-green swath through the water and the fish went crazy, striking at the light. The two guys thought that was hilarious, then one of them sniffed the air. "You smell something?"

The one with the light turned it off. "No."

An old wooden ramp rose from the dock to cinder-block steps leading up a steep incline to an even older house. The smell of coffee carried on the breeze. Two older women and two teenagers sat on the porch playing some game with lots of little multicolored plastic pyramids.

One of the women got up and walked halfway down the steps. "We're about to turn in, Lucas," said the woman. "How long are you boys going to sit out there playing with that flashlight?"

"William said to keep an extra eye out tonight just in case," one of the men, evidently Lucas, replied.

"And then I suppose you'll sleep all day?"

"No," said Lucas. "No, then I'm going to drive into town and work first shift. One sleepless night isn't going to kill me."

These were the werewolves? They were just like normal people. Okay, normal hicks, but normal just the same. I'd expected monsters who went crazy under the light of the full moon . . . not real people. I flew farther down the lake, finding similar scenes. At one house, a couple lay asleep on a futon set out on the middle of their screened porch. A mother sat in a rocking chair in a different house nursing a baby who kept restlessly shifting from puppy to human. "Bert," she called over her shoulder. "Did you find that teething medicine?"

"No, I must have left it in the truck," Bert's voice replied. "Let me get some clothes on and I'll take the boat back and get it."

I flew back to the marina. Eric and Greta were out on the pier untying a canoe. I landed in the center and resumed my human shape, the canoe wobbling as I did. "Are you sure these are the right people?" I whispered.

"Yes," said Eric, climbing into the canoe.

"But they seem . . . normal."

"They are normal." They each took a paddle and we began moving quietly toward the shore. "That doesn't mean they aren't werewolves. Look, I'll try talking to them, but they're not going to listen. We'll have to fight them sooner or later . . . and the only way to keep you and Greta safe is to opt for sooner."

"And we have to kill all of them?"

"No, Mom," Greta said. "You can go home. Dad and I will handle it."

Again with the "Mom" thing. "No, I can deal, but some of them are only teenagers."

"And some of them are younger," said Eric. "But I didn't start this; they did. I tried to make peace. It didn't work."

"Do I need to take care of the teenagers, too, Dad?" Greta asked.

"Not exclusively, just the little guys."

"Little guys?" I asked, a chill running up my spine.

"The children." Eric shipped his paddle and bowed his head, letting us drift upstream on his momentum. He looked defeated and annoyed. "We can't just kill their parents and leave them. They don't stay small and cute, you know. They grow up into big bad werewolves who want revenge for what happened to their pack. If you don't like it, go home."

"I'm just trying to understand." I didn't buy the whole we'll-try-talking-first thing, and killing, not for food, but just flat-out murdering these people, werewolves or not . . . there was no difference between that and . . . I don't know. It seemed monstrous.

"Well, stop trying!" Eric threw down his paddle. "Just stop. It's harder if you think about it. God, you make everything so damned difficult. Part of being a vampire is turning off the piece of you that gives a damn. You do whatever it takes to feed and care for yourself or you go crazy. Tonight it means that I have to murder a whole bunch of people who might just have more right than I do to be walking the planet in the first place, but I can't worry about that. It's you or them. Who would you pick?"

I wanted to say "them" to disagree, but the words lodged in my throat. Deep inside, the same part of my brain that was offended by Drones, that became angry when lesser vampires spoke to me without permission, reared its ugly head. It would kill any of them if survival required it. The vampire within twitched inside my head and peeked out from behind my eyes. "Me," I said quietly. "I'd pick me."

"That's what I thought," Eric said. "Don't try to pretend otherwise. It just makes things . . . shit!"

A mini spotlight hit Eric, lighting him up bright enough for anyone to see. Greta rolled noiselessly over the side into the water the instant before the light would have given her away. She didn't even make a splash. I turned into a cat. Eric pulled his sunglasses off of his T-shirt collar and slid them on. The light came from the same two men I'd seen on the dock. Now Lucas held a crossbow and the other guy held the flashlight.

Eric picked up his paddle and began to row toward the dock. "Either of you rednecks know a guy named William?" he asked as the canoe came closer to their little wooden dock.

"Who wants to know?" asked Lucas.

Eric smiled, his fangs preternaturally white against the darkness. "I'm Roger Malcolm." He spoke with easy confidence, though he was easing the magic gun out of his pants with his right hand. Eric slid it onto the bottom of the canoe. "I just wanted to stop by one more time and talk to William."

"William already told you that we aren't selling," said Flashlight Man.

"What the hell are you talking about?" I meowed.

Greta's head broke the surface in the water beneath their dock, her eyes watching them predatorily through the gaps in the boards.

"You just get on out of here, mister." The man gestured back to the marina with his light. "William will be here soon enough if you don't. We're not selling, to you or anyone else."

"So that's what this is about." Eric nodded to Greta. "Now!"

I ducked back under the lip of the canoe.

"Hi." Greta sounded perky and upbeat when she grabbed their dangling legs. "Whatcha doing?"

They vanished from the dock, the flashlight clattering momentarily on the wood before falling into the water. Shadows moved frantically beneath the surface of the lake and Eric paddled to the dock as quickly as he could, stepping out of the canoe with *El Alma Perdida* in his hand.

"Lucas? Henry?" On the porch, one of the old women gripped the porch rail. "Vampire!"

Darkness came over the canoe. I poked my head back out. Eric leveled the gun at the old woman. "Get William," he said evenly.

"Jimmy, Lisa, run for help!" someone shouted from the porch. The teen wolves charged off howling into the night.

A large black werewolf broke the water behind Eric, as if he'd been fired from an underwater cannon.

"Lucas!" the old woman yelled triumphantly as she too began to change. Eric spun and caught Lucas, slamming him against the dock and latching onto his back. *El Alma Perdida* skidded out of Eric's hand toward the water, but I leapt out of the canoe and onto the dock, trapping it by the barrel with my paws.

Lucas struggled with Eric on his back biting into his shoulder. "How do you like it?" Eric yelled between bites. "How do you like it when I sink my teeth into your fucking shoulder?"

"Better'n a stick in the eye." Lucas shrugged him off and leapt from the dock. I couldn't see the churning underwater battle between Greta and her opponent, but Lucas must have thought his friend needed help. Eric caught him in midleap and smashed him back first onto the wooden dock. Boards cracked, but the dock held.

Greta bobbed up out of the water, clinging to the body of a large brown werewolf who floated facedown. She swam for the dock and pulled herself up out of the water with one hand.

Eric delivered a double-fisted blow to Lucas's temple and the werewolf went still.

Both women from the porch charged down the hill, but only one of them had transformed into a wolf. The other woman was human. I could smell it. Greta met the werewolf halfway and they rolled around together on the hillside. Greta's laughter echoed out over the water. She was having too much fun.

The old woman swung her open hand at Eric. He caught

it with no effort at all and tossed her over his shoulder into the lake. She landed with a splash.

"Help! Vampires! Help!" The teenagers' voices carried clear out over the water. I dove back down into the boat. None of this was happening like it was supposed to happen. Now there were humans here, too?

"Grandma," Greta said, gripping the werewolf's upper and lower jaws and forcing them open too wide. "What big teeth you have."

"Just kill her," Eric said impatiently.

Greta frowned, but did as she was told.

I leapt back up onto the dock and resumed my human shape, complete with jeans and T-shirt. "Both of you, stop this," I cried.

"Go home, Tabitha." Eric grabbed me by the chin, squeezing my cheeks. "Just go the fuck home. I'm sorry I asked you here." He pushed me away. "I never should have turned you. I knew it wouldn't work out. You can't handle this."

"I can do anything I need to do! But this doesn't need to be done. It's stupid. It's murder, not self-defense, not feeding."

"Looks like you got another dud, Dad," Greta said, walking up to the porch of the house.

The woman Eric had thrown in the water floated in the darkness, watching us. Eric pointed at her. "Don't be stupid," he said. "Swim off to the marina or something."

He watched her swim away, looking relieved that he didn't need to kill her. "What do you want from me, Tabitha?"

"I want . . ." *I want you not to push me away,* I thought. *I want you to understand that I'm still me, and then I want to show you what I can do, that I can be like a live girl for you, that I can be warm and sexy and still hunt with you. I want you to be the same reluctant romantic that you always were, the man who isn't always in the right, but tries.*

"Do you want me to be all sexy and dangerous?" He sniffed the air, checking for werewolves. "Am I supposed to be Tom Cruise?"

"No. I . . ." Did he really want me to leave? Was he pushing me away on purpose?

"Am I supposed to go fight crime with you? Open a detective agency? Look for a cure? Because it's not happening. You wanted a monster and you got one!" Waving his gun around as he spoke, Eric came toward me, his intemperate footsteps causing the dock to creak in protest. One of the white plastic barrels supporting it floated out from underneath, dropping the dock closer to the water's surface on one side.

"You're not a monster!" I shouted.

"I'm not?" His voice cracked as he asked. *El Alma Perdida* hummed angrily, but Eric's eyes blazed brightly just the same. His claws came out, and with them, the fangs. He snarled at me, doing everything he could to be less than what he was.

"No. Not really. You're the man I love."

"Oh, please," Eric said, his features becoming human once again. "Maybe you loved me when you were alive, but now you're dead. You don't even smell like you anymore."

"But I—" But I can, I tried to say. Eric cut me off.

"Just shut up, Tabitha," he yelled in a voice so loud that my ears rang. "Listen," he snapped, grabbing me by the shoulder. "Do you hear that?" Howl after howl rang out into the night. "Do you see those?" He pointed out over the water to werewolves in pontoon boats heading our way, some swimming in the lake. "I do not have time to talk about this right now. Some things are more important than how you feel."

And he was right. He was right. This wasn't the time or place. In truth, it was way past time for this discussion, but he hadn't been ready for it, and probably never would be. He didn't like to think about things too hard, especially not emotional things. He didn't want to admit that he loved me, but I knew that he did. He had to.

But I had to rethink my tactics. Chasing him wasn't working. Rolling over and letting him act however he wanted just made things worse. He had to realize that he loved me, had to be willing to admit it to me and to himself. And he couldn't do that with me giving in to him over and over again.

Which left only one way to get his attention.

"I hate you!" My claws raked down his face, leaving behind furrows of ravaged white flesh. He didn't react, didn't yell or scream. He just stood there, an inhuman statue.

"That makes two of us," he spat.

"If you love me, come find me. Otherwise . . . we're finished," I said. I turned into a bat and flew off into the night. I could pick up my things at the Demon Heart and make it to the Highland Towers by morning.

Phillip would take care of me. I knew he would. He knew how to treat a lady. He was nice and sweet . . . and short, fat, and bald, but he would do for starters. If Eric couldn't get a grip on his feelings for me, refused to acknowledge them, never came to get me . . . then a vampire queen deserved better. I deserved better.

32

ERIC:

ILL MET BY MOONLIGHT

Greta and I waited for William on the front porch. We didn't talk about Tabitha. Out in the dark, pawfalls sounded on the damp evening soil. A small armada of pontoon boats and speedboats floated in the middle of the lake, biding their time. Smart puppies. They wanted me surrounded before attacking. Overhead, the crescent moon watched our little war games. I pretended not to hear the rustle of seventy-plus werewolves panting in the night. Greta found an old transistor radio and turned it on.

"I forget," I asked Greta, "is it waxing or waning that's bad news for them, good news for us?" She shrugged.

The same classic rock station popped and hissed to life, treating us all to a little Led Zeppelin.

A wolf, white as snow and large as a lion, rounded the corner of the house.

"Waning is good for you," he snarled. "Tonight's moon is waxing crescent." Huh. Even the moon was out to screw me.

"What kept you?" I asked.

"A meeting."

"It would have saved you three packmates and a guard if you'd been at the marina."

"They are with the Lord now, just as you will soon be with your master the devil."

"Has anybody ever told you how cool it is that you guys talk in wolf form? I wish I could speak English when I change, but it all comes out like animal talk."

"You think this is funny."

"Not really." I pulled the pistol out of the back of my jeans and scratched my temple with the barrel. "I think us fighting each other is pretty damn stupid though. You might be able to hurt me, but I have *El Alma Perdida*."

If he didn't know what *El Alma Perdida* was, then I was screwed and the rest of my night was going to be like the bloodbath at the docks. Tabitha was right about killing them being murder, but wrong about it being needless. Murder can be necessary. If I looked weak to the wolves, like I wouldn't carry out any threat I made, there was no way William would listen.

William didn't blink. "If I shoot you with this," I warned, "you don't go to your reward. You get trapped by the gun. You don't want to spend eternity in a bullet, William. I know you don't."

The other werewolves began to close in, jumping out of boats and onto the embankment. Others came out of the woods.

"You killed my son!" William bellowed.

"No, but you did kill mine," I replied calmly. "I'm still willing to overlook that."

"Dad!" Greta crossed her arms with a loud *humph*. "Can't we just kill them all? They tortured me and they killed Kyle."

"Not yet, sweetheart." My eyes never left William's. "I killed a bunch of werewolves for that already."

William blurred, a mass of growling angry white fur charging at me, going for my throat. If I hadn't had the gun out, I'd never have managed to bring it to bear.

His jaws touched my throat and the barrel of the gun touched his forehead. It charred his fur slightly and he drew back. I had almost been too slow.

"How?" said William. "A vampire can't hold—"

"They can if they wear gloves and don't mind it burning the crap out of them."

"You aren't wearing gloves."

"I'm an exception," I said. "I have it on good authority that John Paul Courtney was my great, great, great-granddad or granduncle . . . or something like that.

"You see, someone has been trying pretty damn hard to

maneuver us into this position. At first, I thought it was because I killed your son, but actually I didn't. I don't know who I killed. He was dressed like a bum, had already killed two other vamps, and jumped me in an alley."

"Fergus." William spat the name out like it tasted bad. "No wonder I couldn't get in touch with him. He's no pack-mate of ours. He's an outcast and a murderer. He'll do anything for money."

"Greta," I called over my shoulder to her. "I'm supposed to remember that name, for some reason. Do you—" Then it clicked. The check! Thirty thousand dollars written to a Fergus . . . something . . . a check on which Roger forged my name. Bastard. "Well, that explains that. So Roger hired Fergus to jump me in the alley. He got Brian to maneuver me into position and . . . Where was I?"

"You didn't do it," Greta answered from the porch.

"Right. I . . . Do you mind backing up a few steps?" I asked William. "Your breath smells like Alpo."

William withdrew slightly, growling low, ears flattened against his head. "You cannot escape."

"I know, I know," I said. "You and your pack will call up more goons from the Lycan Diocese to hunt me down. Blah blah blah."

"Do not mock me, vampire."

"Sorry," I said. I cleared my throat. "Okay, so then I thought that I was being used as a fall guy, that the boyfriend of the vampire who killed your son had framed me to protect his girlfriend, the theory being that I would probably kill you and even if I didn't . . . well, once you killed me you would think the whole deal was over and move on with your life.

"But then I found out about *El Alma Perdida*." I leaned against the wall. It was hard to read William's expression, but since he was listening I kept on talking. "How likely is it that I just happened to stumble into a mess involving an Alpha werewolf, one that I might need all different sorts of silver to kill—blessed, magic, inherited, cherry-flavored, the whole bit, and then wind up with all of it neatly packaged in one gun?

"Now . . . I happen to believe the whole John Paul Courtney thing. I kind of like the idea that I'm related to a badass cowboy werewolf hunter. But that someone would just happen to be using his special gun, that they would just happen to leave a bullet behind so that I could find that gun? It's just too much coincidence."

"You have another explanation?" he growled.

"Yeah, yeah, I do. You know a vampire named Roger, right?"

William growled low in his throat. "Roger Malcolm. He dared to come here, to ask us to sell him our land. He—"

I cut him off. "That's the guy. I think the whole reason I'm down here is because Roger wants me to kill you and enough of your pack that he can bring in some hired muscle and dispose of the rest, snatch the property out from under any relatives you might have, and build his little fancy-schmantsy vampire lake resort."

"And are you here because you wish to protect this 'friend'? Because he is also the one who told us where we could find you the other night."

"Me?" I asked. "Hell, no! Yes, I was planning to kill you, but that's only because after the stunts you've pulled trying to get back at me, I didn't think we'd be able to talk things over. I expected to kill you with the magic gun and then to have to kill your pack so that they'd leave me alone." He bristled at that.

"Now that we're talking, though, we've got options. I figure we can do this one of two ways. Way one I call 'the bad plan.' You don't believe me and I see how many of you I can kill before you take me down. Then, being a Vlad, I keep coming back over and over again. You get the idea.

"Way two, which I must say I prefer, I call 'the give the bastard what he deserves plan.' About forty of your pack members keep Greta as collateral, unharmed, and the rest of us go pay Roger a little visit."

"Dad," Greta protested. "You can't trust them. They'll try to eat me."

"Not if he promises they won't," I told her.

"Dad, no."

"Do it and I'll let you move back into the Pollux," I said cajolingly. "You can have one of the dressing rooms all to yourself."

Greta bit her lip, considering it. With Kyle gone, if I let her move in, she knew I'd let her stay. "And I get to hunt for a whole week, however I want, and you won't complain or be mad about how much I eat."

"Deal," I told her. I inclined my head slightly toward William. "What do you say?"

William resumed his human form. I'd seen other werewolves change back before, the fangs receding and new teeth growing in to fill the bloody holes. In contrast, William's reversion seemed painless. The fur around his eyes lit up from within, spreading outward across his body until the only thing not illuminated were those fierce eyes, the glow obscuring the rest of him. The outline changed, became that of a man. The glow receded and he stood before me in jeans and a white T-shirt, wearing loafers without socks. Very cool. "Assuming I agree to this, what happens after?"

"You let Greta go, deliver her safely to the Pollux—at night," I emphasized, "and agree to stay out of my way in exchange for me staying out of yours."

"In other words, a return to the status quo."

"Yes."

"I can't speak for the Lycan Diocese," William replied, "but I can attempt to explain. I can call off my pack, but you killed Reverend. He was a member of Deacon's pack. Even if the Lycan Diocese decides to forgive you . . ."

"I'll burn that bridge when I come to it," I told him.

"William," one of the others snarled in protest. "He killed Lucas and—"

"Silence," William snapped. "He will pay for his sins. All we do here is agree to let the Lord handle his punishment. If what he says is true, then we attacked him mistakenly."

They argued for twenty minutes, but eventually he convinced them. He convinced me that he could be trusted, too, especially when the packmates he picked to keep an eye on Greta were all wolves who had raised their voices in support of his plan.

The werewolves ferried us to the marina in a pontoon boat, then William let me ride in the back of his pickup, intending to drop me off at my car. We had to make new plans when we got to the abandoned house, though. It seemed Tabitha had decided to take the car with her when she left.

I waved again at the security guards still standing in front of Sable Oaks. This time I got a reaction. They stared openmouthed and called for backup. I think they thought we were invading. With a mutual laugh shared between me and my temporary allies, we drove on.

Which left me with one last problem: Did I really want to help these werewolves kill Roger?

◆ 33 ◆

TIDYING UP

No one was supposed to be at the Demon Heart, but when I pulled around back to park, I saw Marilyn's old Buick in its usual spot, second closest to the door. She always saved the first spot for Eric. I pulled into his parking place and wondered how the fight was going. Had Eric and Greta slaughtered all the werewolves yet? I couldn't imagine the werewolves winning.

Inside the club, all the lights were off except for a narrow band shining out from underneath the door in the main office. The weak thud of Marilyn's heartbeat thumped in my ears, the acrid smell of her cigarette assaulting my nostrils. The door to Eric's bedroom was open. The light snapped on at a touch and I started unpacking my things from Eric's chest of drawers.

I pulled my suitcase from his closet, but I knew everything wouldn't fit. I'd accumulated too much stuff. He'd been so free with money that I now had six times the number of outfits I'd moved in with. My lingerie alone could have filled the suitcase. Packing up my favorites and my jewelry seemed the best way to go. I set aside the blue dress that I'd worn for Eric's birthday and the diamond necklace. I wanted to be wearing them when I saw Phillip.

I went into the bathroom and willed myself to seem alive, my heart to beat, my blood to flow, and most of all for my reflection to appear in the mirror. Doing so diminished my other senses, the sound of my own heart and the blood rushing through my veins drowning out external sounds to near-human levels.

I stripped out of my clothes and studied the figure in the glass. No fat. No cellulite. My breasts were firm and full, and, unlike some dancers, completely natural. The slight sag that gravity normally gave them had been banished by vampirism. My tummy was flat, my muscles toned, and looking over my shoulder verified that my butt was tight and heart-shaped. My long black hair was healthy; it had body and bounce. What was not to love?

I didn't hear her come into the room, but I smelled the smoke.

"That's not the problem," Marilyn said. Her cigarette was out, but the scent clung to her, a cloud of stench.

"Don't you knock?" I reached down for my panties, em-

barrassed by her presence even though I'd shown my body
to thousands of perfect strangers.

"When I feel like it," she said, cackling. "I'm old. People
overlook things when you're old."

"Well, I don't. I—"

"You decided to leave him?" she asked, pointing to the
suitcase. Her eyes loomed large behind her glasses. She
wasn't wearing her false teeth, and it changed the timbre of
her voice.

"Yes." Not for long, though, I thought. He'll come after
me. I walked past her and retrieved my blue dress.

"He won't." Marilyn sat on the edge of the bed, a withered old woman, a witch reading my mind. She smiled a
pursed-lip toothless smile at my surprise.

"How did you—"

"I know him better than anybody," Marilyn told me, crossing her arms. There was no sling, no cast. "Better than Roger
ever suspected." A cough took her, a series of long wracking
painful rasps. "I know you, too, because you're a woman who
loves him. We have that in common." She stood up, slow
and creaking. "So I feel I should tell you this. He won't chase
you, but he does love you."

We had that in common?

"But you hate him," I protested, forgetting the dress in
my hand as I gestured with it. "He disgusts you."

"You don't know me," Marilyn said. She started folding
some of my things, putting them neatly into the suitcase.
"And you don't know him, either.

"Do you know what his hopes and dreams were when

he was alive? Did you see him come back from the Second World War, a man who hadn't believed in killing, but who had believed in doing what was right? We were just friends, then. He was too stupid to realize that when I said I was saving myself for marriage, what I really meant was saving myself for him."

She didn't cry; as emotional as her words were, she snapped them off bitterly. "Did you ever hear him play the piano? Did you even know he could? Did you hold his head in your lap on the day you were supposed to be married to him and cry because he'd been ruined, too?"

"You know I haven't. I wasn't even born then."

"I know." Marilyn's head sagged. "You're young and you're stupid and you think you can treat an eighty-two-year-old man like a teenager. You expect him to run after you, but he can't."

"I don't know what else to do," I shouted. "It's like he wants me to leave, but I know he still cares about me. I've seen him decide to be cruel on purpose and push me away—"

Marilyn slapped me and I slapped her back, the blow spinning her all the way around before she dropped to the ground like a sack of old laundry. Her glasses landed on the bed and I thought that I had killed her.

"Oh my God. Marilyn." I touched her shoulder. "I'm so sorry. I—" And then she slapped me again, her laugh sharp and abrasive, cawing crowlike laughter. I reeled away from her and she grinned, her fierce eyes challenging me. My fingernails had cut her skin when I'd struck her, but the wounds weren't bleeding, they were creeping closed.

"You have to stay and fight for him and you have to win. You have to get Greta on your side and you have to protect him, like I tried to do, but you have to succeed."

"Protect him from what? Himself?" I asked.

Marilyn pulled herself up and reached for the top of her blouse. I thought she was hiding a cross, that she was going to use it on me, but instead, she opened the top button, baring part of a wrinkled, drooping breast, upon which she had a small tattoo of a frog. "Do you see?" she asked. "Talbot told me you killed Veruca. You might have seen, when she died."

"She turned to dust, Marilyn."

"Never mind." Marilyn closed her blouse, deflated, as she spoke. "I can't . . . he won't let me say more."

"Who won't?" I asked. As if in answer to my question, Roger popped up in my mind, seemingly holographic like the vampires at the Highland Towers. He was less powerful than me and had been a vampire for forty-three years. He was shocked to see me, but not as shocked as I was to see his companion. He was walking down Thirteenth Street talking to a young woman who was the spitting image of Rachel. They were arguing and he seemed nervous, almost afraid.

"Nice tits," he said to me and I broke the contact.

"I've gotta go," I told Marilyn. I slipped the blue dress over my head and darted barefooted out the front door.

They'd reached the front of the Pollux by the time I got there. The girl who looked like Rachel wore tight black hip huggers and a midriff top. A small gold padlock hung from her choker and she wore a jade bracelet on her left wrist. Except for the hair, which had been highlighted in blondes and reds, she was Rachel's twin. She smirked when she saw me.

"Hi, slut," she said. "Where ya been?"

Even her voice was Rachel's. But I'd seen her open casket. I'd watched them lower her into the ground.

"Rachel?" I whispered. "But . . . but you died."

"Anyone can get a second chance aboveground, Tab. You just have to be willing to do absolutely anything to get it. Third chances are harder. But I died human, so my path didn't require any special ingredients that I didn't have with me. It's not easy to close the deal when your soul is already hellbound and on-site, but it can be done."

"Rachel wouldn't have gone to hell," I told the look-alike. "She was just a kid."

The smile on her lips was in that uncertain territory between sweet and malicious. "That's cute, Tab. I'm flattered." She turned to Roger. "She gets to leave."

"Like you could stop me anyway," I snapped.

"Kill her," Roger suggested.

I honestly don't know whether he was talking to her or to me, but the Rachel look-alike answered him. "If I do, he'll know I did it, because you insisted that I link with him, make him think he'd made me his thrall. I'm not like your wrinkled-up old fuck puppet, Roger. I'm a witch and you're just a frickin' Master vampire. You can't control me."

Roger opened his mouth to reply, but I beat him to it. "So that's how you look like my sister? You used magic?" I popped my claws. "Well, stay back, witch, because I'm not just a 'frickin' Master.' I'm a Vlad."

The witch laughed like a wicked child, eyes sparkling as if she enjoyed a challenge. "Don't tempt me, sis."

"Do it," Roger urged her. He reached out to her, but drew his hand back before he made contact. He feared her. She sensed it and her nostrils flared. He stammered, "I didn't—"

Her eyes narrowed. "Watch it, dead boy. I'm only helping *you* out because it will help pay my debt. My real boss got me out of hell. You did squat. He said to help you with Eric. Tabitha is not part of the deal."

"You guys are going to try and take Eric on?" I asked incredulously. "The two of you?"

"Roger thinks he is," the woman who claimed to be Rachel answered. "Which is a total joke. I mean, let's be serious. In a fight, even you would kick Roger's ass."

"That's why you're here," Roger said angrily. "You have to help me."

"Not in a fight. Your contract for assistance specifies noncombat. If you want more, you'll have to work it out with my boss." The witch tapped Roger on the nose with her index finger like he was a particularly dumb child. "If he was really just a Vlad, then I might've helped you out. My magic would have had him wrapped around my little finger in under a minute." She ran her hand along Roger's shoulder and he relaxed visibly. The scent of freshly baked cinnamon rolls washed over me, but I couldn't tell where it came from. "But as it is, I have to go all out to influence him even a little bit. I could barely keep him from flying to the other side of the interstate after that mess at the lake. He nearly didn't make it to the right house. So, I'm sorry, but you're on your own."

"Which," the woman turned her attention to me and began massaging Roger's shoulders as she spoke, "is why Roger, here, is going to get his undead ass handed to him tonight."

"He won't kill me," Roger objected, shoving her away with some difficulty, trying to regain his composure.

"Oh yes, he will," the witch countered. "Because you refuse to believe that Eric is an Emperor, not a Vlad. I get why. Accepting what he is means you have to accept that you helped Eric become more powerful than you will ever be, even though you didn't mean to do it."

Emperor, my ass. "You're both nuts," I said finally. "And you," I added, pointing at the Rachel look-alike. "I don't know who you are, witch, or what spell you're using, but you are definitely not my sister."

I stormed back into the Demon Heart and locked the door. Marilyn sat behind the bar, my packed suitcase propped up on top of it next to a bottle of Jack Daniel's. Lord Phillip's diamond necklace sparkled on top of the suitcase. The shoes that went with my dress were sitting on a bar stool.

"You'd better go," Marilyn said after she took a shot of Jack.

"Who is that girl?" I asked.

"I don't know for sure," Marilyn replied, "but she's bad business and that's all I can say. I'm only able to say this much to you because he's careless with the details."

"Who is?" I wondered if she was being infuriating on purpose.

Marilyn cursed under her breath. I know she thought I was stupid, the look in her eyes told me as much, but there was another emotion there that I couldn't read: not fear, but frustration, perhaps? "Don't let her touch you, and stay away from Roger. If you try to hurt him, I'll have to defend him."

"What? Why? Defend Roger? You're just as nuts as they are. You're all in on it!"

"Just go." Marilyn sighed. "Go to Eric. He might not figure it out either, but he can protect you, as he has me."

"I'm not going to Eric!" I shouted. "He's coming to me!"

Marilyn made a hand-washing motion and reached into her purse for a pack of cigarettes. "Do what you want then, Tabitha. I hope you're right about him. I truly do."

Rachel, or the thing that looked like Rachel, knocked on the door. "You still in there, slut?"

Marilyn tore a match out of a Demon Heart matchbook, lit her cigarette and coughed on the smoke. "I hate these things," she told me, "but if you smoke enough of them they can kill you."

"Stop talking to her, Marilyn," Roger shouted from the other side of the door. As if by magic, Marilyn's mouth snapped shut. Her eyes spoke volumes and I finally got it. Somehow Roger was controlling Marilyn. But really, what did that have to do with me? I was leaving.

I slipped on my shoes, put on my necklace, and glared at Marilyn, suitcase in hand. If . . . no, *when* Eric came after me, I'd tell him about all the weird shit that had been going on behind his back, but until then, he was on his own.

I heard Roger fumble with his keys, followed by the metallic click of the lock. I waited until they stepped through the front door.

"Give Eric a message for me?" I asked, looking from Roger to the witch and back to Marilyn. "Whichever one of you is in charge?"

"I'm not giving him any mess—," Roger said. Rachel shut him down with an elbow to the side.

"What's the message?" she asked.

"Tell him I'm going to Lord Phillip's at the Highland Towers."

Roger's lip twitched, but he didn't say anything.

"Fine," Rachel told me.

I nodded and headed out the back way, to Eric's loaner, smiling as I loaded my suitcase into the trunk. Marilyn thought Eric wouldn't come for me, but she didn't know him like I did. She'd only really known him when he'd been alive. My knowledge was more recent. Death had changed him, changed both of us. It might take him a while, but he'd made me immortal. I had nothing but time.

Even when the loaner broke down four blocks from the Demon Heart, it didn't put a dent in my good mood. Carrying my suitcase, I headed toward the Highland Towers, a strong, single, attractive vampire queen. My only thought was how jealous Eric would be when he found out where I'd gone.

◆ 34 ◆

ERIC:

UNFINISHED BUSINESS

I had William drop me off a few blocks from the Demon Heart and I walked them slowly. Roger and I sensed each other half a block away. He popped into my head and I into his, but we acknowledged each other too fast to allow the other to gain much insight into our emotions. We both had things to hide.

Roger was waiting for me at the Pollux. He sat on a wrought-iron bench to the left of the door in front of the marquee. The *Casablanca* title was clearly visible on the poster above his head.

When I was sixteen, I saw *Casablanca* at the Pollux. Rick said good-bye to Ilsa in the end, even though he loved her. He didn't know that he was just a character. He didn't know that Bogart would be in other movies and that on one of those movie sets, Humphrey Bogart would meet Lauren Bacall and fall in love, real love, not celluloid make-believe.

By leaving me, Tabitha had proved herself. Even as a vampire, she loved me, or she wouldn't have been so angry when she stormed off. She was better off without me. If I went after her, I'd regret it. If not today or tomorrow, then soon, and for the rest of my unlife.

"You look like shit." Roger blew a smoke ring from one of his expensive cigars. He offered me one and I shook my head.

"I can't taste them," I told him.

"Neither can I, but I still enjoy the aroma." He put the extra back into the inside pocket of his suit. Roger's lips pursed together, the hazy fragrant smoke flowing lazily from his nostrils. He looked so cocky, so self-assured, daring me to call him on what he'd been doing, to accuse him.

"How'd it go with the werewolves?" Roger took another longer pull on his cigar and held it.

"They're dead," I lied casually. We looked at each other. I stared him in the eye, but his attention was focused on my eyebrows, my chin, somewhere over my shoulder, my shoes, and lastly the concrete.

"Tabitha?" he asked, the words pushing the smoke back out of his lungs.

"Dumped me. It seems that I'm a murderer and an asshole. I pull the wings off flies and glue them back on upside down . . . the whole nine yards."

The ember at the end of his cigar glowed brighter as he took a long steady draw. "That sucks."

I laughed bitterly. "Yeah, it sucks."

"What about the wildflower . . . what's her name?" He looked up, still careful to avoid my gaze.

"Rachel? She's still around. It'll probably take me a month or two to screw that up." I sat next to him on the bench. He suppressed the urge to flinch, thought I didn't notice it, but I did.

"I'm still sorry about Brian." He smirked when I said the name. "I killed him the same night you framed me."

"You were meant to. That's why I befriended him." Another series of smoke rings slipped from his lips, perfect, each inside the other, the way only years of practice can achieve. Damn! And the Cold-Blooded Bastard Award goes to Roger Malcolm.

"So how much is it going to cost me to buy into this Orchard Lake thing?" I asked, trying to make it sound like a real interest. Here was a man I thought I'd known, a man I'd called *friend* since 1937. I wanted to know how long he'd been playing me false. After he became a vampire? Before?

"I underestimated you." He said it thoughtfully and with a complete lack of shame. No remorse at all.

"Maybe you just overestimated the werewolves," I said, trying to match his tone, his total lack of emotion. It was easier, because I could feel Rachel nearby and her influence crept in. Aware of it this time, having been outside her field of influence, I noticed how my control came back in some areas, fled in others: much of my anger was replaced with a desire for her.

Moving the cigar from one side of his mouth to the other, Roger closed his eyes. "Maybe you were just lucky."

"Could be," I allowed. "I always have been."

Roger threw the cigar to the ground. The cherry, still lit, rolled free and lay burning on the concrete. We both watched it burn. "That's something I've always hated about you." He slapped his hands on his knees and rose to his feet. "You get everything you want. You didn't even care about being a vampire." He made an effort to stop himself, to bottle up whatever it was that had been boiling up inside him, but it bubbled out anyway, the rant making him look more alive than he'd been in years. "God, I mean, do you even understand how hard I worked to find just the right sire for myself, to arrange things carefully, to slowly win her trust and work my way in?"

"I bet she really made you work, too," I said, remembering the rituals he had told me about, the ones she made him go through before she would bleed on his cross-inflicted wounds and heal him. "You must have had it rough. Poor Roger." Sarcasm bled into my voice. I couldn't keep up the act anymore. Neither, apparently, could Roger.

"Damn it!" he shouted at me, fists clenched, eyes burning with a light matching the dying ember from his discarded cigar. "I'm a Master vampire. A Master fucking vampire! Sure it's not the top. Not the same as being a Vlad. But it's still the big time. And you, you die in a goddamn car accident . . . and . . . and . . . destiny says screw it! Eric is important. I like

Eric. Eric can't be dead. Let's make him a Vlad! He's a good boy! He deserves it!"

"It could have been anybody, one of the ambulance drivers, a passing bum," I offered. "What does it matter? What does that have to do with anything?"

"There was no ambulance, you dumb shit. No hospital. I watched you lie there bleeding for a damn hour before you stopped breathing and then I watched you for another hour just to be sure. And when I was certain you were good and dead, I bribed the cops, paid the fang fee to have you taken directly to the mortician, and had your ass embalmed so that there would be no doubt, because I was tired of you being so much better than me and you getting everything I ever wanted!"

Cold. Icy cold is how I felt—too astonished or appalled to be mad. "Roger? What the hell, man?" I felt sore and tired. I pushed myself up off of the bench like an old man. "That's what this was all about? You're jealous?"

"Oh. It's funny to you, huh? Poor jealous Roger." I had never seen him like this. Not ever in all our fights had he looked at me with such hatred. It was like walking in on your mother-in-law in the bathroom and realizing she's a guy in drag. It just didn't fit. What had I ever done to Roger? Who cared if he was a Master and I was a Vlad? "You won't think it's funny for long."

"Look," I said soothingly. "Maybe we should get you a vampire therapist or something and just move on."

"God! You'd do it, too, wouldn't you?" He took two agitated steps away from me and spun back around, flailing his arms. "You'd just forget all about it. I bet that if I told you I was sorry you'd forgive me. Inside a month you probably wouldn't remember it ever even happened."

"Pretty much," I answered truthfully. My words hit him hard and it was clear from the insane look in his eyes that he couldn't quite grasp how that could be possible. I didn't want our friendship to be over. I was willing to believe that he was going through some kind of vampiric midlife crisis, that what he was saying about watching me die was bullshit or that he'd been in shock. I wanted him to have a reason, any reason, other than stupid jealousy. *C'mon, Roger,* I thought at him, *just make something the fuck up!*

I didn't see him move. The stake ripped through my T-shirt and lodged in my heart, a familiar feeling for me. Every time it feels exactly the same. Some vampires say it hurts, but to me, it only hurts on the way in and out. While the stake is in there, I just have an overwhelming urge to burp.

"You thought I'd share it with you, that I'd let you buy into the project? After all the shit I've put up with, do you really think I'd let you in? When Orchard Lake becomes Midnight Lake it's going to be the next Highland Towers, Eric, and I can't have you fucking it up. I'm going to be the next big thing! The big kahuna!" Drops of blood stood out on Roger's brow, rivulets of vampire sweat.

Nope, I thought at him, overwhelmed more with apathy than sadness, *what you get to be is dinner.*

He heard the first howl and staggered away from me. The wolves romped in like the Magnificent Seven and the Seven Samurai all rolled up into one big bad case of old-school whoop ass. All wore their human forms, but with lupine grins. William strolled out of the entrance to the Pollux parking deck holding *El Alma Perdida*.

Roger backed away slowly, not running. Was he expecting backup? Ten more of the pack walked out of the deck behind him and another ten stalked from around the corner of the Pollux, all dressed in exactly what they'd worn at their Orchard Lake homes, everything from sweatpants to jeans.

William yanked the stake out of my chest and pressed the gun into my hands. He grinned at Roger. "Hello again, Mr. Malcolm."

"You can't kill me, Eric. I've got connections." Roger stepped into the road, fighting off panic, keeping all of the werewolves in his field of vision. "And I may not be able to kill you, but now I know what you are and I'm going to take that, too—"

I fired *El Alma Perdida*. The bullet struck him in the shoulder and the wound began to sizzle.

"I've been waiting all night to shoot somebody with this gun, Roger," I said. "And there's just nobody I'd rather shoot with it than you."

"I—" Roger tried to speak, but I shot him twice more, the reports ringing out sharp, clear, and satisfying. You see, I've never liked vampires, not even myself. I've never made any bones about that. While I thought Roger was my friend, I'd made exceptions, but now . . . that made him just one more high society vamp in my territory, on my front fucking doorstep. The impact spun him around and he hit the asphalt. His arms flapped up and down as if he were a bat. "Can't change . . ."

"Same thing happened to me earlier," I explained, not the least bit sympathetic as I walked over to him. "Magbidion explained it to me."

"The bullets from *El Alma Perdida* shape-lock anyone they strike," William said. "It kept any werewolves Courtney killed from reverting to human form when the sun hit them."

"He made sure to leave one bullet in the werewolf until the local law enforcement showed up. He'd let them see the monster, and then dig the last bullet out so they could watch it change back into a human with their own eyes," I explained. "That way he could get hailed as a monster killer, not hanged as a murderer." Flames licked out of Roger's wound, and I kept talking as he swatted frantically at the fire. "It was a nice touch when you had Froggy leave one bullet behind to make it look like *El Alma Perdida* was back in Courtney's hands. Too bad the bullets are all linked. Talbot and Tabitha followed the trail right to your bedroom door. Oh, and it's official . . . Froggy was a Soldier. When Tabitha staked her: *Poof*."

Roger tried to speak. "I have a hos—" Tongues of fire climbed up his chest and his words were choked off by cries of pain. Once the flames began to spread, they quickly engulfed him, and the pack, now in werewolf forms, descended on him, heedless of the fire, tearing still-smoking chunks of flesh free with their teeth. Does getting eaten by werewolves count as total destruction? I assumed so. He didn't stop screaming even when he no longer had a throat, the sound echoing out of the empty space at his neck where his throat had been.

Absent the meat, Roger's skeleton writhed on the ground. Several of the werewolves drew back, but William and his core followers devoured even the bones. Roger's cries finally ceased when William crushed his skull between those massive jaws and started chewing. I guess he couldn't have tasted too bad, because they didn't leave anything behind. Note to self: That is not the way I want to go out.

William's pack loped away to their trucks, leaving William alone with me. He laughed when I put the barrel of *El Alma Perdida* against his furry chest. "Now, about Greta."

"Your spawn will be returned to you unharmed," he replied. "I am as good as my word."

"Fair enough." I lowered the gun. "I'm sorry about—"

"Don't come back to Orchard Lake."

So much for apologies. "Keep your pack away from Void City and you've got a deal."

"What would you have done if I hadn't listened to you back at the lake and your magic gun didn't kill me?" he asked.

"I've got an old mercury thermometer in my back pocket," I lied.

William smiled. "And if that failed you?"

"I'd have figured something out," I assured him. "Don't you worry about that."

"I believe you," William said, nodding. "Out at the park, when you commanded the bats to block out the sun, I was afraid you would destroy us all."

"Nah, I only wanted my little girl back."

"She's a monster," he protested.

"Now you're just being mean. Besides, she's no worse than I am."

"I beg to differ," William said. "I didn't see it until I watched you gun down your friend."

"Friend?"

"Fellow vampire, then," he amended. "The look in your eye was the same look I see in the eyes of my pack when they exterminate a vampire. You know they are monsters."

"It's kind of a no-brainer."

"So you say, Eric of the revenant's eyes."

"Huh?" I asked, startled. "Revenant's eyes?"

"When you grow angry, angry enough to grow wings of hate and a skin black with rage, the purple eyes from which you stare are not the eyes of a vampire, but of a revenant, a murdered soul."

"Murdered?" I echoed, not wanting to think about it too closely.

"I only tell you what I saw, Eric."

"All right, so maybe I was murdered, but I'm a vampire, not a frickin' revenant, okay?"

"As you say, vampire. May the Lord have mercy on your soul." I watched him lope off into the distance.

Not a bad birthday, all in all. The werewolves weren't after me anymore, my best friend who really hadn't been my best friend was dead, and I could go back into the Pollux and have my way with Rachel guilt-free, more or less.

"Revenant's eyes," I scoffed and sat down on the bench

where old what's-his-name had admitted his betrayal. Roger. Forget him, I told myself. Just let him go. But my memories of Roger were too tangled up with memories of Marilyn. I couldn't let go of one without sacrificing the other.

Her familiar heart beat across the street at the Demon Heart, a weary skittish beat in comparison to the steady rhythmic thump of Rachel's. I let them both serenade me, Rachel upstairs in my bed at the Pollux and Marily— What was Marilyn doing at the Demon Heart this early?

I crossed the street at a trot and unlocked the front door of the club. She was probably getting things ready for our grand reopening. We could open back up tomorrow, I thought.

Serves me right for being optimistic.

The hair on the back on my neck stood up. Cold white light from the street illuminated Marilyn, tied to a chair in the middle of the room. Blood trickled down her arms and legs where piano wire had cut into her wrinkled flesh. A large band of duct tape covered her mouth. It was frayed along the bottom, tucked under and stuck to itself on the upper right corner. All the little details.

Her eyes screamed at me to run, but I didn't. I'm stupid like that. I never know when to run or when to leave someone behind. That I do, on occasion, manage to do one or the other just goes to prove the age-old adage: "The sun even shines on a dog's ass some days."

Stuck to her chest was a Post-It note with the words: *Happy Birthday, you stupid fuck!* It was signed *Hugs and kisses— Roger.* My vampire speed kicked in and I think I might have made it if Roger hadn't been the one who'd set the trap for me. He'd known me too well.

My claws raked through the piano wire, severing it on both sides simultaneously. I clutched Marilyn close, the smell of stale cigarettes and old age filling my nostrils. The intro music from the old *Superman* radio show flashed through my head. I heard an electronic whine that didn't sound like the alarm system. I rolled away from it, hoping to shield Marilyn from the blast. More than one bomb went off.

I'd never moved with such urgent speed before. We shot past the first explosion as it happened, outrunning it like in the movies, dodging over the runway and into the dressing room. The next explosion went off in there, my every move anticipated, creating a circle of fire, shaped charges designed to hit me from all angles. It wasn't normal fire, either; the way it burned and pierced was a sensation I associate only with crucifixes and holy water.

He'd paid someone to bless the damn explosives. Even so, I lasted longer than Marilyn, watched her burn away. The only thing that eased the pain was knowing that I got Roger first. He was a Master, easy to kill. I'm not.

We Vlads keep coming back unless you find that one special way that will take us out forever. It didn't feel like Roger's method was it for me, but it felt damn close. My body was completely gone; not even a speck of ash remained. I'd been melted before, but there, in the goop, I'd still had a body, just an icky liquid one. Now, I was totally disconnected, a floating ghost.

I hate ghosts.

I hovered over the burning ruins of the Demon Heart, pleasantly surprised to see that the explosion hadn't harmed the Pollux Theater across the street, waiting for my body to re-form and wondering how long it would take. And waiting. And waiting. You know, when I get my self back together, I'm going to find the guy who thought up blessed C-4 and kick his ass.

Happy fucking birthday to me.